bloodlines

A NOVEL

Neville D. Frankel

Events that bookend *Bloodlines* are historically accurate, and several political characters are drawn from reality. Research, interviews and correspondence clarified my thinking, added depth, and made it possible for me to write what I might have imagined but could never have lived. Any errors of fact or judgment are my own.

Also by Neville D. Frankel

The Third Power

For Makson

Who taught me what little I know
of forbearance
and humor

foreword

Having participated in the struggle for justice in South Africa, I am deeply touched by *Bloodlines*. For me, and for the many who sacrificed their lives and families for the freedom of others, this is a profoundly personal and moving story.

The future of many of South Africa's citizens once seemed bleak and hopeless, but *The Truth and Reconciliation Act** began the healing process, moving South Africa forward from violence, divisiveness and hatred. The work of reconciliation is not yet complete--but *Bloodlines* is a call to hope and healing. It is also a work about love and justice, and about the possibility of redemption. It will undoubtedly inspire many, both within South Africa and around the world.

Although *Bloodlines* is a work of fiction, it offers the clearest understanding I have yet seen of what it was like for fair-minded people to live under apartheid, and what they suffered as South Africa fought for and gained

---

*The Truth & Reconciliation Commission was a court-like body assembled after the end of apartheid. Its mission was to offer healing and hope to those who felt victimized by violence, allowing them to come forward and be heard by the Commission. Perpetrators of violence could also give testimony and request amnesty from prosecution.

its freedom. For South Africans too young to have lived under apartheid, this book should be required reading. It does not take long for a whole generation of children to lose the knowledge of their own history, and the significance of what their parents achieved.

Neville is a gifted writer and storyteller, and I am deeply honored to have had a hand in the editing process.

Michael Langa

Professor Michael Langa is a native of South Africa, and was personally involved in the struggle against apartheid. He worked alongside Bishop Desmond Tutu on the Truth & Reconciliation Commission, offering psychosocial support to the victims of apartheid. He served as a consultant and content expert, ensuring cultural authenticity in **Bloodlines***. He has taught negotiation skills on several continents, and now lives in Boston, where he teaches Nonviolence Philosophy at colleges and universities in the Boston area, as well as in the Worcester Public Schools.*

prologue

Johannesburg, South Africa, 1956

A solitary car drives through the southern suburbs of Johannesburg in the late evening hours. It is as sure to draw police as a lone, skittish impala draws predators. This particular car—a Volvo Duett station wagon—glides cautiously through the darkness, obeys all traffic laws to the letter, avoids shopping centers and other areas where a police presence is mandated.

The car is driven by a pregnant young woman; her passenger is a young man squeezing both hands around one thigh like a tourniquet. He sits in the back seat, creating the appropriate impression should they be stopped by the police, because while Michaela Green is white, Mandla Mkhize is a black man. The fact that he is a Zulu of the Mkhize clan, known to his friends by his clan name, Khabazela, is irrelevant. In the eyes of the police, there is only one legitimate reason for them to be in a car together at night. She is the employer; he, the gardener or kitchen boy, and she is driving him to the hospital after a midnight brawl in the servants' quarters behind her home.

None of this is borne out by the facts, which include two boxes in the back of the station wagon, containing thousands of still warm mimeographed pamphlets announcing a protest against a raise in bus fares. The increase is only a few pennies, but for the hundreds of thousands who travel to their employers' homes and businesses as washerwomen, cooks, gardeners, nursemaids and drivers, it is draconian.

"Mandla, are you still bleeding?" she asks, trying to see him in the rear view mirror. "It's not far now."

"Don't worry about me, Michaela," he answers through lips tightened against the pain. "Just get us there safely." He takes a breath, grunts. "I'm bleeding all over your father's car. I hate going to him like this. And I'm sorry for dragging you into this mess."

"You didn't drag me anywhere," she says tartly. "And we have no choice but to go to my father. He's been doing this kind of patch up in his dental surgery for years. Besides, where else could I take you? You have a bullet in your leg, the Special Branch is sure to be after us, and—" she pauses, and he thinks he hears a catch in her throat—"we left a dead policemen in the field behind us."

He is silent, thinking about his first murder, wondering whether there will be others.

"I'm so sorry you had to see that," he says, fading.

"I'm glad I saw it," she says fiercely. "Don't forget, I also saw what he did to you. He would have killed you if you hadn't killed him first."

Mandla lies back with his eyes closed. Michaela relives the events just passed, recalling every moment in terrible detail.

Michaela led the way from the shed where they were working together, through the woods, to the adjacent field where she had secluded her Volvo. She walked as fast as she could, holding the flashlight over her belly. He carried the two boxes of pamphlets, which they planned to distribute to cells around the city. When they reached the car she opened the rear and he put the boxes in the back. As he reached up to close it, however, they heard the screech of police cars pulling up to the garage behind them, followed by slamming doors, shouts, and the sound of furniture breaking.

"Damn them," she whispered. "They're destroying the mimeograph machine. Where the hell are we going to get another one?"

"Never mind that," he responded. "Come quickly, Michaela. You need to get out of here. Get into the car and go home."

"What about you?"

"You can't be seen in a car with me. I'll be fine. Go."

He helped her into the car and as he closed the door there was the sound of footsteps from the trees. She watched through the car window as a policeman emerged from the darkness and collided with Mandla, who fell to the ground. The officer stepped forward and placed a boot on Mandla's hip, having no idea that they were not alone. He spoke, but Michaela, watching behind the closed car window, heard nothing.

Mandla replied, and in response the officer swung his leg back and drove a boot into the prone man's belly. Michaela watched as he tightened his gut against the impact, but the kicks were accurate and brutal. Each one forced the air from his chest, and she was sure that he would soon pass out. She readied herself to scramble from the car, find a log and hit the officer over the head. If she didn't manage to knock him out, at least she would have created a distraction during which they might be able to get away. But when the next kick came, she watched as Mandla grabbed onto the boot and hugged it to his side. Without pause he rolled over, using the momentum of the kick to unbalance the officer, who toppled, pulling a revolver from his belt as he fell. A shot went off, startlingly loud.

Mandla rose to his knees, and as the officer pummeled him in the face, was somehow able to wrap his arms around the man's neck. The blows kept coming; Mandla wanted only to stop them. Finally he jerked his forearms up into the man's throat, twisting as he did so. Bone and cartilage snapped with a sound that seemed to reverberate in his head as loudly as the shot from the revolver, and Michaela saw the body in his arms slump to deadweight. Mandla rose and limped to the car, holding his thigh. Michaela opened her door and in the car light she saw that his trousers were stained with blood.

"Oh, God," she said. "You're shot."

Before she could help him into the car, a black policeman emerged from the trees, armed with only the truncheon in his belt. He saw the body on the ground and glanced up at Mandla. They stared at each other for a long second.

The man knew what work they'd been doing. He hesitated briefly, nodded imperceptibly, and stepped back into the darkness. Mandla raised a hand to his forehead in thanks.

Michaela helped him into the back seat and maneuvered herself behind the steering wheel. Breathing heavily, she drove off. In the rear view mirror she saw the black policeman come out of the trees again. For the benefit of anyone who might be behind him he ran after the car, hand raised as if to stop them.

Mandla awakens lying on a plastic sheet draped over a blanket on the heavy wooden table in the Davidson's kitchen. Dr. Davidson bends over his thigh, and Michaela hovers anxiously at her father's elbow. The blood-soaked pants have already been cut off his leg, and Dennis, the black gardener who has worked for Dr. Davidson for thirty years, is washing the blood from his leg and foot, where it has pooled in his shoe.

Michaela stands at his side, gives him a glass of whiskey for the pain; Dennis takes a position behind him, holds him down as Dr. Davidson removes the bullet from his thigh with a long forceps. When they're done they stitch and bandage the wound. Dennis finds a pair of the doctor's pants for Mandla, who calls the number he has been given for such emergencies, and is told that if he can get to the Rhodesian border, he will be met and taken care of. It is at least an eight hour journey, but Michaela insists on driving him.

"I've done it before," she whispers, not wanting her father or Dennis to know where they are headed. "Besides, there's nowhere for you to hide here. The police will be all over the neighborhood any minute."

Out in the garage, Dennis helps Michaela open the back of the Volvo. They remove the boxes of pamphlets and take out the cover, beneath which is a false plywood floor with a hinge running from back to front at the midline of the car. Michaela folds back the false floor, revealing a narrow, shallow opening just large enough to hide a man. It contains a small pillow, and several blankets to cushion the ride. Mandla is given a bottle of water to drink, which he will refill with urine if he needs to, the false floor is closed and the carpet replaced. Michaela takes rapid leave of her father, who hugs her close.

On the steering wheel is attached a hand-sized, black leather-covered rotating steering ball. Michaela grips it tightly, and through it she feels the grit of the wiry, graying hair on the back of her father's hand, the strength and comfort of his presence. She has stopped only once to refuel and to give Mandla a chance to stretch, and out in the country she stops again to fold back the cover and half open the false floor.

Hours pass, and as she drives on in the harsh pre-dawn light, undulant fields lie still as a photograph; the tan of winter grasses takes on a colorless and lifeless hue. She can see to the far horizon, which gives mass to the sky. The landscape is a frozen scaffold that arches upward to bear the weight of the heavens, and the crescent moon is like a bright light beamed through the perfect arc cut into a backlit fabric. Only the stars move—they pulse and flicker, living pinpricks in such profusion that they have form and density.

The fields begin to alternate with bushes, silvered in the moonlight, and scattered groves of small trees, their shadows dark against the ground. Finally, after the second grouping of large trees between two higher hills, she spots the turning and slows, following the narrow, curving trail around the hills and into a low wooded area hidden from the road.

Up ahead a flashlight blinks, and she breathes a jagged sigh of relief. She's been gripping the wheel so tightly that her knuckles are white, and she is suddenly aware of the cramping in her fingers. They've made good time; more importantly, they encountered no police cars or military roadblocks.

When she stops the car, two men approach. Both wear high laced military boots and khaki fatigues. One of them opens her door and she gets out slowly, stiff and awkward after the long drive. She is quivering with the need to urinate.

Thank God I only have to live with this for another few months, she thinks.

The man at the car door is short, stocky and powerful; he is prematurely balding, and has a boxer's nose.

"Hello," he says, looking at the moonlight on her long brown hair. He watches her body as she opens the door, struggles to turn sideways, and climbs stiffly out of the car. She hates her shapelessness, how awkward she feels, and the ugliness of her maternity clothes.

"Come on," she says. "Let's get him out of the hole."

He grins widely, and in the moonlight his teeth shine against his dark skin. "We're glad to see you. Thank you for bringing him. You show great courage to do this." He gestures with his chin at her belly. "Especially now." His voice is deep and steady, his English heavily accented.

"It was a long trip," she says, "but we weren't followed. I'm just happy we got here safely."

She walks around to the rear of the car and opens the tailgate. The interior light goes on, illuminating the half open floor.

"I need a moment alone," she says. "I'll be right back."

She turns and walks quickly into the forest and steps behind a tree, where she lifts her dress above her waist, lowers her panties and squats, too uncomfortable to be embarrassed. The sound of her water splashing against the forest floor carries through the stillness, and she sighs with relief. When she is through, she stands, lowers her dress, and walks back to the car.

Mandla has climbed out of the hole and sits on the back of the car, his legs stretched out before him. As she approaches the car, the smell hits her—fetid and heavy, of blood, urine, and sweat. She feels her throat closing. I will not vomit, she thinks. Not here, not before him, and all he's gone through.

"Raymond, are you a sight for sore eyes," he says. His voice is hoarse.

The man laughs, a deep, throaty sound. "Khabazela," he says, addressing Mandla by his clan name, "it's good to see you, too. But what the hell have you been doing in there? It smells like a zoo."

The night air is fresh and moist; Mandla breathes deeply, then attempts to move his legs. He groans loudly. "Feels like I've been lying in that position for a week," he says. "Michaela, I'm so sorry I messed in the car. I had to go, and with the floor closed over me, I couldn't get the bottle in place."

"I'm just glad we got here in one piece," she says.

"You better get along," says Raymond. "You're not safe here."

The second man has not introduced himself. He is tall and lithe compared to his companion, and slightly younger. Under his military cap his shadowed face is smooth, but his voice is educated, and has the ring of command. "The border's only over the hill. We'll get him some help. Thank you for what you're doing."

Michaela reaches into the car, takes the soiled blanket gingerly by a corner, drags it out of the hole, and drops it on the ground. Then she closes the false bottom and rolls the carpet back. It will reduce the smell on the long journey home—and besides, it needs to be closed in case she encounters a roadblock. She stumbles quickly to his side.

"Heal quickly," she says. "Come back as soon as you can. We need you."

"I will," he says. "Be safe, Michaela. And thank you."

Then, without a word, Raymond helps Mandla up, supporting him on one shoulder; the other man hefts both rifles and they disappear into the woods. She runs to the car, her heart racing, and has the presence of mind to leave the lights off as she drives back along the trail towards the road.

one

STEVEN

Boston, 2001

T hese events occurred in Johannesburg and along the Rhodesian border in 1956, three months before I was born. My name is Steven Green; the young woman, Michaela Green, was my mother. It was not until I reached middle age that I discovered the wounded man was a political activist who later became her lover.

You might wonder how I know the details of our little trip to the border when I was still *in utero*. It's a long tale, and it has to do with the legacy my mother failed to leave me.

In an impassioned struggle against apartheid, it was inevitable that my mother's clandestine activities would catch up with her. Eventually she was arrested, and with a wrenching suddenness, she disappeared from my life. Much of my childhood was spent mourning her, and I guarded what little recollection I had of her as if it were a pearl of memory embedded in me, the physical embodiment of a courageous and outspoken mother killed in the long struggle for freedom.

When I was seven, in 1962, my father, Lenny, moved us from South Africa to Boston to start a new life. He taught engineering at MIT, we seldom spoke about the past, and we lived alone and womanless. For over forty years, I thought I was the son of a dead mother. Then everything started to unravel. At first slowly, and then very fast.

I remember little about our first few months in Boston. My father rented a smallish two-bedroom apartment in Cambridge, and although I was unaware of it, we lived frugally.

By the time I was twelve, he had saved enough to make a down payment on a little cottage with a garden just off the beach in Dennis on Cape Cod. We spent almost every weekend there during the school year, and as much of the summers as he could afford.

In my memory, winters were pretty much shades of gray until we bought the cottage. Then I began to see the possibilities of color, even in the bleak, early-dark winter skies that hovered over the Atlantic. Perhaps it was the beauty and isolation of the Cape, which was still an undiscovered gem in the 1960s; perhaps something in my father came to life once he felt himself attached to a piece of land. Or, perhaps it was that he and I began to spend more time together when we went to the cottage, mostly in silent communion while he worked and I drew or painted, or in lockstep as we walked the beaches and the streets that were deserted and silent for much of the year.

In any case, we never discussed our relationship. My father was intensely private, a guarded personality, and as I matured, I took his example and respected his space as he respected mine. Now that I have children and know what it means to be involved in their lives, I recognize that he raised me with a distant kind of love best described as benign neglect.

When he and I were together, I often felt that something was missing. But in time, the missing ingredient took on a character of its own. Instead of being an absence that bound us together, it became a presence with its own specific gravity. Eventually we formed a molecule with my father on one end and me on the other, and the force that kept us apart was so palpable that it might have been a magnetic field in which we were drawn together with no option but to repel each other.

For years I thought—assumed—that the thing between us was the absence of my mother; that because we both missed her and mourned her death, that the loss bound us together. But it was a different kind of loss for each of us, and the real barrier between us was not her absence. It was that we lived two vastly different versions of reality, which, because they were irreconcilable at the time, we were unable to broach until much later.

My father refused to discuss what happened on the last day I saw my mother, and so I have no knowledge of what he experienced or remembered.

As for me, I remember that my mother dropped me off at kindergarten that morning, and I have tried without success to recall whether she kissed me goodbye. Of course, neither she nor I knew that it was her last day, but over the years the question of whether I received and returned her kiss became more and more important to me. Perhaps it was a childish attempt to cement my connection to her. Eventually I came to accept the absence of that final kiss as a part of her legacy.

What I do remember of her are a little boy's sensations of the caress of her skin, and the feel of her hair; and her breath, which had about it the warmth and sweetness of our garden in mid-summer. When I think of the way her lips opened when she smiled, and of her breathy laughter, it gives me a catch in the chest even today. I remember her physical intimacy. Ironic, because what I craved from her as I was growing up was to know her mind—to talk to her, to hear how she might have advised me to live my life.

The few appeals I made to my father on the subject of my mother's death revealed little of consequence, and eventually it became a concrete fact in my life that he would never reveal what happened. So what does a seven, or a ten, or a fourteen year old boy do when he has no information about the death of his mother? He lies awake at night, trying to recreate her last hours. Which I did, night after night, into my teens.

They say memory is not fixed—that it can be changed, or even created. I created my own private internal story of my mother's death out of scraps of what I overheard; from the earliest cowboy movies I watched, where I ignored John Wayne coming to the rescue, but only saw the massacre of Indians; from the newscasts in movie theatres—of international events, police brutality, African genocides, foreign wars. Later, I incorporated what I learned about torture and intrigue from spy movies, thrillers and television news. It was all equally valid grist to my mill, and I chewed it all up and turned it into a series of memories that changed and became increasingly sophisticated as I grew older. These memories became my nightmares.

Despite my father's attempts to avoid talking about South Africa, I couldn't help but come to a vague understanding of its politics, and as I did so, my nightmares became more factual, and more violent. My mother, driving through the darkness, stopped by a car full of uniformed white men. Terrified, but always brave, she refuses to open the trunk. They break it open, discover a man cowering beneath a hidden floor. Sometimes they shoot her right there and leave, and I have to bury her; sometimes they cart her off to prison, where she is brutally interrogated, has cold water dripped on her forehead, and goes mad before they finally drown her, leaving me to dispose of her body.

In the fifth grade, my class was assigned to prepare an oral report entitled *My Family History.*

The report was supposed to be a personal interpretation of family history using interviews with parents and other family members, as well as research gathered from other sources. I was at a distinct disadvantage—I had no other relatives to interview, and getting family information from my father was like pulling teeth. But motherless and with my strange foreign accent, I already stood out in class, and I refused to be branded in addition as the one with no family history, so I worked with a tenacity that surprised even me, spending every afternoon in the school library.

Mrs. Tolliver was the school librarian, a stern, angular woman with iron-gray hair. She understood instinctively that this project was more than simply a school assignment, and she became my accomplice. She found books for me, showed me how to use them, and took me one afternoon to the Cambridge Public Library. She must have sensed that I was a visual child who best expressed himself through drawings, and that I was in search of a past.

She laid before me books of photography and drawings of South Africa, and I saw the city I came from, Johannesburg, surrounded by huge mine dumps, the crushed rock that remains after the extraction of gold. I saw the gorgeous coastal cities and beautiful beaches of Cape Town and Durban; wild stretches of rolling farmland of the Free State and the profusion of wild game in a book on the Kruger National Park. I took it all into myself and it became autobiography, filling what had been empty. But I was most taken by the Drakensberg Mountains southeast of Johannesburg, in KwaZulu-Natal, near the area once known as Zululand. I was spellbound by the majestic wilderness of towering, jagged peaks and rolling *veld*. I didn't understand it, but as an adult I recognize that something in its massive and permanent isolation struck a chord in me.

No one, not even Mrs. Tolliver, knew what I was preparing for my report, and I wanted it to be a surprise to everyone.

When my father said that he had a meeting on my scheduled presentation date and would be unavailable, I was heartbroken and furious. And despite my outraged beseeching, he was adamant that his meeting could not be changed. The next afternoon, Mrs. Tolliver noticed my lack of concentration as I sat in the library over a book of South African history.

"You seem so distracted, Steven," she said. "If your presentation isn't finished, you'd best pull yourself together. It's only a few days away."

"I don't want to do it," I said.

She sat down beside me. "What is it, Steven?" she asked. "You've worked so hard on this project. What happened?"

"My father can't come," I blurted out. "I know it's not for him, it's for me, but if he can't be there to listen, I don't want to do it at all."

"You know," she said quietly, "perhaps we can reschedule your presentation to a time when your father can be there. What do you say?"

Years later my father regaled me with a story about the telephone call from Mrs. Tolliver. He told the story as if it was a joke, impervious to what it revealed about him.

"I knew the minute I heard her voice," he said, "that she was a tough cookie. She explained the problem, and there was no way she would let me off the hook. 'Steven's teacher has set aside six presentation days in all,' she said. 'On which ones will you be available?' She gave me the dates, but I told her that I had classes to teach, and graduate students to meet with. 'Mr. Green, I've been watching your son work on this project, alone, for over a month,' she said. 'I don't know all that your family's been through, but this is Steven's attempt to find his past. He needs you to witness this presentation, and I will do whatever I can to ensure that he gets your audience, even if it means that he has to do a second presentation one evening in the library. So, Mr. Green, which is it going to be?'"

My father finally agreed to a time. I had no idea what happened behind the scenes—how my teacher managed to arrange the switch with another child—but eventually it was my turn to present *My Family History*.

I rose in my jacket, white shirt and pressed khaki pants, a nervous little boy, hair slicked back, walking proudly to the front of the class. Mrs. Tolliver caught my eye and winked at me. My teacher stood to the side, ready to remove the white sheet that had been placed over my presentation before class began.

I don't remember exactly what I said; the notes I made are long gone. But I do recall that I spoke about the injustice of apartheid. I spoke of the Pass Laws, requiring all black people to carry a document specifying when and where they might live and work. I talked about the fact that white and black people could not live in the same house; about separate public toilets, and park benches labeled for black or white use, and the fact that black people were only allowed to do menial, low-paying jobs. And in a small voice, in my father's presence and in the presence of others, I spoke about my mother. That, I remember.

"My mother was a brave woman who believed in equal rights, and in the freedom of all people, of all skin colors. She was willing to fight for what she believed in, and to break laws that she thought were unjust. She helped people in trouble to escape from the authorities, and she worked hard to bring knowledge of what was happening in South Africa to the rest of the world. She taught me that it is important to try and make a difference, and she showed me that if the difference is worth making, then it's also worth dying for.

"But South Africa is not just a cruel government of unfair laws. It is also a beautiful country of wonderful people."

I beckoned to my teacher, who came to the front of the class and removed the sheet covering my brown paper roll. There were several small pictures taped to the roll—a picture of Johannesburg, which I described as the city I had been born in, two pictures of African tribesmen in traditional dress, the beaches, a pride of lions. But the three pictures I was most proud of, the ones that stood out most prominently, were my paintings of the Drakensberg Mountains—Champagne Castle, Giant's Castle, and the cloud-covered Sani Pass, from which mountains, rolling hills and rivers are visible into the far distance. I had painted them in brilliant colors, the greens deep and dense; the grasses in the foreground typical of the dry gray-green and tan colors of Africa.

"The country I come from," I said in conclusion, "is filled with many different people and racial groups. Lots of good people have been hurt or killed doing what they feel is right. But one day they will succeed in their struggle." I looked at the back of the classroom, directly into my father's eyes. "And then," I said, "then we will be able to go home again."

After a brief moment of surprised silence, one of the parents began to clap, and the whole room joined in. No other presentation had been applauded, and I was filled with pride.

In the back of the classroom, Mrs. Tolliver dabbed at her eyes with a tissue—but my father was pale, trembling visibly, and, as the tears ran down his cheeks, he wiped them away with his shirtsleeve. It took me a long time—over forty years—before I understood precisely what he was crying about.

I took a very different professional direction from my father. Having always been interested in art, and having painted and sketched since I was a small boy, it was only natural that I become a painter. But my father, ever the practical man, insisted that I equip myself to be a teacher of painting in case my own talent turned out to be less than adequate.

As a result, I concentrated on fine arts in college, eventually did a Master's degree in modern American painters, and my first job was teaching undergraduates at the Boston University School of Fine Arts. In that sense, my father and I are similar—we both earned a living as academics, even if our subjects were very different.

Luckily, whatever talent I might have had, combined with a need to paint that has been one of the few constants in my life, has proven sufficient. My paintings of Cape Cod sell as well in Chatham as they do among the desert paintings that fill the galleries in Santa Fe, and their sale provides an additional source of income that adds a nice cushion to my academic salary.

To see me, you wouldn't think I had lived through anything out of the ordinary. I look like what I am—forty-eight, white, male; a boyish face, pleasant expression. My wife Dariya tells me that my age shows around the eyes, which are a little baggy and crease when I smile. I like my face, but it's nothing special. Fair complexion, receding light brown hair, a little gray at the temples. A bit under six feet tall, broad in the shoulder, skinny hips and thighs, beginning to run to fat.

As I sit here writing, I am wearing an often washed, once sky blue oxford shirt, open at the throat, with sleeves rolled up to the elbow. Chino pants, khaki colored, with an old leather belt. Running sneakers too well used to run in. Not important, I suppose, but my wife, who is a journalist and knows such things, tells me that revealing these details makes the tale seem real and give it immediacy. Besides, she says, when we're gone and our great grandchildren are reading this, they'll want to know something about the ancestor who told the tale.

She makes this kind of statement in all seriousness, with her dark eyes wide, heavy eyebrows furrowed in concentration, and a somber expression on her face. Her Russian accent is still thick, and while some of her words sound as if they've been strained through honey, others seem to emanate from the back of her throat, somewhere between a sexual moan and a guttural growl. Her skin is fair and smooth, her wavy hair, brown with reddish highlights, is cut short and falls to cover the tops of her ears. The counterpoint between her appearance and her speech is like sugar and spice; sweet melody set off by the excitement of a drumbeat.

Dariya loved my father, perhaps in part because he made the decision when I was a child to leave the African continent for safer shores. The relationship they established was good for them both, and I appreciated it because it relieved some of the awkwardness that sometimes crept into the interaction between my father and me. As grown men, we had developed a kind of reticence with each other that was a natural outgrowth of the way he raised me. Once my father discharged his paternal responsibility, he disconnected. There was no animus, anger or bad feeling—we became independent of each other organically, in the way lion or bear cubs or other warm-blooded wild animals do. It was as if he recognized that at some level his job was done, that I no longer needed him, and that it was time for each of us to make our own lives.

Over the years, we met once a week for lunch at a little Greek restaurant near the apartment. When Dariya and I married, he occasionally came to our home for dinner, and Dariya, lacking parents or family in the US, adopted my father as hers. Although he cut me loose to live my own life, he recognized that others might need him. Dariya needed to be a caring daughter, and he had responded in kind. And once our children were born, I watched with amazement—and perhaps some resentment—as he turned into a warm, interested and loving grandfather.

When Sally was six, he sat at her little play table and had a tea party with her as if it were the most important event of his week, drinking pretend tea from tiny cups and taking little bites from an Oreo cookie as if were a serious French pastry. And then, not to be outdone, Greg, who was two years younger, insisted that Grandpa throw a ball with him. I watched my father throw a rubber ball to his four year old grandson with a gentleness and patience that I would have sworn were absent from my own childhood. As it turned out, very little of what I believed about my childhood was accurate.

My father's life seemed to me uneventful, if not downright boring. For forty years he was a professor of engineering who only traveled outside Massachusetts when he was invited to lecture elsewhere. He had few visitors and fewer friends, and I knew virtually nothing about his past.

He was an only child; his mother died before I was born; his father, my grandfather Papa Mischa, died shortly after we left South Africa. His closest relatives had been his father's two sisters and their families in Moscow, whom he had never met. Even the existence of family in Russia had come to light only when, as a teenager, I discovered him weeping over a letter he had received from Moscow, reporting on the death of one of his aunts.

For as long as I can remember, he was unwilling to discuss anything to do with the past, burying the details of my mother's living and dying. Now, in middle age, I've made my peace with his secretive nature. No matter how curious I might once have been, I realized that unearthing his story, with all its bones and baggage, would have meant reliving much of the pain of his separation from my mother and the difficulty of the years that followed.

I wish that he had tried to share his story with me while he was alive. It would have been a fascinating journey, and I might have confronted him with questions whose answers I can now only imagine. But it was a journey we didn't take together because he never raised it. And when he was diagnosed with pancreatic cancer, he didn't share that with me, either, until his disease was so advanced that he could no longer deny it, and by then it was too late for any treatment.

I wept at my father's grave, which surprised me; but what surprised me more was that the intensity of my grief continued for months.

Most of the issues I had as a child and as a teenager had been resolved years earlier, and I accepted anything that remained unresolved as the limitations that were a part of every relationship between adult children and their parents. Or so I thought. But my response following his death was an indication that much between us had remained unresolved, and my grief was made up of many strands. I felt that he had died, as did my mother, leaving me alone; and, like her, he left unanswered questions in his wake.

The truth is that he did want to share his story with me, but I could never have imagined why.

Shortly before he died, he told Dariya that he had left a bulging file in a drawer in his desk. He wanted to make sure that after his death, I would sit down and go through the folder, and she assured him that she would make it happen.

In the folder were several yellow, lined pads covered with notes. There were photographs and newspaper clippings, and a carefully wrapped pile of old letters. And there was the manuscript, in three parts. The first was neatly formatted and printed; the middle, also printed but unedited, must have been written when he was still well, but feeling the pressure of time. Then there was the final section, written in bed with his laptop on his knees, which he had left in the file folder on a flash-drive.

I was surprised by the quantity and variety of what he had left me, but I was not yet ready for it. I needed time to settle the estate, go through his personal effects, give his clothes to charity, and sell his condo. And I needed time to grieve.

Several weeks after my father's death, before I had begun trying to read the file again, I answered the phone to an unfamiliar voice that addressed me as if we were lifelong friends. It was obviously a long-distance call, but I could make out a voice that was remarkably slow and clear, the English strongly accented in a way that was unfamiliar to me. It was the South African accent I was accustomed to, with the addition of something far more exotic.

"Hello. Do I have the honor of addressing Steven Green?"

"Yes, this is Steven. Who am I speaking to?"

"I'm so glad to hear your voice, Steven." The voice was deep, and slow, and it contained a hint of warmth and humor, almost a teasing quality. "Finally. You may not yet know of me, but my name is Mandla. Mandla Mkhize. I am called Khabazela by my friends. There was a time—not an easy time—when your parents and I knew each other well, and we worked together for the same cause. I'm so sorry to hear about your father. I would have liked to see him again."

"You knew my mother?" I asked.

"It is a complicated story," he said, "Which I hope to one day share with you." There was a long pause. "Yes, I knew her."

"I'm afraid my father never mentioned your name to me. How can I help you?"

"I think it's more about how I can help you." He paused. "Tell me, Steven," he said warmly, "how are you?" His voice was deep, and there was gentleness and knowing in his tone that put a lump in my throat. I was silent a long time, but he waited patiently.

"I was very sad to hear of your father's death. I had hoped to put the past behind us and to reconcile with Lenny, but he has preempted me." He paused. "I will have to reconcile without him. But we South Africans have become used to asking forgiveness from—and forgiving—those who are no longer among us."

"Yes," I said. I had no idea what he was talking about. "Did you and my father quarrel?"

He didn't answer my question, but after a moment he continued, his voice calm and even.

"I have known of you always, Steven, while you have just discovered my existence. I have hoped for many years that we would have occasion to speak. We will meet soon, I am sure, and I have no doubt that we will have much to say to each other. I am eager to see you again."

He was a stranger, yet he spoke to me with warmth and even affection, as if we had some deep and meaningful connection. I didn't understand it, but I felt as if we had known each other forever. I had no way of responding to his words, and I was silent.

"Your father told you nothing about me," he said. It was as much a question as it was a statement.

"My father never spoke about his life before we left South Africa," I said. "But I've discovered that at the end he apparently had a change of heart, and he spent the last months of his life writing a document for me to read."

"And has this document raised any issues that you might want to discuss?"

"I've been too busy concluding his affairs to read it yet," I said, "But what makes you think there would be issues I want to discuss with you?"

In answer he chuckled deeply.

"Please don't take offense at my laughter," he said. "I've been waiting for your questions for decades—but I'm laughing because they reveal so clearly that you have not yet read your father's history. Some things will be resolved as you read, and when we meet, I will be happy to answer any that are not."

"I can't imagine why you're so sure that our paths will cross," I said, "although I'd be happy to meet with you. Perhaps you can tell me about my mother—my father never spoke about her. And if you have any insights into him, I'd be interested in those, too." I paused. "My father didn't have many friends. To be honest, I'm a little surprised to hear from you."

He chuckled again. "I thank you for the invitation, if that is what it was. But it is not as simple as getting together to drink coffee—I live in Soweto, just outside Johannesburg." When he continued, his voice took on a serious tone. "At this precise moment, you have no interest at all in meeting me. But that will change. All I ask of you, Steven, is that you suspend judgment until you finish reading what he left you. And when you have finished reading, I invite you to call me."

I wrote down his number, and when I asked for the spelling of his name, he had to repeat it several times.

"I understand that this is frustrating for you," he said, "and I would conclude it today, but it is not mine to end. Please, trust me when I say that this is the beginning of the openness you desire, and that when this process your father started comes to conclusion, there will be no more secrets. Okay?"

"I don't have much choice, do I?"

"I'm afraid not," he said. "And Steven, there is one more thing I would ask of you."

"What's that?"

"When you were a child, you called me Khabazela. It's what you called me when we last met, at a small farmhouse outside Johannesburg, when I rescued a little boy who had climbed too far up a pear tree and couldn't get down without some help. I may have changed since then," he laughed, "but not as much as I assume you have. I would like for you to call me Khabazela again."

At the mention of being rescued from a pear tree a wave of images and sensations surged through me; I felt buffeted by them as if by driven water, and when they receded I was left dry, but shaken. There was the feel of a comforting hand on my ankle and a voice urging me to step down to the next branch. I didn't remember the farmhouse he mentioned, but I saw it—a little frame house secluded in a forest of smallish trees and bushes. Many were fruit trees in full bloom, and I was aware of the colors—oranges and reds, dusky purple and yellow—and of the mixed sweetish odors of wild fruit on the trees and on the ground. There were four or five children with me, and we were playing hide and seek. I was surprised to see that they were black children, because I don't remember having anything but white playmates.

Nestled among the trees was a small, peeling wood frame farmhouse, and standing beside the front door were two people talking intently to each other—one was a tall black man. As soon as my memory registered that the other figure was my mother, the current seemed to cut out, and the image disappeared. I had no idea where it came from, or where it went. And for the first time I realized that although I had no memory of this man, I did know him.

"Khabazela," I said, trying out the name. It was strangely comfortable on my tongue.

"Yes?" he answered.

I didn't want to tell him what I remembered; not yet, not until I had a better understanding of what had happened. And I was just beginning to have an inkling of how much I didn't know.

"I was calling you by your name," I said, "as you asked."

"Thank you, Steven," he replied. "That means a great deal to me. Now go and read your father's words to you. We will talk again."

We ended our conversation, and I sat in silence for a long time. I had the sense that I was on a journey I hadn't planned, along an unmarked road. I had no idea where I was going, and wondered whether I would be the same person when I arrived at my destination.

There was only one way to find out. I reached for my father's manuscript, and began reading.

two

LENNY

Boston, 2001

Steven:

When I first began writing this, I wanted to do it in partnership with you, to give you the personal and family history that I have so long avoided sharing. I wanted to be face to face with you as the reasons for my avoidance became clear. I had a fantasy of being able to relive the experiences, see the expressions on your face, and, I hoped, be the recipient of your forgiveness while I was still able to appreciate it. What I really wanted was to feel the relief of being held to account. Selfish, I suppose.

Sadly, I lacked the courage. You long ago stopped asking questions about the past, and you have indicated by your actions, and by the distance you maintain from me, that you feel at peace with what you don't know. Perhaps I should have let well enough alone, but it became clear some months ago that I could not go to my grave in silence. This will make no sense to you now, I know, but you will at some point learn about our history from a perspective different from mine. I know nothing about how this other perspective will paint me, but I can be sure that it will not portray me as I would wish. And if I want a fair hearing, I need to speak out now.

I waited too long; should have begun long ago, when you had time in your life for me, when you were younger, less experienced, and less impatient than you are now with me. I'm disappointed, but that's not your fault. What I did initially was intended to be an act of self-sacrifice, but in failing to be honest with you it turned into an expression of cowardice, and the passage of time has only compounded my duplicity.

My medical prognosis is bleak. The type of pancreatic cancer I have offers few treatment options beyond an awful, disfiguring surgery—and I'm not much interested in a procedure that might extend my life by dragging out my dying. I don't want you to remember my end that way. There will be enough for you to deal with after I'm gone.

I intend to spend what time I have left getting this story—my confession, I suppose—down on paper. You can read it when you're ready, and I have little doubt that once you start, you'll find it sufficiently engrossing to carry you through to the end. In advance, I ask that you not judge me—us—too harshly. I hope for your own sake that you can find it in your heart to understand and forgive. It's a gift I have not been able to give myself.

With all my love
Dad

Johannesburg, 1953

I fell in love with your mother as I watched four uniformed police-men escort her out of the Witwatersrand University newspaper office in Johannesburg. She strode tall and defiant in their midst, taken into custody for writing an editorial critical of government policy.

I had read the editorial the previous day and been struck by the writer's courage, and by the naiveté of the writing—and I knew that it could only have been written by Michaela Davidson. Her topic was the forced removal of 50,000 mostly black residents from their homes in Sophiatown. The area was to be bulldozed and a white suburb built, and the inhabitants moved to a new area called the South West Townships, which in later years became notorious as Soweto.

I knew that there would be some kind of backlash—the government didn't take kindly to criticism. But I expected that they would punish her through the university administration in the form of censorship or reprimand. Instead, infuriated by this young student's refusal to be silenced by threats of disciplinary action, the police raided the university newspaper office. And they did it late on a Friday afternoon, when there would be few students or faculty around to object to her arrest.

Your mother and I didn't know each other well. I was older by a few years, and I had always been uncomfortable with women. But our paths crossed frequently, and it would have been difficult not to take note of her. She was attractive and daring, she smiled easily, her laugh was open and enthusiastic. And in our socially conservative culture, she had no hesitation about flaunting convention. I thought I was invisible to her, but she told me later that she had been watching me for years, a shy, studious boy a few years ahead of her.

I had just dropped a book off at my professor's office and was about to push open the front door and walk out of the building when she was escorted down the corridor, two officers in front of her and two behind. Her flushed face betrayed her fear, but she walked with her shoulders straight and her head held high, and as she reached me she came to a sudden stop. The officer directly behind her stepped on her heel and tripped, reaching a hand out before him and shoving her shoulder. He almost bowled her over, barely righted himself, and swore under his breath.

He was clearly ill-disposed to this pretty, privileged girl with her Jewish name, her English accent, and the trouble she was causing. She was playing with fire, breaking the law, undermining the principles he held dear.

"Keep going, girlie," he said. His English had the particularly heavy guttural accent common to those whose first language was Afrikaans.

"I'm going to give a message to my friend," she replied coolly, "so that someone knows where I am." She turned to me. "Lenny, please call my parents and let them know I've been arrested. They're listed under Samuel Davidson. If he's not home, he'll be in his dental office."

"You know this young woman?" one of the officers asked.

"Of course I know her," I said. "What's going on? Where are you taking her?"

Both officers looked at me, scowled, and stepped forward to stand at her sides. They took her by the elbows and began to pull her along. "Call my parents, Lenny," she shouted over her shoulder, struggling to release the grip on her elbows. "They're taking me to the prison at Marshall Square. Michaela..." she shouted again, "Michaela Davidson."

I was paralyzed at first, mortified that I had neither the bravery or physical resources to help her. The policemen hustled her into the back of their wagon and drove off. I rushed home to call her parents.

Their home was in Cyrildene, an older suburb outside Johannesburg, and her father's office was at the same address. He was listed as a Doctor of dental medicine. I called the house and the housemaid answered the phone. Dr. Davidson was in his surgery seeing patients, she said, but she could take a message for me.

"This is an emergency," I answered. "Please get him. Michaela's been arrested."

I heard the slap of her slippers echoing on the stone floor as she ran from the phone, calling to Dr. Davidson. There was a brief silence, and then the sound of his shoes approaching on the flagstones.

"Hello?" he demanded. "What's this about my daughter being arrested?"

"I was just at the university with her—"

"This better not be a joke," he said, angrily. "Who are you, young man? What's your name?"

"Lenny," I said," flustered by his tone. "Lenny Green. I wouldn't joke about this. Michaela asked me to call you."

"This isn't the kind of news one expects from strangers," he said.

"I'm not a stranger, sir," I said. "I'm a friend of Michaela's. I'm in the school of engineering at the University. As I was leaving there this afternoon, four policemen were escorting her out of the building. She called to me, asked me to phone you and let you know that she's been arrested. She's being taken to the prison at Marshall Square."

"How was she?" he asked. "Did she seem all right? Had she been mistreated?"

"I don't think so," I said. I thought of the way she walked, her shoulders held straight and high, her flushed face revealing both her fear and her fury. The idea that they might have treated her badly hadn't crossed my mind. In the 1950s the opposition was still largely peaceful, and white middle class women were treated respectfully, even if they were protesting.

"It must be that editorial she wrote about Sophiatown," he said anxiously. "I told her she was crossing the line." He paused, as if at a loss. "Lenny, was it? Green?"

"Yes, sir."

"Thank you for the phone call, Lenny. I'd better make some enquiries and get over to Marshall Square. Good bye."

I spent the evening thinking about the way she held herself, the dark hair framing her face as she looked back at me. Walking between the muscular officers whose authority gave even more weight to their already substantial bulk, she seemed diminutive and fragile, but there was a way in which her sense of resolution and grace were made even more powerful for being housed in so slight a body. I kept hearing her voice calling my name, and realized that I wanted to hear her say it again. She had referred to me as her friend, and I wondered whether she had done so because she wanted the officers to think we were friends, or because there was indeed a possibility that we might be.

The next day when I was through with classes I walked by the newspaper office to see what had happened to her, but she wasn't there. None of the other students in the office had heard from her. I was surprised by my disappointment as I left, and went home, planning to call her that evening. But I didn't have a chance, because she called me first.

My father was a widower—my mother died in a car accident when I was in my last year of high school. The night Michaela called, my father was out taking inventory at the furniture store, as he did twice a year. It was something I had helped with throughout high school, but when I reached university my father insisted that I stay home and study. Usually

I insisted, and ended up helping out for a few hours at the end of the day. But that evening I was at home, working on a paper evaluating stress measurement in steel railroad trestles, an area in which I eventually specialized. When the phone rang, the last person I expected to find on the other end of the line was Michaela.

"Hello?"

"Lenny, this is Michaela. Michaela Davidson."

"Michaela," I said, rising from my chair at the kitchen table. "I'm so relieved to hear your voice," I said. "Are you okay?"

"I'm fine," she said. "I wanted to thank you for yesterday, and to apologize for imposing. I hope you didn't mind the way I asked for your help."

"Not at all," I protested. "You didn't have much choice."

"I suppose I didn't." She paused, and for an awkward moment we listened to each other breathing.

"Did they treat you with respect?"

"Respect?" She laughed. "That's the last thing I expected from them. They're bullies. My father came down to the police station as soon as you called the house. They only kept me in a cell for a few hours."

"They put you in a cell?" I said, feeling more confusion than anger. "Like a common criminal? For what—writing an editorial in the school paper?"

"Don't sound so shocked, Lenny. Where have you been? It's happening all over the country, and this is just the beginning."

"But on university grounds? To students? Women? It's madness. Where was the university administration?"

"Scared into silence, like the rest of the country," she said. "Did you read the editorial that got me arrested?"

"Yes," he said.

"What did you think of it?"

I wondered whether to be truthful, or to simply praise her, and quickly decided that this—and she—were too important to be glossed over.

"I thought it was well written," I said, gathering my thoughts.

"We both know I'm not asking about the writing."

"It was good, Michaela. You interviewed people about to be thrown out of their homes, and that put a human face on the problem. Great interviews, by the way. No one could question the intentions of the writer, or her courage." I paused. "But I'm not sure the editorial will achieve anything, other than making you some dangerous enemies."

There was silence on the other end, which I took as a sure sign that she was displeased with my response. But I underestimated her tenacity and determination to get it right, and to get what she wanted.

"Will you be at the university tomorrow?" she asked.

"In the afternoon," I answered. "How about you?"

"I'll be in the newspaper office after three," she said. "Will you meet me there?"

"Wait for me," I said. "I'll come by when my classes are over."

I was in the last year of my engineering degree; your mother was just beginning her third year in the school of music. We were an unlikely match. In my graduating class photograph I stand in the back row, tall and serious. Looking today at that young man, I see long, smooth cheeks, deep-set eyes, and what looks like a wide, easy smile, and nothing of the reticence I felt inside. Your mother used to say later that my face was unusual—it combined serious intensity with the possibility of wild abandon. Throughout my life, mostly unknowingly, I have used this contradiction in my appearance to unnerve people and put them off balance—but it was just this contradiction, she said, that attracted her.

Like most students, we both lived at home. I was an only child, and although my father and I were close, he was not a talkative man. Once my mother died, he spent most of his time in the furniture store they ran together. I don't think he ever fully recovered from her death. We lived together amiably, but the house was haunted by my mother's absence, and I spent as little time at home as I could. I was focused on engineering and on my career, and while I might have been interested in socializing, I had neither the time nor the confidence. I did have friends, but most of my contact with them was playing cricket on weekends. In my spare time I read—but until I met Michaela, I made no connection between the political philosophy I was interested in, and the realities we lived with.

In contrast, your mother was a whirlwind. She thought quickly, moved rapidly, and spoke her mind. She gave the impression of knowing where she was going. At the university she knew everyone, began writing for the paper in her first year, and was voluble and opinionated. She loved music and had chosen it as her area of study, but I don't think she ever intended to use it to earn a living, and in fact she never did. She had an attractive, open face, wide brown eyes and an infectious smile, and with her fair skin, her enthusiasm, and her slender figure, there had never been a lack of boys in her life. Luckily for me, she found them all immature and shallow.

Like me, your mother was an only child; your grandfather, Samuel Davidson, was a dentist, your grandmother, Selma, a teacher. Even in the early 1950s when such activity was unheard of, Selma made it a condition of employment that her domestic servants be willing to learn the educational skills they were denied as black South Africans. Four evenings a week after supper, sitting around the kitchen table, she taught reading, arithmetic and basic science to a group that also sometimes included servants from neighboring homes, if their employers approved.

As soon as your mother was old enough, she watched the classes, then she sat in on them, and finally, as a high school student, stood in as a relief teacher. And of course—it could only have been recognized in hindsight—the contact she had with domestic servants over the kitchen table at night gave her a respect for their intelligence and their person-hood that was denied the rest of us.

Both of your mother's parents were opposed to the political direction South Africa was taking. Your grandmother was by far the more radical of the two, and your grandfather was horrified when it became clear that their daughter intended to put into practice what she had heard spoken in their home. He tried to dissuade her. The times were dangerous and the laws more stringent; the opposition had achieved frightening increases in power. The stakes were higher, he said, and she did not yet understand what price she might have to pay.

But in the end, her father's opposition was not equal to the combined weight of her mother's radical commitment to change, and the anarchist leanings of her mother's Russian parents. Michaela was so much a rebel by nature that it would have been strange had she not gravitated to the more extreme position.

Eventually your grandfather Samuel realized that he could do no more for his daughter than he could do for his wife—that his job was to love them both, provide for and protect them as best he could, and, ulti-mately, let them live their lives. While Michaela was still at university, however, he thought he could still have an impact on her behavior and on her choices. About that he was mistaken—but about much else he could not have been more accurate.

At the time we left South Africa, Steven, you were too young to understand its history. And when we reached Boston you were so intent on becoming an American that current events outside the United States were of no interest to you. As far as I know, you never took a course or read a book about the country of your birth. But to understand what those committed to changing the country were up against, you need to know a little of the past. This is my understanding of how we arrived at the events that landed your mother in jail.

South Africa's history is a succession of minor events that were unforeseeable, yet inevitable. It started with the need to prevent scurvy, a vitamin C deficiency that was the scourge of sailors on long voyages. In 1652, the Dutch East India Company established a re-provisioning center at the tip of the continent to provide fresh food for Dutch ships sailing around the tip of Africa. It came to be known as the Cape Colony.

Within a few years, employees began agitating for permission to start their own farms, and soon the company started offering settlers free passage to the Cape Colony. It was a new, wide open place at the tip of fertile Africa, and settlers came in droves to escape a Europe that seemed to them crowded, tradition-bound and burdened by its history. Others, like the French Huguenots, came seeking freedom from Catholic persecution. They merged with the descendants of the Dutch until all that was left was the Dutch pronunciation of their French names.

When Napoleon conquered the Netherlands in 1795, Britain sent troops to Africa to ensure that the Cape Colony didn't fall into French hands. Twenty five years later, the first British settlers began to arrive. By then, the Netherlands had formally given the Cape to Britain. The Dutch settlers, the Boers, resented British colonial rule, and because Boer farmers were dependent on slavery to work their lands, they especially resented the interference of abolitionist missionaries.

Boer farmers had enslaved the two yellow-skinned indigenous people, the San and the Khoikhoi, using them as house servants and farm workers, and many farms were ruined in 1833 when the British Empire abolished slavery. A few years later, seeking freedom from British rule, several thousand Boers loaded their belongings into ox-drawn wagons and traveled inland in what came to be called The Great Trek. As they spread north from the Cape Colony, the Boers became the Afrikaner nation, and their history is one of battles with the black tribes they encountered, among them the Zulu and the Xhosa and the Shangaan.

Through the teaching of the Dutch Reformed Church, the Afrikaners came to believe that they were the modern Israelites, a Chosen People to whom God had given South Africa. Their hardships—battles with black tribes as well as with the British—were the trials they had to endure before the Promised Land could be theirs.

When the Union of South Africa was established in 1910 as a self-governing country and a part of the British Empire, the constitution put control completely in the hands of a deeply divided white population. They spoke different languages, had different cultures and religions, and while the Afrikaners were primarily farmers, the British gravitated to industry and commerce.

In the years leading up to the Second World War, Afrikaners began leaving rural areas for the cities. Because they lacked training, they were at an economic disadvantage to the better educated and more culturally sophisticated British; worse yet, they found that they had to compete for jobs with blacks. This was politically unpalatable. In the election of 1948, their party, the Nationalists, came to power with a promise to strengthen what had until then been separation of the races in fact, if not in law.

The election was really a minority victory since blacks, who made up eighty percent of the population, were denied the vote. Nevertheless, the Nationalists wasted no time putting their much more severe version of apartheid into the legal code. It became a crime for different racial groups to live together; sex across color lines became a punishable offense, and they established a system of job reservation to ensure that the massive black labor force was relegated to the lowest paying, most menial jobs.

Entire black communities were forcibly moved from their homes into newly established Homelands, culled from land that was barely arable, with limited mobility because of the Pass Laws, and no opportunity. It was this forced movement based on race that occasioned Michaela's editorial about Sophiatown, one of the oldest black settlements in Johannesburg.

Your mother's father Samuel was a quiet man. He preferred to be in the background, which is where he lived most of his life. But he and your grandmother, Selma, had just picked up their daughter at the main police station in the center of Johannesburg. It was not an experience for which life had prepared them.

Michaela told me what happened, and much later, after you were born and your grandfather believed for a brief moment that her days of dangerous protest were over, he shared with me his recollection of the conversation they had on the way home from the police station.

"Teach your daughter some respect for the law," the duty officer had said. "The time for these games is over. If you can't control her, we will. Now take her home with you and make sure she keeps her *kaffir*-loving ideas to herself. Understand?"

Neither of your grandparents had ever been treated with such contempt, and they were angry and shaken.

"I hate that the police were so awful to you," said Michaela, filled with indignation. "And I'm sorry that I had to call you to bail me out."

"You did the right thing, Michaela," said her mother. "Of course you had to call us. But how did you expect them to treat you? They didn't invite you to a bloody tea party. If you're going to fight against a police state, you have to be prepared for retaliation. They're not going to lie down and let you roll over them."

"She's not fighting anyone," said her father. "This is over and done with, Michaela. You're out of it in one piece—this time. God only knows what they'll do next time they get their hands on you. It's a lesson to all of us. No more incendiary editorials," he warned.

"You want me to just keep quiet and watch as families and communities are destroyed?" she said as they drove home. "That's not what I've learned from you. You taught me that if we cower when tyrants flex their muscles, nothing will ever change. It may be more dangerous now, but these black people are being treated like cattle. Don't we have a responsibility to stand up for them?"

"Time to get off your soapbox," he said. Michaela told me later that never in her life had he spoken so sharply to her. "The people running this government are fanatics. They think they have God in their pocket, and they believe they're passing His laws. They don't care about anyone's welfare but their own—and you know that even in their churches they preach that the blacks are an inferior race put here for their convenience. These people have a different name and a different uniform, but they're motivated by a belief as hideous and deluded as the Nazis'. They're full of themselves and their destiny, and they've given us fair warning tonight. In their theatre the only place for blacks is backstage, and there's standing room only for people with our political beliefs. For Jews, there's no room at all. We're out in the parking lot."

He looked at her, and in the darkness of the rearview mirror, she could see that he was trying to smile.

"Their political beliefs will eventually backfire and kick them right in the backside. But in the meantime, they hold all the cards." He was silent, and she stretched out a hand from the back seat and squeezed his shoulder as he drove.

"Thanks, Daddy," she said. "I'm sorry if I scared you."

"Don't think you didn't scare me, too," said her mother, turning in the passenger seat so that she could look back and forth from her husband to her daughter. "The difference between your father and me is that while I'm concerned for your safety, I'm also proud of you. I don't want you to stop fighting these bastards. I just want you to do it with intelligence, and I don't want you to do it alone. You can be far more effective if you join—"

"No, Selma." Samuel interrupted his wife sharply. "There will be no political organizing tonight. Please. Not after this. Not now."

Your mother was alone in the university news office when I arrived, sitting with her back to me, typing furiously. I stood in the doorway, staring at her. She was using an old manual typewriter—an Underwood—you had to work hard on those machines—and even from behind I could sense her determination. Her hair was cut short, revealing a tanned, slender neck, and she sat with her back straight, swaying slightly as she typed so that her head remained motionless as she concentrated on what she was writing. But for the staccato sound of the typewriter, she might have been dancing.

Pursuing her was risky, and I had never been a risk-taker. She was beautiful and headstrong; everyone knew her. Men with a lot more to offer than I did were in constant pursuit—men with charm and good looks, some of them from wealthy families. I couldn't imagine what she wanted from me. Several times I almost turned and tiptoed out, but

I didn't leave, and eventually I called her name. She stopped typing, turned around, and her face lit up when she saw me. I wondered whether she was really glad to see me—or whether this was how she was with everyone.

There was no small talk with your mother. Not then. Not ever. She always got right to the point, I think because she felt there was so much to do. And that first day we sat down together, she wanted to get right to work—to discuss what I liked and didn't like about her editorial. At first I was flattered to see how interested she was in what I had to say, but after awhile I realized that no one before me had the courage to tell her that her approach wouldn't work, or to explain why. Other people had complimented her on her willingness to tackle a topic as controversial as Sophiatown, but warned her that what she was doing was dangerous. But I soon learned that there was a reason why no one gave her any feedback on how she could be more effective: she didn't make it easy.

"What's wrong with being straightforward?" she argued. She had small hands; her fingers were slender and graceful, and she used them for emphasis as she spoke—as exclamation points, full stops, question marks. "I have strong views of what's right and wrong, and I express them clearly. That's what an editorial is supposed to do, isn't it?"

"Yes," I explained patiently, "but it's only a first step. You have to do more than state your case clearly—you have to make it convincing in a way that people can hear."

"The police were apparently convinced enough to arrest me."

She glared at me and pursed her lips in a gesture that would become a hallmark of her determination, and I learned eventually that it was a sign for me to back off. But at the time everything was too new, for both of us, and I stumbled on, not knowing where I was taking us.

"Don't delude yourself," I said. "Being arrested isn't a sign that you've written well—it's only an indication that the authorities are threatened by your subject matter. Even a badly written editorial that was critical of what's happening in Sophiatown would have brought them down on you like a ton of bricks."

"Thanks for the vote of confidence," she said sullenly. "So how would you have made this more convincing?"

"You need it to tell a story," I said, "what does it feel like to people being tossed out of their homes? You have to interview more of them and tell their tales, in their own words. Bring in other voices, more authoritative than yours—quote liberal politicians like Helen Suzman, who's probably as outraged as you are. You have to persuade your readers that this is bigger than just you. You're not an isolated voice—you reflect the views of many people, some of them influential."

I paused and looked at her, fearing that she'd had enough of my frankness and was about to tell me to leave. But she was looking at me with interest and curiosity.

"Go on," she said. "What else?"

"You're writing for the provincial white audience in this country—but you can't bring about real change that way. You need the opinion of the civilized world behind you. That means you have to provide some historical perspective; condemn what's happening here in a way that lets the whole world see what the Nationalists are really doing."

"What is it you think they're doing?"

"Can't you see it?" I asked, incredulous. "It's so obvious. The British abolished slavery over a hundred years ago, and these people are trying to bring it back in all but name. But Michaela," I said, softening my tone, "you have to find a way to do all this without getting arrested. And I don't know how to do that."

"If speaking my mind will get me arrested, then so be it," she said. "It's still legal to express an opinion in this country. If they don't have a reason to detain me they have to let me go. That's the law."

She banged her closed fist on the table, and I found myself reaching over to cover it with mine. Her hand was small and warm, and she opened and closed her fist within my grasp. It felt like a bird fluttering against the cage of my fingers. Her eyes were wide, and the heat radiated from my face as I spoke.

"They can close you down as easily as this," I said softly. "What you really need right now is to shut up and listen."

I looked at the delicate curve of her jaw, at the promise of her full mouth, and what I did next surprised me as much as it did Michaela. I was shy and inexperienced, and I felt clumsy. But the impulse to kiss her was irresistible. Through the dark lashes and into the depths of her liquid eyes, there was a dawning recognition that she knew she was about to be kissed—even before I was aware that I was going to kiss her. And her kiss expressed the more generous part of a personality that was often harsh, angry and uncompromising. Her lips were soft and yielding, and with her tongue she signaled that she would be as passionate in love as she was in argument.

Our first kiss, sitting at the scratched table in the press office, with my hand covering her fist, typified our relationship. Somehow she managed me into things before I even knew I was being manipulated, and I found myself being assertive in a way I hadn't thought possible. She would say later that no other men she went out with were able to match her; they just buckled under her tireless onslaught.

What was telling, about both of us, is that she wanted me to withstand her battering; she admitted that I was the first man she didn't want to overpower. To my amazement, I became what she needed me to be.

I was proud and gratified to see that your mother found something worthy and acceptable in me. We were so different, and she was far ahead of me in so many ways. I found her reckless, but her activism showed a degree of courage that I lacked. She was convinced that I was naïve, but she valued my ability to think strategically. That combination, she felt, might make me a willing student, someone she could persuade and bring along to the point where I too would respond to the crushing injustice of the shameful world we lived in. And then, she hoped, I would be willing to take risks, too.

I looked up at your mother and wondered how she came to know it so clearly, and so much earlier than I did. But the truth was that I had known for a long time what was and wasn't shameful. As a little boy, growing up in a small town outside Johannesburg, I'd experienced first-hand what living in this world had done to us, both black and white. I learned that in a world where unwritten laws governed the conduct between the races, every word has a consequence. But I didn't know what those consequences were until I had caused terrible harm to someone I loved.

Let me tell you a story about how I learned not to speak the unspeakable when I was just a child.

Johannesburg, 1945

I was in my pajamas, sitting curled in a chair in the kitchen with Roslyn, the black woman who had worked for us since before I was born. It was late, way after my bedtime, and my school friend, Alex, who was spending the night, was already sleeping.

Roslyn was a plump woman in her mid-thirties, with full cheeks and smooth skin. Most of the time she wore a serious, worried expression, but when she smiled her whole face opened up, and her cheeks dimpled. She wasn't smiling now—in fact, she was studiously ignoring me. She stood over the ironing board in her starched light blue and white uniform, iron in hand, smoothing sheets and pillowcases, ironing my father's shirts, putting creases in my trouser legs, refusing to look up at me.

"Go to bed, Leonard," she said wearily. "There is nothing you can do to change my mind. I'm going to tell your father when he comes home."

"You don't have to be to be so mean," I said.

"Me, mean? What about you? You supposed to be in bed half past eight. Instead you been playing around, making messes with your friend, being rude to me. You don't care about me—but I have to take care, cleaning up your mess, running about after a big boy like you, when I have ironing to do for your mother. She's not going to be pleased that it's not done, and I'm tired. No. It's enough with you. I'm going to tell your father when he comes home. Maybe he beats you with his belt; it will be a good lesson for you. Maybe next time they go out, you behave better than tonight."

In my mind, there was no next time. I had been badly behaved all week. My father had made clear that if we misbehaved, it was the last time Alex would sleep over, and that in addition I would be punished. What form the punishment would take I didn't know—although my father was not overly strict, he knew that I was easily shamed, and that withholding his approval was generally punishment enough.

But there was something in me that wouldn't allow me to do what Roslyn said at that moment, some kind of pubescent rebellion I couldn't stop. I wanted to get what I wanted, and was suddenly for the first time reckless enough to speak about what was ordinarily taboo in our little world —something that made me voice words forbidden by the social contract that bound us.

"It's not my fault, Rosy, that things are the way they are. I didn't make them this way. I didn't choose to be born white, you know, any more than you chose to be born black. And I didn't make the laws that force you to live in a different place, and make it so that you have to work in my parents' house."

She looked at me strangely.

"What you talking about, Leonard?" she said, and went back to her ironing.

I was in unknown territory, beyond what was acceptable, and my heart was beating wildly. There were few things that could not be said to an African servant—yet Roslyn was family, and I knew even as I spoke that I was overstepping the bounds of propriety set by my parents.

"I'm talking about the way things are, between white people and black."

She looked up at me again, briefly, out of the side of her face, and I could see the tiny red veins in the whites of her eyes.

"Go to bed, Leonard," she said wearily, waving me away with the back of her hand. "I'm tired of you tonight, and I have work to do. Your mother and father will be home soon—don't let them find you still awake. Go."

Roslyn stood bowed over her ironing board, repeatedly running the iron back and forth over my father's white shirt, stopping every few runs to dip her hand in a bowl of water and flick moisture on the fabric. Eventually she looked up at me, briefly, reproachfully.

"What?" I said. "You're forced to live in a poor township, far away from here, and to work in our house and live in a little room in the back-yard. You have to watch us living together as a family, but you can only see your children one day a week. And they don't have all the things that we have. If I were you I would be angry, too—but that doesn't mean you have to take your anger out on me by telling my father I've misbehaved."

When I started talking, I didn't quite know what I wanted to say, or what impact it would have, or even whether I would be doing my cause any good. It was quite possible that Roslyn would be infuriated by these words from a child, and that she would be undeterred from her intent to tell on me when my parents came home. What I didn't expect was that she would say nothing; that she would refuse to look at me; that huge, clear drops would fill her eyes and roll down her cheeks to form a dark puddle on my father's starched shirt, and that she would do nothing to stop them.

Even at twelve I recognized her helplessness; saw in her tears a loss too deep for words to express. And I felt a sense of power at the reaction I had been able to elicit from her. I had plumbed the depths of her life; forced a tacit admission that her time was spent in involuntary servitude. I had spoken the unspeakable, revealed the fiction created by both master and servant so that we could survive each day—the servant unashamed by what she allowed herself to suffer without rising up in fury against her masters to reclaim personhood and birthright; and the master, una- shamed by what he was willing to impose upon a people regardless of the cost to his own humanity.

"I'm sorry, Rosy," I said. "Please, don't cry. I didn't mean to make you sad."

"Yes, you did," she said, "and now look."

She put her iron down on the stand and picked up my father's shirt, a brown angular burn visible on one shoulder. I knew that Roslyn was proud of her ironing, and that she never burned anything. She dropped the shirt into a basket at her side, and for a moment rested both hands on the ironing board, her head lowered and her weight hanging from her shoulders.

"I'm sorry about the shirt, Rosy. It got burned because of me. Please, don't worry. I'll explain to my mother that I was annoying you," I said bravely, "and that you got distracted."

But Roslyn ignored me.

"You can have what you want, Leonard," she said softly. "I will not tell your father about tonight. Not a word about your bad behavior. And nothing of this conversation."

She refused to look at me, but I could see that her eyes were swollen, her cheeks still wet.

"Now go to bed."

I rose from my chair and walked towards her, intending to give her a hug before I went back to my room. But she closed her eyes and looked down, the tears still falling from her cheeks like morning dew from a plant, uprooted and shaken. I turned and made my way through the kitchen, up the darkened corridor to my room, and climbed into bed. I didn't know then what rape was, but I knew that I had violated her— exposed her against her will, robbed her of something essential to her sense of well-being. In the process, I had soiled myself.

Roslyn didn't tell my father about my bad behavior that night, nor did she mention our conversation. But neither could she face me. Despite my efforts to engage her, to apologize, she turned away from me, and when I became insistent, she locked herself in her room. I stood out-side her door, entreating her to talk to me, and received only silence in response.

After that night, she wouldn't speak to me or look into my face. Shortly thereafter, she asked my mother for a reference, saying that she no longer wished to work for a family with children. She gave no reason, and my parents respected her decision. They asked me whether anything had occurred between us, or if I had in some way offended her, but I was too confused and humiliated by what I had done to tell them the truth. They could never have imagined what actually happened, and I never told them; never shared it, until now, with anyone else.

I knew she had three children who lived in a township with her mother or her aunt, and on her day off each week she traveled six hours one way by bus to spend a night with them. I never learned which township it was; never asked her children's names or their ages; never saw their pictures. Thoughts of my childhood are incomplete without her; I carry her face with me every day of my life. Her voice, her accented English, her dimpled cheeks and her laughter, the flowery smell of her hair oil, are a part of me. I didn't know her by any name other than Roslyn. And I never saw her again.

Johannesburg, 1953

After that first kiss, Michaela and I spent many hours together at the office and in coffee houses, and at the homes of like-minded friends. Your mother was always willing to take risks—she wanted to make bold statements, take action. We discussed our plans and the best ways to achieve them, and if I hadn't been there to inject moderation and caution, she would have been the one to lead the charge, to be in the vanguard, and to be the first one shot. I was much less politically motivated than she was, but I was also politically astute in a way that she would never be.

"You're not going to get them to change their plans for Sophiatown," I told her and a group of fellow students one night around the table in a local café. "Not by writing editorials or by demonstrating. It's a done deal. You think you can change their minds, but you can't."

I tried to explain why it was too late to stop the relocation. The government wanted to satisfy an adjacent community of poor whites who resented the proximity of the black community. They were already planning to bulldoze the area and build a white suburb over the ruins—which they ultimately did, naming it Triomf—Triumph—in unvarnished arrogance. The plan was to move residents out of the freehold of Sophiatown, where they were allowed to own land, and into a township where they would be denied property rights—where it was easier to monitor their movements. The strategy of the Nationalist Party was brilliant: take advantage of the strength of tribal bonds to fragment and weaken the opposition, and make it impossible to mount any united resistance to apartheid.

When I was through explaining how I thought it worked, Michaela leaned back in her chair, folded her arms, and looked at me quizzically.

"You've never been to Sophiatown," she said, "so you're talking theory—you've never seen the reality of what they want to destroy. You've never seen the communities that will be bulldozed." Her large, dark eyes filled as she spoke, and she wiped the overflow from her cheeks delicately with the backs of her fingers. "You've never looked into the faces of people who've lived there for fifty years, who own their homes, and who are about to be forced off their property as if they had no say in the matter, no feelings, no legal standing. Or the children whose neighborhoods are going to disappear; friends who'll end up living apart from each other because they belong to different tribal groups, or have a slightly different skin color."

"I haven't seen those things," I responded quietly. "But seeing them isn't going to change the reality of what's about to happen."

She slowly shook her head, and smiled at me knowingly. "You may not be able to change the outcome by visiting the place," she said, "but standing shoulder to shoulder with people, seeing their faces, will change your reality. You may still talk about issues and possibilities, but once you've been there, your issues will have faces. And faces make a difference."

"Okay," I said. "Write about those people. Put their voices in your stories."

"I'll do better than that," she said as she stood up and began to gather the papers on the table to take home with her. "This week we're going to the Odin Theatre. I'm going to show you the face of this country—the face they intend to beat into submission."

"Okay," I said. "Where's the Odin Theatre?"

"You really don't know, do you?" she said with a grin. "It's at the center of Sophiatown."

That first visit to Sophiatown changed the course of my life—not only because I saw so many black faces and black lives, but because for the first time, I saw who your mother really was. Most of all, it was the moment in my life when I first understood what it meant to be South African; when I recognized the richness of the identity that was being denied all of us. There was no going back from that moment.

Blacks made up eighty percent of the population, but they were invisible to us. We might speak a few words in one of the Bantu languages—Xhosa or Zulu or Shangaan—but we knew nothing of their customs or their mythology; nothing of their families or where and how they lived. Sometimes we didn't know their family names, or even the names of their children.

There were exceptions, of course—people who recognized the inhumanity of apartheid, and who did their bit to make a difference. But for the most part it was a sort of willed ignorance—because if you acknowledge how evil the system is but continue to live in it and benefit from it, then you have to live each day with your hypocrisy. Most people aren't evil enough—or strong enough—to do that, and it was easier to simply ignore the problem. We all did.

Sophiatown, 1953

Sophiatown was a hodge-podge of people—black, colored, Indian, Asian, and they all lived in relative harmony. They belonged. It was one of the few places in the country where they could own their homes and the land they lived on. I didn't understand quite what that meant until Michaela and I drove up to the center of Sophiatown that first time in her father's Volvo.

It was the first time I saw Christ the King Church, where Father Trevor Huddleston preached, and where Michaela helped in the Mission School. Father Huddleston was an Anglican priest who had brought his ministry from England, and he was the first white religious leader to come out strongly against apartheid. He was way ahead of his time, and the first time I met and heard him speak was on that winter evening at the Odin Theatre.

When your mother and I arrived in Sophiatown we drove straight to the home of Dahlia and Charlie, a young couple who worked for Father Huddleston. Dahlia was short and energetic, with a sweet face and an easy smile; Charlie towered over her, a big, serious man who moved quietly as if he didn't want to reveal his true size. I remember thinking at the time that being so tall must have been even harder for a black man; that it's difficult to fade into the background when one stands out in a crowd.

We were the only two white guests in the house. Our hosts were gracious and pleasant, and I felt truly welcome. They greeted us warmly, looked into my eyes instead of down at my feet as they would have in Johannesburg. It was a new and freeing experience for me.

The house was modest and poorly furnished; the floor of unfinished board and the table a heavy, ancient thing with a flowered oilcloth attached by thumbtacks. We sat down in their home to eat before the meeting—the first time I ate a meal in the home of a black family. As I sat eating thick chicken soup and bread out of a chipped white enamel bowl, I remember thinking the most striking thing about it was that it seemed so normal. Your mother insisted upon helping to serve and clean up after the meal, and she laughed with them and their friends as she would have with her friends at university.

We left the house as a group just before the meeting was scheduled to start, and your mother and I walked hand in hand through the streets of Sophiatown.

"Come," said Charlie as we reached the entrance to the theatre, "let me introduce you to the speakers, and to Father Huddleston."

Father Huddleston was tall and exceedingly thin, his black cassock hanging on his shoulder blades as he stood outside the main door in deep conversation with two men, both black, one slightly younger than the other. As we approached the little group, four armed policemen walked toward them, and several of our party moved in front of us, as if to protect Michaela and me from what was about to happen. Our white skins were conspicuous enough, but they were all aware that your mother had already been arrested because of her editorial and wanted to shield her from view. We all watched from a distance, but my heart was pounding. I had no idea how quickly a situation could deteriorate, or how ugly it could get, and this was closer than I had ever been to a confrontation with the police.

The commanding officer was a balding middle aged man with light brown hair, a beefy face, and a trim, graying beard. He wore a serious expression, but one side of his mouth was raised in an expression of contempt. It was clear that both men were known to him, and that he resented having to deal with them. He spoke brusquely, completely ignoring Father Huddleston.

"Walter Sisulu and Nelson Mandela, I'm placing you both under arrest," he said. "You should know better than to be here—you're both banned from attending public gatherings."

He gestured with his hand and the other three officers stepped forward, but Father Huddleston stepped between them.

"These men have done nothing. And you should be aware," he said accusingly, "that the orders prohibiting them from attending public functions have expired. If you arrest them you will have to arrest me, too."

"I suggest you stick to your business, Father," said the officer. "Stand aside."

Father Huddleston refused to move, and the police took him by the elbows and began to force him out of the way. What happened then opened my eyes to something I had not thought possible. One of the two black men—the one he had addressed as Nelson Mandela—took a small step forward, faced the commanding officer, and looked calmly into his eyes. He was young and tall, but there was something in his presence greater than his size or his age. The officer was accustomed to using race, position, uniform and manner to intimidate people, and in his stance there was a promise of violence. But Mandela continued to look calmly into his eyes, and eventually the officer faltered and took a step back. He seemed to be stepping out of a force field, and there was relief on his face as he gestured to his men and they released Father Huddleston.

"Thank you, officer," said Mandela. He spoke softly, but the weight and gravity of his voice compelled those within hearing to listen. "I appreciate your leaving Father Huddleston out of this. I'm sure that you would not wish to make a wrongful arrest, and I can assure you that the orders banning our appearance at public events have expired. We would not be here tonight talking to you if our bans were still in force."

Police records were notoriously bad, and the officer in charge must have been aware that his knowledge of when banning orders began and ended was imprecise. He hesitated for a moment, but this rabble rouser was humiliating him before the men in his command, and his face reddened.

"Don't step out of line, Mandela," he said. "And don't think you can cross me. I'm watching you." Then he turned on his heels and left, his men following behind.

I was amazed and awed by the experience—I had never seen a black man confront a white police officer, and I couldn't tell whether I was more surprised by the courage it took, or by the fact that the earth had not opened up and swallowed him as a consequence.

This was the first time I had come across Nelson Mandela, and although his courage surprised me, his strength and dignity did not. It was a quality I was used to in black men. Only later did I recognize the determination and character it must have taken to rise each day into indignity and slight and yet to maintain even a vestige of self-respect. Perhaps they had no choice—at least for some men, perhaps maintaining dignity was what allowed them to rise each day in the first place. For others, the appearance of dignity turned out to be simply a mask for rage that was inexpressible.

Father Huddleston looked in our direction, smiled, and beckoned. We walked over and he gave your mother a brief hug.

"This is Michaela Davidson," he said proudly, introducing her to the men with him, "a fine young woman who volunteers at the Mission School. And you," he said, "must be Leonard Green. Welcome."

I was still sweating uncomfortably from our encounter, but the two men who had been singled out stood by calmly, as if we were attending a garden party instead of a racially charged political meeting. I shook hands with them both, and we went into the theatre as if nothing had happened. The crowd welcomed Father Huddleston, who introduced Nelson Mandela as a young leader in the opposition movement. I don't remember Mandela's words, but I do recall the hush that came over the audience as he spoke, and like them I found his message inspiring. It was more about human dignity and freedom than it was about the politics of the impending forced removal from Sophiatown.

For me, that day was filled with firsts. My first outing with your mother; my first visit to Sophiatown; my first and only meeting with Nelson Mandela. Back then, Mandela still believed that change without conflict was possible. It was several years before he recognized that dialogue and peaceful demonstrations alone would not be sufficient to bring apartheid to an end. I had no idea who he was, but I have carried with me since the impression of his profound gravitas and quiet power.

I went to Sophiatown because of your mother, and she was right. Once I met the people, my theories took on human expression. But by then, I had fallen so deeply in love with her that I would have followed any example she set.

Sad to say at the fading of my life, the truth is that your mother is the only woman I ever loved. I last laid eyes on her almost forty years ago, and they have been lonely years for me. You will see, Steven, as this story unfolds, that I bear full responsibility for depriving you of her presence, and of her love. Living without her has been punishment enough—both for the things I have done, and for the things I should have done, but didn't.

three

LENNY

Johannesburg, 1953-55

I began spending time at Michaela's home, and came to know her parents, Selma and Samuel. Michaela became very fond of my father, Papa Mischa. Within the year we became engaged, but there seemed no rush to marry, until Selma became ill and was finally convinced to see a specialist. They thought at first it was kidney failure, but additional tests revealed that kidney failure had been caused by the inoperable cancer filling her abdominal cavity. She was given several months to live.

She wanted to dance at her daughter's wedding, and Michaela wanted to give her that pleasure while she could still dance. We had a small, elegant wedding, and a month later, Selma died. Your grandfather Samuel took it hard, but he continued his dental practice, working long hours, and he continued to take as patients many who could only pay in kind. I always wondered how he made a living, but somehow he and your grandmother always had enough, and once she died, he didn't need much. He continued to live in the house, and Dennis, who had been his gardener since your mother was a little girl, took care of him. Your grandfather was a warm, gentle man, and he and Papa Mischa became close friends in those years. Often we had them both for dinner; sometimes we all met at Samuel's house, where Dennis and the cook would argue in the kitchen until they agreed on something that the Doctor would enjoy.

I went with Michaela to public demonstrations, lectures, and small meetings held in secret. But it wasn't until July of 1955, when the Congress of the People took place on the *veld* outside the little village of Kliptown, on the outskirts of Johannesburg, that I understood how big the groundswell was, and how threatened the government was by it.

This was to be a national convention, and it had a grand purpose—to vote on a Freedom Charter that set the tone for the South Africa of the future. We decided to show our support and became Freedom Volunteers, planning the event, and acting as convention officials at the site.

At the university, Michaela wrote a carefully worded editorial in support of the convention. By then she had already spent a night in jail, and she recognized the need for caution. But tempers were high, and even a cautiously worded editorial could elicit some nasty responses. In this case, the police left her alone—but she received several letters from the right-wing fringe. One of them was delivered to the newspaper office and addressed to her, and even after fifty years, I recall it word for word. It said:

When you ask the kaffirs what laws they would make if they were in charge, you give them big ideas about freedom. Don't you know what they want, you stupid Jew? They want your house. And when they come and take it from you, like the Nazis did, your feelings will be hurt. You people never learn. Why don't you mind your own fucking business? Just keep up your money-grubbing and stop interfering in politics. Watch out, Jew girl—this is not your country. If you don't like it, get out. And if you don't know what good manners are, we can teach you.

Michaela disregarded the note, although it confirmed what her father had told her.

On the day she received the note, we had dinner plans with her father, and Michaela showed her father the note. After dinner, he insisted upon taking us for a drive to the outskirts of Sophiatown, which was in the process of being bulldozed.

The sun was just setting as we arrived. We got out and walked around to the side of the car facing the ruined city, and your grandfather took out a silver case and offered us a cigarette. Michaela was surprised, but he thrust the case at her again, and she took one.

"You're a married woman, Michaela," he said. "I know you smoke, and you certainly know your own mind. And after the correspondence you received today, you're entitled to all the privileges—and responsibilities—of adulthood."

I pulled out my lighter and lit our cigarettes, and as we smoked, we leaned against the car in the evening silence, looking at the ruins. The church tower was still standing against the sky, and a few of the better houses, but block upon block of shacks were bulldozed rubble, and the dust rose into the evening sky.

"You know the population statistics as well as I do," your grandfather said. "Thirteen million blacks; three million whites; fewer than a hundred thousand Jews. We're a drop in the bucket here—and we're only safe as long as we don't make a big splash." He took a deep draw on his cigarette and slowly exhaled. "This People's Congress you're involved in is about to make a huge splash— and you're being shortsighted if you think you're only putting yourselves at risk." He pointed to the acres of destruction before us, red dust rising into the sunset. "You know better than I do what's gone on here. But I don't want you to forget what they've done. The world watches, and doesn't give a damn. This government has forced the residents of Sophiatown out—and they'll find a way to move us Jews out, as well. It wouldn't be the first time in our history—we've been expelled from better countries than this. I've made my life, and I won't tell you how to live yours. But I can't help wondering whether the writer of your little poison pen letter is right—some of us just never learn. Please, don't you be one of them."

But the more opposition Michaela faced, the more determined she became. She just held her head a little higher, put her chin out a little further, and kept going.

Your grandfather's concerns didn't stop us from volunteering at the convention when three thousand people from all over the country descended upon this little town on the *veld*. They came by bus, by car, by the truckload. Some came by foot. Most of the delegates were black, but there were representatives of Indian, colored and white organizations, too.

Michaela thought it would be a major turning point in South Africa, as important as the 1776 Continental Congress when Thomas Jefferson wrote the Declaration of Independence, and James Madison's writing of the Bill of Rights thirteen years later, all rolled into one. She hoped the impetus for change was so strong that time would compress and the impossible be accomplished–and we would be there to watch it happen. The police were there, too, but on the first day, all they did was take photographs and write down names and a record of whatever they heard. I thought the People's Congress was too much of a threat to the government—they would shut it down before it started, and it would never happen. But they were smarter than we gave them credit for. They wanted to catch the organizers in the act, and make a show of force. Which they did.

On the second day, in the afternoon, a cordon of police armed with rifles surrounded the crowd, and several went up to the podium. They pushed the delegates off the platform, and the officer in charge took the microphone.

"You're being held here on suspicion of treasonous activity," he said. "No one leaves until we have the identity of every person here."

Each section of the Charter had been approved by the time the raid took place, and the goal of the convention was achieved. But for the next few hours, the police took down the identities of every person present and confiscated whatever written material they could find. We were forced to line up at a table they set up at the entrance, and only after providing proof of identity were we allowed to leave. When I reached the table I identified myself, the officer took down my information, and a photographer took my picture. Then it was Michaela's turn.

"Name?"

"Michaela Green."

The officer leaned back and with his thumb tipped up the brim of his khaki police hat. He was older than we were by about fifteen years, which would have put him in his late thirties. I remember him well—we met several times after the convention. He was a muscular, big-boned man;

thick bellied. He had reddish hair and freckles, pale blue eyes, thin lips, and I watched with distaste as he looked your mother up and down.

"So, this is Mrs. Green, who used to be Miss Davidson," he said with a serious expression, and in a dense Afrikaans accent. "I've heard all about you. Read several of your little Socialistic pieces in the university paper. I wondered when our paths would cross. Let me congratulate you on your marriage, Mrs. Green. Tell me, does your father, Dr. Davidson, know that his daughter is here today, serving food to our *kaffir* communists while they plot treason?" Michaela stiffened at the mention of her father's name, but I squeezed the back of her arm, and felt her lean into me, acknowledging my signal. The officer missed nothing.

"No need to be alarmed," he said, pointing to his mouth. "See these?" He opened his lips to show his teeth. "Your father keeps them in good shape. He's my dentist. He gives me really good advice about healthy living. That way, I get to keep my teeth." He crossed his arms over his chest and looked up at her. "You should think about living healthy, too, Mrs. Green. Keep your teeth that way. And I suggest that you watch out who you keep company with." Then he smiled a nasty grin. His teeth were the best thing about him. "You can go now—if we need more information from you we'll be in touch. And tell your father Officer Viljoen says hello."

The police raid on the afternoon of the second day marked an intensification of the government campaign to wipe out all opposition. Once the convention was over, the government began to gather information. They searched for evidence of sedition and treason and for anything that could be interpreted as a violation of the Suppression of Communism Act. And a year and a half later, in December of 1956, the Treason Trials began. They charged a hundred and fifty-six people with High Treason, and accused them of plotting to use violence to overthrow the government, and to establish a Communist regime.

We were small fish, and were never investigated—but many of our friends were. No one who read the Freedom Charter could have believed that it was an instrument of Communism—but it was a document incompatible with apartheid, and deeply at odds with the ruling party.

The government stated unequivocally that the Freedom Charter threatened the security of the state. Those opposed to the government watched the trial with shock and disbelief. For many, including Michaela, it gave the lie to any possibility of peaceful change, and showed the country for what it was—a police state camouflaged as a democracy.

The Treason Trials lasted for over four years, but the prosecution found itself unable to make a reasonable case against most of the accused. The court found no evidence that the African National Congress—the ANC—planned to violently overthrow the state, and it ended with the dismissal of all charges.

In the early days of the Treason Trial, we were invited to a party to celebrate the dropping of all charges against a friend, a journalist who had been charged with treason and sedition. When we arrived at his modest suburban home just outside Johannesburg, doors and windows were open to the warm, summer night, there was jazz playing on the phonograph, and the living room and verandah were crowded. Blacks, whites, coloreds and Indians laughed and drank together, dancing and making toasts to freedom. It was the South African version of a love fest, and I realize now that we were like children, living in a dream world. We behaved as if the mere act of dancing and laughing together would make it acceptable to the world we lived in; as if a glance of affection across the color line, or the joining of white lips to black, would somehow be their own validation.

Perhaps they should have been, but they weren't. Pretending that apartheid didn't exist would not make it go away—in fact, it did the opposite. One of the neighbors, enraged by the mere idea of blacks and whites partying together, called the police.

Halfway through the evening, all hell broke loose. There were shouts from the garden, the front door was forced open, and camera flashes went off like firecrackers as reporters pushed their way into the house and took pictures of black and white men and women partying together. I looked around for Michaela and saw her immobilized at the instant a camera flashed in front of her. She stood before a potted palm tree, eyes opened wide in surprise, and there was a smile on her face. She was dancing with a black man wearing a short sleeved white shirt, and against his dark skin she seemed pale and insubstantial. Someone grabbed the glass from my hand and emptied my whiskey out the window as the police arrived. Interracial drinking was against the law—had they found any alcohol we would all have landed in prison. Somehow, thankfully, all the alcohol disappeared in time, and the police left, taking the reporters with them.

The next day, the newspaper featured a front-page photograph of Michaela—a photograph you may already have discovered. What you can't know from the photo is that by then she was already pregnant, and it wasn't long before I was the subject of gossip and snickering.

I was in my second year on the engineering team at LeRoux and Raphael, a company that specialized in building bridges. The size of train engines and the weight they were drawing had increased beyond the capacity of bridges built in the early part of the century, and I had been hired as one of the junior engineers on the team working to increase the stress capacity of trestle rail bridges. The senior design engineer didn't hesitate to tell me that it was my responsibility to keep my wife in line.

I was embarrassed by the publicity, humiliated to have my wife's photo spread across the front page of the paper, and jealous to see her dancing with another man, her bare arms wrapped about his shoulders. But worse was the surprising recognition that what bothered me most was who she was dancing with. It was Mandla Mkhize.

four

LENNY

Boston, 2001

Winter has come to Boston, and a heavy snow falls outside my window. Each day I put a piece of myself into this manuscript, and it increases in heft and in consequence that I won't be here to witness. At times I wonder about cause and effect—whether I'm writing the manuscript because I have cancer and want to get it all down before I die; or whether the act of writing is itself the cancer, drawing the life force from me.

I imagine, after I'm gone, that you will sit together and read what I've put down here. Perhaps that's just wishful thinking, but it's what I need to imagine in order to keep going. And what I imagine is that my intrepid daughter-in-law will be way ahead of me.

I imagine you, Dariya, after reading each section of the manuscript, running off to scour the databases you have access to. You'll be searching for confirmation of what I've written; for proof that the events are true, and for names and places and facts that put you in front of the story. You will find news of apartheid and struggle, dissension and protest—but you will notice something bizarre as you scour the newspapers, and you may not recognize at first what you find so disquieting. You will find that in South Africa, just as you saw in Moscow, people continued to live their lives in even the most chaotic of circumstances. In the midst of headlines about apartheid policy, violence, protests and arrests, people took care of commerce, went to sales, watched the stock market and the cricket and rugby scores, celebrated and mourned.

Eventually you will realize that what so disturbs you is what was not reported. Between the headlines on apartheid—the politics of race—and the articles that reflected everyday life, there was a huge silence that had swallowed the entire black population. There was so little recognition of their existence in the news that they might have been a small population living out their lives on our border, instead of being a massive presence confined to scattered pockets throughout the country. The newspapers— all of them—reflected an almost absolute refusal by the ruling minority to recognize that there was a price to pay for their privileged lives, and that the bill was about to come due. You might see, between the lines of newsprint, that the future history of the country was writ large and clear. You might even find it astounding that from a distance, the direction of events was so predictable, but that at the time, those in power were able to pretend for so long and with such success—and at such a price—that they were in control.

And if you can tell from the newspapers you're reading which way the political winds were blowing, you will feel a twinge of excitement when you reach March, 1960. That was the tipping point—and if your instincts are correct, they will tell you that this was also the point at which Michaela had thrown caution to the wind, and become involved in the activities that led to her downfall.

Sharpeville, 1960

What happened in March, 1960 came to be known as the Sharpeville Massacre. It changed everything in the country, and in our lives. Before Sharpeville, the country was divided; afterwards, it was polarized. It was the point at which the struggle against apartheid became a war. Not my war—there wasn't enough room in our marriage for that. It was your mother's war. And although neither of us was directly involved with what happened that day, we had friends who planned and executed parts of the demonstration. One of them you already know, if not by name. He was the black man the news photographer captured dancing with your mother at our friend's party—and it was that picture, on the front page of the newspaper, that was to prove so destructive a few years later.

I've had no desire to follow his activities, and all I know about him is that he is still alive and healthy. He will apparently outlast me, which, I suppose, is neither here nor there. Some of my ambivalence will become clear as I explain what happened that day, the day that made Sharpeville famous.

The demonstration was intended to be a peaceful show of civil disobedience against the Pass Laws that made it mandatory for every black man to carry a reference book. Men would leave their passes at home, march to local police stations, and demand to be arrested. The idea was to overwhelm the police with thousands of peaceful men who were breaking the law, and who should by rights have been taken into custody.

No one knows what really happened during the protest. About 6,000 people—many of them women, children and elderly—were gathered outside the police station at Sharpeville. A few days earlier, several policemen had been killed elsewhere in the country, and the police were scared and jittery. When the demonstration began, there were half a dozen policemen inside the station. Earlier that morning the authorities were so concerned about the size of the crowd that they sent in a squadron of low flying planes, but had no success in dispersing the throng. By the time the killings occurred, reinforcements had arrived—there was a force of three hundred men and several armored cars. Standing on the roofs of these armored cars were soldiers armed with submachine guns. Anyone involved with civilian crowd control would have told them that it was a recipe for disaster—but those in authority were not thinking like civilians.

The people were curious—they'd been told that someone would be arriving to make an announcement about the Pass Laws, and they were waiting. Minutes before the shooting, the man in charge of the Special Branch had been able to walk through the crowd, arresting members of the Pan African Congress. He said later that he was able to do so because although the crowd was noisy, it was not violent.

There was apparently no command to fire—perhaps what sparked it was the sound of a door slamming, or a car backfiring. Perhaps someone threw a stone, and it bounced off the reinforced steel of an armored car. But suddenly one policeman opened fire, and fifty others joined in. The people in the crowd thought the police were firing blanks, and didn't move until they saw bodies dropping around them. You can find photographs in the news reports of a young policeman on the roof of his armored car firing into the crowd. The whole event lasted for forty seconds, in which time seven hundred rounds were fired, killing sixty-nine people, a third of them women and children. Another hundred and eighty were wounded—again, about a third women and children. Most were shot in the back running away. Some of the dead were women carrying children in blankets on their backs—in several cases, mothers and children were killed by the same bullet. And there were accounts of soldiers initially taunting the wounded as they lay on the ground, telling them to get up and be off.

Later, there was an inquiry, and the Lieutenant Colonel in charge was questioned. He said he never gave the command to fire—but he made some comments that sound ludicrous today. Even at that time, his words were astounding. He said the character or the mentality of the blacks didn't allow for peaceful gatherings; that anytime they got together in a crowd was an opportunity for violence. And when the presiding judge asked whether any useful lessons had been learned from the experience, he responded by saying that perhaps next time they would have better equipment.

Things changed after that day. The government was petrified. They placed the country under a State of Emergency, banned all opposition organizations and clamped down as hard as they could. Those of us involved in the struggle realized that it was the end of an era—and it was the event that decided Nelson Mandela to abandon his long held non-violent stance. After that day, Mandela began to advocate acts of sabotage against the government. Not long afterwards, he went to Algeria, where he was trained in sabotage and guerilla warfare. The ANC went underground—but it didn't die. Sharpeville gave birth to *Umkhonto we Sizwe*,

Spear of the Nation, the ANC's military wing. That's how the struggle became a war.

So, you ask, what does Mandla Mkhize have to do with all this? The answer is, everything. Or, nothing. You decide.

Your mother and I were home that day, and we knew nothing until the telephone rang. I answered it. It was a call from an official with the ANC. I recognized his name, and knew that Michaela had worked with him. He was rushed and nervous, apologized for his hurry, explained what had happened at Sharpeville. At first I didn't understand why he was calling, or why he was speaking to me. But it became clear that he wasn't supposed to be talking to me—he had misunderstood his instructions.

"Mandla Mkhize asked me to say to you that he was at the demonstration, as planned—but he was not hurt, and he managed to get away before the police began rounding people up. So the first message is that he is safe. And the second is that he wants to meet tomorrow at the usual place."

"What usual place?" I asked.

There was silence as he recognized that he had made a huge error and delivered a message to the wrong person. Then he hung up.

I must have been an idiot, because I still didn't understand the message, and for another moment, I didn't get what it implied. As I lowered the phone I looked up at Michaela, puzzled, thinking that together we might be able to decipher what it meant.

"What do you think he's talking about?" I asked. "What usual place?"

She stood across the room from me, one hand covering her open mouth. Without answering me, she rushed from the room. Then I understood.

That moment is embedded in my flesh like a razor. Outside the window there was a willow tree, and the late afternoon sun shone through the glass at an angle that gave the light in the room a warm, greenish hue, as if we were underwater. Your mother wore a light brown skirt and a soft, beige blouse, and as she ran past me I smelled her perfume—an almost undetectable fragrance of gardenia—and it mixed with her skin in a way that made it her personal scent. Until that moment I thought I was the only man in the world who could smell that fragrance and know what it was to make love to the woman whose body created it.

After she rushed by me, all I could do was to stand there. You were five, Steven, sitting on the Persian rug, playing with a set of big wooden blocks. They were white—the carved letters were royal blue, and the numbers were red. You loved those blocks.

We never discussed it again. I don't know for sure what 'the usual place' was, and I don't know whether she went to him the next day as he asked. But Sharpeville put the country at war with itself; and that telephone call changed my life, and yours, Steven. It wounded our family and devastated me—and for the first time, it crossed my mind that perhaps we should cut our losses and leave while there was still something to save. I don't know whether your mother would have come with us had I asked her, but I was too paralyzed to act. I waited too long; events overtook us. By the time I did decide to leave the country it was too late, and forgiveness was long beyond me.

I have no doubt you and he will eventually meet. He will tell you much that I'm not capable of sharing with you, and much that I don't know, and he can shed light on events that occurred both before we left South Africa, and after we arrived in Boston. I believe you knew him as a child; you may have met several times, although I was never present. I didn't learn until much later that your mother had taken you to see him. He is a charming man. You will like him.

When the occasion presents itself, I have a message for you to give him.

Tell him I want to set the record straight—that I long ago forgave him for what he might have done; that I hold him responsible for nothing. He did not then, and does not now, have the power to put a sour taste in my mouth or bitterness in my heart. I've always been the only one capable of that. If I taste sourness and choke on bile as I die, they are the recognition that I am less a man than I would have liked to be. I've been unable to live up to the standards I set for myself; unwilling to honor the truth that is the underpinning of all we did and all we risked to make South Africa a free country. I've had to live with that truth and with its consequences for over forty years.

Tell him I said perhaps it's a good thing my dying is happening now, because if South Africa were to ever become the paradise it can be, I would not be fit to live there. I leave it to the next generation, and to the one after that, to discover what has become of the place I left. And when you do finally get there, you will discover precisely what it was that Mandla did or didn't do. Perhaps you, too, will find it in your heart to forgive him.

five

STEVEN

Boston, 2001

I was curious, but I wanted to read my father's manuscript quickly, deal with whatever it was he needed to tell me, and then shake the emotional baggage off me like a wet dog and get on with my life.

Dariya knew that it couldn't possibly be so simple. She understood that my father's revelations carried more weight than I anticipated, and that if I took it all in at once I would miss half of it and still be left reeling. She suggested gently that we read together, slowly, taking time to discuss and digest each section. She said it would give us time to think about what he had written, and to absorb the emotional impact of whatever he had kept to himself for so long.

As usual, she was right. We began by reading a short section of the manuscript together after dinner, once we'd put the children to bed. We sat at the kitchen table and she read aloud, while I cut and peeled a piece of fruit. When she came to a stopping point we would remain sitting and eat the apple or pear I had sectioned. But after this particular revelation that my mother and Mandla Mkhize had apparently been lovers, I couldn't remain still, let alone eat.

I rose from the table and loaded the dishwasher in silence; she watched, peering at me from over her reading glasses. As I began washing pots and pans she came to stand beside me, and I handed them to her to dry.

"Are you alright?" she asked finally.

I nodded. "He remembered," I said.

She glanced in my direction, and I wondered why she put down the dish towel and walked towards me.

"Remembered what?" she asked softly.

She stood before me and took my face in her hands, and as she wiped my cheeks, I realized that the salty taste in my mouth was tears. I wept silently, with no awareness of my grief. I was numb.

"He remembered my blocks," I said, burying my face in her hair. "And he remembered what they looked like."

Dariya put her arms about my neck. "I love you," she said.

"You're in love with a man who's over forty, standing here crying about his blocks," I said. I laughed, and what emerged was a cross between a chuckle and a sob. "What an idiot."

"Your father remembered that you loved your blocks," she said, "which I find out of character for him. But you're not crying about the blocks. You're crying for a little boy who lost his mother, and a man who lost his wife."

"My poor father," I said. "I had no idea."

"He was carrying a lot all by himself for a long time."

"I've always thought of my mother as an avenging angel; I was angry with her because she died early and left me. I guess she left him, too—long before she was killed."

"Now we know what he's been hiding," she said. "There must be some relief in that for you."

She took my hand and led me upstairs, and she latched the bedroom door. Still numb, I stood and watched as she quickly undressed herself, and I felt the pink heat coming off her body as she undressed me, pulled back the top sheet and blankets, and led me to the bed. She turned out the lights, and in the darkness she made love to me with her hands and her full, bountiful mouth, and then she straddled me and kissed me with her tongue. Filled with love, and with joy and thankfulness that I had Dariya in my life, I put my hands on the warm rounds of her hips, and we rode gently into the night.

My job was to go about my life, take care of my family, paint my canvases and teach my students, and somehow integrate my mother's infidelity into my history. I was furious with her—but I kept reminding myself that she was long dead, that I never knew who she really was, and that it was all emotional baggage, sentimental and immature at best. I'd be doing myself a favor if I could empty my head, discard the whole story, and give up on my attachment to a small boy's fantasy, carried into middle age. It didn't do much good—everything I painted looked like an angry earth-colored blob, which accurately reflected my state of mind.

Dariya, on the other hand, was ever the good researcher. My father had understood her well, and he was correct in assuming that she would continue her research even as we read his manuscript. Confident that the truth was out in the open, she searched for documentation that supported my father's version of events. She immersed herself in the periods leading up to and following Sharpeville, but she shared none of her discoveries with me. Dariya's silence continued for several weeks, during which time I was essentially absent. I was withdrawn and silent, and when I occasionally caught her looking at me intently I glared at her, and she dropped her eyes without saying a word. And then, one weekend at the beginning of Christmas break, she said she had some things to show me.

We rose early—Sally and Greg were up at the crack of dawn, ready to take advantage of every hour of vacation. We ate cereal and cooked scrambled eggs and toast together, and by the time we finished with the breakfast dishes the children were content to leave us for friends and video games. I made a fresh pot of coffee and carried two steaming cups into Dariya's small office adjoining my studio. Newspaper headlines and articles from old South African newspaper databases lay in a neat pile beside her printer.

"You've been busy," I said as we sat beside each other at her desk.

"Very," she said. "I have these moments where something your father writes about is confirmed by the historical record, and all of a sudden I'm right there, watching history as it happens." Her eyes were bright with the adrenalin of discovery, but her movements were flustered and anxious. "I've gone through daily newspapers page by page. It was a frightening time, and I understand why he felt such a need to get you out of that environment."

"Did you find references to my mother?"

"I've discovered something, but I'm not sure exactly what it means. Let me show it to you as I found it," she said, "so you can understand the sequence of events the same way I do, and come to your own conclusions. Okay?"

Dariya flipped quickly through her pile of newsprint. "Sharpeville changed the political climate," she said. "The government was petrified, and they became even more restrictive than before. Then they put out a warrant for Nelson Mandela's arrest. He went underground, and the next day they printed a transcript of his statement."

Dariya pulled out the next article, featuring a picture of the young, bearded Nelson Mandela. It was an impassioned call urging the black population to mobilize their resources, and to withdraw all cooperation from the Nationalist government. It was a call, finally, to make the work of government impossible.

"They forced Mandela underground, and that was the beginning of violent opposition. Then look what happened."

Dariya placed the articles in front of me one by one, and I read them in silence. Over the following months there was a surge in acts of sabotage. Most were conducted at night, against military and electrical installations, utilities, munitions factories, or police stations. It was clear by the nature of their targets that they were following Mandela's instructions to make governing impossible.

But the government response was predictable. Minimum punishment for sabotage was raised to five years, and the death penalty was invoked. Some of those responsible were captured and tried; many were imprisoned without trial, executed or disappeared. When I was finished reading, Dariya held one last piece of paper in her hand. She said nothing, but removed all the pages from the desk, and placed this single sheet in front of me.

"This is a news clipping from early 1962," she said quietly. "It's the only reference to your mother I could find."

It was from page five of the Johannesburg *Star*, and the date was March, 1962, when I was seven years old. I have no memory of the events surrounding it. The clipping fitted snugly onto a piece of white photocopy paper, and at the top, side by side, were two photographs, one of a young black man, and one of a young white woman. Neither photograph was clear, but the woman was identifiable as my mother, and beneath her picture was her name, Michaela Green. I knew before I saw it that the name beneath the picture of the young black man would be familiar, and it was. Mandla Mkhize.

I felt a sense of relief when I first glanced at the clipping because I assumed that the typescript below the pictures was a report of my mother's death, and that, finally, I would discover evidence of how she was killed. Then I read the news report. The article was titled "TRIED AND CONVICTED". Clearly, it was not a report on their deaths. They had both been charged with miscegenation and with sabotage.

According to the story, they blew up an electrical plant, and then made their way under cover of darkness to a farm known to be one of the ANC's safe sites. Several hours after the explosion, members of the Special Branch observed them having sexual relations in the bedroom of a small house on the farm grounds. They were arrested and taken into custody. Mandla, a known member of terrorist organizations, had orchestrated the act of sabotage, and as the leader, he was given a life sentence. My mother had associations to banned organizations, but she was not known to be a member herself. She was identified as an accomplice, and they were more lenient on her. She was sentenced to ten years in prison.

If she served her full sentence, she would have been released in 1972, and I found myself calculating how old I would have been, had she survived. Seventeen. I was a junior in high school, about to lose—or having just lost—my virginity on the royal blue carpet in my bedroom.

"Stevie?" Dariya stood behind me, waiting, and placed a hand gently on the back of my neck.

"So she didn't just cheat on my father with this man," I said. "They blew up an electrical plant together. And they went to jail."

Dariya didn't say anything.

"My father never said a word about any of this. He must have been trying to protect me. She must have died later, maybe in prison."

"I've looked," she said, "gone through the paper page by page, and found no other mention of your mother. She seems to have just disappeared. I did name searches during the ten years she would have been in prison, and after, and found nothing there, either." She paused. "I did find a mention of Mandla, though," she said. "He won a teaching award—I think it was from the Natal Regional Ministry of Education—sometime in the early 1990s."

"I've spoken to him—so we know somehow he survived." I paused for a moment, and Dariya also remained silent. "But what happened to my mother? Did she die in prison, or did something happen to her once she got out? I can't let this rest here just because the newspaper doesn't give us an answer," I said. My voice was hoarse. "She can't just have disappeared."

"I'll keep looking, if you want me to."

"Where would you look? You've already gone through the newspaper page by page."

"There are other sources," she said.

"Like what?"

"Mandla. You can phone him. He should know. And there may be retired news reporters who worked for these newspapers. And there are other databases that I could get access to." She paused. "If you want to follow this further."

"I don't have much choice," I said. "I can't let this rest here. But let's finish my father's manuscript first. Perhaps it will answer some questions. And if it doesn't, maybe it will give us a better idea of where to look, and what to look for."

six

LENNY

Johannesburg, 1960

After Sharpeville our lives fell apart with bewildering speed. At times I wanted to punish your mother—but even when I knew she was away from my bed and from our child, it was beyond my imagining that she would be willing to risk her family, her life and her freedom to meet with that man in forbidden places. All I could do was pace up and down the hallway of our house in a murderous rage—but even then I didn't consider doing anything that would have separated her from you.

What I felt went beyond confusion and betrayal—I was incredulous. In our world what she was doing was not just scandalous, it was inconceivable. Marriage between them would have been illegal; sex between them was a criminal act; if they had lived together openly they would have been arrested and convicted. What was left to them? Short of settling in another part of the world, their only alternative was to continue hiding their affair, and that was hardly a long-term solution. In fact, there was no long-term solution—unless they believed that they were about to change the world, and that love between them would shortly be sanctioned. But that would have been delusional. It was clear to me and to everyone else, that for a white woman and a black man to have an affair was to destroy both lives—but somehow, she was unable to see it.

I still loved your mother, and she hadn't disavowed her love for me. I didn't want to divorce her—all I wanted was to understand what she was doing, but there was no one I could confide in, and nowhere to go for help. I went to the library, read books on psychology; searched through medical books on the sociology of sex. I wondered whether she had been brainwashed; considered that perhaps she had fallen in love with him because she saw him as a heroic figure fighting for his people's freedom.

The only conclusion I could live with was that your mother and Mandla shared a commitment to freedom and were strongly opposed to the government and its policies—and that, being thrown together in stressful situations, she had mistaken those feelings for attraction, or love. All I could hope for was that she would come to her senses before it was too late.

But she didn't. By the time I discovered the truth about their activities, and the sordid details of their relationship, it was already too late. She had carried her activism and her contempt for the law past the point where either compassion or anger would make any difference.

Your mother was out of the house that night—the night they blew up the electric plant. When she didn't come home, I assumed they were together, and I went to bed. Just after dawn, two cars full of Special

Branch officers pulled up at the door, barged in, and began to tear the house apart. They forced open closets, broke through walls, pulled up linoleum flooring. They smashed photographs and paintings in search of hidden messages written on the back, and they ripped open the seams of my suits to see if we'd sewn notes in the lining. They wanted to know where she was; searched for evidence and documents that showed proof of her membership in banned organizations. They probed for any indication that we were involved in the systematic campaign of sabotage being waged by Spear of the Nation, and took away with them boxes of books and journals on socialism and Marxism, the politics of protest, and liberal philosophy.

I was a terrified young father, alone with my son, and the men going through my home were rabid to find evidence. They became more and more frantic and angry as time passed and they found nothing. Eventually the man in charge sat me down, took off his hat and threw it on the dining room table and stood above me, glaring, his arms crossed over his chest. I was so disoriented that at first I didn't recognize him.

"Mr. Green," he said, "We met at Kliptown a few years ago—you were there demonstrating at the Congress of the People with your lovely wife. Your father-in-law is my dentist."

He must have thought me a pitiful creature, because he showed more compassion than I expected.

"My name is Viljoen, Anders Viljoen. Remember me?"

"Yes," I said. I could barely look at him.

"We have proof that your wife is involved in a plot to bring down the government," he said. "Were you aware that she took part earlier tonight in an act of sabotage?"

I shook my head.

"You don't know where she was this evening?"

Again I shook my head.

"And I assume you don't know where she is right now.   Is that correct?"

"Yes," I said.

He pulled out a chair and sat down beside me.

"Mr. Green," he said softly, "you have my deepest sorrow for what you're going through. You have no idea what's going on here, or what your wife's been up to. Do you know why I'm so sure of that?"

Again, I shook my head.

"Because your wife couldn't tell you anything about what she's been engaged in. No wife could. You know what I mean, Mr. Green?"

"Are you suggesting this is more than politics—that my wife is sleeping with another man?" I said. "What evidence do you have?"

"I think we can safely say it's both," he said. "Sex and politics. And as for evidence, we're collecting it.   You're not in the kind of trouble she is— but if you withhold evidence, then you're no better than she is, and you will be prosecuted, too.   Then what will happen to your son?   The boy deserves one good parent. So, what can you tell me about where she might be?"

They interrogated me for what seemed like hours, but I told them nothing.   It was dawn before the police left, and I was exhausted, and scared.

The truth is that I had an idea where they might be—I'd been to the farm to deliver documents and to attend meetings myself. But the only way to warn them was to go there myself—and if I was followed, or caught, I'd go to prison along with her. And I had a third life to consider, Steven—yours. Neither your mother nor I had any siblings, and the only family we had was my father, Papa Mischa. He was already ill, and there would have been no one else to take care of you.   If we'd both gone to prison, what would have happened to you?

I chose to take no action; made no attempt to find or contact your mother. Even after all these years, I don't know that what I did was right—it's possible that I might have saved her from being arrested. But I did nothing. I've lived my life wondering whether I should have acted differently. But when I examine the options that were open to me, and at what I knew—or thought I knew—at the time, I'm still unsure. For years afterwards, it was one of the things that kept me awake, staring into the dark as if I could find an answer in the blackness.

I knew that if she didn't return soon, she was either in jail or dead. Whatever happened, it was possible that the police would return later to arrest me. It felt as if the end of the world had come, and there was no way I could pull myself together enough to function at the office. You were a deep sleeper as a child, and somehow you managed to sleep through the chaos. But when you woke you were shocked to see the state of the house, and you wanted to know where Mommy was. Your nanny was as shocked as you were, but she got you off to school, and once you were out of the house I managed to shower and change. It was the longest day of my life, and in some ways it never ended.

Around noon, the Special Branch returned, and Viljoen sat me down again.

"I'm sorry to be the one to break this to you, Mr. Green, but your wife was arrested earlier this morning. She was with a man named Mandla Mkhize. You know him?"

"I know who he is," I said.

"They had just blown up an electric plant," he said, "and apparently couldn't wait to get into bed together."

That's how I found out that our life together was over. I sat for a long time with my head buried in my hands, not knowing what to do or say.

"I can imagine how unpleasant this is for you," said Viljoen. "Perhaps you can get some of your own back on this terrorist Mandla Mkhize by telling us what you know of their plans, and where they meet. Anything your wife might have told you that might be of consequence."

I had nothing to say; nothing to give. It felt as if I had been robbed. Your mother took everything from me—wife, family, self-respect, good name, even the cause we had fought for together I could no longer claim as my own. I said nothing, and Viljoen made clear that he had nothing but contempt for my weakness.

"I'll do my best to keep you out of jail, Mr. Green. But your son deserves more than this from you, and so does your lovely wife. She may be misguided and easily misled, but if you can't stand up to defend her honor and let her know how much she means to you, you don't deserve her. And by her own actions, it's obvious to me that she feels the same way." Then he walked out with the other members of the Special Branch. All I could wonder was whether I hadn't fought hard enough for your mother's love.

Michaela was arrested early that morning, and she was held in a cell at Marshall Square, the main prison in Johannesburg. They could have kept her for an extended period without letting anyone know. But in their own minds they were lenient—they allowed her to call me at home the next day, from a public phone in the prison. I could barely hear her over the sounds echoing down the corridor behind her, and she spoke in a small, scared voice, which didn't make it any easier.

"I'm so sorry, Lenny," she said.

"I'm sorry, too," I said. "But it's much too late for sorry."

There was a long silence. I didn't know how to end it, so I spoke what was most on my mind. "Viljoen came to see me," I said. "I couldn't give him any information, being completely in the dark about what you were up to."

She said nothing.

"He said a man who really loved you, and a father who deserved Steven, would have been strong enough to protect you from yourself. Was he right? Could I have done anything to stop you from turning our lives and our marriage to shit?"

I could hear her weeping over the phone. Aside from the guilt she felt over what this would all do to you, Steven, there had already been sabotage cases where people were sentenced to death, and she was terrified. I had to overcome my anger and tell her not to worry about us; that we'd manage. She never did respond to my question—but then, I probably wouldn't have liked her answer, whatever it was.

Our lawyer went to see her—he called me later and told me that she was being treated as well as could be expected. He said the police thought they had a strong case—that's why they were willing to divulge the fact that they had her in custody. They had nothing to gain by putting her through a lengthy interrogation.

Within days the news was out, and I knew very quickly who our real friends were. Some dropped us like hot stones. Others didn't drop us so quickly, but they thought they had a right to criticize, or to condemn outright what she had done. One of my senior partners told me that the whole incident reflected very badly on our firm, and he suggested that I should have kept a tighter rein on my wife, the way he did on his. Very few people I knew believed the sexual charge was legitimate, but if it was, no one I knew condoned it. The few who shared, or at least understood our political objectives, rallied around us.

The government wanted to put a rapid stop to the acts of sabotage, and the prosecution was very efficient. The court wasted no time. They brought your mother to trial within a week, and it lasted all of two days. There were eyewitnesses to the sabotage, evidence that both your mother and Mandla had planned it, and at least one photograph of them in bed together, taken through the window of the farmhouse just before the arrest. And that was it. She was sentenced to ten years in prison—and I had to decide how and where I was going to raise you, and what to do with my life.

Your mother was supposed to be transferred from Marshall Square to the women's prison the morning after sentencing, but she never arrived. I was convinced that the police killed her; they accused me of having been involved in her escape. They kept our house under surveillance, shadowed me from morning to night, and for weeks I had no idea what happened to her.

Then one day about two months later, I was in charge of the engineering plans for repairing a railroad bridge at an isolated site in the *veld* about two hundred miles south of Johannesburg. The foreman said one of the workers had found some cracks in the support pillars at the bottom of the ravine. He wanted me to come down and see if they were just surface cracks, or if they weakened the structure.

I climbed down the side of the ravine with him, a tall, heavy set Zulu man old enough to be my father, in a torn overall, shabby and stained, covered with rock dust. His head was shaved, and he had a thin, carefully shaped salt and pepper mustache. He carried himself with easy confidence, and he reminded me of Mandla. I found myself becoming angry as we slid down the side of the ravine.

"This better not be for nothing," I warned. "I don't have time to waste."

"Yes, *baas*," he said loudly, turning to look up at me. There was mockery in his voice, and a wide grin on his face, and when he smiled, his mustache disappeared. Then the smile disappeared, too, I looked into his eyes, and I knew that he was not what he appeared to be. When he spoke again, his voice had dropped to a low murmur.

"Just do as I say, Lenny. When we get to the bottom, for the benefit of anyone watching, I will point to a crack at the base of the pillar. While I'm talking, you follow my hand as I point upward. You understand?"

I was so taken aback by his speech and by his demeanor that I could only nod. Nowhere but in clandestine ANC meetings had I experienced this kind of interchange with a black man. I wondered briefly whether he was here to tell me that your mother was dead, or whether I was about to be killed, and the potential reasons why anyone might want me dead flashed through my mind. I had failed to warn your mother and Mandla when the police came looking for them; they suspected that I had been the one who gave away their location to the police; or perhaps, I thought, this was Mandla's way of getting rid of me so that he could have your mother to himself. I even wondered if your mother wanted me dead so that she could steal you away and go live with Mandla in some less restrictive place.

When we got to the bottom, we stood together in the shadows at the base of a massive concrete pillar that rose forty feet above us and narrowed at the top where metal support girders emerged and arched widely across the ravine. He pointed to a small surface crack at the concrete base. As he spoke, he followed it up, and when it came to an end at about waist level, he continued to raise his hand, pointing at an imaginary crack that meandered back and forth across the width of the pillar, and rose to disappear into the scaffolding high above our heads.

"I have information for you, Lenny," he said. "Look at the crack while I speak. You are curious, and concerned—but please show no emotion on your face. You understand?"

I nodded, looking intently at the concrete.

"Good," he said, and he leaned in to me.

His clothes smelled of sweat and the distinctive smoky odor of burning *veld* grasses, and I found it strangely comforting. He had a rich voice, but he spoke softly, his words urgent and rapid.

"Michaela is safe. I saw her yesterday—she is in good hands. She asks me to tell you that she misses you; that she sends you her love, and her sorrow. She asks that you kiss your son for her."

I stepped toward the pillar and scratched at the base with a screwdriver, hiding my face from view. When I had my expression under control again, I stepped back and resumed my place beside him.

"Where is she?" I asked. "Is she still here, in the country?"

"I can't tell you—it would be better for you not to have information the police might extract from you. The government is embarrassed to have the world know that she escaped—but they're hunting everywhere, so we're being extra cautious. They suspect that you were involved. Your phone is not safe. You're being followed, and they watch your office and your house day and night. The police are also keeping an eye on your son."

"Steven? What for?"

"They think Michaela might come for him. Guard him carefully, but tell him nothing. If the Special Branch finds an opportunity, they will isolate and question him."

That was all. He told me nothing else; said that he was in danger by merely being there; wouldn't let me know where or when I could see your mother. As soon as it was safe, he said, they would get another message to me. Then we climbed back up the ravine, and he disappeared. In the weeks that followed I searched eagerly for him in the desperate hope that he might have news for me, but he was gone. He would never have revealed his real name, and I never learned who he was.

It was common knowledge in the community that your mother had been convicted, and the children at school with you all knew what she had done. They taunted you about your mother being a convict and a terrorist—and worse, there were lurid stories going around about her having been caught in bed with a black man. They said your mother was a *kaffirboetie*—the closest translation is nigger-lover; and they joked that your real father was a black terrorist.

I'm sure you didn't understand any of it—and neither did your class-mates. But you didn't have to understand it in order to know that it was a terrible thing. As for me, at work I was suspect; my colleagues knew that I was being followed, and the senior partners were leery of the attention I was drawing. The police could have picked me up and put me away for ninety days at a time—and then where would you have been? Our lives had become intolerable, and it was clear that we needed a new start.

Slowly, I began to tease out the possibilities, discovering where I might be welcome. My advanced degree in engineering and a fair amount of experience in the narrow area of railway system bridge maintenance, made me employable all over the world. I wrote to people I knew in Boston, in Houston, in San Francisco; spoke to colleagues who had left the country and were working at engineering firms, or teaching in universities.

MIT was expanding their Graduate School of Engineering, and I submitted an application. They offered me an Assistant Professorship. It was more, and faster, than I had expected, and it forced me to rethink what had happened to our lives. I realized that any love I might still feel for your mother was wasted on her. She had gone too far; pushed my tolerance beyond its limits. I was done. And before we left, I wanted to let her know that we were through. But she still hadn't made any attempt to contact me.

Wherever I went I kept looking for the man who had taken me down the ravine; I was constantly on the watch for new faces, or for eye contact that might indicate a message was coming. When someone brushed up against me or touched my elbow in the street I searched my clothing in the hope that a note might have been quietly slipped into a pocket. At home, or in the office, whenever the phone rang, my heart jumped in anticipation of hearing your mother's voice on the other end. But there was nothing.

About a month after your mother disappeared, your headmaster, Mr. van Rensberg, called me one evening. He suggested strongly that I be present at a meeting in his office the next day. The meeting had been called by Miss Coetzee, your teacher, and she demanded that an officer from the Special Branch be present. Mr. van Rensberg was very uncomfortable—said he had no idea what the agenda was, but suggested that since there would be a member of the Special Branch there, and considering our current family circumstances, it might be wise if I were to consult my attorney.

We met in his office—small and crowded, a typical elementary school headmaster's office, not meant for five adults. There were only four of us at first—me, my attorney, Miss Coetzee and the headmaster, who might have been great with children, but seemed very uneasy with us, or perhaps with the situation. It was clear that he didn't know how to address the meeting, and had no idea what was supposed to happen, so we sat in silence until Miss Coetzee, who had a formidable look in her eye, said that an officer from the Special Branch—Lieutenant Viljoen—was having a smoke outside.

"Viljoen?" I asked. "Big, red haired fellow?"

She nodded, surprised that I knew him. My worst fear was that you had shared something incriminating with Miss Coetzee, and that she was about to give us up. As we waited, I wracked my brain for any information I might possibly have let slip to you, and how to protect us all from it when it came out, whatever it was.

Lieutenant Viljoen walked into the office without knocking, and sat in the only open chair.

"Mr. Green," he said, "we meet again. I hope you and your son are well."

"Thank you," I said. "Yes, we're doing all right. Under the circumstances."

I realized that he thought exactly what I did—that Miss Coetzee had called the meeting in order to give us away, and I was filled with panic.

Mr. van Rensberg started the meeting awkwardly, going round the room and introducing each of us, but he quickly handed control over to Miss Coetzee. She was calm, but she was as determined as usual, and not to be trifled with.

"Let me be very clear about why I've requested this meeting, and why I've asked for it to be in the presence of Mr. van Rensberg and Lieutenant Viljoen."

"Just tell us what happened in your classroom, Miss Coetzee," interrupted Viljoen. "That's what we're here to find out."

She gave him a piercing glance and there was a look of surprise on his face as he seemed to physically deflate.

"The purpose of this meeting," she continued, "is to share with everyone here exactly what has transpired in the last two weeks, and to let those of you who don't already know that, regardless of what my politics may be, I am first and foremost a teacher. Mr. van Rensberg already knows that." She turned to him. "I have always found you most supportive, Mr. van Rensberg, and I have never been more in need of support than I am now. May I anticipate your continued goodwill?"

"I don't see why not, Miss Coetzee," he stammered, turning to the Lieutenant. "Miss Coetzee is one of our most experienced teachers, and she is devoted to her students," he said.

"I'm sure Miss Coetzee is an excellent teacher," he said smoothly, smiling at her. "And I'm sure that nothing is more important to her than the safety of her pupils."

She continued as if he had not spoken. "I have been a teacher for over thirty years," she continued, "and in that time my only concern has been the welfare of the children in my charge. For as long as I am able to teach, I will continue to do whatever I can to further their health and their education."

She turned to Viljoen again. Her back was ramrod straight, her cheeks pink with indignation, and there were tears of fury in her eyes.

"But I am not a spy. Even for the sake of state security I will not inform on my students for the police or the Special Branch or for any other organization." She turned to me. "Nor will I lie for them. Is that understood?"

"What are you talking about, Miss Coetzee?" asked the headmaster, sitting up straight for the first time. "Has someone asked you to inform on the children? Or to lie for them? And why?"

"Miss Coetzee, no one has asked you to be a spy," said Viljoen quietly. "I think you misunderstood the request we made. All we've asked is that you—"

"I'll decide whether or not I've been asked to spy," she retorted. "What do you call your request to me last week—your request that I share with you anything Steven Green might say about the whereabouts of his mother?"

"You went directly to one of my teachers on an issue of this nature," said Mr. van Rensberg, his thin face darkening as he glared at the Lieutenant, "without going through my office?"

Viljoen rose, his bulk filling the room. "You all seem unaware that this is a criminal matter," he said. "I've been charged with conducting a search for convicted terrorists who've managed to escape, and I have the authority to obtain information any way I deem necessary for the protection of the public."

Mr. van Rensberg ignored the Lieutenant and turned again to Miss Coetzee.

"What did you say about lying for your students? Who asked you to lie?"

"No one has asked me to lie," she said. "But I wanted to make it clear to Mr. Green that even though I will not be an informer for the police, neither will I lie about anything his son may say in my classroom."

"Wait a minute," I said. "I haven't asked you to lie about anything my son might have said."

"Exactly what did Steven say in your classroom, Miss Coetzee," asked Viljoen, "that you are so reluctant to tell us?"

Again, Miss Coetzee ignored the Lieutenant, and turned to me.

"Mr. Green," she said, "I grieve with you about what's happened in your family. And if what Steven says is true, then I am with you in your loss."

"I ask you again, Miss Coetzee," said the Lieutenant, "exactly what did Steven say?"

"You don't need to answer that, Miss Coetzee," said my attorney, "at least, not without having your counsel present."

"I'm not afraid of speaking," she responded. "And nothing I have to say will cause any harm to Mrs. Green, or be of any use to the Lieutenant." She looked at me again. "Mr. Green, I must tell you that unless you have information about your wife that is not public, I think you are doing Steven a grave disservice by telling him that his mother is dead."

"Dead?" I said, catching myself. "I have no idea whether she's dead or alive. I don't even know where she is—the Lieutenant himself said that they're hunting for her. And I certainly haven't discussed it with Steven—he's a little boy, and he's got enough to deal with. Who told you that she's dead?"

"Steven," she answered.

"That's what he told you?" interrupted the Lieutenant, unable to hide the disappointment in his voice. "That's what you called this meeting for? To discuss the fantasies of a sad little boy who misses his Mommy?"

Lieutenant Viljoen strode to the door and turned back to us, one hand on the door handle.

"Mr. van Rensberg, I'll thank you not to waste my time again unless you have substantive business to discuss. And as for you, Mr. Green, I'm sure we'll meet again. Good day." Then he walked out and closed the door noisily behind him, and there was an audible sigh of relief.

Once he was gone, Miss Coetzee told us what had happened in her classroom. You've never given me any indication that you remember any of this, Steven, which I find surprising considering the nature and content of the family history class project you did in Boston several years later, when you were in the fifth grade.

Miss Coetzee gave you an assignment to talk about the work your parents did, and, she said, she had purposely worded it that way because there was one child in the class whose father had recently died. Very few mothers worked for a living, and she knew from experience that most children would choose to talk about their fathers. She assumed that you would, too. She told you all to go home and interview the parent you were going to talk about, and she gave you specific questions to ask. You must have discarded the questions, and you never interviewed me.

On the day you were supposed to give your report, you came in very quietly, with purpose written all over your face, and you behaved with great courage. You were far from the biggest child in the class, and some of the boys had been giving you a difficult time—you know, children sometimes overhear their parents talking, and they repeat what they hear. There must have been some talk about your mother, and Miss Coetzee found you on several occasions during playtime outside on the playground alone and crying. Once or twice she stopped you and another boy fighting, and had to punish you both for misbehaving in class. When it was your turn to talk, you walked bravely up to the front of the room.

"I know your Steven," Miss Coetzee told me, "and I saw that behind the courage and determination, he was just a little lost boy, longing for his mother."

Sitting in the headmaster's office, Miss Coetzee repeated what you said, and I've never forgotten the little speech you made. If I close my eyes, I can remember hearing her, voice shaking with emotion, as she recited your words.

"All people are created equal, and they all deserve to have enough to eat, and a good education like the one we get at our school. It shouldn't matter what color their skin is. My mother believed that—but not everyone agreed with her. And some people who don't believe that took her away and killed her. I loved her a lot, and she was brave and she worked hard to help everyone, and now she's dead and I miss her."

Then you stopped, and you walked out of the class. Miss Coetzee was deeply affected by your performance, and she waited for you to return so that she could praise you in front of the classroom. But when you didn't return after a few minutes, she became concerned that you might have done yourself harm, so she had someone from the office take over the class, and she went looking for you. She almost didn't find you—but as a last resort she walked the perimeter of the school—you probably don't remember, but there was a high brick wall around two sides of the school, and a row of old blue gum trees on the far side of the playground. Anyway, that's where you were. She found you hidden behind one of the trees, sitting cross-legged in the grass, leaning against the trunk. The only reason she headed in that direction was that she heard something clinking against the wall, and that's when she looked in your direction.

"He looked so sad," she told us. "He had been crying hard, and he was still sobbing deep in his chest as he threw marbles at the wall. So I sat down beside him, and I really wanted to take him in my arms. But that wasn't what he needed—your boy needed to know that he would be okay, no matter what happened. We sat together in the sunshine, and he continued to throw marbles, and eventually I joined in.

"When he calmed down, I put my hands on his shoulders and looked into his eyes. And I said to him, 'Steven, look at me.' As he turned to me, the tears ran down his cheeks and he wiped them off with his shirtsleeve.

'Nothing wrong with crying,' I told him, and I wiped my own cheeks, too. 'See?' And then he managed to smile.

"'I don't know whether or not your story is true, Steven,' I said. 'But no matter what anyone says, you must believe that your mother lived her life with courage and with her eyes open. You have those same wide open eyes, and you have her courage inside you. You're a brave little soldier, my boy. You're very sad now, but I know that you're going to be just fine. You make sure to remember that. You hold your head high, Mr. Steven Green, and put a smile on your face, because you're the son of a very brave woman. Now, you pull yourself together, and when you're ready, come back and join the class.'"

Miss Coetzee rose and returned to her other students. You got up and ran after her, and she said that when you walked into the room, your head was held high, and there was a brave smile on your face.

I can only imagine how much pain you were in. You had to deal with the absence of information, because I wasn't telling you anything, and neither was anyone else. On top of that, you were being teased at school, and your classmates were accusing your mother of misdeeds you didn't even understand. Where you got what you said, I will never know. You didn't hear it from me—perhaps some of it came from conversations you remembered having with your mother.

You've shown no indication that you remember any of these events, Steven. I can imagine you asking, as you read this, why I never told you that the story of how your mother died was your own invention.

Perhaps you can understand now why I was so reluctant to watch you make your presentation in Mrs. Tolliver's class when you were in the fifth grade. I knew it would be a more elaborate version of the same story—but for me, it was sadder than you can imagine. It was déjà vu—with an older and more articulate you, in a different country, before a different audience. The only thing that was unchanged was your pain and isolation, and your sense of being different from everyone else; and your need—your constant need—to put the issue of your mother to rest. But you were insistent, and Mrs. Tolliver was unrelenting, and so I came. Reluctantly. And I sat in that cramped little desk at the back of the classroom, and when you were through all I could do was cry. For the lies, and the secrecy; for how much they cost us over the years. And for how much they cost us still.

seven

STEVEN

Boston, 2001

As Dariya and I read my father's retelling of Miss Coetzee's story, I began to recall my second-grade classroom. At first, I didn't know whether the images formed out of the mist of imagination, or whether they came from memory.

"I do remember her," I said. "She kept a bright blue bag full of marbles tied to her belt, and at recess she used to walk around the playground. Sometimes she would play marbles with us. She sat down next to me and opened her little bag, and she asked me what I was aiming for. I showed her the reddest brick in the wall, and we took turns throwing marbles at it."

"So your father wasn't making this all up?"

"Not the parts I remember."

"What about your little speech? Do you remember that?"

I shook my head. "No—but if I did make the speech, I can't believe I would have forgotten it."

"You were under tremendous stress, Steven—there's a lot you might have forgotten."

"Perhaps," I said. "So when did my mother die? And how? It must have happened much later."

Dariya just looked at me. "Let's keep reading," she said.

"I can't right now. I need your help in the studio. We need to select the paintings for my show at the Danforth Museum next week, and then I have to deliver them."

Dariya came with me to the studio, where I had selected what I thought were the five best and lined them up against the wall. She was seeing them for the first time.

"They're masterful, Steve. Great color. They jump from the canvas, but somehow you've kept the subtlety. I love them." She stood before them, swaying her hips as she glanced from one to the next.

"Is there a 'but' in there?"

She crossed her arms, rubbing the knuckles of one hand against her chin.

"No buts—just a question. What do they say? And when did you start with all the abstract shapes?"

"I don't know," I said. "Since the summer, every time I start a landscape or a seascape, I find myself painting a tower in the water, or a huge monument in a valley—anything to fill up the emptiness. I want to use space differently, you know? But what you call abstract shapes, really aren't abstract at all. Look closer."

I showed her that every shape in every painting was organic—that I had just changed the scale of things, viewed rock walls and umbrellas, bottles and windmills and towers and seashells, from different and unusual angles, shaded and tinted them in unexpected ways.

"What happened?" she asked. My paintings were arrayed against the wall and I glanced from one to another, seeing suddenly that they were an attempt to get below the skin of the landscape, to stick my arm deep into the painting and pull out what was hiding there. And underlying that was a belief, or at least a hope, that my search would reveal something worth seeing.

Dariya had moved out of my line of sight, and was standing behind me. She put her arms about me, leaned over so that our cheeks were touching.

"Steven," she said. "There's something I want to talk to you about."

"What?"

"Do you think your father was hiding something else?" asked Dariya.

"You mean something besides the fact that my mother was unfaithful to him?"

"Yes."

"And besides the fact that he never told me I made up the story of how she died?"

"Yes."

"What makes you ask?"

"Don't you think there's something strange about the way he's written his story?"

"He was a very private person," I said. "I've thought as we read through the manuscript that writing this history must have been like having his teeth pulled."

"No," she said, "it's more than that. It's not just strange—there's something calculated about the way he's revealing the story. As you read it, don't you feel in the slightest way that you're being manipulated?"

I put my hands on her shoulders and looked at her skeptically.

"Don't make fun," she said. "You know, if you're any good as a journalist, you quickly develop a sense of whether people are withholding information. You know I'm good. And I'm telling you he's holding something back." She paused. "Something else."

"Perhaps he is," I said. "Maybe he was just trying to postpone writing about what happened to my mother for as long as possible. Remember, he was never able to talk to me about her."

"He was dying as he wrote this—he didn't know how much time he had, or whether he'd be able to finish. Wouldn't it have made sense for him to write about the most important things first?"

"Who knows what he thought was important? Dariya, I'm not a writer—I have no idea what was on his mind."

She agreed, reluctantly, that I was probably right.

"We don't have to wait, you know," I said, grinning at her.

"What do you mean?"

"If you're so sure that he's waiting to reveal something else, we could skip to the end of the manuscript. That way we might find out what it is in our own time, instead of on his schedule. Would that make you feel less manipulated?"

She shook her head. "I already thought of that," she said, "but it would feel too much like cheating. I suppose we just have to go along with his plan and keep reading."

It struck me that there were several advantages to writing a history and leaving it for me. First, he avoided having to face me, and second, as long as I read it in the sequence he gave me, I had no choice but to discover each piece of the story in precisely the order in which he decided to reveal it. Despite himself, he had managed to remain in control. What Dariya didn't—couldn't—tell me was that she had already figured out what else he was hiding. She was trying to prepare me for what was to come, and it wasn't far off.

eight

LENNY

Boston, 2001

We come now, my children, to the almost end of my part in this story. I say almost because there are still two things to be addressed. None too soon.

You were just here, Steven, sitting at my bedside, watching over me as I write feverishly, looking on as I die. I want so much to face you and tell you the truth, but I lack the courage, even now. Instead, I spread my arms wide, intending it, I suppose, as an invitation to hug you. I wanted so much to hold you close to me, to feel your love and to have you feel mine, before everything changed. But you looked at me with alarm—if you think back, you will remember it—and the moment passed. You looked with pity and dismay at my narrow, shrunken chest, and I raised my shoulders in a long, painful shrug. You watched my wrists sticking out from my pajama sleeves, bony and thin. I felt—and you must have seen—a man not so much cold-blooded, as bloodless, drained of all fluids. Then, like a skeletal, avian thing coming to rest, I lowered my arms like wings, bent them into a fold at my sides, and closed my eyes. When I awoke you were gone, and Dariya had taken your place.

I've known since we left South Africa that we would eventually have this conversation. I didn't know how long we'd have to wait for it, or what the tenor of the discussion would be. And I hoped it would be in the form of an interchange, where you could ask the questions I've successfully avoided answering all these years, and I would have the opportunity to explain. This is far more difficult—like giving an interview, but without an interviewer. I have to provide all the answers, without benefit of questions or accusations.

You say you have no memory of finding out that your mother was killed fighting apartheid—it's always been a fact of life for you. There's a reason why you have no memory of the event: no one ever told you that she was dead. I just failed to find the right time to tell you what did happen. Why didn't I tell you before? There were many reasons—I leave it to you to decide when the first possible moment was to tell you the truth.

Was it when we first arrived in Boston? South Africa was still dealing with sabotage and violence then, and the atmosphere was as repressive as ever. Your mother had disappeared, and the police were unwilling to suspend their search. They wanted her alive, or they wanted proof that she was dead.

The growing community of South Africans in Boston knew who I was and what had happened to us, and many of them were still in touch with people who hadn't left. One word about your mother and it would have been all over the country, and the police would have intensified their search. I imagined how angry you would have been to discover as an adult that your mother had been captured because I told you the truth, and you shared it with a school friend. So in the early years, I said nothing.

Perhaps I should have told you when you were old enough to keep it secret—when you were twelve, or fourteen, or seventeen. Or should it have been my birthday gift to you when you turned twenty-one? I don't know. And the longer I waited, the more difficult it became.

There was also the matter of what your mother wanted. She did manage to get a message to me before we left the country, and we spoke briefly on the phone. I was in a garage outside the city—I don't have the faintest idea where she was, and she was afraid to tell me.

"You've destroyed my life as well as yours," I told her angrily. "Why didn't you just light a bomb under us? At least it would have been quicker."

"I didn't mean any of this to happen," she said, "I'm sorry, Lenny, but it happened and I can't undo it. I don't have much time. Tell me—how's Stevie?"

"Oh, his life is one big party," I answered. "The Special Branch follows him wherever he goes, he's bullied at school by children who repeat the profanities they hear at home about you, and he misses you terribly. Other than that, he's doing fine." She didn't answer. "Did you expect that he would accept all this madness in his life without missing a beat? For Christ's sake, it's turned my life upside down, and he's only seven years old. What the hell were you thinking?"

I didn't hear her voice again for almost forty years. All that time, she's been an absent presence in our lives, and she has weighed heavily on us both. She did write occasionally. In her letters she made it clear that she thought you were better off without her; left me to decide when to tell you the truth. She left me responsible for ensuring her safety; left me to carry the lie; left me to live with the consequences of your reaction when you found out the truth; left up to me the decision of when to break our silence.

What right did she have to leave it all up to me? One can understand why she wanted to remain anonymous at the start—she was in danger of her life. But that danger ended in 1992 when apartheid ended and Mandela was elected. Then it became safe for her to give up her false identity, admit who she was, and resume her real name. Where was all her vaunted courage then? Why didn't she come forward and tell you the truth?

I don't know the answer, Steven. All I do know is that your mother is still alive. It will be up to you to find out who she became, and what her life has been like. If you want to.

nine

STEVEN

Dennis, 2001

We had driven down to Dennis that weekend, and were reading the manuscript early Saturday morning while we were still in bed, and Sally and Greg were sleeping. We read aloud to each other, taking turns. And because Dariya was reading, I will forever remember the revelation that my mother was still alive, in her voice. As she finished the section, she put the pages down and looked at me silently.

"You knew, didn't you?" I asked.

She nodded slowly.

"When?"

"I'm a journalist, Steven. If the facts don't add up, I have to look at other possibilities, even the unlikely ones. I told you I was pretty sure that your father was manipulating the story. I didn't buy his story of your mother's disappearance into thin air—but we agreed that he would reveal it all in the end." She shrugged. "And that's exactly what he did."

"You tried to tell me."

"You weren't ready."

"I'm still not ready," I said. "How can she suddenly be alive? What am I supposed to do with all those years of grieving?"

"You'll know what to do," she said. "It just needs time to sink in."

"There's a piece of me that doesn't want this to be true."

"Steven, we don't have to do anything except continue to live our lives. I think you should go now."

When I could, I met her eyes. "Go?"

"Go," she said quietly.

"Where?"

"You were going out to the low tide to paint this morning," she said. "Do yourself a favor, go. We can talk when you get back."

"No. There are only a few pages left," I said. "Let's finish before I go out. I want it done. I want it to be over."

ten

LENNY

Boston, 2001

When I realized that I was dying, I found the courage to call your mother. I felt an obligation to tell her that I had only months to live. Other than her intonation and the way she said your name, her voice was unfamiliar to me, and I recognized nothing in her of the woman I once knew. We talked briefly about my illness, and she made the appropriate sympathetic noises. Then there was heavy silence, filled with all the unspeakable accusations and recriminations.

"Why the call, Lenny?" she asked. "You didn't call just to let me know you're dying. What about Steven?"

"I don't have it in me to tell him, Michaela," I said.

"Tell him what?"

I laughed, harsh and angry. "If you've forgotten, I guess it wasn't all that important, was it? I promised I'd tell him the truth when the time was right. It was an easy promise. All these years I've felt guilty about keeping it from him—and even when it was safe for you, I didn't have the courage to do it."

"Are you saying he still doesn't know?" she said, her voice hushed. "I thought you told him. Years ago. Not an hour passes," she said, finding her anger, "without my thinking of Steven. And you...you never told him about me?"

"I could never find the right time."

"So he doesn't know."

"No."

"He doesn't know," she muttered, talking more to herself than to me. "He still thinks I'm dead."

"That's right," I said.

"He never made contact with me because he didn't know—and all these years I assumed it was because he decided that he had no interest in knowing me."

"It just became too difficult to juggle all the pieces, Michaela—to keep clear what was true and what wasn't. I'm sorry."

"You're sorry? You promised you would tell him." Her voice was low, quivering with anger. "You bastard. You let him live all his life with this lie. And me—you don't owe me anything, but you made me a promise. All these years you led me to believe you had told him the truth. How could you?"

"I haven't led you to believe anything," I said, finding my own anger. "And you're right—I owe you nothing. I kept your secret, protected you, for decades—but I don't see any calls from you since it became safe for you to resume using your own name. What's it been, twelve years? As you once said to me, none of this was intentional—it just happened," I said. "Now it's too late. And I'm just too tired."

"So you called to tell me you don't have the balls to tell our son the truth? Even now?"

"I called to tell you that I'm not likely to reveal the truth to him at this point, Michaela. You can decide whether you want to tell him yourself."

"You may be willing to go to your grave with Steven believing I'm dead," she continued, "but I'm not. I'm going to write to him and tell him what happened. If you choose to say nothing, all he'll have from you is silence—but by now he must be used to that. Are you really willing to die and leave him without a word of explanation? For God's sake, Lenny, if you don't have the courage to face his anger, write it down. At least that way, after you're gone, he'll have both versions of his history. I'm content to let him know my side of the story—he can decide for himself whether or not he wants to know me."

That was our conversation. And now you know where the impulse to write it all down came from. I would probably have been content to let this history die with me—but I still have sufficient self-respect—call it ego—that I'm not willing to leave you in possession of only your mother's version of the story. I'd give almost anything to read what she plans to send you, but that's one of the many things I will never accomplish. All I can do is make sure you have my story, too.

One other thing I need to share with you before I go. A deep and most shame-filled thing; a thing so repulsive to me that I have hidden it even from myself all these years, carried its weight within me like blackened slime. It is my last, secret, and most despairing failure.

I adored your mother—would have followed her anywhere, and taken you with me. And if she hadn't invited me along, I would have raised the issue myself and told her we were coming. I would have gone with her wherever she went after she escaped from prison, and taken you with us into hiding, or into exile. You might have grown up living in some of the most beautiful landscape in the world, on a farm in the wilds of the Drakensberg, under an assumed name—but you would have had two parents. I would have forgiven her anything. Or so I thought.

When it came out that she had been unfaithful to me, I was surprised—and heartbroken. Ultimately, I found that I could forgive her all but one thing. It was a recognition that ripped away my cover and exposed me as a fraud and a hypocrite.

I was as deeply committed as your mother was to the cause of freedom and equality, and I fought as hard as she did for it. It was one of the central themes of our life; it bound us together, and it was always present. I don't think a day went by without a meeting or a phone conversation or a clandestine message being passed. And we really believed that the time would come when all people, every color and race, would live together in friendship and harmony and peace. But not, apparently, in adultery.

Mandla and I were friends, and I admired, even loved him. He was a courageous man, committed and gentle. But when it came down to the wire, she chose him over me. Over us. Turned out I could have forgiven her almost anything, including an affair—but I couldn't forgive the fact that the affair was with a black man, and it mattered enough to put forgiveness beyond my grasp.

That's what I'm ashamed of; the thing I despise in myself; what I can't forgive. It makes me so much less than the man I wanted to be. Perhaps your mother saw that failure in me; perhaps that's why she couldn't have me accompany her. When shown the Promised Land, I failed to recognize it. My punishment is that I was denied entrance.

I know very little about your mother's life, other than that she owns a farm in KwaZulu Natal. It's in an area called Balgowan, in the Midlands, near Cleopatra Mountain. It overlooks the Drakensberg Range. I remember the location—we once took a holiday there—but the real reason for our trip was the man hidden under the floorboards of our trunk. He had escaped custody after being badly beaten by the police, and we took him to an isolated village so that he could disappear until the hunt for him subsided. You were in the car with us—an infant. I wonder, what could we have been thinking? We would have been put away for years had we been discovered. But that was in another country, at a different time, and the details of what happened, and why, recede into confusion. Yet I retain a vivid memory of the place. It is remarkably beautiful, and you, of all people, will appreciate the grandeur of the landscape. Think of me as you stand amid the hills, painting the sweep of sky.

I have a final message for you, my son, and one for your mother. Tell her that the last thing I said to her at the end of that telephone conversation forty years ago was accurate. I never wanted to see her again, but I have missed her. And I did love her for the rest of my life. The only person I have loved more is you.

eleven

STEVEN

Dennis, 2001

I made my way down the path towards the beach, carrying my portable easel. I've painted the ocean at all times of day and night, in sunlight and cloud, in moonlight, at dawn and dusk, in good weather and bad. I've tried to define its moods during sunshine and storm, attempting to isolate and capture the defining characteristics of each season by simply looking at the way light—or its absence—reflects off the water. What I've discovered, and sometimes captured on canvas, is that light is alive; that it can be both the source of energy, as well as the palette on which the sky paints. It sometimes glances off the surface of the water, or it can be absorbed, soaking into the body of the ocean.

At times, reflected light colors the ocean; at others, the water itself seems to be the light source, beaming reflected light into the air.

I don't know whether I've succeeded, but people seem to like what I do, and there is as much demand for my more ambitious paintings in New York as there is on the West Coast. When I'm between larger projects, my sketches and smaller paintings—the ones I do as exercises in preparation for bigger work—sell in galleries at Wellfleet and Provincetown. I've been lucky, so far.

Would my mother like this place, I wondered? And what would she think of my success as a painter? Would she even care?

For the last few years, I've been working on a series of paintings done from the low-tide line, looking back at the beach. I'm at the mercy of the tide for most of these paintings, because I have to wait until low tide to set up my easel. On this part of Cape Cod, at the inner elbow of a curved arm of land with Provincetown at the tip of loosely curled fingers, low tide is a major event. The tide goes out about a mile, and at its lowest point, the mud flats seem to extend forever. The sea, when it is visible in the far distance, is no more than a dark blue line on the horizon; on clear, windy days, the dark blue line is punctuated by whitecaps.

To get to the low tide mark I have to drag my equipment out over the tidal flats. Time is limited once I set up my easel, because from where I paint, there is only a two or three hour working window between low and high tides. On several occasions, I've become too enmeshed in my painting and lost track of time, and had to slog back almost a mile through knee—and sometimes thigh-high—water, loaded with equipment. More than once, I've had to float my easel behind me. I've become wiser now, sometimes going out with a camera, taking a series of shots, and working from those back at the studio. But there's still no substitute for painting on site, being able to relate the canvas directly to the subject.

This morning, the dawn horizon was swatches of orange and mauve and deep purple, and at the center where it was brightest the orange hue was beginning to shade to yellow, becoming too bright to look at. I cupped a hand around my eyes and looked up at the trees on either side of the path, peering into the foliage. The birdsong was loud, gleeful and raucous; I loved their profusion, delighted in their quick, eager movements, and my chest filled with elation as I watched them soar.

I walked down to the beach, carefully removed my sneakers, and set them beside each other in the shelter of the rocks. Then I made my way across the rocky sea wall and started out over the mud flats towards the low tide. A flock of seagulls, two or three hundred birds all facing into the wind, rose lazily as I approached, some stepping along the sand with flapping wings before they took off, most simply opening their wings to the wind, and rising effortlessly. They were wary, perhaps, but not alarmed, as if they were doing what they were supposed to, without really believing that it was necessary. They rose in waves, like a blanket being shaken, and came to rest just beyond the point from which they had taken off. The flock parted as I approached and reformed behind me.

I strode out across the sea grass, splashed through the rooted seaweeds that floated gracefully at high tide, but now lay formlessly on the wet sand. Beyond the weeds, the sand was white and already dry. I stepped over the giant sun-whitened clam shells that stuck out of the sand like bottle fragments; walked gingerly wherever I thought there might be hidden clam shells lying flat, just under the surface, waiting to crack and splinter beneath the unwary foot.

At the softer, white sand, I stopped and looked carefully at the designs the receding tide had made. It had formed in beautifully symmetrical wavy lines and patterns, and any section could have been lifted from the beach and framed. The sun, now above the horizon, was still low enough to cast long shadows, and the light and shadow on the corrugated sand, extending down the mud flats until it was too distant to be seen, was magical. And now I was at the low-tide line, the cutting edge of the Atlantic Ocean, where the seabed declines so gradually that there were no waves, only small ripples on a smooth, lake-like surface, interrupted at intervals by the tail end of ocean swells, echoes and remnants that came to lap at the shore before subsiding into the sand.

This is where my father came to reflect deeply on his life, to remember, and to regret. This is where he grieved for his lost life; where he relived the love he felt for my mother, and his anger and grief over losing her, and where he must have revisited the decisions he made that so affected us, and our relationship. As I set up my easel and looked out at the sun-drenched seascape, I thought about my parents. My father had never been able to let me see who he was, but in his manuscript, he was able to give me an understanding of what motivated him, what he feared, who he needed to protect—my mother—and who he most loved.

In the writing of his story, he retained control of the way information was divulged, forcing me to learn the history before he revealed the truth about my mother. In so doing, he defused the rage I might otherwise have aimed at him for withholding information. What he and my mother had done to me was unforgivable, and he knew it. There were reasons that had once been clear, but they became murky and questionable with the passage of time. Now he had explained them, and the rationale was again clear—but the consequences of those decisions were permanent.

I had promised to call Mandla —he knew how the manuscript would end. I was still reeling from the idea that my long dead mother lived on a farm in KwaZulu Natal, and that I could actually call her and ask her the questions I had rehearsed over and over as a child. Only now the question, "How could you leave me?" had a very different meaning. And while I wasn't sure I wanted to hear her answer, there was a part of me that couldn't wait to pose the question. All I had to do was decide whether I wanted to contact her. And then I had to decide what—if anything—to tell Sally and Greg.

Thick blotches of cadmium yellow, pthalo green and scarlet erupted up through the surface of my painting; they fought to escape the confines of the canvas. And superimposed on this chaos, looking as if it had been chiseled into the pigment, was a controlled filigree of burnt umber and titanium white, and swirls of manganese and cobalt blue. There was rage on my canvas; rage and sorrow and guilt. And the fury of an impotent child. Dariya was waiting for me on the beach when I came back.

"Thank you for trying to tell me," I said.

"You couldn't hear it until you were ready."

"Yes."

"While you were out there, I thought about when I first knew. It wasn't just how your father was revealing information—it was also your conversation with Mandla," she said. "He asked you to suspend judgment until you finished the manuscript, so he knew that your father would keep whatever revelation he had until the end."

"And he got it just right—finished in time to lapse into a coma."

"I think it's the other way around," she said. "The only thing keeping him alive was his drive to finish the document. When he was done, there was no reason to keep fighting. He just let go."

I imagined my father fighting against pain and morphine to retain control of his thoughts and his fingers. The document he left on his computer for me was error free—no typos or grammatical mistakes. It was a measure of his determination.

"I suspected everything," she said, "except the last thing."

"Which last thing?"

"What was probably most difficult for him to bear—that his whole life he professed a belief he never really subscribed to, and couldn't live by."

"You mean his feelings for Mandla."

"Yes. He was a closet hypocrite—and he lived in the shame of that all his life."

"I wonder whether Mandla has any idea."

"You could ask him," she said.

"I suppose."

"Are you going to call him?"

But I hadn't gotten that far.

"Steve? You are going to call him, aren't you?"

"Yes," I said, "I'm going to call him."

I put the phone on speaker so that Dariya could hear, and made the call. A woman answered, and I asked to speak with Mandla.

"May I tell him who it is?"

"Yes," I said. "Steven Green."

"Steven," she said with delight. "This is Miriam, his wife. He will be so glad you called. Hold on a moment–I'll find him."

While I waited, I wondered who his wife was, and what had happened between him and my mother. But I reminded myself that what I knew of their affair was forty years old, and that anything could have happened in the interim. It struck me for the first time that my mother might not only be my mother, but someone's wife, and the mother of other grown children.

"Steven," he said warmly. "I'm so happy to hear your voice."

"You asked me to call, when I finished my father's manuscript."

"You've read it, then."

"I have."

"I don't know the details, but I imagine that I feature as the villain in your father's history."

"It's not so cut and dried," I said. "His feelings for you seem to have been far more complex than that." I cleared my throat. "You asked me to call you by the name your friends call you, Khabazela. My opinion may change, but the impact you've had on my life doesn't encourage me to think of you as a friend."

"I'm sure that's true. And I am sorry for my part in the events that separated you from your mother so long ago." He stopped. "It was a very long time ago, Steven, and much has happened since. In all our lives."

"I suppose it has," I said. "Tell me, why did you ask me to call you when I was finished reading? Are you trying to make amends for the past?"

"In some ways, perhaps I am. But there are other reasons for my call to you, and for my request. I was certain that your father would mention me, and if you had chosen not to call, I would have assumed his portrayal of me to be so villainous that you found yourself unwilling to speak to me. That would have posed its own difficulties, but I would have called you eventually. I have learned that people can work out their differences, if only they're willing to talk to one another. And although you may not know it yet, you and I have common interests. Anyway, you did call—and even if you know nothing else about her, you know that your mother lives."

"I'm not sure what I know," I responded. "I've been told that she lives. Whether I actually believe it—or whether I care—is another question."

"That is about to change," he said.

"How?"

"For obvious reasons, I had to wait until you had completed reading your father's history. Now that you have, I will be sending you pieces of the story that your father couldn't have known. Part of it is your mother's; part of it is mine. You may find it strange that I am so involved in this, but your mother and I have been important players in each other's lives, and I think I can shed light on Michaela that neither she nor your father could."

"So you want me to withhold judgment until I've read your versions of what happened?"

"Correct. I don't know how your father positioned all the facts, but even if he presented them even-handedly, there is another side to the story. I'm sure you have mixed feelings. It's all very new to you, but as you can imagine—or maybe you can't—Michaela has hoped for years to hear from you one day."

"I'll take your word for it," I replied, "but that's hard for me to take in." I paused. "After more than four decades of no contact."

"We have lived very different lives, Steven," he said, "but this is as new for me as it is for you. Perhaps I should start by speaking for myself, and let your mother speak her own words. I can tell you that, having been close to her all those years, and having heard about you, I have hoped that you would call. I have wished it for your father, whom I would have liked to see again—but I have wished it also for your mother, and for you, and for myself."

"You think she wants to hear from me?"

"With all her heart. I would stake my life on it."

"You know her that well?"

"I know her very well."

"Despite being married to someone else."

There was a brief pause; I wondered whether I had offended him.

"Much can happen in four decades," he said. "We can't explore your life, or ours, in one telephone call, and we shouldn't try. I hope that you and your family will visit South Africa, and we can come to know each other better. Before you arrive, however, I'm sending you some of the story in writing that will I hope cast light in a few dark corners. In the meantime, would you take some advice from an old man?"

"I'll listen," I said.

"For years I was deeply involved in Truth and Reconciliation hearings in this country, and I have seen many confrontations between people harmed by our struggle, and by those who did the damage. You and your father—and your mother as well—are as much victims of that time as those who lost family to state-sanctioned violence. This was all set into motion long ago, by political movements bigger than the little human lives they upended, and by emotions that we do not always effectively control. I have learned, Steven, that those who emerge whole from this process of confronting loss, are the ones who remember that you cannot change the past, but you can control how you respond to it. That's something you can do for yourself, and that you must do for your children."

We drove home late Sunday afternoon, stopping at the seafood diner for an early supper. We ate fresh corn as we waited for our fish and chips at an outside table. Dariya gave me plenty of space, and I watched the children chatter on about the week to come at day camp. Greg was sitting next to me, concentrating on his corn. Sally sat across from me, next to Dariya, and she kept looking at me out of the corner of her eye. She had bright blue eyes and honeyed skin, and before she ate her corn she put her hands behind her head and clipped her hair into a pony tail, the clip in her mouth and her eyes on my face.

"What's up with you, Dad?" she asked as she completed the job, running her fingers over the clip to make sure her pony was tight enough.

"What do you mean?" I asked.

"You always say we don't keep secrets in this family, but you're doing just that." She tossed her pre-teen, all-knowing head. "I've seen that big book Grandpa Lenny left for you—and I know you and Mom are reading it out loud to each other, which is really cute. But something in the book's made you really unhappy, and you won't tell us what it is."

"I noticed, too," said Greg. In order to speak he had to stop rotating the corn through his teeth and held it poised in both hands before his mouth, ready to start again.

"Please eat your corn like a human being," said Dariya, "not like a combine."

"What's a combine?" he asked. "Is it like a transformer?"

"It's a machine, Greg," said Sally patiently, "for picking lots of vegetables on a farm."

"I'll show you one when we get home," said Dariya. "Why don't you tell us what you noticed about Dad?"

"Well, usually when Dad comes back from painting in the morning he leaves his canvas on that, you know, that special thing—that ledge—he built in the fireplace room. He leaves it there to dry, I think, and we can all look at it and see if we like it. But yesterday he hid it from us."

"I didn't hide it from you," I said.

"Then why did I find it in the little bedroom under the stairs?" asked Greg.

"What were you doing in the little bedroom?" asked Dariya. "You never go in there."

"Dad's painting wasn't anywhere else in the house, Mom," he said, explaining slowly so that we would understand. "That was the last room."

"So you were looking for Dad's painting, right?" asked Dariya.

He nodded in agreement.

"Why, Greg?"

"I always look at your paintings, Dad, just like you always look at mine. It's like, you know, we tell each other what we like, and what works, and what doesn't work. Like you showed me."

I imagined Greg scouring the house in search of my missing canvas, and I was touched by the idea that he took our interaction around painting so seriously.

"I see," I said, looking at Dariya and finding her staring at me. "That's great."

"So tell us," asked Dariya, "what did you think when you found the painting?"

"At first I was surprised," he said. "I didn't think Dad painted it." He wrinkled his nose in thought and lowered his corn to his plate. "There were too many bright colors—you know, the main colors—and they didn't all smoosh into each other smoothly like Dad's colors usually do. The colors crashed together, as if they were mad. And all these weird dark designs were trying to cover them over, and all I could think about was that the bright colors were mad because they wanted to get out from under, and they didn't know how."

Dariya grinned at me from across the table, her face bright with pride.

"Wow," she mouthed silently.

"That's pretty accurate, Greg," I said. "I was feeling a lot of those things when I painted it. But I wasn't hiding it from you—I was hiding it from myself."

"Why, Dad?"

"Looking at that painting," I said, "made me think about some things that I really didn't want to think about."

"Things you read in Grandpa Lenny's book," said Sally. "Right?"

"Right," I said.

"What things?" asked Greg. "What did Grandpa Lenny write that you didn't want to think about?"

I looked at the puzzlement creasing my son's smooth forehead—my serious, often silent son, who looked like me, with my coloring and my disposition; about whom I sometimes worried because he seemed sad.

"Nonsense," Dariya would say. "Stop projecting your own sadness— he's just thinking."

Sally had reminded me that in our family, we don't keep secrets; and according to Mandla, for the sake of my children I needed to remember that while we can't control the past, we can control how we respond to it. It was clear that in the present, that translated into telling the truth. There had been no secrets among us, and there would be none now.

"We did make a discovery today." I looked at Dariya to see whether she was signaling me to hold back, but she was smiling, so I went ahead, not knowing quite where I was going. "We've told you that my mother, your Grandma Michaela, who was married to Grandpa Lenny, died a long time ago, when I was a child, right?" They both nodded. "Well, that's what we thought for a long time. But part of what Grandpa Lenny wrote about was what really happened to my mother. She didn't die. She's alive."

Greg reached across the table and took Dariya's hand. She looked at him and smiled, and I knew that he was comforting her because I had had my father, and now I had my mother, but Dariya had neither. She was still an orphan.

"Where was she all this time?" he asked. "Was she lost or something?"

"Well, for a long time she was hiding," I said, "but now she doesn't have to do that anymore. She lives on a farm. In South Africa."

"Wow, Dad," said Sally, "how great is that? Just as Grandpa Lenny dies, and we think we have no more grandparents, we find out that we have a grandmother."

"On a farm," said Greg in amazement. "Do you think she has animals? Or maybe it's a vegetable farm, and she has a combine."

"When can we visit her?" asked Sally.

"Do you want to?" I asked.

"Of course. Who wouldn't want to see their long-lost grandmother?" She looked at her brother for confirmation. "Right, Greg?"

"I suppose," he said cautiously. "Does she know about us?"

"I suspect she does," I said.

"Then—" he stopped, trying to find the words "—then why hasn't she come to see us? You know, like grandparents are supposed to? Like Grandpa Lenny did?"

"I don't know the answers," I said. "That's why I said Grandpa Lenny's book made me think of some things I didn't really want to think about."

Sally's little girl face across the table suddenly took on an adult expression, as if she had in an instant catapulted out of childhood and into the next state of being.

"I'm sure there was a reason, Dad," she said, looking at me out of big brown eyes.

"I'm sure you're right, Sally," said Dariya, turning to me. "From the mouth of babes," she whispered.

"I hope you're right," I answered, "but I don't really know. I guess when you meet her, you can ask her. How does that sound?"

About two weeks later, DHL delivered a package from South Africa containing the manuscript I had been promised. As I opened it, I imagined the man behind the voice I had come to know, and I saw Mandla as an old man, writing with a fountain pen on parchment, in a formal and old-fashioned script. But I couldn't have been more wrong. The manuscript was composed on a computer, and he had sent me a photocopy printed on both sides. It was spiral bound, in an elegant cover of soft, textured, honey-colored leather. Carefully handwritten on the front in dark brown ink, was the following inscription:

To Steven
In Truth, and for Reconciliation
Mandla Mkhize

I put the manuscript back in its package, unopened. Later that night, once the children were in bed, I showed it to Dariya.

"What a beautiful cover," she said, running her hands over the leather as she read the inscription. "Mandla put a lot of thought into this," she said. "I think he must be a very special man."

In answer, I opened the front cover and began reading.

twelve

MANDLA

Soweto, 2001

Dear Steven,

When we spoke on the phone, I mentioned the Truth and Reconciliation Hearings. I was referring to them in relation to Lenny's confessional writings. I was thinking, I suppose, of the opportunity they provided him to tell you, in his final moments, the truths of his life. I had not originally intended to relate the hearings to my own life, but there is a natural connection.

Initially, I thought that this writing would be my way of educating you. I thought I was creating a doorway through which you could enter the world your mother has inhabited and see how she became the woman she is now. I thought I was writing about Michaela.

The road your mother and I traveled diverged a long time ago, but in many ways our paths ran parallel, and at times we trod in each other's footsteps. But having now written my own version of events, I realize that I could not tell her story without revealing part of my own. And so I discover what Lenny already knew—that this kind of writing is by definition confessional.

In sending this to you, I have no expectation that my words will repair the past. Much of my life has been spent committing acts of violence that in other times would have been unthinkable, and that even as I was committing them ran counter to my own essential self. For years I justified what I did in the name of freedom, in the service of people and country. But the acts are mine; the blood on my hands long ago congealed into scabbed wounds that are a permanent part of my flesh. In my frequent nightmares, the blood I have shed is my own, and it runs glistening, thick and hot from my veins. I sweat and tremble into wakefulness to reach for the solace of my wife's arms, and until now she has been the sole repository of my night terrors.

In all the years I have waited to speak to you, it never entered my mind that I might come to see you as my confessor, or that in the process of revealing to you my love affair with your mother, and the life we lived together, I would find the relief and self-forgiveness for which I have searched unsuccessfully for years. I suppose, Steven, that in the parlance of South African national forgiveness, this is my personal Truth and Reconciliation Hearing.

Sophiatown, 1954

Imagine that hundreds of children stand and wait silently at your doorstep; their school is closed, and it is forbidden for teachers to open any institution that looks or operates like a school. Many of the children have had no breakfast, because their parents left to catch the bus for work at 5:00am. What do you do with them? I didn't know the answer, and I had already been teaching in school for five years. But that's what we were faced with in the 1950s when I first met Michaela.

She was volunteering in the afternoons at the Mission School at Christ the King Church, and she wanted to help. And I will tell you, I came very quickly to love her, which did not simplify matters. But in those days, nothing was without problems.

It was government policy that beyond certain forms of basic labor, there was no place for the black man in the work force. It was the kind of stupidity that led to the end of apartheid, because it was an unsustainable fiction. But they were smart enough to recognize that unless they controlled the education of young black laborers, their vision would not last. So every school had to be licensed, and was compelled to teach the curriculum set by the Ministry.

Education was compulsory for white children; for black children it was not. In fact, it was discouraged, and most black children who were being educated were enrolled in Mission schools. A few unemployed teachers held private classes in abandoned garages or empty halls, but when it became mandatory for schools to be registered with the Ministry, many of these schools and classes chose to shut down rather than to teach a required curriculum. Now, in addition to two-thirds of the children who weren't attending school, we had to address the needs of children whose schools were closed.

Under those conditions, teaching was all but impossible. We set up cultural and social clubs where the children could gather, being careful to avoid anything that would give the appearance of schools. No blackboards, no desks, no books. When the Mission school closed in protest, several women from Johannesburg came to help me and the other teachers. Michaela was one of them.

She was in her second or third year at university, but she felt that her real work was here, with us, and she attended classes only because it was expected of her. It got her into trouble—but no one could ever tell Michaela what to do. Not then, not later, and not now. You will have the opportunity to see for yourself.

At the beginning the club we started in an abandoned garage had about twenty children—but soon there were fifty, and then a hundred and then two hundred children. We had no equipment and no money; we had too few teachers, and eventually, no place big enough to meet. Michaela collected money from those in the white community who were supportive of us, but it was a constant struggle. We bought pipe cleaners by the hundred dozen, and finger paints, and old newsprint that we tore into big sheets. We played games with the children, sang songs that helped teach them numbers and letters. We got donations of milk, fruit, and cheese so that they had something to eat for lunch. Sometimes we gathered outside, in the priory yard; other times in the recreation hall. Occasionally we used an abandoned barn that still smelled of horses, but it was at quite a distance, so we only went there when it was warm and sunny.

Michaela was wonderful with our children. She was filled with love for them, and so energetic, and she gave them everything she had. Perhaps she worked no harder than we did—but these were our children, not hers—we had a duty to them, but she took on the burden voluntarily.

I found that in the most private and hidden parts of my heart, there began to grow a deep love for her. Even today in the new South Africa such a love is a difficult thing, but back then, we would have been courting disaster. There was also no reason to assume that my love would be returned. I knew that if I did really love her, the greatest gift I could give her was to hide my feelings, and so I did.

But it was inevitable that over time we grew to be close friends. When the day ended, we would clean up together, waiting until the other teachers had left so that we had a few moments to talk. It was foolish, and dangerous. A black man and a white woman talking together in an empty hall was an invitation to trouble in those days. But on the surface at least, nothing was happening between us, so in Michaela's mind, we were doing nothing wrong. Even so, we were aware of the danger, and we were cautious.

At first our conversations were awkward, because our lives had so little in common. We would talk about the children, and what we had done or not done that day; what had gone well and what experiment we would not try again. She asked me questions about the children's lives, and I would try to answer with kindness—but because I felt so close to her, there were times when I could not hide the anger from my voice, or the bitterness from my words.

Most of the time she was so involved with the children that she forgot about the circumstances of their lives, and was able to be happy and encourage them. But one day a little girl came and sat on her lap, and told your mother that she wanted to grow up and be a doctor.

"I didn't know what to tell her," Michaela said to me. "What I thought was, she'll be one of the lucky ones if she has five years of schooling, and it'll be a miracle if she finishes high school. She must have seen something in my face, because the light went out of her eyes, and I felt as if I'd killed her dreams. Sometimes it feels so hopeless that I just want to run away and hide. Mandla," she said, "how can I teach these children about hope and possibility, when in my heart I feel that they have no future?"

"That's a good question," I told her. "As a black teacher, I ask it every day. And every black parent in this country faces it every time his child asks a question. He feels like a coward, too—but he knows that there is no point in running away."

I think my tone was angrier than I realized, because she drove away unhappily that day without saying goodbye, and I thought I would surely not see her again. But the next day she was back, and she thanked me for being honest, and I apologized for being angry and abrupt. But we understood each other, and it became easier to talk after that.

Sometimes we argued, because although she was enthusiastic, she was not attuned to the political consequences of what she did. At one point she showed me an editorial she had written about what we were doing at the cultural clubs—she planned to print it in the university newspaper in order to encourage support among those able to help pay the costs.

"Be careful, Michaela," I told her. "Most of the whites think it was foolish for our Mission school to close—they say it's better to get a terrible education than none at all. I'm not sure how much support you'll get—but you will certainly attract more attention from the police. Police patrols are already on the lookout for cultural clubs—you know they drop by every few days. But so far all they've done is wander in, look around, and leave. If you attract attention to us, they'll close us down."

But Michaela was very stubborn. She went ahead and published the editorial. After that she came in with a big grin on her face, and a fistful of money—she wanted to let me know that there were people out there who did care. But if I was wrong about attracting support, I was right about the police. They arrived a day later, three cars from the Special Branch, filled with men in uniform, with their rifles and their dogs, their German shepherds on short leashes, and they closed us down. We quietly herded the children out of the building. The rest of us were silent—we were used to this, and we knew, there was nothing to do. But once the children were outside, Michaela showed her fury, and her lack of caution.

"What kind of people are you?" she shouted at them. "Your dogs are terrifying the children. Does it take a dozen men with rifles to control a few unarmed teachers?"

The police were busy looking around, watching over their dogs, observing as we escorted the children through the entrance and into the courtyard. They ignored her. When all the children were accounted for, Michaela and I turned to go back into the hall, and a young policeman followed us inside. He carried his hat under his arm, and his blond hair, cut short, was sticking in all directions. I had heard his commander address him as de Jaeger. He was tall and muscular, he walked with a predatory swagger, and I didn't like the fact that he had followed us alone. As a matter of self-preservation, I had learned early to identify men who were most likely to be brutal and abusive, and all my instincts told me to run, but I couldn't leave Michaela alone. I urged her to keep walking, hoping that he would turn back, but he stayed with us all the way through the empty hall, almost to the exit door at the back wall.

Before we reached the door he called out to her, and we stopped and turned to him. He walked toward us, grinning at Michaela, ignoring me as if I were invisible. But I was used to that.

He looked at your mother the way you might examine a sheep, or a cheap woman you're thinking of buying for the night. You know, in my mind, the Afrikaans policemen were all badly informed, badly led men doing evil work, but they were not all inherently evil. Many were churchgoing men who really believed they were doing the work of God. But there were those who got a charge from their authority, and they were unable to resist taking advantage of their position. This man was one of those—he was dangerous in his potential abuse of power, and I was powerless.

"So," he said to your mother, "you're the pretty kike *kaffirboetie* I've been hearing so much about. What you need, Miss, is to have the fear of God put into you." Then he reached down and grabbed at his crotch, and he grinned at her. "You know what I call this? This is the Fear of God."

Your mother frowned, not understanding at first, and then her eyes and her mouth both opened very wide as she realized what he had said. She looked stunned—I don't think any man had ever spoken to her like that before. I would like to claim that I defended her honor, but I was paralyzed with terror, because if he felt comfortable saying these words in front of me, I was as good as dead.

As I watched him, the ugly smile faded and for a second he looked puzzled, and then anger blazed and his face swelled with rage. When I glanced at Michaela, I realized why and wanted to step over to her and cover her mouth, because she was smiling, and then, as she realized just how crude and infantile his words were, she burst into laughter.

It was the worst thing she could have done. De Jaeger turned very red, his face and his forehead and his scalp too, even in the dim light of the hall, and his mouth became thin and evil, and he drew his fist back to hit your mother.

I couldn't stand by like an invisible man and watch him strike her. I stepped between them as his fist came down very fast and hard, and the blow hit me in the side of my neck, where the collarbone joins. As I fell and lay on the ground, choking, I knew that his fist would have shattered her slender jaw. He was breathing hard as he stepped around me and drew back his leg to kick me. I tensed myself, waiting for the pain in my groin, because that's where his boot would have landed. I was about to close my eyes when there was movement behind him, from the corner of the room.

What appeared to be a tall, thin woman in a long black dress moved rapidly toward us with her arm outstretched, and when she reached us she leaned into the officer and pushed him away from me.

De Jaeger was still on one leg as he prepared to kick me, and he lost his balance and fell so that he was lying beside me. I looked up to see who the woman was, and saw that it was not a woman, but Father Huddleston in his black robe. That moment, as the Father looked down on de Jaeger and me lying on the ground together, I will remember always. And I will never forget what he said.

"Time to rename your organ, my son," the Father said calmly, in a very English accent. He had a deep voice, and it echoed through the hall. "And perhaps you should teach it some different music." He bent down and stretched out his arm and grabbed de Jaeger's hand and pulled him up and stood there with him, hand in hand. The Father was the taller of the two, and he looked down into the young man's face, red with anger and embarrassment and, I thought, perhaps fear.

"The fear of God is not yours to dispense, although you could do with some of it yourself. Your behavior is unbecoming, and your superior will not take kindly to a report of it. Now get out."

De Jaeger pulled his hand away and turned to leave, but not before he glanced down at me with such fury that my bladder opened. I felt the urine coursing down around my hips and pooling on the ground beneath me, and I remember thinking that my own humiliation was complete. We watched in silence as de Jaeger stamped out, and then the Father and Michaela bent down to me.

"Are you hurt?" he asked. "Can you rise?"

"I can rise—give me a moment," I said, and my voice was hoarse and quaking. "Thank you, Father. I think you saved my life. I didn't know that you could move so swiftly."

"We're just lucky that these people feel no need to hide their presence," he said. "I came running as soon as I heard them."

"Mandla," said Michaela, kneeling at my side. She was pale and shaking. "This is all my fault. I'm so sorry. I should have listened to you and not run that editorial. Now the whole school is closed. We've lost it. And look what he did to you."

I was very weary, and in pain, but I sat up. She was crying, and without thinking, I stretched out my hand and wiped the tears from her cheeks. It was the first time I touched her face. Father Huddleston took a sudden breath, and I quickly withdrew my hand and turned to look at him. In the half-light his eyes were wide, and his face was as pale as his white collar.

"Dear God," he said, closing his eyes, "how very ugly the world seems at times."

He was silent—I thought he was praying, but perhaps he was just searching for the right words to say to us. When he opened his eyes he looked back and forth from Michaela to me.

"Your care for each other is touching," he said in a hushed voice. "But you must know that in every time and place, there is at least one kind of love that cannot speak its name. I don't have to tell you that here, today, what you feel for each other is that kind of love. My children, whatever you do, be very careful."

He helped me up, and we went outside. The sun was still high in the sky, and the light was blinding. We could hear the police cars going down the street. As we saw your mother to her car, we both leaned into the window to say goodbye. I cleared my throat before I spoke.

"I think you should not come back for a few days, Michaela," I said. "I don't know what we will do with the children, but I fear for your safety—and mine—if they come back again and you are here."

"Mandla is right. Stay away for a few days. Attend some classes." He smiled. "Be a good student for a change." As he patted her shoulder through the open window, his smile disappeared. "Now go, Michaela," he said. "Go with God, and remember my words."

She nodded, and we watched her drive off. Father Huddleston walked with me to my mother's house, only a few blocks distant. I was in great pain—my collarbone was broken—and I was scared for the future. I knew that Michaela would stay away, and that while she was in Johannesburg, she would spend time with Lenny. I had no illusions about anything between us, but she had taken my hand; I had touched her face, and Father Huddleston had said that what we felt—for each other—was love. At that moment, it was enough.

After Michaela left, the police returned every day. Father Huddleston never mentioned the incident again, but he must have spoken to the district commander, because de Jaeger disappeared. We found out later that he had been reprimanded and transferred to another district.

Michaela planned to let a few weeks pass, and then to come back, but many things intervened to prevent her return. Her mother, your grandmother Selma, became ill, and before she died your parents were married. I saw their marriage notice in the newspaper, and your mother wrote me a letter. Then, in February of 1955, the relocation of Sophiatown actually started, and for those of us who lived there, everything else took a second place. I remember like yesterday watching as the lorries began to move 60,000 people across the *veld*, to Meadowlands. Today Meadowlands is one of the townships in Soweto, but back then, it was nothing but a barren stretch of ground.

The land had been cleared—and I remember row upon row of sterile little cement houses with corrugated roofs. There weren't enough houses, and those that had been built weren't ready for occupancy. But the architects of apartheid were ready to bulldoze Sophiatown, and the people had to be moved somewhere. Anyplace was good enough.

That day, my friends, the day the relocation began, for the first time in my adult life, I wept. Something inside me broke, and when it healed, it was a different substance, harder and stronger than before. The Sophiatown removal took away from me any faith in the future, and I found myself thinking often in the time after of the question Michaela had asked me—because I realized then that I could no longer be a teacher of children without hope. Before I could teach again, the future would have to be different. I didn't think then that we would ever be able to change it, but I was ready to risk everything in the attempt.

It was several years before I met Michaela again, and by then, we were both changed. I went through combat training in preparation for the violence that was to come, and I traveled out of the country, to Mozambique, and Botswana, and even to China. When I returned I was a different person, competent in the world. I had learned the use of explosives; learned how to collapse a bridge or destroy a police station. I became a marksman with a rifle, and with a revolver. More importantly for me, I learned hand to hand fighting; I knew how to silently immobilize a man. They taught me to kill. Never again—never—would I lie silent on a floor and tense myself for a kick in the groin. I might die in the process—but I would not die alone. The fury that ate away at my insides when I felt helpless was transformed into a cold rage. I had learned that if any war was just, this one was—and I became a soldier on the front line.

But while I was away, I learned also about myself—that although it was important for me to know the techniques of combat and self defense, I discovered that violence should be my way only if everything else failed. I was no longer teaching children—but I was at heart a teacher, and my weapon of choice was words. I knew that we were getting closer to our goal, and I gave silent thanks to the proponents of apartheid who were forcing us up against the wall. The harder they pushed, the sooner we would find in ourselves the strength to push back. And I knew that when we were ready, they would not be able to mount enough force to stop us.

During that time I had to support myself, and I had to appear legitimate to the authorities. I worked for a time as a gardener at a large public park, where I could meet with people easily, to give and receive messages. Later, I was a chauffeur—I drove a car for a Johannesburg law firm, where one of the partners was active in the freedom movement. And I worked in a garage that we used as a transfer station to move banned people around; to get those in danger out of the country. And it was there, at that time, that Michaela entered my life again, only this time, Steven, she was carrying you in her belly. She was physically changed, and surer of herself.

But despite the changes in both of us, nothing had changed between us. That was immediately clear.

The garage had two bays. On the day she arrived, there was a truck in one bay, concealing an injured man who had just escaped from the authorities; the other bay was empty, waiting for the transfer driver to arrive. I didn't know that it would be Michaela—I had been told only that the driver was experienced, and that the car had a concealed compartment in the back. But when she arrived and the mechanic drove her father's Volvo into the bay, I recognized it at once.

So I went out and looked through the window separating the garage floor from the waiting area, and there I saw her. Her pregnancy was obvious, her hair was shining and she glowed the way pregnant women sometimes do. I was so very happy to see her—but the police were still patrolling and I didn't want to attract attention, so I turned to walk back into the garage. That was when Michaela looked up and saw me.

If we had been standing side by side, nothing could have stopped me from putting my arms around her. And from the look of great surprise and joy on her face, I knew that, had I embraced her, I would have felt her arms around me in response. But that moment was illicit, and our emotions forbidden; to act on them would have been foolish.

I turned to the garage and went in, and with help from a fellow worker, transferred the man to the hidden compartment in the back of her car while she waited outside. When it was all ready and the boxes had been repackaged in the back, I went out to tell her. She was sitting in the waiting area with three other people, reading a magazine, and all four of them looked up as I opened the door. I knew that once she drove away, I might never see her again.

"Madame," I said to her, "your chariot is ready." In that place, and at that moment, it was the closest I could come to a declaration of love.

thirteen

MANDLA

Johannesburg, 1959

Michaela and I did eventually have a love affair—but it didn't start until you were three or four, Steven, when the resistance movement had gained maturity. We didn't plan it, but we found ourselves thrown together at the same meetings and protests; involved in hiding or transporting the same people; participating in the same background work to spread the word.

At one point the government increased the bus fare charged on black-only buses that carried people from the townships to where they worked in Johannesburg. We were organizing a peaceful strike against the fare hike, because those who used the buses had no alternative transportation, and the increase, although small, created a real hardship.

Late one night, a few weeks after my reunion with Michaela at the garage, she and I found ourselves working together with four others printing pamphlets to protest the fare increase. We were using a mimeograph machine in a shed on the grounds of a home in a suburb west of Johannesburg. One person cranked the handle, another made sure that paper was feeding cleanly; a third collected the mimeographed sheets, and the remaining two packed and carried boxes.

The shed we were working in was a makeshift office, lit by a single bulb hanging from a rafter, and the mimeograph machine was set up on an old green metal desk directly beneath the light. All around were cartons of paper and supplies for the mimeograph machine. Each time we filled a box with pamphlets, one of us took it out of the side door and stacked it there. When we had filled two or three boxes, we made the trek to the back of the property, where an empty lot was covered with waist-high grasses and scattered trees. Michaela had driven her car through the grass and parked it beneath the overhang of a huge mulberry tree. It was a moonless night; the car was virtually invisible.

Of the six people there, I was the only black man, and it was foolish for me to be in a white suburb, working so late at night. The plan was for me to spend the night in one of the servant's rooms, and in the morning it would have been easy to leave. But a neighbor reported our activity, and sometime after ten o'clock the police arrived.

Michaela and I were at the back of the property, loading a box into the concealed compartment in her father's s car, so I didn't witness their arrival. But we heard the squeal of tires as the police cars pulled up, and the sound of the shed door being forced open as half a dozen armed men stormed in. I heard a crash, which I knew must be the mimeograph machine being knocked to the floor.

Michaela was worried about the mimeograph machine—it had been expensive and difficult to obtain—but my first thought was for her safety.

If they found the concealed compartment in the car, both she and her father would be arrested; and the police would know how we had been getting our people out of the country, right under their noses. The idea would become unusable, and we would have lost a valuable tool.

Sooner or later someone would realize that there was a side door to the shed, and they would follow the path to the back of the property. The car had to be moved—and we had to get away. She didn't want to go without me, but I insisted, and she had just gotten into the driver's seat and closed the door when we heard the sound of booted feet running along the path.

We were too late. Michaela hadn't started the car, and I hadn't taken a step to hide myself when something hit me in the back with tremendous force, lifting me into the air. I fell to the ground on my face and remained where I had fallen, taking count of my body. I was shocked and in pain—but I remember thinking that this was the second time Michaela had watched me being beaten by a member of the South African security force. The first time I had been a boy—this time I was a man, and I had been trained in the art of killing. More importantly, perhaps, I knew deep in my bones that this was one battle in a long war, and that they would have no mercy on me. This time, I thought, I may die, but I will not lie still and be beaten.

The footsteps edged closer, and a boot nudged my kidney. It was a firm nudge, cautious and curious, but there was authority behind it.

"What are you doing here, boy?"

I turned and looked up to see a policeman standing over me. It was too dark to see his face, but he was a big man, with a very deep, angry voice. He was alone—but not for long. We had very little time.

"I asked you a question," he said. "What are you doing? Stealing the car?"

I slowly raised myself onto all fours until I was kneeling.

"Can I get up, *baas?*" I asked quietly. "I have my pass in my pocket."

He put his foot on my back and pushed down hard until I was on the ground again, and then lifted his foot away. He kicked me twice, hard, and I heard myself grunting. Out of the side of my eye I saw the foot move back a third time and as he prepared to kick me again I rolled away, grabbing it under my arm as I went, and twisted hard as I rolled it under me, jamming the heel into my side. Under the combined force of my weight pulling and twisting him in one direction, and his own weight forcing him in another, his leg came with me, and I felt the crack of breaking bone and the jarring snap of cartilage in his knee. He grunted in pain as he went down. This was the first time I had used what I knew to purposely hurt someone, and I remember being shocked at how easy it was, and by the animal sound in his throat.

As soon as I felt him land, I released his leg and rolled onto all fours and then up onto my feet, only to look down into the muzzle of his revolver. He had snapped it from his holster as he stood over me, and the safety was off. My eyes went instinctively to his. I saw that he was frightened and hurting, and I felt rather than saw the tightening of his forefinger on the trigger. I dived toward him and knocked the revolver away, but not before there was a flash in the darkness, an explosion of pain in my left thigh. But I had no chance to see what the damage was because he grabbed me around the waist with one arm and punched me in the face with the other.

I drove my elbow down into his throat with all the power I had, and felt the cartilage give. He coughed, choking, but still kept pummeling my face. By now I was above him; he had his arm about my neck, and he was squeezing so hard that I couldn't breathe. I knew that I wouldn't be thinking clearly for many more seconds. Somehow I managed to wrap my arm under his head, grabbed hold of his chin, and twisted as hard as I could. From within his neck there was the cracking sound of breaking twigs, the arm about my neck released, and he was suddenly still.

All I could hear was my breathing, and then there were shouts from the direction of the house, and footsteps. I rose, unsteady, and when I put my hand down to the burning pain at my thigh it came away warm and wet. Now we had no choice—I would have to leave with Michaela, putting her in great danger.

As I limped towards the car, a black policeman emerged, truncheon in hand, from between the trees. Not allowed to carry firearms, black policemen had become expert with the truncheon. He stopped short, taking in the scene before him. In a fraction of a second he realized that the figure lying on the ground was the officer.

I waited for him to tackle me, but he didn't. He looked up at me, then back to the trees, then back again, going through the choices open to him, and I knew we had a chance. He was aware of the work we had been doing, and who I was. I could see the conflict working in his face. He was putting himself at great risk, and I had to move before he changed his mind. I opened the back door, maneuvered myself into the seat, and signaled Michaela to start the car.

The black policeman looked back, listening for the sound of running feet. It was silent, and as he walked backwards into the shadow of the trees, he raised a hand and waved me away. I touched my forehead in thanks and he nodded. We drove away, and just as we lost sight of him, I saw him raise his arms and start walking slowly towards us, as if calling us to stop for an unseen audience.

The neighborhood was relatively new, with many empty lots and unpaved roads, and badly lit. We drove slowly, making as little sound as possible, and left the lights off until we were out of the area. But if we had managed to avoid a chase, we were still in danger—a white woman and a wounded black man driving alone in a nice car this late at night, we were a magnet for the police.

I had no idea how badly I had been shot. I was still bleeding, and although I could think clearly, I was aware of feeling light-headed and shaky. The pain seemed to have disappeared, which I knew was not a good sign.

"Where are you going, Michaela? We need to get you off the street."

"I'm taking you to my father," she said.

"No, I don't want to involve him."

"We don't have any choice," she said. "You've lost a lot of blood and you're still bleeding. I've got to get you to a doctor, and the only other choice is Soweto. I'll be even more obvious there. I can't take you to Baragwaneth Hospital—we'd both be arrested. And I'm not going to let you bleed to death."

I had been to meetings at your grandfather's house before Michaela and Lenny married, so I knew where they lived. But I knew she was right about his being willing to help me because when Michaela was teaching in Sophiatown, she arranged for him to come and do some dental work on those who needed care. He treated the children one morning a week for several months, and very often I was the one who would bring them to him. I came to know him well, and to respect him.

There were no highways back then, so we had to make our way around Johannesburg along deserted residential streets until we reached Dr. Davidson's neighborhood. It took about thirty-five minutes, and by the time we arrived I had passed out.

When I opened my eyes, I was lying on a plastic sheet spread out across the heavy oak table in the middle of Dr. Samuel Davidson's kitchen. Dr. Davidson was bent over my thigh, a lock of long grey hair hanging like a curtain over his forehead. Michaela stood at her father's side, looking down. She smiled anxiously at me.

"How do you feel?" she asked.

I raised my eyebrows and shook my head from side to side.

"Michaela, give him a glass of whiskey. It'll dull the pain." Dr. Davidson looked at me. "You're a lucky man, Mandla. Another inch to the right and you would've bled to death."

"Thank you," I said. "I didn't think when we came to secret meetings in this house last year that you'd ever have to stitch me up."

Following her father's instructions, Michaela put a hand beneath my neck and raised my head so that I could reach the whisky. I took a sip and gagged on it.

"I'm not much of a drinker," I said.

"Then hold your nose and swallow," said Dr. Davidson. "The bullet's lodged in your quadriceps, and we need to get it out." He held up a pair of forceps. "I don't have enough anesthetic on hand, so drink up. You're going to need it." He turned his head to the kitchen door. "Dennis," he called. "I need you in here."

Dennis had been Dr. Davidson's gardener for thirty years, and this was not the first time he had assisted in surgery. He came in from the garage, where he had been cleaning the car, a muscular man in overalls, his hair mostly white, and washed at the sink.

"I got all the blood off the seat," he said, drying his hands. "The car's good as new."

"Thank you," I said.

Dr. Davidson beckoned, and Dennis moved to stand behind me.

"Give me your hands, my friend," he says, looking down with a smile. "I'm the only anesthetic you get today."

He stood close to the end of the table, took my hands, and gently pulled at my arms until they were stretched out behind me.

"Put your arms around my waist and grasp your hands behind my back," he said. "When you feel pain, you squeeze. You can't squeeze too tight."

He leaned over, took the skin at my waist between his thumb and forefinger, and pinched hard.

"Hey, what are you doing?"

"He's giving you another source of pain to distract you," said Dr. Davidson. "You'll thank him later. Here goes."

Dennis pinched harder and I felt the forceps enter my thigh. I gasped, squeezing my arms so tightly about his hips that Dennis was forced up against the edge of the table. I couldn't help but writhe against the pain, and out of the corner of my eye I was aware that Michaela had turned away.

"Keep still, man," said Dr. Davidson, "you're just making it harder." He withdrew the forceps. "You almost made me lose it. Here it is." He looked carefully at the bullet to make sure he had the whole thing, and dropped it into a stainless steel dish as his side. "We're done. Dennis, where's the kit?"

Seamlessly he and Dennis worked together to stitch and dress the wound.

"My pants will be too short for you," said Dennis, "but here's a pair of the Doctor's trousers." He helped me pull the pants leg up over my band-aged thigh, and smiled at his employer. "He won't even know they're gone," he said, leading me to a chair.

"Dennis, get rid of this stuff," said your grandfather, ignoring the comment as he rolled up the plastic sheet. "You know where to dispose of it. Mandla, you can be sure the first place the police will search after they hit Michaela's house, is here. You need to get out of the city."

Michaela looked at me. "Where is it safe for you?" she asked.

"I should make a call," I said, looking around for the phone.

Michaela walked over to a telephone table in one corner of the kitchen and carried the phone to where I sat, bandaged leg stretched out before me.

"Wait until we're gone from the room," said Dennis. "The Doctor and I don't want to know where you're going."

I waited until they had left, removing all evidence that any surgery had taken place. Then I dialed the number I had been given for just such an eventuality, and the phone was answered by a man speaking Zulu. In a subdued voice that was short but alert, he asked who I was. I gave him the coded words that identified me, which I have long since forgotten.

"What do you need?" he asked.

I told him where I was, that I was wounded, and needed safety.

"We have no transport available now," he said. "If you can hide safely for a few days we can get to you. If not you'll have to find your own way to the Rhodesian border."

I beckoned to Michaela and told her what he had said.

"The Rhodesian border?" she whispered.

I nodded. "That's where they'll meet me. Can you get me there?" I asked. "If not, Dennis can hide me in the servants' quarters in any one of a dozen houses, and the police will never find me."

"The police will search the whole neighborhood," she said. "We need to get you out of here."

"Are you up to it? It'll take the rest of the night to get there."

"There's not much choice," she said. "If you can lie still in the compartment for that long, I can drive it. I've done it before. Let's go."

"Dennis," said your grandfather, "take them out and help them into the car. I don't want to know where they're going, and you shouldn't either. Mandla, I know you're doing good work. Good luck to you." He took Michaela in his arms, hugged her to his chest, and looked into her eyes. "Please, my love, be careful." Then he waved us out, and I saw him watching your mother, his eyes filled with tears.

Dennis led us out to the garage. We opened up the hidden compartment and Dennis removed the boxes of pamphlets so I could curl up and squeeze into the cramped space. They lowered the compartment doors above me, and in the darkness, I heard them spread the mat down so that the back of the car looked like any Volvo Duett station wagon. Michaela started the car, and I huddled in the dark as we headed for the Rhodesian border.

Many things might have been different had Michaela and I not gone to your grandfather's house that night. It took years before I understood the details of what happened, and I had to put together pieces of the story myself. I spoke to Dennis, and many years later, after things changed, I had a conversation with Officer Viljoen, who had been in charge of the investigation at your grandfather's house that night after we left. Our discussion revealed much that would have otherwise have remained hidden. It was one of the benefits of the Truth and Reconciliation Hearings that came about once Mandela was elected.

Three police cars arrived at the house an hour or two after midnight, and when they arrived, your grandfather came quickly to the front door to answer the loud knocking.

"Dr. Davidson," said Officer Viljoen. "I'm sorry for the inconvenience, but you can put the blame for this search on your daughter's thoughtlessness. If she would confine her activities to her home, and take care of her family instead of trying to solve everyone else's bloody problems, we wouldn't be here bothering you tonight."

Your grandfather stood up straight, an elderly man in striped pajamas, with his white hair uncombed, calm as a cucumber, and he looked up at the Lieutenant in his pressed khaki uniform and his official Special Branch hat.

"The only one being thoughtless, Lieutenant," he said, "is you. I don't sleep well since my wife died, and I'll not likely get back to sleep tonight. So you and your men can do your searching, and then I'll thank you to please leave me in peace."

So they began to look around the house, six or eight policemen searching for anything your mother might have left there and for anything that might incriminate your grandfather. They didn't think he was guilty, but it was a way of getting to her. They took whatever they found that contained names and addresses. In a closet they found old copies of newspapers, and several journals that had since been banned. They paged through liberal magazines for mention of communism or socialism, or any writings critical of the government or of apartheid; they searched for anything written in support of social justice, equality, or protest. They looked through diaries, paged through every book on every bookshelf, opened up photograph frames and searched behind the photographs for hidden documents. And through it all, your grandfather watched quietly. But when the officers asked for the key to his dental studio, your grandfather refused.

"That's where I draw the line," he said. "I earn my living in there, and no one goes in except me and my assistant. It's a sterile environment. My instruments are expensive and delicate, and I'll not have your men turning the place upside down."

He was angry, his face was red, and he was holding and rubbing his shoulder. The police insisted on searching his studio, and he was ordered to sit down in the kitchen and stop interfering with their investigation.

As he sat at the kitchen table there were sounds of a scuffle outside, the back door opened and two policemen dragged Dennis into the house. They had knocked him around, and his lip was bleeding. He stood at the back door with one man while the other went off to fetch the Lieutenant.

"I'm sorry, Dennis," your grandfather said. "'This is my fault."

"Don't worry," he answered. "Everything is OK. *Baas*," he said to the policeman, "I am feeling weak—can I sit?"

Without waiting for a response, your grandfather rose and carried a kitchen chair to Dennis.

"Sit down, Dennis," he said, and he did.

They questioned Dennis, wanting to know where he had been and why he was tip-toeing back into his room after midnight, and he smiled slyly and said he had been visiting his girlfriend. They found nothing in the dental studio, and very little in the rest of the house. But then

Viljoen came in and jerked the chair out from under Dennis, who fell to the ground. Viljoen was livid.

"You interrogate a *kaffir* sitting down while you stand?" he shouted at his men. "Are you fucking mad? And you—" he pointed down at Dennis "—you think you can sit while your betters stand? Get up!"

Dennis rose warily and stood before Viljoen, who proceeded to ask questions about how long he had been in your grandfather's employ, and what work he did.

"Do you ever go into the dental studio? Help the Doctor to fix up your friends at night after they run from the police?"

"No, never. Not in the studio. And *baas*, the Doctor never fixes up my friends."

"You lie through your bloody teeth, boy," said Viljoen, and boxed him in the face.

"Stop that!" your grandfather said, rising and stepping between them.

Viljoen elbowed him roughly out of the way just as one of his men came in from the garage.

"Lieutenant, you better take a look at this."

"I'm coming," said Viljoen, pointing to your grandfather and Dennis. "Bring them both with us. Whatever we're going to see they already know about."

Your grandfather stumbled out the back door, holding his chest; they pushed Dennis after him. The garage was empty, but along the side wall were the two boxes Dennis had removed from the back of the Volvo so that he could open the hidden compartment for me. An officer was standing beside one of the opened boxes, holding in his hand a mimeographed sheet of paper. Within the box thousands of sheets were visible. Viljoen took the paper from his officer and read an announcement of a demonstration against the increase in bus fare to be held two days hence. Your grandfather realized what happened, and he must have been suddenly fearful that the discovery of the pamphlets placed Michaela in jeopardy. It was too much for him.

"Oh, God," he whispered to Dennis. "What have we done?"

He was weaving back and forth, falling even as Dennis turned and caught him.

"What is it, Doctor?" he said, lowering your grandfather to the ground. But he was unwilling to let his employer's head rest on the cement floor and so he lay down with him, one arm spread out under his neck as a pillow. Your grandfather was grimacing in pain, holding on to his chest with one hand. With the other he gripped Dennis's forearm.

"If there's a next world, perhaps it will be better for us both, old friend," he said, one side of his mouth already dying as he tried to smile.

"Dr. Davidson, what is it?" Dennis cried. "What can I do?"

"All done now," your grandfather said hoarsely. "Nothing more."

He was a very fine man, Steven, and when his heart gave out you were not yet born. One of your mother's greatest regrets was that you never got to know him.

They buried your grandfather in the big Jewish cemetery outside Johannesburg. It was a strange ceremony, and very sad. Although there was nothing in the news of what had happened, people came from everywhere to honor him. They were Jew and non-Jew, speakers of English and Afrikaans, Indian and black and white. Mourners couldn't stand together—blacks stood in a section behind the whites—but everyone was united in their love for your grandfather. His patients were there—he treated everyone, and when people were unable to pay, he didn't charge them, or he charged them what they could afford, which left everyone feeling a sense of dignity. Dennis was there, too, weeping; he loved the Doctor like a brother.

Your father was there, of course, and many of your parents' friends—but Michaela had been arrested driving back from the Rhodesian border after dropping me off, and the authorities denied her permission to attend the funeral. It was a little bizarre, because many senior police officers had been your grandfather's patients. Your father said a number of high ranking officers apologized when they offered their condolences. They were not so much concerned about your mother, but felt that refusing to allow his only child to say the mourner's prayer at his graveside was a sign of dishonor and disrespect to Dr. Davidson.

They were right—and it was also a sign of arrogance and contempt. But in those days, there was more than enough of that to go around.

They did not keep Michaela for the full ninety days, and she never spoke to anyone about the experience. Even your father said that she refused to talk about it. I think they let her go after six weeks because she was pregnant and they were not yet sure how to use the Ninety Day Detention. That would come later.

I was in Rhodesia for several months, recovering and training, and when I returned, the ANC gave me false papers and a new name. No-one knew that I had been mimeographing pamphlets that night, or that I had been wounded, or involved in the death of the policeman. But by then I was well known by the police, and the ANC felt that a new identity provided one more level of protection against discovery.

I found work as a driver for a law firm, and was frequently called to drive one of the senior lawyers, Mr. Griswold, home in the late afternoon.

Mr. Griswold knew who I was, and he knew my history. We often talked in the car. He was highly respected, and when I drove him, he sat beside me in the front seat, which was very unusual.

One day after I had been working for him for about six months, I was waiting for him outside the building, and when he came out of the front door he was with a young woman. I got out of the car in my black chauffeur's uniform with a black cap, and came around to open the door for him.

"This is Mrs. Green," he said. "You'll be taking her home after you drop me off." I looked at the young woman, to see your mother smiling at me with such happiness in her face that I couldn't speak. I just nodded. I was shaking as I closed the back door and went around to the driver's side, and I had to take a moment to steady myself before I turned on the engine.

I don't know what Mr. Griswold knew about us—at that point there was little enough to know, other than that we had worked together in Sophiatown, and afterwards. Mr. Griswold had known Father Huddleston, and I knew that he and Dr. Davidson had been friends. But I said nothing, and neither did Michaela. From their conversation, I gathered that they had been meeting about settling your grandfather's will. She was an only child, and there were no other blood relatives except you—there was some talk of a trust, and Mr. Griswold was the trustee—but I knew nothing of such things, and I was not very interested. I did look at Michaela in the rear view mirror, and she looked back into my eyes and smiled at me. She was pale, but beautiful; her eyes were lively and bright, and no one would have guessed that within the previous year she had spent six weeks in prison, or that she was the mother of a four month old infant.

When I think today how tightly we were bound by fear back then, and by taboos, it is difficult to believe, and hard to explain. Michaela and I were so relieved to see each other safe, and there was so much we wanted to say to each other, so many questions, even putting aside the fact that we might have desired each other. But even alone in a car together we felt as if we were in a glass cage, visible to everyone.

After I dropped Mr. Griswold off at his house, there was nothing I could do, no way to physically express my affection for her. All she could comfortably do was lean forward and put her hand on the shoulder of my jacket, and when the car was going, I felt her thumb on the skin of my neck. It may seem today like very little—but when everything is forbidden, even a small taste is like a feast.

We talked briefly—but there was too much to say, and not enough time. It was a short distance to her house, she was already late, and it was enough for us to touch each other and to be together.

"I'm so relieved to see you," she said, and I began telling her how sorry I was about her father, and to explain how much I regretted that she had taken us in the car to his house, but she stopped me.

"Not here," she said. "I don't want to get home crying. But I want to know what happened. Where can we meet?"

Many people don't know it, and others wouldn't believe it, but at that time we had safe houses scattered throughout the country. Some of these safe houses have become infamous as a result of being in the press after a police raid, but many have never been identified. No one knew them all, but because of what I did, I knew of several—and over the next few years, your mother would come to know them, too.

One was a working farm with several buildings on the property—the farm was run by a young couple, but jointly owned by several men with connections to the underground.

On my next day off I would be staying at the farm, with a meeting planned for the early morning, and before she left the car that evening we arranged to meet there. The farm was just outside Johannesburg, about a half hour from Michaela's house, and we agreed that unless I called to warn her off, she would come there at midday.

I waited all morning, fearful that she would decide not to come—but she did come, and I watched through the window as her car appeared in the distance and drove down the unpaved road toward the farm buildings. She passed the main farmhouse and continued on the dusty path that ran through a field of *mielies*—corn.

I remember that it was summer, and the corn was high, and as she drove through I lost sight of her car. When she reappeared she pulled into the empty barn to conceal the car, as we had discussed, and walked out into the hot sunshine. She was dressed as if she had been playing tennis, in her whites, with tennis shoes, and she headed toward the shaded wood frame house where I waited for her. It was a small house, built years earlier for a farm foreman, and it was set in a clearing among old jacaranda and blue gum trees. More recently, smaller, faster growing wild trees and shrubs had sprung up, and she stopped as she approached the house to look up into the branches of wild pear and acacia trees. When she reached the door she knocked, opened it and came in, and closed it carefully behind her.

I came from the window where I had been watching her and took her hand in mine, but she put her arms around my neck and slowly, as if she would break, I took her in my arms, and I could feel the heat of her through her white blouse. We stood a long time, breathing together, and we were both shaking. It was too much for me—too much relief, too much desire, too much danger. I released her and stepped back, and offered her some tea. She nodded, and we went into the kitchen, and she sat at the old yellowwood table while I put the kettle on to boil. I had expected it to be awkward between us, but it was as natural as breathing.

"I am so sorry about your father," I said.

I poured the milk, added tea and sugar, placed the cups on the table and sat down across from her.

"I am responsible for bringing much pain to you, Michaela."

She sipped her tea, and I watched her purse her lips on the side of the cup. She drank carefully, not wanting to stain it with her lipstick.

"You were wounded," she said, "and your life was in danger. Where else could we have gone? And the police didn't come to my father's house searching for you—they had no idea you were even involved. They went to my father's house in order to intimidate me. Also," she said, "my father was ill. He had very high blood pressure, and he was in pain when he came into the garage. His heart attack was already happening; nothing could have stopped it. So I don't blame you for any of that. I'm just happy that he was there to prevent you from bleeding to death." She paused, turned her tea cup around, and looked down at the table. "You were his last patient," she said.

"Yes."

She drew the fingers of both hands like a comb through her hair, and I remember watching her body as she raised her arms. She was still breast-feeding you, and I could see that her breasts were full. She leaned back in her chair and looked into my eyes.

"I can't stay for long," she said. "I have to get back to feed Steven."

It was the first time I heard your name.

We said nothing for some time, and then she reached for the leather handbag on the seat beside her and fiddled with the silver clasp. I recall thinking that if I had a wife it would be impossible for me to buy her such a handbag, because what I earned in two weeks would not be enough to pay for it. But at that moment, it didn't matter.

I watched her take out a pack of cigarettes and shake two from the opening. Her hands were delicate, but her fingers were long and sun-tanned; the fingernails rounded and well-cared for, like all the other white women I had ever seen, but they were unpainted, which was unusual back then, and they looked natural, like a young girl's. She had a lighter in her bag—I saw it—but instead she found a pack of matches and removed a match, put both cigarettes in her mouth and lit them.

You cannot imagine, today, how intimate that act was, or how electric our touch was when she handed me the cigarette lit from her mouth. We looked at each other for a moment, and I took in all the details of her face—strands of soft hair loose at her temples, high cheekbones, the curves of her lips, which I could have stared at all day. I looked at the shadows beneath her eyes and the length of her dark lashes, and then I peered directly into her eyes, and she returned my stare frankly and with openness. The color rose in her cheeks and she looked away, pushed back her chair, and got up from the table.

I thought she was going to leave, but she just stood, leaning on the back of the chair. She slipped off her tennis shoes and walked slowly back and forth across the wooden floor as she spoke. Her legs were long and tanned.

"I tried to tell Lenny what prison was like," she said, "but it was so terrifying to him that he couldn't listen."

It was silent in the room and there was no noise from outside, and she spoke very quietly. "I've told no one else about it until now—and I'm sure there's not much I can tell you about being in jail that you don't already know." She paused, looking away from me out of the window, and all I could see was the silhouette of her face against the glass. "They took away my watch, and each hour seemed to last for weeks. They kept me in isolation. It was cold—they moved me around and some cells had a blanket, some not. I slept a lot—but eventually I couldn't sleep at all, and then the time passed even more slowly, especially the nights.

The food was inedible—cold tea, thin, lukewarm soup, congealed fat, stale bread—but I couldn't wait for it to arrive because it broke up my day and I knew I had to eat whatever I could for my baby. I even looked forward to the interrogation sessions because they were the only chance I had for human contact, even if it was unpleasant. They had the power to withhold everything from me—food and water and air; light and silence;

even the freedom to go to the toilet was taken out of my hands. And I understood in my guts what it means for a prisoner to identify with his captor—and what a terrible responsibility it is to have power over another person."

She paused, smoked again, still facing the window, her shoulders hunched, arms folded in front of her as if to protect her heart.

"They treated me like a naughty little girl at first—if I gave up the error of my ways, they would find it in their hearts to be lenient, and forgive me. They promised me paper and pen, and books to read. But I didn't have much of the information they wanted, and when I refused to give them what I did know—names, dates, and places—they became angry and abusive. That's what Lenny couldn't bear to hear about.

"They called me all the things you might expect—whore, kike, *kaffirboetie*; told me that I was bringing shame to my father's memory, and to the memory of my people. I wondered over and over who they thought my people were—Jews, English-speaking whites, or all the white-skinned people in the country—but it didn't matter what they thought because if I knew one thing, it was that nothing I did would bring shame to my father's memory. When that tactic didn't work, they accused me of being a negligent wife and a bad mother. They said it would have been better if my grandparents had all been killed in concentration camps during the war. I told myself, while they shouted in my face and leered at my breasts and my legs, no, I'm not a bad mother or a bad wife. I haven't betrayed my father—he would be proud of me. And I haven't betrayed my people—the struggle for freedom and fairness is the essence of Jewish teaching."

She came around to my side of the table, and she took my hand.

"Then they asked me if I supported the anti-apartheid movement because I was one of those deviant white women who wanted to sleep with black men."

She tugged gently, and I rose to stand close to her.

"I didn't tell them," she whispered, "but there's only one black man I'm interested in." And she led me into the bedroom.

I will spare you the details of my love affair with the young woman who was your mother, except to say that Michaela was a woman of extraordinary conviction and passion, and she was beautiful besides. In fact, the passion she felt for whatever she was doing was an inseparable part of her beauty, and it showed itself in her face with each change of expression. After being in prison, your mother was no longer only the daughter of a privileged family, wanting to do good in the world—she had become a freedom fighter. And in the time we had together, I learned a great deal about her.

She continued to love your father, even when her involvement with the movement became tiresome to him, and her devotion to the little boy she carried around with her wherever she could was complete and absolute. She was always the best mother to you that she could be, without giving up our political struggle—for that she had to make tough choices every day, and it was a bitter conflict in her life.

By the time Michaela and I became intimately involved, we had friends in jail, or being tried. Some were under house arrest; others had been hurt or killed, and there were those who had been forced to leave the country. The mood was such that we didn't know when we might be picked up and imprisoned—or even whether we would survive into the next week. As a result we operated under siege mentality—we went from day to day with the mindset that exists in the midst of battle, where conventional rules that govern human conduct seem petty and unimportant.

Eventually we were captured together after blowing up an electrical plant and both sent to prison. But perhaps you know about all that already from your father.

In the story of what happened to us, there are many truths. One is that Michaela betrayed her husband and I betrayed my friend, and for that, we paid a heavy price, both then and afterwards. I ask forgiveness of those, like you and your father, who suffered as a consequence. But I have no regrets, because there is another truth: against all odds, at an impossible time, we found and loved and had great joy of one another. For that, I can never apologize.

fourteen

STEVEN

Boston, 2001

Before I married Dariya, I had affairs with women who were single, and I had affairs with married women, too, a few of them the mothers of young children. As an artist I've painted nude women for over thirty years, and have seduced—and been seduced by—some of them. If asked, Dariya would confirm that I am no prude. I thought I was well enough entrenched in my time, and my sense of propriety broad enough, that nothing could shock me. I was wrong.

What's the appropriate response to Mandla's revelation that the mother who abandoned me as a child seduced him while I was still suckling at her breast? Did the milk intended for me drip from her full breasts as they lay together in the little cottage bedroom? Whatever they did could hardly have been leisurely, since she had to hurry back and feed me. When she came back to me, I wondered, did she smell of him? As I took her swollen nipple in my infant mouth, did I sense anything different about her? And did it make a difference that the man she had been with wasn't my father?

These questions came to me unbidden, and as they rolled over me the images they conjured were tortuous. As I watched myself writhe with them, I recognized in myself the symptoms of the spurned lover, and knew I was being ridiculous. Here I was in my fifth decade, having spent my youth and adolescence pining for my dead mother, wondering whether I knew as I sucked at her breast that she had just been intimate with another man.

Dariya was unsympathetic; worse, she was amused. She let me mope around for two days, but her patience ran out as we sat in the kitchen after breakfast on the second day, drinking coffee and reading the *Boston Globe*.

"Come on, Steven," she said. She looked at me tenderly, but the smile on her mouth told me that she thought I was being infantile. "It happened almost half a century ago. Michaela was a young woman who fell in love with another man. Mandla said they were living with a siege mentality—it happens in dangerous times. Yes, the woman we're talking about was your mother, and you happened to be an infant, and yes, you were suckling. But it wasn't all about you then, and it's not all about you now. Time to move on."

For a moment I glared at her. She may have been right, but a little compassion would have been nice. She rose from her chair, sat on my lap.

"For the record," she said, "I think it's cute that you're jealous of your mother's young lover, who by now must be close to eighty." She kissed me, and I put my arms around her.

"Much better," I said. "I think you've cured me."

"That was the idea." She rose. "So what's next? Didn't Mandla ask you to call him when you were through reading what he sent you?"

"He did."

She looked at her wristwatch and handed me the phone. "It's mid-afternoon there."

My conversation with Mandla was not long. I told him that I had finished reading. I offered no reaction to his writing, and he had the grace to ask no questions.

"I look at your website occasionally, Steven," he said. "Michaela does, too, with great pride, I might add. As a painter of seascapes, you'll appreciate it if I tell you that we're trying to paint a picture of the past from many angles. You've seen it from Lenny's viewpoint, and from mine. But you've not yet heard from the most important player."

"In my father's last conversation with Michaela," I said, "she threatened that she would send me her own accounting. He said he decided to write his story so that I'd have his version, too. I guess I have her to thank for that." I paused. "Somehow I don't think my father expected that there would be three versions of the story."

"There is only one story, seen through three sets of eyes. I don't think one telling contradicts another—but I hope that each adds its own richness to your understanding."

"So what happens next," I asked, "in this carefully choreographed revelation?"

He laughed, a chuckle deep in his chest. "I like your sense of humor, Steven," he said. "I'm sitting at my desk looking at what Michaela's written, which I picked up from her last week. I'm taking the liberty of interspersing a few of my own notes—chapters, I suppose—explaining events that she's not aware of or found too difficult to write about. I think you'll understand what I mean. I'll be done in a day or so, and will send the package air express. With the exception of what I've added, the package is exactly as she gave it to me. You should have it next week. Once you've read it, Steven, I will have done all I can. The next steps will be up to you."

Mandla was right—I needed my mother's story to round out whatever picture of the past was being painted. Impatient, almost resentful, I waited for the package to arrive. Dariya reminded me that I had waited all my life to hear my mother's story, and that a few days more or less wouldn't make a difference.

"Perhaps you were right that my father was manipulative in his writing," I said to her. "But I feel manipulated from all directions—as if the three of them were in collusion, arranging to tell their story so that events are sequenced to make them look good."

"There's no collusion between your father and your mother," said Dariya. "Your father wanted to confess, and at the same time present himself in the best possible light to you. I imagine that your mother will want something similar for herself. Mandla may be helping her to make her case, and perhaps that's manipulation—but he's doing it openly."

Greg noticed that I had been impatient and preoccupied, and raised the issue in his own way at supper one night, as he laboriously cut his spaghetti into pieces so that he could eat it tidily.

"How come you're so sad, Dad?" he asked.

"What makes you think I'm sad, Greg?"

"You're not smiling these days," he said. "And you don't seem very interested in me."

"I'm not sad," I said. "And of course I'm interested in you. I'm always interested in everything you do. But right now, I have a lot on my mind."

"You don't seem sad to me," said Sally. I watched her as she carefully twirled spaghetti around the fork in one hand, while the tines were supported by a spoon held in the other. "You just seem impatient, as if you're waiting for something to happen." She looked up at me and stopped twirling. "Are you?" Then she maneuvered the fork into her mouth, chewing and watching me as she waited for a response.

I cleared my throat. "As a matter of fact," I said, looking at Dariya for direction, "I am waiting for something."

"What?"

"Remember the book Grandpa Lenny wrote," I asked, "the one he left me to read?"

They both nodded.

"Well, the grandmother you've never met, Grandma Michaela, is sending me the book she's written, so that I can learn all about what's happened to her before we meet again."

"I don't understand all this writing stuff," said Sally. "Why didn't they just tell you the stuff instead of writing it all down?"

"Is our grandma writing it all down now because she knows she's going to die," asked Greg, "just like Grandpa Lenny did?"

"No, I don't think that's why she's writing," said Dariya. "But sometimes people find things difficult to say, and perhaps it's easier to write them down."

"When you're writing something to someone, you're not really looking at them, are you, Mom?" asked Greg.

"That's right, honey," said Dariya. "Why?"

"Well, it's hard to say some things to a person when you're looking in their eyes," he replied. "You know, like when I do something bad and have to say I'm sorry? It's easier to say sorry if you're not looking in the person's eyes."

In response, I got up from the table and walked around to my son, knelt at his side and wrapped my arms about him.

"Let's not talk about Grandma Michaela any more tonight," I said into his ear. "I'm not sad, and I want to know something. What have you been doing that you think I'm not interested in?"

"Lemme go," he said laughing as he squirmed in my arms.

"Never," I said, and I kissed his warm, salty neck, breathing him in. Letting him go was the last thing in the world I ever intended to do. And I promised myself that there would never be a need in our lives for written apologies to my children.

Again, Mandla was as good as his word, and the package arrived ten days later. Had I been expecting the same carefully bound, leather-covered manuscript from my mother that I received from him, I would have been disappointed. But what I found when I opened the package was a far more likely presentation from the woman my mother turned out to be. What I withdrew from the package was covered in thick plastic, and within it was a thick sheaf of paper, sandwiched between two sturdy pieces of cardboard cut from a packing carton. Three huge, red rubber bands surrounded the cardboard. When I removed them and laid the cardboard aside, I found the manuscript.

Each chapter was held by an oversized brass paperclip at the top left, the whole thing clipped together by a galvanized binder clasp with the handles folded down. As I flipped through the pages, I could see that she had written and edited it on a computer, and I imagined her—someone—printing each chapter as she completed it. When I noticed that there were two different fonts, I slowed down enough to realize that Mandla had interspersed his sections among hers, and the font he used was the same one he had used on his own manuscript.

Again, I put it away unread. The package was delivered on a Thursday, but Dariya and I didn't get a chance to look at it together until early Saturday morning. We opened it again as the children slept, and we drank coffee in bed.

fifteen

MICHAELA

KwaZulu Natal, 2001

My Dear Steven,

I write this to you, my son, now in your forties, with children of your own. You've been in my thoughts each day since I last saw you when you were seven, but you'd be within your rights if you refused to think of me as your mother. I understand that your father wrote a memoir of sorts, which I'm sure has left you with an unflattering opinion of me. Mandla Mkhize—he has by now probably invited you to call him Khabazela, and that is how I will refer to him—Khabazela and I have a lifelong connection, and our lives are interwoven with a complexity that's difficult to explain. I don't know precisely what, but he's apparently added parts of his own story to the mix in an effort to rehabilitate me in your eyes.

You know very little of me, despite the writings of these two men, who lived with me in very different times, and under dissimilar circumstances. Knowing your father as I did, I doubt whether he ever told you much about my background or my family; I know from my last conversation with him that up until a few months ago, you were still convinced that I died before you were seven. That came as something of a shock to me. He and I had agreed that when you were old enough, and when he thought the time right, he would tell you the truth so that you could decide for yourself whether to make contact with me. For whatever reason, the time was never right, and I've lived for over ten years—since Nelson Mandela came to power and I was safe from prosecution—with the fiction that he had told you the truth about me, but that you'd made a conscious decision not to know me. I don't know much about you, but I can be sure of at least one thing: you have no idea why I made the decisions I did, and you have no concept of the circumstances in which those decisions were made.

This is not my life story, and it's not a fairy tale written in the hope of love and forgiveness. I can't ask for either—it's not my way, and I don't want your forgiveness for the life I've chosen. What I do want is your understanding, if it can be had.

I didn't know it then, but with the distance of age, I can see that I started out as a driven, uncompromising young woman who wanted to make a difference in the world; fought hard against my father, whose idealism I inherited, but not his fearfulness and timidity, nor his reluctance to stand up to authority. I was loved by a young man molded in my father's image, a good man who was not as exciting or as radical in his politics as I felt the time required. And with no thought of the consequences to him or to me or to you, our young son, perhaps just to show him how weak he was, I found another man who was far more radical than I was. I thought, then, that I was willing to put everything at risk for a moral cause and a political movement more important than any of us individually, and the bonus was that he and I loved each other. But perhaps I had it backwards. It may have been that we loved each other—and the bonus was that we had a cause important enough that it allowed us to justify putting everything at risk. Whichever truth it was, my story will tell that we risked everything. And though we made huge strides for the cause, much of what we risked personally, we lost.

Johannesburg, 1962

The night we were arrested was my first venture into violence against what we called—it sounds so contrived today—the infrastructure of apartheid.

Khabazela and I planted a bomb and destroyed an electric-generation plant, plunging the southwestern neighborhoods of Johannesburg into darkness. By the time the bomb went off we were a half mile away, riding bicycles through the deserted pre-dawn roads towards the small foreman's house on a farm outside the city, a safe house used by the ANC.

Whether an informer gave us up or whether members of the Special Branch of the South African police had been following our movements, we still don't know. For a moment when they broke into the house, it crossed my mind that Lenny might have betrayed us—but your father was not capable, then or now, of such an act.

I remember still, with numbness and shock, the expressions of disgust and outrage on the faces of young, uniformed men when they broke into the bedroom to find us naked on the bed. It happened in an instant—they ripped him from my body, pinned him to the floor, stamped their boots on his naked feet and kicked his exposed genitals. Others grabbed at the sheet I had drawn up to cover myself, forcing it from my clenched fists so that they could look with lustful ownership at the body they thought I had defiled. And I did not know which was worse—that they treated him as a mongrel or me as their own personal thoroughbred.

They arrested us and took us to the main jail in Johannesburg, where we were separated—I was taken to the white women's prison; he was dragged off to the infinitely worse prison reserved for black men.

They gave us a rapid trial, presented all the evidence against us. There was the testimony of early morning walkers who claimed to have seen us at the electric-generation plant, Khabazela scaling the fence, and me throwing a bag over the fence to him. There was no bag thrown, and none found, but it was considered a minor discrepancy. They had been watching us; knew that we spent time at the safe house, knew that he had been sent out of the country for military training; knew that he had a saboteur's knowledge; had found beneath his bed in his sister's house in Soweto mimeographed pamphlets with detailed instructions on building and detonating time-delayed explosives. That was the evidence against us for treasonous activity and sabotage.

Then there was the charge of miscegenation, about which they went on at much greater length. They presented evidence of a long-standing, intimate relationship between us that went back to my years at university, when I volunteered at the school attached to the Anglican Mission in Sophiatown where he taught, and where I first met him. But for purposes of the prosecution, it was irrelevant that years passed before anything happened between us. At the trial, Lenny was portrayed as a respectable man, a good husband and father; I was the whorish white wife, the despicable mother, who had given in to a lustful and godless impulse—they made it sound subhuman—for which I was willing to throw away my life and to leave my son motherless, and my husband alone.

Then there was the damning testimony of the police who had broken into our not so safe house. They claimed to have found us, having just committed an act of terrorism, in the midst of copulation so frenzied that we were unaware of their presence. They had entered the house silently and with frightening speed, and it is true that we didn't know they were there until they were standing in the bedroom with us. But through the lens they shone on us and on our lives, it all seemed venal and ugly, twisted and brutal. And it was sufficient to convict us for a long, long time.

Lenny came to see me in prison. He had been more than a passive observer to my political activities; had been involved in them himself, and at some level we both knew that we took the risk of being discovered and jailed. But this was more than civil disobedience. This involved violent protest, and as far as Lenny was concerned, violence was beyond acceptable, especially since we had you, Steven, to think about. What he felt about me was, of course, equally clear. Poor Lenny. I felt sorry for him when he came to see me in prison—he was lost, mortified and furious.

"You've ruined more lives than just your own," he said. "I'm only glad your father isn't here to see what you've done. All this time I thought you were deeply committed to the cause, but it was more than that, wasn't it? It was pure selfishness. What a fool I must seem." He leaned closer to the bars that separated us and continued in an angry whisper. "They're going to put you away for years," he said. "You've deprived Steven of a mother. You've left me alone to take care of him. You've humiliated me. My credibility is shot. What the hell am I supposed to do? Where am I supposed to take him?"

I had no answer then, and I have not found one since. But even if I had an answer, it would not change the emptiness of those early years, or massage away the sensation of a lump in my chest whenever I thought of you, Steven. Nor will it bring back to me the missed years of your childhood.

The baby I birthed and suckled grew into a lanky little boy with fine, light brown hair and solemn eyes. I see you respond to something funny, throw back your head, mouth open to reveal white, even little teeth, and the peal of your delight washes over me like liquid joy. In my memory I reach for you, and I have carried with me through the decades the feel of your soft hair brushing my cheek, the warmth of your neck, the feel of your small fingers on my face. From kissing your eyes when you cried, I still taste the salt of tears, and sometimes—walking through the street, opening the refrigerator, greeting a friend, embracing a neighborhood child—I am brought up short, unable to breathe, by the recall of how you smelled, of fresh bread and summer days, of hay and the sea and warm strawberries; of dry leaves, apple and melon.

All gone to ash. Smoke, vapor, wind, air. Nothing. The little boy I remember trapped in an instant of time that never was, grown now to a man I do not know and would not recognize.

We were convicted in short order, me for ten years, Khabazela, as the black mastermind, for life. I learned later that Lenny brought you to see me the day after we were convicted, to say goodbye before I went off to serve my sentence. But when he arrived with you in tow—you were six at the time—they were told that I had already been taken from the holding cell to the distant prison where I was to serve my time. For years I imagined Lenny's confusion and terror at hearing this news.

It was not until two days later, when they summoned him to the police station to interrogate him about my whereabouts, that he discovered we had escaped, and that there was a country-wide manhunt for us. It was the first and only simultaneous, coordinated break from the white women's and the black men's prisons, and it humiliated the police. They were furious, determined to pursue and find us. It could, they said, only have been engineered from inside, and in fact, it was.

If the trial and the judgment against us were unusually rapid, there was a good reason for it. Several weeks earlier, Nelson Mandela had been arrested, and he and his co-defendants were on trial when we were arrested. There was so much publicity around his trial that our prosecution received very little attention, and the security forces were so embarrassed by our escape that they did everything in their power to keep it out of the press. Khabazela didn't tell me until years later, when it no longer mattered, that he and Mandela were in the same prison. The ANC had spent too much time and money on both men to allow them to spend the rest of their lives in jail. When they sent a message to Mandela asking whether an escape should be planned, he thought about all the ways in which an escape might be beneficial to the organization, and he arranged to have a conversation.

In his soft-spoken, determined way, Mandela had already convinced his jailers that he and his co-defendants be allowed an hour a day walking in the yard. Now he arranged to have the same privilege extended to other prisoners, and he made sure that he was beside Khabazela during their daily walk. Their conversation took place over two days. He started by speaking in very general terms, explaining how he intended to make his case.

"I can do most good for our cause by standing on principle, speaking the words that our people and the world need to hear," he said, whispering out of the corner of his mouth. "We will eventually bring this regime to its knees by withholding the massive power of our labor from their fields and their factories. The industrialists and politicians are petrified;

they already recognize the economic disaster that will follow if we're able to organize. Until now, they've been able to prevent us from showing a united front, but they'll eventually fail. And when we do show a united front, Khabazela, the world needs to see that we're a legitimate political force, willing and able to confront the regime."

"I agree," he replied. Mandela had addressed him by his clan name, and he replied in kind. "But Madiba, what do you want me to do?"

"A prison break is being planned. Our organization wants me to escape, but the leadership does not recognize that if I run away, I lose all credibility as an honorable participant in this dialogue. In fact, it will be the end of dialogue—the regime will have succeeded in their quest to have the world see us as terrorists and criminals. You, my friend, are a different case. We still need men and women in the world, helping in other ways. Tell me," he asked, seeming to change the subject, "if you were to find yourself out of prison, would you continue our work with the same energy you have brought to your efforts thus far?"

"Madiba, how can you even pose such a question to me? I'll do what you ask—whether that means remaining in prison with you, or escaping and working on the outside. But there is the matter of Michaela Green. She's an innocent bystander in this matter of sabotage, and she will not do well in prison. I would hate to see her spirit broken." He hesitated. "Besides, if she's free to travel around, she can be a real asset to our cause. She's already made a significant contribution and saved many valuable lives."

Mandela smiled at him as they walked. "There are no innocent bystanders in war, Khabazela. Didn't she consent to the acts of sex in which you and she engaged?"

"She did," he whispered, looking down at his feet. "But they were not merely acts of sex—they were also expressions of love."

"I don't need to tell you that there can be no acts of love between a black man and a white woman under this regime. Didn't Father

Huddleston tell you that years ago, when he said in any age there is more than one kind of love that cannot speak its name?"

Khabazela started at the reference to Father Huddleston, looking up in surprise. Nelson was taller by at least a foot, and he looked down with a grin.

"You know that the Father and I are friends," he said. "Yes, Khabazela, I know what happened in that empty hall, and I've watched you and Michaela Green since Father Huddleston saved you from a beating all those years ago. And I agree with you—she's a courageous young woman, and likely to be a great asset to us. But she's also hotheaded and foolhardy, and without guidance she'll end up in trouble. You may love each other—and for that, I offer you both my condolences. That love will make the work you have to do easier, but it will also make your lives more difficult. Perhaps unbearable. You may wish in years to come that you had remained in prison—but I want you to take this opportunity. We will arrange for a simultaneous break from the women's prison. If all goes well, you and she will travel separately to your uncle in Zululand. Once there, you will be contacted and further arrangements made. Go with God until we meet again."

Their conversation ended abruptly as the guards gathered to escort the prisoners back to their cells. Nelson was taken in one direction; Khabazela, in another.

Several months after our escape, Nelson Mandela was sentenced to five years in prison. You know that he had been instrumental in forming Spear of the Nation, the ANC's military wing, and within the year, he was brought back to stand trial with other leaders of the organization for plotting a violent overthrow of the government. That's when he was sentenced to life in prison.

The world knows that while he was serving his life sentence, Mandela could have obtained his freedom by changing his political position, but he refused to compromise. What they don't know is that even before he was sentenced, he was determined to take the high road, and that he refused the opportunity to escape. What's also not known is that he was instrumental in organizing an unpublicized prison break that resulted in the escape of one black man and one hotheaded, foolhardy white woman.   They did not see each other again until three decades had passed.

I was completely surprised by the plan; had no idea who was behind it, or whether Khabazela was involved. All I knew was that a few hours after lockdown one of the guards handed me a roll of clothing and told me to change, and left the door to my cell unlocked. Shortly afterwards there was a complete power outage in the jail. All hell broke loose, and a woman in a guard's uniform escorted me silently through the darkness and out a side door to a waiting car. We turned down an alleyway and dropped the woman off at the maintenance entrance to an office building on Eloff Street. I thanked her, but she shook her head.

"No," she said. "It is I who must thank you, because what you do, you do for all of us."

Then she was gone. I lay down on the rear floor and covered myself with a blanket. The driver, whose face I never saw and to whom I uttered not one word, drove in tense silence through the pre-dawn streets of Johannesburg, and I fell asleep eventually, exhausted and drained, despite the hard floor and the discomfort of the drive train that ran down the center of the car.

When the blanket was roughly pulled off me I thought I was discovered, but I sat up to see that we were in a darkened garage, parked beside a grayish delivery truck with the words "L. Feldman, Ltd., Importers" printed on the side.

"Quick, lady." The driver spoke quietly without turning around, but I looked up to see his dark, tense eyes in the rear view mirror. "Out the car and into the back of the truck. Lock the truck door from the inside and climb under the blankets. Someone will come this afternoon to give you food."

Before I had closed the door behind me the car pulled out of the parking space, and for a moment, as I made the four foot dash to the rear door of the truck, I was completely exposed. What, I thought, if the truck door is locked? I was an escaped prisoner—the police would arrive, see me, and shoot to kill. But the door had been left ajar, and I closed and locked it behind me. The truck was empty but for a pile of padded wrapping blankets on the floor, the kind used to protect furniture, and I lay down among them, covered myself, and waited.

I didn't know it then, but I was in an indoor garage on the ground floor of an apartment building in upscale Killarney, a community just outside the city, and it was a perfect place to wait for nightfall. In the hours I spent there only a half-dozen cars came and went. At mid-afternoon the driver's door was unlocked from the outside and a woman in a blue uniform with a white apron and cap—a servant in one of the apartments upstairs—put her fingers to her lips, and beckoned for me to follow her.

We saw no one, and she took me up in the service elevator to the roof of the building where the servants' quarters were, and where few of their white employers ever ventured. I used the bathroom and washed my face, and she returned me to the truck, leaving me with a thermos of tea, a chicken sandwich, and a smile. I ate and drank and fell into an exhausted sleep. The uncertainty was more than I could bear, and sleep was the only way to make the time pass.

When I woke, the truck was moving. It was dark, but there was a sliding door between the driver's compartment and the cargo area, and it was half open. I peered through the gap to see that we were driving at high speed along the highway, and that there was only darkness on either side of us. The driver was a young white man with long, pale face and a thin beard, in a gray delivery uniform and a khaki driver's cap.

"So," he said. "She wakes, finally." He turned to gaze at me, and beckoned to the passenger seat. "Come sit up front. We're well out of Jo'burg, but we've got a long drive ahead of us."

"I don't know who you are or why you're doing this," I said as I maneuvered myself forward, "but thank you."

"You're welcome. But better you don't know who I am." He shrugged his thin shoulders. "We're on the Durban road headed southeast. I'm to take you as far as Mooi River. You know where that is?"

I'd seen signs for Mooi River when we drove overnight to Durban on school holidays, but I'd never been there. All I knew was that it was an isolated farming village off the main road.

"I know where it is," I answered. "Where do we go from there?"

"That's where we part company," he said. "I go on to Durban to pick up a truckload of sweets and biscuits at the dock. It was conveniently left off the big truck that picked up our delivery yesterday, so if we're stopped I can explain where I'm going."

"And me? Where do I go?"

He shrugged. "I don't know," he said. "And for now it's probably better that way."

His instructions—from whom, he couldn't or wouldn't say—were that when we arrived after a five hour drive through farmland and open *veld*, he would be handing me off to someone else. It was less information than I needed, but it was all he would give me.

It was still dark when we reached the turnoff to Mooi River and left the main road. After several miles on a pitch-black deserted mud lane, he pulled the truck off the road and cut the lights and engine. For what seemed like an eternity we waited in silence, listening to the rhythmic clicking of cooling metal, and to the sound of the cicadas through the open window. Then, from behind us, came the sound of an engine, approaching slowly.

"Here they are," he said, relief in his voice.

"Who's 'they'?" I asked.

"Don't know," he said. "But you're about to find out."

The vehicle crept by, a face peered curiously into the driver's window, and then an ancient truck pulled up and parked in front of us.

"This is it, Mrs. Green," he said.

"You know who I am," I said, feeling stupid. How could I have imagined for a moment that I was unknown to him?

"The whole country knows who you are," he said grimly. "And they'll know a hell of a lot more about Michaela Green when tomorrow's paper is delivered." He reached across me and opened the door. "You're in for a difficult time, Miss. I wish you the best of luck."

"Thank you," I said, stepping down into the dark unknown of a new life. It was only a few steps, and I could have refused to take them. In fact, at any point I could have turned off the path I was on. I could have made my way to Swaziland and flown out of the country; I could eventually have gone to the United States, which is where Lenny finally decided to go and start a new life, unable to handle the pressure of being the husband of the disappeared Michaela Green.

But I don't remember at any point even considering a path other than the one directly in front of me. Perhaps what my father called my incredible bull-headedness was really not that at all, but was instead a lack of imagination. I could never see a way to do other than tackle what was directly ahead of me. There was no going around obstacles; I had to force my way straight through them. This has been a life-long pattern. Perhaps it was a genetic predisposition; maybe it was simply called into being by the brutality of the system I was born into. In retrospect I could have lived my life no other way, but it has exacted a heavy price.

When this journey began I was the white, privileged daughter of educated, upwardly mobile Jewish immigrants, living in the suburbs of Johannesburg, completely insulated from the realities of South Africa's gross inequities. For the white middle-class, these horrors—the arbitrariness of life and law, the uncertainty and constant fear, lack of safety and hope, the poverty and violence and disease—did not exist, but they soon became commonplace to me, and I learned to go among them as easily as walking from sunlight to shadow and back again.

I climbed up into the passenger seat of the ancient truck and closed the door. The seat sloped uncomfortably towards the gearshift; the backrest was ripped, and I could feel the compressed stuffing hard against my spine. We took off slowly, the sound of the engine a deep-throated rumble interrupted by the frequent misfiring of badly gapped spark plugs. I was sure that the noise would attract attention, but the driver was unconcerned. In the darkness I was able to identify him only as a burly white man of indeterminate age. He would have been content, it seemed, to drive me to wherever we were going without exchanging a word. But eventually, the silence between us, punctuated by the sound of the truck engine and the whine of downshifted gears, became deafening. He spoke first.

"So," he said, his voice deep and unexpressive. "This is pretty dangerous stuff you're involved in, hey?"

I was surprised to hear from his accent that he was an Afrikaner—much more likely to be violently opposed to change, and at far more risk from his community if he were seen with me.

"Seems you'd know as much about putting yourself in danger as I do," I said. "Why are you doing this?"

He turned to me in response, and for the first time I saw that he was in his forties, sandy-haired and unshaven, and that his mouth was firm, serious, even angry.

"I don't like your methods," he said, glancing at me through clear blue eyes, "and I don't agree with all the changes you want in this country. But that doesn't mean I think you ought to be serving ten years of hard time with real criminals." He shook his head. "Pretty woman like you—I don't understand it. But it's your business. Not mine."

"Yes," I said. "But thank you, anyway." I was surprised—and touched—that he was willing to put himself in danger and to help me despite political differences.

"You're going to have a hard enough time as it is," he said. "I'm just driving a few hours, dropping you off, and then going straight back to my farm."

"Where are you supposed to drop me?"

"You don't know where you're going?"

"I've no idea," I said. "Nobody told me. I've been taken from one place to another by a series of people I don't know. It hasn't been pleasant, but I suppose it's better than being where I was."

"If I were you, I wouldn't feel too thankful. Not just yet—not until you get to where you're going. I don't know your final destination, but it's probably the only place in the country that's safe—the middle of nowhere." He grinned at me. "Right in the heart of Zululand."

It seemed we traveled forever, first on the highway, then on narrow dirt roads that traversed hillsides and curved through mountain passes.

I saw nothing but what the truck headlights illuminated. We drove up steep inclines and along cliff edges, and although I was sure that we were climbing, there were times when the overall direction seemed downward, towards the sea. We made our way along mile after mile of rough country track, and for the last few hours I was in a daze as we rocked and bumped over paths that were first gravel, and then sand and mud.

It was still dark when we pulled over, into darkness and silence so thick that I could have stretched out a hand and touched it. There had been no lights or dwellings for miles, and it had been an hour since we passed another car. I was about to ask where we were when there was a gentle tapping at my window, the door handle clicked, and as the door was slowly drawn open, the indoor light came on. Into the narrow shaft of illumination at my side stepped an elderly black man wrapped in an orange blanket. He wore a dark woolen hat, and his cheeks were covered by tight grey twirls of sparse beard. In his mouth there was an ancient straight-stemmed pipe, the top of its bowl burned and uneven, and as he puffed on it he drew in his cheeks while he stared at me. His eyes were deep-set, pouched and reddened, surrounded by coarse folds within which was set a network of fine wrinkles. They were thoughtful eyes; there was no judgment in them, and for that I felt grateful. Eventually he nodded solemnly.

"*Sawubona*," he said. I see you. And he gestured with his head that I should come with him.

My driver nodded to me, and as I thanked him and dropped down to the ground he slowly pulled away, turned around, and headed back the way we had come. It was freezing on the mountaintop, the silence absolute, and I was alone with a dignified old Zulu who spoke no English. He wasn't simply tall—he towered over me. Bending to my level so that I could see him gesture in the darkness, he beckoned for me to follow, and he led the way down a path that paralleled the road for a few hundred feet and then turned into the brush, through a narrow ravine. We came to a stream and he strode nimbly over the peeled log that spanned it, and again I felt grateful—this time that he didn't look back to see me struggling to keep my balance.

Eventually he stopped at a fork in the path, where a small donkey was tethered to a tree-stump. Attached to the blanket saddle was a canvas bag which he opened and from which he pulled a heavy woolen blanket. He unfolded the blanket and draped it about my shoulders, bent to untether the donkey, and gestured for me to mount the animal. I shook my head, preferring to walk, and he frowned, at first puzzled by my refusal. Then he shook his head emphatically, and it was clear that he was unwilling to continue unless I rode.

"All right," I muttered eventually as I stepped over to the donkey. "I'll play by your rules."

I put my foot into his clasped hands, with which he hefted me up to the animal's back. Then he smiled at me through his pipe-stem, took hold of the donkey's tether, and led the way down the path. He was right, of course—the warmth of the animal's belly between my legs was comforting in the cold, and I soon realized that I could not have matched the old man's pace. In the darkness his orange blanket seemed to float in slow-motion around his elongated figure as he took smooth, long-legged strides that ate up the distance, his bare feet shushing rhythmically on the path.

Only a man used to making long journeys on foot could move with such speed and constancy. From the sound of the donkey's hooves I knew that there were stones and twigs on the path, but the old man's pace remained unaffected by what he stepped on, and I remember imagining the protection afforded him by the thick, yellowed calluses that had formed on his heels, and beneath his forefeet and toes. I couldn't have imagined that in a matter of months I would be able to match both his speed and the toughness of his feet.

Dawn was just breaking when we came across a cluster of huts on a hillside. They were traditional Zulu huts, a framework of sticks wired together into a frame and covered with woven grasses down to the ground. There were seven in all, one in the center larger than the others. I had seen these structures from the road, passed similar smallholdings on the way to volunteer at the church in Sophiatown, learned about them in school. I knew that the larger one belonged to the father; the smaller ones to each of his wives with her small children, and that perhaps there was one for older boys and another for older girls.

There was a fire burning at the center of the cluster, and as we arrived two people rose from the fireside—an elderly woman with a traditional raised, flat headdress on her head, and a slender young man. I moved toward the fire and opened my blanket to let the heat warm me. Before he led the donkey off, the old man and the woman spoke together in low voices, and although I knew a few words in Zulu and was familiar with the sounds of the language, I understood nothing of their dialect. But it didn't matter—for the first time in hours I felt warm, and would have been happy to curl up beside the fire and fall asleep on the ground. When they were done, the woman approached me and beckoned for me to follow her. From the fireside she picked up a bowl covered with a cloth, and led the way to one of the huts. The young man followed us at a distance.

The hut was high enough so that once inside, I could stand straight. In the center there was a circle of stones in which burned a small fire, and most of the smoke seeped out through the grass walls. What was left warmed the air and gave off a thick smoky odor that was familiar to me— the black people I met often smelled this way, and I realized for the first time, with some shame, even in my exhausted state, that it was because they carried the smoky smell in their clothes.

I learned later that smoke prolonged the life of the hut, kept termites out, and discouraged insects from eating the grass walls. The hut had a mud floor and was furnished with a low, roughly-made table, and two upended logs that served as chairs. To one side was a grass sleeping mat on the floor. The woman pointed to the table on which there was a galvanized tin pitcher filled with water, and she placed the bowl beside it. Then she called to the young man who was standing at the entrance and he came in, respectful of both the woman and of me.

In the firelight I saw that he was not yet a young man, but a tall boy just past puberty, thirteen or fourteen. He stood uncomfortably, waiting, with the old man's humorous mouth and piercing eyes, but his eyelashes were long, and his cheeks smooth. He wore short pants that ended above his bony knees, and a stained long-sleeved white shirt that hung on him; the shirt-sleeves were thickly rolled up and were still long enough to protect his wrists from the cold. He walked into the hut with awkward, long-legged grace.

"Do you speak English?" I asked.

"I speak," he said, his high voice not yet changed.

The woman addressed him, several long sentences, waving toward me, pausing to change or amend what she wanted him to tell me.

"*Gogo*—my grandmother—she says you must eat—" he pointed to the bowl on the table "—and then you must sleep."

"Thank you," I said. "But why—" I remember trying to formulate my questions—who were they? Why were they helping me? Who had arranged my escape? What was to happen to me? But I was chilled to the bone, hungry and in shock, too weary to find the words.

In response the woman led me to one of the upended logs and sat me down, and as she uncovered the bowl, she spoke to the boy. I thought I heard her say my name, and as she spoke, she placed the steaming bowl in my hands and motioned with her thumb and the first two fingers of her hand that I should eat.

"She says for me to tell you," said the boy, "a man comes. Tomorrow. Now you eat, and then—" he pointed to the bed "—you sleep."

He backed out and left. The woman waited until I had eaten, picking up mouthfuls of the thick warm porridge with my fingers. It was *mielie* porridge, pap, and I had seen black servants eating it almost every day of my life, either hot or fermented, mixed with vegetables or meat, always with their fingers, or sopped up with bread—but I had never eaten it. Now the warmth and texture of this whitish, heavy, bland, slightly salty dish seemed to infuse my body with strength and calm. When I was through, the woman led me outside and showed me where to relieve myself, and pointed to a bucket filled with cold water so that I could wash my face and hands. Then she took me back to the hut, watched me curl up on the mat, covered me with a blanket, and left.

My life was at a dead end, and falling asleep felt like a death from which I might not wake. I could not even imagine my parents' grief, had they been alive to see where I was. And then there was my Grandmother Rachael. She would have been overwhelmed by disapproval and sad-ness—but I don't think she would have been surprised.

She was a seamstress, a woman with no schooling, but she was an important person in my life, and she had a tremendous influence on me. Her world centered on the plain, rundown brick building that housed the synagogue. In her life she took nothing on faith but faith itself, and she had a ferocious belief in *tikkun olam*—the obligation to be involved in the work of healing the world. She took food and companionship to the sick and elderly, and people in need were all the same to her. It was irrelevant to her whether those she helped were members of her synagogue, Jews or gentiles, black or white.

She knew things about me that I have only discovered—or been able to admit to myself—as an old woman. I was comforted by the thought that her devotion to me was as fierce as her disapproval, and that her love would have been no less because of where my life had taken me. As I lay on the mat in circumstances that she could never have imagined, unable to sleep, I remembered sitting on the couch in her small living room when I was in high school.

"Why is it not enough for you to be content with what you are?" she asked.

"I am content," I answered. "I'm just curious, that's all. What's wrong with learning what other people believe and how they live?"

"Hear me carefully, Michaela," she said. "You do well at school, but you struggle against being a student. You write for the school newspaper, beautifully, but you don't feel like one of the group, so you stop writing and you become curious about playing piano. You join the orchestra, you don't feel like one of the musicians, you look for something else. You go to Tuesday afternoon classes at the synagogue, but you feel different from the girls and boys there, so—what is next for you? Where do you go?"

She thrust the spread fingers of both hands through her hair in frustration. "Michaela, you're already where you are supposed to be." She took the skin on my forearm and rolled it firmly between her thumb and forefinger. "You are here, where you belong, inside your skin. That's what you're really trying to change." She pointed a finger at me and spoke very slowly. "There is no place else to go," she said. "Underneath your skin is where you need to be happy first, before anything else. You will have no peace, Michaela, until you stop fighting to become something other than what you are."

Grandma Rachael was deeply grounded by the certainty that she had a purpose in the world. She knew instinctively who she was, where she came from, and where she belonged. She gave me many gifts, and she offered that one, too. But even her considerable energy and determination were not enough to make me comfortable in my own skin.

As I tossed and turned, the grass-filled mat beneath me rustled each time I moved. I finally fell asleep with her face before me, remembering the camphor-filled smell of the one-bedroom flat she and my grandfather lived in.

I slept without moving, the deep, dreamless sleep of exhaustion, and when I woke, stiff and hungry, the hut was filled with warm, mid-afternoon light. There was a figure sitting on one of the logs, watching me. When he saw that I was awake, he smiled, rose, and came to kneel on the mat beside me.

I looked into his face, and thought at first that I was dreaming— the man who owned this face was on his way to serve a life sentence in prison—he couldn't possibly be here with me in this hut.

"Khabazela?" I whispered.

"I am here, Michaela," he said.

For a long time we said nothing. We looked into each other's eyes; he held my hand; I stroked his cheek. The silence between us was an expression of relief that we were together—but it was also reluctance to discuss the impossibility of our situation.

I was a fugitive, estranged from my husband. The grief and terror— and the awful sense of loss I felt as I anticipated the start of a ten year jail sentence—were now gone, replaced by uncertainty, and fear of what the future held. I even allowed myself to wonder how long it would be before I saw you, Steven, and to imagine the circumstances of our reunion. But no matter how hard I thought about you, I could not find a way around the facts.

In the months that followed, I spent much of every day lying on my mat in the hut Khabazela and I shared, my eyes closed, tortured by images of you and of your life without me. Sometimes I imagined you tearful and sad, missing me; at others, I thought of you living with your father and some other woman, happy enough with whoever had replaced me. I couldn't tell which image was more painful, but eventually, sleep came and gave me release.

All I had left was Khabazela, and I would not willingly leave him—but it was clear that if we wanted to remain together, we would have to create our own reality, and that it could only exist outside the boundaries of what was legal. I could not then have imagined what survival would demand of us, but I was to learn firsthand how vulnerable I was to corruption and cruelty.

sixteen

MICHAELA

Zululand, 1962

The old woman who had greeted me the previous night turned out to be not so old. Her name was Lungile—The Good One— most of her teeth were gone, and she was in her fifties, although she didn't know her exact age. She was the senior wife of my guide of the previous night, Sthembiso, who, when he worked in the gold mines, was called Promise.

Both he and Lungile were wonderful to us. When we first arrived, all I saw was an uneducated and impoverished couple, with nothing to offer me but their meager hospitality. I was grateful—but it would have been impossible to imagine at the beginning that by the time we left, I would come to see them as energetic and gracious, and to love and respect them. I'm not sure that they ever truly understood what we had done, or why it was necessary for us to hide from the authorities. But Khabazela's father and Sthembiso were related—they belonged to the same lineage—and we were accepted as family. We stayed with them in their homestead among the hills of Zululand for almost nine months, and in that time I was reborn.

At first, I knew nothing of their language or customs. Khabazela could do little to help, but he watched me, and that was perhaps more important. After all, we had never spent more than a few hours at a time together. He might have seen my strength and determination as a volunteer in Sophiatown, or as an upper-middle class white woman enraged by a corrupt power structure. And he might have felt that he loved me. But what he had in mind for us was not time-limited—it was a commitment to a lifestyle, far more dangerous and challenging than anything I had known in my previous life. It would take place in isolated and rural locations, in the absence of any community of support, and in an environment where we would be in harm's way much of the time. Before he put his proposition to me, he needed to see if I had the commitment, the willingness and the strength to manage the difficulties he knew were in store.

For my part, I watched him, too. When he was with others, and when he was with me. And I watched myself when we were together. I thought I loved him, but in truth my knowledge of him was superficial. I knew his body, and the texture of his skin, and his hair; and I knew the feel of his lips on my mouth, and on my flesh; I knew what passion looked like in his eyes, and gentleness; knew that he was a patient teacher, that he was angry and brave; that he had wept in my arms after killing his first man, the police officer who would otherwise have killed him.

Lungile took care of me. It was a two and a half hour walk over the hills to the nearest road, and young boys watching the cows were also watching for strangers, so it was unlikely that anyone from the outside world might see me. But with a pair of binoculars on a distant hill, it might have been possible for someone to notice my white skin. So at the beginning, each morning she intercepted me as I left our hut, and took me into her own, where she darkened my skin, rubbing my arms, legs, neck and face with a thin solution dyed with tree bark and roots. Over my clothes, I wore a torn old work shirt of her husband's and over that, a stained apron, and a woolen hat to cover my hair. Only then would she stand aside, hands on her hips, look at me, smiling so that I could see her pink gums.

"*Hau*," she would exclaim, satisfied with her work. "*Yebo*." Yes. And she would wave me out of the hut.

The homestead was on a hillside, with the huts in a rough circle, and what I had not seen on my first, exhausted night was that in the center was a *kraal*, a pen bounded by wooden stakes, in which the cattle were kept; the lower part of the circle was open, and contained a patch of tilled soil in which, at various times during our stay, Lungile grew *mielies*, beans and sweet potatoes. Gentle, rounded hills rolled off in all directions to the horizon, and although at first I had thought that we were alone, it became clear in the light of day that other homesteads were scattered among the hills, and that they were joined by a network of paths.

In the western distance, the silhouette of a massive range of mountains was visible, sometimes clearly, and at others indistinguishable from high cloud cover. These were the Drakensberg, which to the whites looked like a dragon's back—but the Zulus called their mountains the *uKhahlamba*—the Barrier of Spears.

Winter is the dry season in Zululand, and although the temperature drops precipitously at night, it is crisp and clear during the day when the sun shines. The winter grasses were tall and wheat-colored, with an occasional hint of pale green, and standing outside my hut in the bright sunshine I recall feeling an overwhelming impulse to extend my arms and rise into the air as I watched the gently rolling hillsides waving and thrashing in the wind that billowed across the landscape. It would have been so easy to give myself to the wind, to become weightless and be carried upward and away.

Early in the day the silence was broken by the sound of the cattle, and by the barefoot young boys whose job was to care for them. In the mornings the boys encouraged their cows along the paths, herding them in single file, to the hillsides where they would spend the day grazing. These were Nguni cattle, which had accompanied the migrating forebears of the Zulus as they traveled down from the northernmost reaches of the African continent. The journey took place around the fifteenth or sixteenth century, and no one knows how many hundred years it took for them to reach the land where they finally settled. Perhaps as a result of the journey, the cows were hardy and resistant to disease, and many had a distinctive, mottled coloration. They were also the measure of wealth among the Zulus; herding them was a privilege, and the boys watched over their charges with pride. At night, before the sun went down and as the temperature began to fall, they would return along the same paths, singing to each other and calling to the cows by name, voices echoing among the hills.

It was a peaceful place of never-ending skies, silent hillsides, and streams that ran clear and pure. Its people were imbued with the dignity and wildness of this astoundingly graceful land, and it all seemed far distant from the turmoil of unjust laws, and the poverty, sadness and disease they spawned. Johannesburg and Soweto were like the memory of a distant, festering wound—but even then in Zululand, the signs of disharmony were present.

Most of the able-bodied men were gone for months at a time, some to work in the sugar cane fields; many to labor in the mines, living in barracks under almost penal conditions. Women from the cities were brought in to service the miners—women who themselves had few other choices. That was bad enough—but it was nothing compared to the current situation. When the AIDS virus arrived, the men returned from the mines to their multiple wives in the hills of Zululand, bearing lethal gifts.

One evening about a month after we arrived, as the cows were being returned to the *kraal*, one of the young boys ran into the homestead at full speed, his bare feet making no sound. Lungile was in the gardens when he arrived, and I watched as they spoke quietly together, his bare chest heaving as he gave his message. He had run a long distance, and began to shiver as he spoke. She placed a blanket around his shoulders, and then he sank down beside the fire.

Ignoring me, Lungile ran to our hut, calling out as she ran, and when Khabazela emerged they stood together and talked. I watched, knowing that the herd boys were on the lookout, that they signaled each other silently from hilltop to hilltop, and that they had been alerted to watch out for people who might be after us.

"The boys have seen a group of men in uniform," he said, lowering his head as he entered our hut, and beckoning for me to follow him. "There are five white men on horseback, with bearers and pack animals."

"Do we know who they are?" I asked, following his example as he rolled his blanket.

"No," he said, and stepped back to look around the hut. There was nothing that might identify either of us. "Could be the Special Branch searching for us; but even if it's the regional police doing a routine patrol, they've been asked to be on the lookout for us. If they stop for the night, they'll be here by mid-morning—but it's a full moon, and if they keep going, they might be here in a couple of hours. We have to go."

"Where?" I asked.

"Where they'll never find us," he said in a low voice. "But we'll be in good company—it's the forest where King Cetshwayo took refuge in 1883, when the Zulu leadership was destroyed."

I didn't know of Cetshwayo, and I had only heard mention of the nearby forest as a dark place of spirits and ghosts. I was full of fear as Lungile took two yams still in their skins from the fire, stuffed them into the blanket I was carrying so that I wouldn't burn myself, and waved us off. The boy had risen from the fire and led the way, and I followed them to the top of the hill where Khabazela took my hand in the evening chill as we made our way silently through the waist-high grass.

We had been walking together every evening, and I was no longer as easily winded as I had been when we first arrived. I was used to his pace; I had learned to hear his breathing over the sound of my own exertion, and to breathe in tandem with him. Walking together calmed me and gave me a sense of purpose.

We followed the boy along a cow path across a lengthy crest, further than I had yet ventured from the homestead, and eventually broke off to forge our way through the grass up the side of a steep hill. When we reached the top, the boy lowered himself to sit on the ground; Khabazela followed suit, and pulled me down beside him.

"Look," he said, and pointed into the horizon.

The Zululand sky is vast, and although the sun was no more than a blinding sliver about to vanish behind the distant peaks, a pastel glow colored the underside of the cloud cover just above and rays of light shone down onto the forest that spread out before us. The tops of the trees—the forest ceiling—extended out almost horizontally from where we were, but from our vantage point, I could see that the hillside continued on a downward slope beyond where it became the forest floor. It ran along the valleys and up the hillsides, bounded at the higher points by steep, grassy fields. It was an isolated mist-belt forest, found only in high mountains. The density of the growth, and the almost immediate height of the trees, made it dark and virtually impenetrable.

"Nkandla," he said. "Many of its trees are hundreds of years old."

"It's beautiful," I said, "at least, it looks beautiful from here."

"Yes, in the light. From within, it is less lovely. And the forest floor is treacherous."

He turned to the boy and they spoke together, and the boy gestured down the hill, pointing with a closed fist to a narrow trail that ran along the forest border and seemed to come to a sudden stop. Then he arched his body, rolled his thin shoulders, seemed to be pulling himself along by outstretched arms that gripped a series of invisible branches and roots. I shuddered involuntarily at the sinuous movement. I knew that he was showing us how we would have to crawl along the darkened, moist floor, threading ourselves among the roots, through the trees and the vines that locked them together until we had inserted ourselves so deep into the body of the forest that we became invisible from the outside; so deep that we ourselves were unaware of which direction was out, and which would take us further into the darkness.

We rose, and Khabazela placed his hands on the boy's shoulders, thanking him in a grave voice for showing us the way. The boy's eyes widened with pride, and he held his lean, smooth cheeks tight so that he wouldn't show how pleased he was—but he couldn't maintain it, and as he smiled, his teeth gleamed in the last reflected light of the day. Then he turned and ran back up, disappearing over the crest of the hill.

The Nkandla forest was full of more than trees and vines. There were several species of deer, and leopard, some of the older people remembered seeing elephant, and there were many cautionary tales of rocky cobras, puff adders and black mambas. The path we followed was actually the route the wild pigs took to their lair, and rather than stopping abruptly, as it seemed to do from a distance, when we reached its apparent end-point we were at the forest verge, and we followed it on into the trees.

Within seconds we were in darkness, the temperature dropped immediately, and we were enveloped in the thick smell of the place—the smell of moist soil, wet bark covered with lichens, rotting vegetation, and a musty animal odor that could have come from wild pigs and baboons. At first I found the smell insufferable, but within a short time it became just one more part of the forest background. The trail was inaccessible to us—it disappeared into a tunnel of roots and vines so low to the ground that we would have had to crawl on our bellies to enter it. We stopped to see where we were, our hands entwined.

"That way," he said, pointing at a wall of vines and trees, "but you'd better put your blanket over your neck—you're going to need both hands."

"How do you know this place?" I asked, stopping to do as he suggested.

"I was here often as a boy," he said, taking the woven reeds hanging from my blanket roll and looping them over my head and one shoulder. "We used to play here, and we sometimes slept in the place I'm taking you to. After all these years, I hope I can still find it."

I followed as he clambered through the living barrier. It closed in on me so that I felt bound and constricted, and I couldn't seem to expand my lungs to get sufficient air. The growth was thicker and more dense than I could have imagined, and I found myself having to arch my body as the boy had, sliding one shoulder up over the roughened surface of a horizontal vine, in order to pass through a narrow opening between vine and branch, even before I had extricated my legs from the dense tangle of roots behind me.

Unlike the hillside homestead, which was warmed by the sun even in the midst of winter, this place never saw the sun. The ground never dried, and our clothes were drenched from contact with dripping ferns, wet elephant-ear leaves, and the rotten and moist deadwood underfoot. It was strenuous work, and when we stopped ten or fifteen minutes later—an interminable period—we were hot and sweating, despite the chill. We were in a circle of ferns and hanging vines at the base of an immense tree trunk that rose leafless and branchless into the darkness.

"How far do we have to go before we're safe?" I asked.

"I think we're here," he said, "if this is the right tree. There should be a rope ladder hanging down—there's a sleeping platform high up, and we can pull the rope up after us."

Khabazela pulled a flashlight from his pack, and directed the light first before us to show the way, and then up at the tree in search of the ladder. The forest was so thick around us that the light was completely insulated from outside view.

We were not alone. Several times the light reflected off a pair of yellow eyes in the undergrowth, and we heard the unsettling sounds of scurrying paws—or claws. It took us a few moments to make our way around the complex root system, which reared up out of the ground like an exoskeleton—narrow struts and buttresses attached at ground level, or arches that extended up to join the trunk far above our heads. We had somehow circled around and approached so that instead of the ladder being directly in front of us, it was on the other side of the tree. But we found it, a thick hanging vine with a sturdy branch bound to it crossways by rawhide or reeds at two-foot intervals.

I went up first, holding the highest rung I could reach, bearing my whole weight on my arms and hands, and pulling my feet up behind me.

When my feet were firmly perched, I reached up with my arms to the next rung and pulled my feet up another level, until I had no sense of where the ground was, or of how far up I had climbed. He held my ankle firmly when I hesitated, shining the light up so that I could see the ladder above me, and I forced myself not to look down, or to wonder whether the single vine was strong enough to hold us both. Eventually, I reached the platform and pulled myself up to lie rigid in the darkness.

The platform was about six feet long, and slightly less wide, about as big as a good-sized bed, made of thick branches lashed together, and cradled in a nest where three huge limbs forked away from the main trunk. When we were both sitting together, Khabazela turned on the flashlight briefly so that we could see the extent of our limited world, and as he did so, pointing it at the trunk, I saw something that made my blood congeal.

"Look," I whispered, and pointed at what the light reflected—two narrow, vertical eyes. Snake eyes. As I watched, a triangular head emerged slowly, a thick head, with speckled blotches on its flat top, the sides brightly colored green and orange.

"Don't move," he whispered.

I couldn't have moved if I'd wanted to—but I watched the puff adder rear its body so that I could see its pale underbelly. As I listened to the deep hiss of warning and danger, I was aware of a wide open mouth, of fangs, and then the whole platform trembled as the huge snake struck. And then it was gone. The flashlight clattered to the platform, its light reflecting the rictus of pain on Khabazela's face as he lay on his side, his hands already forming a tourniquet below his knee, and just above the bite on his calf.

"So, Michaela Green," he whispered, drawing himself up to a sitting position. He grinned through the pain—but all I saw was a death mask. "What would your father the dentist, who took a bullet out of my thigh and saved my life, tell you to do now?"

His question was rhetorical—we both knew what my father would have told me to do, and we both knew that I had no choice. I thought of leaving his dead body alone on the platform; of climbing down in terror from the tree to find my way alone through the tangled nightmare below; of returning alone to seek refuge with Lungile; of losing him, living alone; being abandoned. But even as the images rolled in rapid succession through my mind I was refusing them, moving rapidly to his pack to find his knife, which I opened and wiped on my shirtsleeve. There was no water—no fire to sterilize the metal.

He removed one hand from his leg to take the flashlight from me, and he held it while I tore the leg off his trousers. The bite was on the back of his calf, halfway up and deep in the muscle tissue. I wound the fabric around his thigh just above the knee, thinking that it would give us a few more inches—and a little more time—to prevent the venom from traveling through the blood stream, then twisted the cloth around a small piece of wood as tightly as I could until it bit into his flesh, and he grunted in discomfort. I pushed him into a lying position and on to his side so that I could get to the back of his leg, bent him forward and guided his hand to the tourniquet.

"Can you hold it in place?"

"Yes," he said. "Go."

The circle of light on his calf revealed two deep, blooded punch holes, the skin around them already pinkish and swollen. I hesitated—there was only one right way to do this, and so many ways to get it wrong. What if I didn't cut deep enough? Too deep?

"No time to think, Michaela; this is a time to act." His voice was firm. "Cut deep, and draw out the poison. I will be fine."

I did it. Stuck the knife blade into his calf until it scratched the bone, sawed down through the muscle, wiping blood away so that I could see where I was cutting. When I had an inch long incision, I pulled it out and made another incision at ninety degrees. It was a perfect X running right between the punch holes, and I knelt down and opened my mouth to his flesh. With my tongue I felt the sharp outlines of the incision and tasted the salt warmth of his blood, and I shuddered at the thought of what I was doing.

I sucked at the wound until my mouth was full and I turned from him and spat out over the edge of the platform. Then I took a deep breath as I returned to my work, and sucked again and when my mouth was full of blood, instead of rising and spitting I let it dribble from my lips, taking care not to swallow. The tourniquet did its job and finally the flow staunched, and I had to work hard to get any blood at all. When my lips were numb and my tongue and cheeks ached from the effort, I stopped. He was shivering, muttering under his breath, his hand tightly cramped over the tourniquet. I helped him release it, covered the wound with a piece of pants leg and tied it loosely round with two strips of cloth.

I spread the blanket over us both and turned off the flashlight, thinking how much of an intruder I was in this place of absolute darkness. Baboons moved around through the trees, rustling and thrashing branches as they swung from tree to tree, and their hoots and screeches cut through the darkness. The song of tree frogs, crickets and swarms of insects was so intense that it seemed to bounce off the night, and to make the blackness around me shimmer.

He was still muttering as I put my arms around him. He turned to me, shivering, and said something unintelligible as I lay beside him. All I heard was the word 'close.'

"I didn't understand," I said softly into his ear. "Are you cold? Do you want to come closer to me?"

"Yes," he mumbled, "closer. If the snake takes me in the night. Promise me."

"Promise you what?"

"That you will bury me beside my King, Cetshwayo."

"I promise," I said. "But you're not going to die in the night." And I went to sleep, wondering if he would still be alive in the morning.

I woke stiff and freezing, to a cold, dull early morning light that made its way down through the forest ceiling. The platform was shaking. Beside me Khabazela was hot to the touch; he shuddered and gasped, and his skin was beaded with perspiration. His eyes were open and met mine when I looked at him.

"I need water," he said through quivering jaws, and stopped to swallow. "I think this will pass. You got almost all the venom."

He had lost blood—how much, I had no idea. But blood loss and fever sweats meant dehydration, and I had to find a way to clean his wound. Congealing pools of blood dotted the platform, and it was covered in ants and flying insects.

"Go further down the hill—there will be a stream at the bottom. Break branches as you go or you'll never find your way back." Then he waved me off and rolled himself into a fetal position under the blanket.

I took the knife and climbed back down to the forest floor. I didn't notice until I began to clamber through the undergrowth that my arms and legs were scratched and bleeding. But as I scrambled and contorted my body over and under the twisted branches and vines, I reopened wounds from the previous night, and there was soon a cloud of blood-crazed mosquitoes hovering around me. I snapped dead branches to mark my way, and when I finally reached the bottom of the hill stumbled into the stream that Khabazela had known would be there. I wondered how he had known—but I learned later that upwelling streams followed the gorges through all the valleys of the Nkandla.

The water ran clear, but was almost obscured by ferns and vines. I couldn't reach it from the bank, and had to scramble into the middle of the stream, where I drank deep, stopping in mid-swallow as I realized that we had brought nothing in which to transport water. We were not supposed to have suffered snakebite; were not supposed to have one of us trapped on the platform, unable to fend for himself.

I looked around me for something to use as a water vessel. On the other side of the stream was a stand of tuberous plants with huge leaves—the largest was at least a yard long and two feet across. After several failed attempts I managed to wrap one into a cone without tearing it, but when I tried to fill it with water it collapsed under its own weight—and I realized that even if the leaf could bear the weight, I probably couldn't. I needed something to give the leaf form and shape, something that would retain moisture until I could get it back up the hill.

My shirt.

I ripped it off, rinsed it and rang it out several times. Then I put it into the leaf cone and submerged the whole thing into the stream. When I raised it above the water, it was heavy, but it also maintained its shape. I knew I would lose some of it on the way back, but I had no choice. It was the best I could do.

The return journey up the steep hillside to the platform was interminable. I cradled the waterlogged leaf cone in one arm and followed my trail of broken branches, maneuvering myself up the hill one vine at a time. I interrupted a family of wild pigs rooting along the forest floor, broom-ended tails aloft, and they dispersed in front of me, snorting. Several times I thought myself lost and was about to panic and call out when I found the next broken branch and continued uphill. Eventually I located the tree, and had to stop and catch my breath at the bottom before attempting the climb. I grabbed the vine with my free hand and pulled myself up the makeshift ladder, bearing my weight on one arm each time I hoisted my feet from one rung to the next.

When I reached the platform he was still shaking, and hot to the touch. Water dripped from the bottom of the cone as I held it over his face. He squeezed the base and caught the stream of water in his open mouth, and I found myself grinning with a sense of accomplishment so intense that I can still taste it today. When he had drunk what he needed, I unwrapped his leg and washed the snake bite and the incisions. There was no way of knowing whether it was infected; it was still swollen and discolored. But the water helped to reduce his fever, and as the shivering decreased, he became more alert.

"Thank you, my Zulu lady," he murmured, turning to look at me. "Today you have become a Zulu."

"Khabazela," I said softly, turning from him to hide my face.

Although he had told me that he loved me, this was the first time he had addressed me in his own language; the first time he had called me his lady. His Zulu lady. Many times since then I have wondered why his words touched me so deeply; wondered what it was—still is—that makes me so want to be what I am not, and can never be.

"Time to eat something, Khabazela," I said, breaking one of the cold yams into pieces.

We ate together in silence. When we were through, he reached out and touched me, and he smiled.

"Now I will tell you a story," he said. "It will pass the time, and take your mind off worrying about me. I told you that we would be in good company here, because this is where King Cetshwayo came to find refuge. Remember?"

"Yes, I do. And do you remember that you made me promise last night that I would bury you beside him? Well, I would have been happy to oblige," I said. "But I have no idea where he's buried."

"So Lungile has not shown you Cetshwayo's grave."

"No—she hasn't shown me anything. How would she know where it is?"

He drew back from me, and although I didn't know why, it was clear that I had misspoken.

"You have not discovered yet that very little is as it seems," he said gently. "Even though Lungile and her family give us hospitality and protection, you see her only with your western eye. You see an illiterate farmer who lives in a grass hut, and wears a garment around her waist made of cow stomach. But if you could see through Zulu eyes, you would see a woman born into the Shezi clan; you would know that her grandfathers were spear makers to the Zulu kings. You would see a woman who lives her history every day."

The effort of speaking exhausted him, and he paused to take a deep breath.

"As a Shezi, Lungile is the custodian of King Cetshwayo's grave. Each day she goes to the grave site. She keeps it clear of weeds and overgrowth, and makes sure the cattle stay away; she guards it and watches over it. And every day when she tends her duties, she carries the history of her people into the future."

He stopped and we looked at each other, and from across a vast distance he reached out his hand and took mine.

"I would like to bring together our two impossible worlds," he said.

"Yes." Doubt filled me, and in the midst of it, a surge of hope that what he proposed was indeed achievable—and that perhaps we might make it happen ourselves. "Me, too."

"If it is to happen at all, it will be one person at a time." He paused, and his expression softened. "You may love me," he said gently, "but only when you have learned to see through both eyes will you understand us. And only then will you and I be able to make ourselves useful here." He caressed my hand, and looked into my eyes with an unstated question. "If we are to try and live this," he said, "we will live in the shadows, and in secret; in the darkened courtyard between the back door of the main house and the servants' quarters; in the invisible places between the lines of the law."

It was the first time Mandla—Khabazela—gave me any indication that he had been thinking of the future, or that he had even considered a future that included me. For my part, I had been too shocked and bereaved by the course my life had taken to even think beyond tomorrow. But now that he had raised the issue, I was terrified by his suggestion, and by the questions it raised. How would we live? Where? What pretense could we concoct that would be both believable to the outside world, and acceptable to us? A clandestine affair, made up of occasional brief encounters, was one thing—but living together in secret and carrying the knowledge of a relationship that could be shared with no one, was another thing entirely.

I shook my head, and we sat together high up on a swaying platform in the middle of a dim forest lit by greenish light that seeped into the treetops as smoke seeps out from the reed walls of a hut. Like two children in a world of make believe, with my back resting against the tree, and with his head in my lap, he told me about Cetshwayo, the last of the great Zulu warrior kings, who was forced to watch as the British dismantled the Zulu nation. And when he died in 1884—poisoned at the hands of his rivals, or by the British, no one knows for sure—his body was hurriedly transported from Eshowe, where he died, to the Nkandla Forest. On the back of an ox cart he was carried across thirty kilometers of trackless *veld* and thrust into the ground without ceremony. They left the ox cart atop his grave as a marker, where it served its purpose for close to a century. Its remains were still there.

We spent three days in the treetops of the Nkandla. When the police search party had given up and left, one of the boys came to tell us that it was safe for us to return, but Khabazela was too weak to climb down the tree or to make his way out of the forest alone. Sthembiso sent a rescue party, and I watched with relief as they built a stretcher while we explained to them what had happened. They carried him out into the light and back to the homestead, where he fell into an exhausted sleep.

There was rejoicing that we had returned, that Khabazela had survived the snake bite, and that I had done what was necessary to care for him. Sthembiso prepared to slaughter a cow for a ritual celebration. There would be meat, and as much beer as could be drunk.

When I first arrived in Zululand I knew nothing of Zulu ritual or belief. The only way I could process what I saw was to relate it to my own background, and all I knew of such things I had received at the hands of my grandmother Rachael, who was raised on the Jewish traditions in the ghettos of eastern Europe before the war. Without her faith, life would have been formless and she a lump of clay, and she took it into her body like a sacrament. The rituals she practiced shaped her belief, wove the fabric of her life, offered purpose and beauty.

When the celebration began, I watched it through the lens my grandmother had given me. What I saw was primitive and crude—but much of it was so familiar to me that at moments, I felt I had come home.

On the morning of the celebration, women swept the huts and cleaned the grounds. Around midday the guests began to arrive. Lungile and the other wives had brewed huge pots of traditional sweet millet beer, and they brought it out and passed it around in clay vessels. Cattle were herded into the enclosure and the gate shut, and the guests watched, talking and laughing.

The noise of celebration ceased when Sthembiso emerged from one of the huts and walked gravely towards us. He wore a skin around his shoulders, on his head a dressing of feathers, in his hand the long, ancient homestead spear, passed down through the generations, and used only for ritual slaughter. Behind him came Khabazela. My breath caught in my throat when I saw him, looking down at the ground, sporting several long feathers in his hair. He wore only a narrow leather thong that hung from his waist, hardly covering him.

Together they came into the enclosure, where Khabazela was seated on an upturned log beside an old man. Sthembiso wandered among his herd of thirty-two cows; he could identify them by the shape of their ears, the feel of their udders, their sounds and the smell of their breath. With a familiarity borne of long practice, he touched them as he walked through the enclosure, passing his hand across their backs, mumbling under his breath. Eventually he stopped, took a dramatic step backwards, and raised his spear into the air. Behind us, a musician began drumming a rhythmic beat.

Sthembiso danced, chanting under his breath in time to the drum, an elderly man rocking back and forth, stamping his feet on the ground and twirling his arms in the air. He could easily have been a bearded Hassid in a black frock coat and hat, dancing with face upraised in ecstatic acknowledgement of the spirit world; and my imagined Hassid could have matched each Zulu chant with a Yiddish song that expressed his own adoration of the Almighty.

He danced over to a big reddish animal with symmetrical horns, the sacred cow that never worked because it belonged to the Shades, the ancestors. He stood beside the animal, one arm across its neck, and he spoke softly into its ear. As he spoke, a white cow with black markings along her flanks separated herself from the herd and ambled across the byre, coming to a standstill on Sthembiso's other side, and there she stood, chewing her cud. Sthembiso turned and placed his hand on the neck of the white cow.

"We have excited the Shades," he said in a breathless shout, "woken them with the stamping of our feet. They have chosen this cow for their meat. Is she not beautiful and fat?" He stopped and reached out his hand, and one of the men handed him a clay bowl filled with beer. He poured it onto the animal's back, spread it with his hand over her neck and shoulders, and back over her flanks. "We anoint this animal with beer, which is the drink of the Shades." He turned on one foot and pointed dramatically. "Look! It is as we have said—there sits our son, Mandla Mkhize, full of health; today he will eat among us, and give thanks with us to the Shades who live among us and with us, and who have acted in these days to bring us health, and meat, and drink."

He turned, leading the chosen cow with him to stand before Khabazela. He beckoned to the old man, who rose, and Sthembiso gravely gave him the spear. The old man walked around the cow, passed the spear between the animal's rear legs, being careful not to touch them. He passed his hands over her udder, muttering, and walked to her side, where he passed the spear between her front legs to ensure the cattle's fertility. Then he placed the tip of the spear on the cow's neck where the main artery comes close to the surface, and without apparent effort, he thrust it deeply into the animal's flesh. Blood pumped from the wound and sprayed across the enclosure, the cow bellowed loudly, her forelegs buckled and she fell to her knees.

The slaughterer held the spear in place, and when he was assured that the cow's bellowing had been sufficient to call the Shades, he inserted the tip of the spear between two vertebrae, twisted deftly and severed the spinal column. As the white cow's rear legs buckled and she came down, the spectators shouted approval, and several men came into the enclosure and maneuvered her so that she fell onto her right side. The other animals milled around uncomfortably at the smell of blood, and Sthembiso called for the boys to come and take the herd out to graze.

The slaughterer opened the cow's belly, carefully cut out the gall bladder and poured its contents over Khabazela's shoulders and onto his hair.

Muttering, he gestured that Khabazela should open his mouth, which he did, and the old man sprinkled a few drops of gall onto his tongue. Like a trusting child; a paschal lamb.

Unbidden and unexpected, unsure of their origin or why they appeared, the words of broken psalms formed in my mouth. You prepare a table before mine enemies; my head you anoint with oil. It's all of a one-ness, I thought; the same things, seen through different lenses. Grandma Rachael, were she still alive, would have been horrified by the mere idea.

On a shard of clay from a broken pot, Sthembiso placed pieces of organ meat, beckoned to Khabazela, and together they returned to the hut. They put the potshard on the fire so that the Shades might be called by the burning meat to partake of the feast with us. The guests remained silent while the two men remained in the hut, waiting for the meat on the hearth to begin sizzling. It was like the Passover Seder, the cup of wine, filled to the brim each year so the children might run to open the door for the Prophet Elijah, if he were to arrive and announce the com-ing of the Messiah. I remember the excitement of waiting, breathlessly watching the cup to see whether Elijah would enter the house and take a sip of wine.

Smoke wafted from the doorway of the hut, and the odor, familiar and vaguely unpleasant, was the smell of the symbolic shank bone bak-ing unseasoned in my grandmother's oven before the Passover feast. The Shades would smell the smoke, recognize it as theirs, and come lick their meat and beer. Then the living could resume their celebration.

The horns and part of the skull of the slaughtered cow were mounted above the door of our hut. The empty gall bladder was tied around Khabazela's right wrist, and Sthembiso tied a strip cut from the cow-hide around his left. He insisted that I, too, have a piece of wet hide tied around my wrist. It was a great honor, I was told, to be given a hide bracelet from a ritually slaughtered animal, and I accepted as graciously as I could. For days I went about with the smell of rotting meat in my nostrils. Khabazela joked that I could not refuse to sleep with him because of his bad smell, since I smelled just as bad. But eventually the smell dissipated, or else I became used to it, as I became used to much else, and our lives returned to what had come to feel normal.

Over the years, I've come to understand the significance of what took place when we emerged from the Nkandla Forest. It forced me to see Khabazela in a new light, as a far more complex person than I had initially thought, and I didn't know what to do with his particular complexity. This man, whom I loved, who on the surface was as Western as I was, had depths that I could not imagine. No matter what promises we might make to each other, he had age-old ties and loyalties far deeper than any commitment he might make to me. I knew deep in my blood—and I accepted—that if I chose to spend my life with him, it would be with the understanding that I might be called upon at any moment to give him up to the tribal demands that preceded mine.

He would have laughed at me had I raised the issue of his potentially divided loyalties. But I had seen in him the presence of the traditional Zulu who shared a body with the humorous, gentle, and determined idealist I knew, and it filled me with an intense sense of loss. I was aware of the duality he lived with, and I had to accept that I was irrevocably shut out from a part of his life.

Lungile waited until the winter had passed before she took me to the silent hilltop to see Cetshwayo's grave. She waited until she knew me better; until I had learned Zulu, and we could speak to each other. There were words that needed saying, she told me, and she thought it appropriate that they be said at the grave of a Zulu King.

The grave itself was nothing to look at—a small, grassy plot on which lay the remains of the oxcart, surrounded by a makeshift fence to keep the cows out. It was well cared for, but I remember being puzzled by the contrast between this primitive and desolate site, and the pride with which Khabazela and Lungile had spoken of the man whose life it marked. A hush enveloped the site like a thick fog, and I imagined shouted slivers of distant voices cutting through the silence. With my new eye, I paid my respects, kneeling beside all that was left to mark the site—a rusted wheel rim, a moldering axle, and miscellaneous bits of wood and metal.

Lungile sat me down at a distance from the grave, in the shade cast by a huge sausage tree, its elongated seed pods hanging from vine-like stems. It was early morning, and the long, mottled shade we sat in was distant enough from the tree itself that we were far from the spot where, should they fall, the heavy seed pods would land. She leaned back on her arms, legs stretched out before her.

"Michaela, my daughter," she began, "I have troubling dreams, and they push me to speak difficult words, to explain things of the Zulu to you." She looked down at the ground, rubbing her bare feet against each other. There was thoughtfulness in her voice, and she said each word slowly, so that I would understand. "You have lived two seasons with us, and we have learned, you and I, that what binds us together is greater than that which makes us different." She laughed loudly. "Did I think I would live to have a white daughter? Never! And did you come to us thinking that you would find a Zulu mother? No! But so it is." She paused, picked up a twig, and began drawing in the sand at her side. "Among us it is the work of mothers to explain to young girls the things of women and men."

"It is the same with us, Lungile," I said.

"Good. You are no longer a young girl, but in the ways of women you are still a child. It has been given to me to teach you these things." She paused. "The Shades are the molders of children. Do you know of this?"

"No," I answered, "nor do I understand what it means. It's strange to my ears."

"I will explain," she said. She shifted herself into a more comfortable position, and raised her hands above her head to illustrate her words. "When the sky brings clouds to us, the rain comes, and it makes all living things grow. This you know, because you have seen it. We say of this, that the sky is working with water. And as we talk of what is between man and woman, we say that the man is working with water. In this way there comes into the womb of the woman the water of the man, to mix with her blood. This makes a child grow."

Lungile fell silent. Finally, she reached out her hand and touched my wrist. "It is these things, the water and the blood, that the Shades use in the molding of children. Do you see how it is, my daughter?" she murmured.

"Yes, mother," I said. "I see how it is." But she continued to stare at me, shaking her head, and I realized that I had not seen what she wanted me to. She clapped her hands, once, startling me.

"No!" she said loudly. "I have not told you well what I mean. I must use other words, or you will not hear what I have been given to tell you. It is like this." She licked her lips and turned to face me. "When Khabazela is with you together in the hut where you sleep, he works with water with you. Is it not so?"

"Sometimes it is so, Mother," I said, and felt the heat rising in my face. "But there will be no babies, so how can there be a problem with the Shades?"

She reached over and slapped my face. I don't know even today how forceful the blow was, but it stung, and I was shocked.

"Why do you humiliate me, Mother?" I asked, keeping my anger under control. I had seen her slap other young women, who took the treatment in stride, but this was the first time she had raised a hand to me. "How have I offended you?"

"You have not offended me," she said loudly, "but you offend the Shades! Do you want to bring on yourself the worst of the sicknesses of women, which is the curse of childlessness?" She clicked her tongue, shaking her head from side to side in irritation. "There will be babies! But you are like a small child—you speak in ignorance, and so you force me to swat your words away to protect you from yourself."

It was a foregone conclusion that we would never have a child. One of the ironies of making sex between races illegal was that an interracial child became evidence of a law broken, and although parents might be punished, the child bore the consequences. There were multiple cases in those years of children being taken from their parents because they bore physical characteristics closer to those of a different racial group. They were torn from their families, relocated to live in a different racial area, with a family whose color, facial features and hair were deemed closer to their own. It was horrendous while it happened, and difficult to believe today—but back then we had already felt the long arm of racial laws. We had no desire to complicate our lives—or the lives of children—by bringing them into so unjust a world. As a result, either he used a condom or I used a diaphragm, but we didn't discuss it until much later. Talking about why we could never have a child would have been far too painful, and we both avoided the subject.

I was taken aback by Lungile's words, but I still didn't understand what her real concern was until she tried again to make it clear.

"Your people do not live with their Shades in the same way that we do," she said, "in their homesteads and in their houses. Is it not true?"

"It is true, mother."

"Then where do the Shades of your ancestors go to live after they leave this life?" she asked.

I tried to explain to her that there was no one way of thinking of ancestors; that they did not feature as prominently in most religious beliefs as the presence of Shades in Zulu life.

"But if this is true," she said, "who does the molding of children in the womb?"

"We believe," I said, "that—*Inkosi AmaKhosi*, the Lord of Lords— takes care of the making of children, and that He does it by uniting the egg of the woman, which lives in her womb, with the seed of the man, which is in his water."

"*Hau*," she scoffed, "this is not correct. You are confused. You speak of eggs and seeds working together. You mix animal and plant, as if the big seeds on the sausage tree—" she pointed at the seed pods hanging above us, and then down at a small bird pecking at the base of the tree "—could do the working of water with that little female guinea fowl there, to mold a living thing." She laughed loudly, incredulous at the impossibility of what I was suggesting, and waved her hand vigorously back and forth. "No, my daughter, this cannot be the correct teaching of your people."

She stopped, sat in silence for a moment, rolled several strands of long green grass between the palms of her hands until they formed one strand, and then looked critically at what she had made.

"I know how it is between Zulu and Zulu," she said thoughtfully, "but I cannot tell you how it is among others. Between you and Khabazela, I do not know how a child will be molded; nor do I know if the Shades will find each other in your womb. Among us it is not told what happens when the Shade of a Zulu meets with the Shade of another people."

She knelt, rose to her feet, and stretched. "I have unburdened myself, and I have no more to say. More answers must come from others, who see deeper than I. Sthembiso has decided that together you and Khabazela will go to see a great *sangoma*, a very old woman, who will perhaps know of these things. The place where she lives is far— come, my daughter. We have preparations to make."

We did see the *sangoma*, although it didn't happen for several weeks. Khabazela was secreted away somewhere negotiating the next step of our lives with the leaders of the ANC, and it would not be until after we visited the *sangoma* that he explained to me what they had agreed to, and what choices I had.

In the meantime, I found myself longing for you, Steven. I wanted to look into my child's face and hold him in my arms, to know that he was well and that he didn't hate me. But traveling to Johannesburg to see you would have placed us both in danger, and bringing you to Zululand was out of the question. When Khabazela said quietly that the best we could do was arrange a phone conversation with Lenny and Steven, I jumped at the suggestion.

It took a week to arrange. A news reporter visited Lenny, saying that he wanted to talk about me. During the interview he slipped Lenny a note telling him to be at Sal's Garage on the outskirts of Johannesburg at noon on the day of the call. There was no guarantee that the call would actually take place. We were at least a day's journey from the nearest phone that was not on a party line—one that would allow us to have a private conversation.

Sthembiso and I started out after midnight on the long trek out to the main road, which we reached at sun-up, to find our contact waiting for me in an old Ford pickup. We drove south until we reached a town large enough to have a post office with a public phone, and we arrived several hours before the call was scheduled. My driver went off to have breakfast, but he dropped me at a second hand clothing store where I bought a skirt and jersey, new underwear and a pair of comfortable shoes. Then I went next door to the town hotel and rented a small, inexpensive room with its own bath. I had my first hot bath since my escape from prison months earlier. If I hadn't been anxious about the phone call I would have luxuriated in the bathtub, but as it was I washed my hair three times, scrubbed my skin until it was red, then dressed and waited until it was time to go.

We had decided not to drive all the way together in the truck. The post office was for Whites Only, and my guide would have been arrested had he set foot inside. I walked two blocks to the post office. Anything could have gone wrong. The phone might have been out of order; there might have been a long waiting line; Lenny might have been delayed. But the post office was empty; the phone not in use, and Lenny arrived at the garage on time. I would have been better off had the conversation never taken place, but the arrangements for the call couldn't have gone more smoothly. I followed instructions to the letter—I called the number of the garage and then hung up; someone called me back and hung up to let me know that Lenny was ready; and then I called again. The phone was picked up and I heard a muffled voice. "I think this is for you."

Then Lenny came on the line.

"Where the hell are you, Michaela?" he asked. He sounded weary and strained.

"I can't tell you where I am, Lenny."

"Great," he said. "Can you tell me what your plans are?"

"I have no plans. And if I had plans, I couldn't share them with you over the phone. It wouldn't be safe."

"That's par for the course. Whatever your plans are," he said bitterly, "they haven't included me for some time now, have they?"

Much of what we said, I don't remember. But some of Lenny's words that day are carved in bone on the inside of my skull.

The fallout from what I had done, he said, made it impossible for him to remain in the country. Most of our friends had supported him when I was on trial, and some had continued even after I was convicted. The police didn't publicize our escape, and the media never printed a word—but because the investigation continued, and everyone associated with us was questioned, it soon became known among our circle that even after a guilty verdict, I had been involved in a brazen escape. Apparently, few people wanted to be associated with a man whose wife was unwilling to take her medicine and fade away into obscurity. Lenny quickly discovered who his true friends were; the others simply disappeared. His mentor and the senior partner in his engineering firm accused him of jeopardizing projects for which the firm was bidding—told him bluntly that he should have had the balls to put me in my place while the marriage was still salvageable. The management team was almost universally contemptuous of him.

"I didn't mean any of this to happen," I said.

"That's rich," he said. "Perhaps you can explain to me how you fuck a man without meaning to. Dear God, Michaela, what the hell were you thinking?" Anger and despair were so clear in his voice that I had to distance the phone from my ear. "You've destroyed my life as well as yours, to say nothing about what you've done to Stevie."

"I'm so sorry, Lenny." My voice was a whisper, trying not to be heard, instinctively shying away from what I didn't want to know. "How is he?"

"He's traumatized. The Special Branch has us both under constant surveillance. They follow me to work and him to school, hoping that you'll try and make contact. At school the children are merciless. They taunt him every day with words they don't even understand—it just shows what they must hear at home. They call you a traitor." He spoke the words slowly, enunciating carefully. "Whore. Adulteress. *Kaffir* lover."

I listened to the recitation in silence, wondering whether, at some level, Lenny was using the words to make his own accusations.

"I have to get Stevie out of the country," he said eventually. "I've been offered a teaching job in the States, at the Massachusetts Institute of Technology. We're leaving next month."

"Of course," I said, unable to raise my voice beyond a whisper. "I understand why you have to go. But will you tell Stevie that I love him? That I never meant to hurt him?"

"He's not ready. He's got enough to cope with." Lenny hesitated briefly and then continued, remorseless. "I wasn't going to tell you this, but he's convinced himself that you're dead. He's told his entire class that you were killed fighting apartheid, and that he's proud of you."

My breath caught in my throat. "Where did he get that from?"

"Not from me. He made it up—it's the only way he can deal with what's on his plate."

"When you get settled you'll tell him the truth, won't you?"

"Of course I'll tell him the truth," he snapped. "I'm not about to live with the lie that you're dead. When he's ready, we'll have a talk and I'll tell him the truth."

I was silent, wondering, what truth will you tell him? And how will you know when he's ready to hear it?

"That's it, then," I said. "I'll write you at the Massachusetts Institute of Technology and let you know where I am."

"Fine. I'll give him your letters, and if you ask me about him I'll write back and let you know how he's doing." He paused. "I can't speak for Steven, but I'm done with South Africa. I will never return." He breathed a jagged breath, and in the silence that followed I recognized the sounds as Lenny choking back his tears. When he was able to speak, he cleared his throat. "I'll probably love you for as long as I live, Michaela, but I never want to see you again. You've done enough damage for one lifetime."

In response I wept silently, shook my head into the phone as if he could see me disagreeing with him. But whatever pain I might have felt at his words, I could not dispute the damage he accused me of. He waited, listened to me breathing, but I couldn't speak. Eventually the phone went dead.

"Goodbye, Lenny," I whispered.

I remained in the kiosk long after we ended the call, the receiver hard against my ear, listening to the dense silence that comes through a disconnected phone. It wasn't until a man knocked impatiently on the glass that I forced myself to cradle the receiver, push open the sliding door, and place one foot in front of the other until I was standing outside the post office, blinded by the brilliant sunshine. It was a warm summer afternoon, but I was shivering, chilled to the bone.

I thought then that in your mind, the mind of my seven year old son, I was dead, killed in the fight for freedom. Alive, I was a disgrace and an embarrassment; it was much easier to live with the memory of a dead hero. I tried to imagine the macabre conversation in which I came to life. Would you be disappointed or relieved? Or just furious that I had sabotaged your attempt to create an acceptable mother?

"Hello, Stevie," I would say. "I'm back. I never died—you just imagined that I was dead because it was easier than living with reality."

"Reality?" you would respond. "My reality is that you're dead, and I'm proud of the way you died. Would you rather have me live with the fact that you were a terrorist? That you betrayed Dad? Had an affair that was not only illicit but illegal—without thinking what it would do to me if you were caught? Stay dead," you would say, "it's easier that way. I'm over my grief. Dad and I will have a good life together. Who knows? Perhaps he'll find another wife who'll be a better mother than you ever were."

I was numb and silent in the truck on the long return drive, and I don't recall being led through the darkness on Sthembiso's mule. By the time we reached the homestead and I crawled under the blanket beside Khabazela, I knew that one choice, at least, was no longer mine. You and your father had made it for me.

seventeen

MICHAELA

Zululand, 1962

Why we went to visit the *sangoma* I still don't know, but that we would go was never a question. I thought the whole exercise was pointless, but Khabazela was able to understand science, politics and history, and at the same time hold fast to a belief in the most traditional of Zulu practices, without one cancelling out the other. If I had not learned to respect this in him, I had at least learned that the apparent contradiction was not a topic for discussion, and that he would do what his tradition called for, even if it went against his Western half. So I went along, willing to participate in whatever way I was asked.

We left before noon, a few days after I returned from my telephone conversation with Lenny. It was a warm summer day, and there was a haze along the crests. Our path wound around the hills, linking one homestead to the next. The hum of insects traveled with us; butterflies floated from flower to flower, seeming to rise on updrafts of heated air. Big white cow lilies dotted the flanks of the hills, interspersed with the purple, pink and yellow of wildflowers. Occasionally we came upon a gathering of steenbok or impala in the shade of a tree, one lone male watching for danger. For the first time in months, I didn't feel like a foreign object dropped into a strange environment—instead of standing out, I felt as natural a part of the landscape as the grass or the deer. I was comfortable in my skin, at home in the hills, and surprisingly happy. We had not been together for more than a few hours in a long time, and this was an adventure.

We walked until after dark, and when we arrived discovered that Sthembiso had already sent ahead a black goat as payment for our consultation. We were not alone—this *sangoma* had a reputation throughout Zululand, and people came from much further than we had to seek the Shades' counsel through her. Knowing that there would be other supplicants waiting, and not wanting to parade my presence before them, Sthembiso had arranged for us to stay alone in a small dwelling outside the main homestead. After we had eaten that night, as we sat together on a flat stone beside the fire, Khabazela tried to prepare me for the next day.

"How do you imagine this meeting?" he asked me.

"I expect an old woman in gypsy clothes to tell me that I've had many previous lives, and that in one of them I was Cleopatra's handbag," I said. "But nothing would surprise me. I suppose there'll be an old woman throwing bones on the floor, and staring at them. She'll have snake skins, and grated antelope horn, and foul medicines, and we'll leave with dire predictions about the future. She's probably planning to warn us never to have children, because they'll be born monsters."

He shook his head, smiling. "I think this talk that Lungile had with you of not having children is making you want children more." He turned to look at me, stroked my calf. His fingers were warm, familiar. I quivered, even in the warmth of the fire, and he put his arm about my shoulders. "That would be in character," he said softly. "Wouldn't it? You've always wanted what you can't have."

"Always," I whispered, turning my face to him, teasing. "That's the only reason I'm here. I don't really like you at all, you know—all I want is forbidden fruit." I smiled in the darkness as I ran my hand down his thigh.

"You think we're going to see a witch doctor, performing magic and sleight of hand," he said quietly. "But the real ones don't claim to have any powers of their own—they believe they're chosen because they have the ability to communicate with the Shades. They're diviners—all they do is act as a medium for what the Shades want to say to their children."

"Why does there have to be an intermediary?" I asked. "Why can't they communicate directly with the spirits of their ancestors?"

"It's a little strange," he said, amused, "that although you have no direct communication with your ancestors, you wonder why we don't."

"You're the ones who have diviners," I responded. "All I'm doing is asking why you need them."

"Such a white question," he said, tightening his arm about me. "Maybe we'll find out tomorrow whether we need them or not."

We waited almost until noon the next day before the *sangoma*'s trainee came to tell us she was ready to see us. That morning, a thunderous summer rainstorm had started; the clouds were low and dark, seeming to fly along just above our heads; there were heavy winds and lightening, and the homestead seemed deserted. I had only just learned that lightning and thunder are signs that *Inkosi Amakhosi* is angry, and during such storms, people sit silently in their homes and wait. We thought that the *sangoma* would wait until the storm was over to see us, but when she summoned us we waited for a lull in the rain, and then ran to her hut, which was set apart from the other dwellings, on higher ground.

Cow skulls with horns still attached were tied to the doorframe, some ancient and dried, others relatively new. White beads were woven into the roofing thatch, and a small section of thatch on one side of the entrance had been inserted backwards, so the seeded ends hung over the edge of the roof. The hut was darkened, and when we entered, we were greeted by a sharp, acrid smell. It was pungent, but not unpleasant—a combination of burned herbs, sweat, smoke, and sweet beer. Khabazela sat in the man's place to the right of the door; I sat in the woman's place, to the left. At the back of the hut, the place of the Shades, a fire was burning, and beside it there were several earthen containers, and bundles of dried herbs and medicines. To the right of the herbs, on a grass mat, a small woman sat in a squatting position on a raised platform.

She was bent over, peering at something on the ground in front of her. Her grey hair was a wild nest in which were woven dried cow bladders and medicinal roots. Around her neck she wore snake vertebrae threaded on rawhide, and she had many bracelets on her wrists—copper, cowhide, gall bladders, woven hair from cow tails. She spoke throughout our interview, either talking to herself in a mumbled monotone, or addressing us. Several times, she gathered the collection of small bones on the floor and let them drop casually before her, then carefully examined where and how they had fallen, their relationship to one another, and whether any had landed outside her circle. She did not look at us once; only at the end did she raise her face to us, and even then her eyes were closed.

We sat in silence for several minutes, listening to the thunder and lightning, and to the sound of her mumbled words. There were moments when I would have laughed, but I didn't want to risk giving offense, and so I kept silent. Khabazela spoke first, his tone hushed.

"Mother," he said, pointing to me, "she speaks our language, but not well. I ask your permission to speak your words in English for her, so that she can understand. It will not be a sign of disrespect."

In response she raised her shoulders, making a dismissive gesture with one arm. Her lack of concern was unmistakable. If there was a message, she would deliver it—but she didn't care if he translated for me; didn't care whether I understood or not. We had come a long distance to hear her words; one of us, at least, had some investment in what she would say. But she had no connection to us, and her detachment made me uncomfortable. If she bore no responsibility whatever for the message she was about to deliver, then there were no limits to what she might say. It struck me, finally, that this was not some playful exercise, and that it might have unintended consequences for which no one would be responsible.

As she spoke she underwent a series of bone-wrenching trembles and quivers, as if to emphasize that others were speaking through her. Despite the quivering, her voice was strong and steady, devoid of emotion, and disembodied.

"She is filled with sorrow," she said, raising her right arm and extending it towards me, fist closed, "for her first child." These were simple words, and I understood them, but Khabazela, looking down at the floor, repeated them for me in English. "She says you are filled with sorrow for your first child."

"The boy is not lost," she said. "He will return to her from very far distances when she is an old woman."

Khabazela, still looking at the ground, repeated the words I thought I must have misheard.

"Not until I'm an old woman?" I heard myself say. "How does she know about Steven?"

She ignored me, threw the bones again, and stared at them. "She should not waste her sorrow on this child. In time there will be sufficient reasons—other reasons—for sorrow."

He repeated her words, and she raised her left arm so that she was pointing a closed fist at each of us. I understood little of what she said, and even after Khabazela translated, sentence for sentence, I had more questions than answers.

"She says that together with—another woman—another mother—you and I will raise two children. Two sons—" his halting voice told me this was more than even he had bargained for "—who will have work to do among us in the early parts of their lives. We will have a grandchild from one of these sons, who has the gift of giving vision to others. He will be one who parts the grass that others may see into the distance. She says we should give him a name that reflects this gift, as a tribute to those who bestow it on him."

She threw the bones again. As she studied them the sound of the rain increased, beating against the ground outside and pelting the thatch above us. Rolls of thunder boomed overhead as we waited. Khabazela raised his eyes from the ground and we stared at each other. I thought, for the first time, that I was looking at my future.

When she spoke again it was with her right arm raised, pointing at us. I understood only isolated words—evil times, and blood, and hardship. Khabazela sat with his head bowed as he listened, and I waited for him to translate. He may have been weeping—but whatever he was feeling, he was incapable of further speech until we left.

Finally the *sangoma* stopped speaking, dropped her arm into her lap and raised her head for the first time, her eyes closed. Her trembling ceased, and when she spoke again it was in the high, uneven quaver of an old woman. "I am empty. Go."

We made our way along the path on the long walk back to the homestead. The thunderstorm had passed, but clouds swirled thickly above us, and there was a strong wind and the continued threat of rain. We had made our way there playfully, enjoyed each other's company like children tripping through the sunshine; we walked away swiftly and with purpose, burdened by the gifts of her prophecy, and by what they revealed about our future. I was still dazed that she knew about Steven, and whether or not she was accurate, her prediction that he would return to me when I was an old woman put me in touch, yet again, with the magnitude of my loss.

I glanced occasionally at Khabazela, but he was walking fast, engrossed in his own thoughts, and I had to struggle to keep up with him. Eventually I stopped to rest, and when he realized that I was no longer at his side, he stopped and retraced his steps. We sat together on a flat outcrop of rock, overlooking a steep valley at the bottom of which a tributary of the Tugela River wound its way through the hills.

"I don't know whether we will have a life together," he said, his voice muted in the wind, "but she says we will raise children together. And that we will have a grandchild."

"With another mother?" I asked. "What does that mean?"

He shrugged. "We'll find out what it means," he said, "in time."

"It probably means nothing," I said. "We've never even talked of children, and now we're discussing what to name a grandchild."

"She said that he would have the ability to remove obstacles so that other could see. So if there is a grandchild, we will name him Penya." He spoke placidly, without concern, as if we could actually plan our lives. "But before there is a grandchild," he said, smiling, "there must be a child." As rapidly as it had formed, the smile vanished. He frowned deeply, his mouth tightened in concern.

"What did she say to you at the end?" I asked. "The part you didn't translate for me?"

"Her words were difficult," he said. "Difficult to hear, and very difficult to repeat to you."

"Well, you can't keep them from me," I said. "What did she say?"

"I wasn't keeping them from you, Michaela. It was just that I couldn't speak for a moment, and I couldn't find the words."

"Can you find the words now?"

"She said this time is filled with evil. She said it would get worse, that there would be great hardship, and much killing, both black and white; that brothers would shed each other's blood, and Zulu the blood of other Zulu. She said that although this evil seems long, it is only for a breath of time—and that just as strong winds die down, as thunderclouds pass, as locusts feast and then leave, it will come to an end. But when it is gone, it will leave behind other, deeper problems for our children to face."

He paused, reached over and stroked the side of my neck just below my ear, and I leaned into his fingers. He smiled in acknowledgement, but it was a sad smile.

"She said when I have doubts about what I'm doing, the ancestors want me to remember that the work I do is for my people—it honors those who came before, and prepares the ground for future generations. But for us, Michaela, who are still here for a small space of time, there is not likely to be much change. What we do here—if it benefits anyone—is unlikely to make a difference in our lives."

"How very comforting," I said. "A long prison sentence seems more and more appealing. Now that we've escaped, perhaps we ought to go live on a Caribbean beach—forget about making the world a better place for others. Maybe it's time to think about ourselves."

Khabazela rose and squinted into the wind, his hands in his pockets, looking down into the valley. He stood sideways to me, his shirt blown tight against his stomach and chest, bellied out in back.

"I didn't mean to offend you," I said.

"I'm not offended, Michaela," he answered, still staring down into the valley, "but I am frightened."

"Frightened?"

"That you will go," he said, turning now to face me, "when I tell you that unless you can remain here with me freely and with an open heart, I would prefer that you take the opportunity to leave." He raised a hand to forestall my objection. "If you choose to stay with me, the ANC will provide you with a new name and identity so that you can live in the open. But I want you to be able to make the decision freely, and I have worked hard to convince them that whether you choose to stay or go, you should have the right to start again, with a new identity, and with new papers." He paused. "You could stay in South Africa, go and live in Durban or Cape Town under a new name, and make a new life for yourself. You could go to Australia, and get Steven to join you. Or to the United States. I don't know if you would even need a new identity elsewhere—here we are escaped terrorists, but perhaps in other parts of the world you would be seen as a freedom fighter." He moved towards the path, avoiding my eyes. "My way is clear," he said. "I must stay, but you have a choice. I would not hold you, and I will honor whatever you choose to do."

He walked rapidly down the hill without looking back. I rose and gazed down into the valley, where he had stood staring at the river. For a moment, as I thought about the gift he was offering me, I felt the flutter of freedom in my chest, and the thrill of a new beginning. Anything was possible. He had offered me the gift of a new life, away from turmoil and hardship; given me the chance to put the past behind me, to rejoin my son, whom I longed for. His timing was perfect—what woman in her right mind would refuse the offer of a different life, away from the *sangoma*'s dour forecast?

But the offer of ease and opportunity did not include him, and the thrill of freedom was fleeting. Because he was giving me another choice—to start anew with him, or to repudiate him, all he stood for, and the life he was offering me.

But Lenny had made it clear that he never wanted to see me again, and you had convinced yourself that I was dead. Reunion was no longer possible. I followed Khabazela down the hill, across the wild, rolling landscape, back to Lungile's homestead, and to our Zululand life.

eighteen

MICHAELA

South Africa, 1964

I've wondered often since then why I chose the path I did. Looking back, I think a combination of factors, real or imagined, worked their magic in my head until there was only one real option.

In my mind I had lost you; I loved Khabazela, and he had offered me a life; that life included meaningful work for the ANC, and the possibility of children, which until then seemed out of the question. I saw how placidly this strong and rational man accepted the *sangoma's* predictions, going so far as to choose a name for the grandchild she foretold. That I was a confused young woman is not in doubt; I was adrift, aching to hook my life to something that would give it meaning. Khabazela offered all that, and more.

If I was going to accept his offer to spend our lives together, I had to find a way to make it work—but the whole idea was impossibly unrealistic. We needed money to create the framework around which we would build our pretend life, and I wanted to do it on my own terms. I needed a home and a place where he and I could be together without attracting attention. We would be doing whatever the movement required of us, which included hiding freedom fighters and political figures, transporting those under surveillance out of the country, and much more that I could not then have imagined.

As a paramilitary commander in Spear of the Nation, Khabazela was required to travel within and beyond the borders of South Africa. He needed a role in which he could be invisible when he was present; the kind of role in which no one would miss him if he was absent. That meant we needed space, isolation, and a cover story that was sustainable. We agreed that we would have the best chance of success in a rural area, and I decided to buy a farm.

True to their promise, the ANC provided me with a false identity. And because the way to successfully live a lie is to make it as true as possible, my story was that I had owned a farm near the Rhodesian border with my husband, who had been killed in a farming accident. Now alone, I had sold the farm and was trying to decide what to do with my life. The ANC provided me with a new name—I was to become Grace Michaels—and with the forged papers to prove it. I came to know the story well, to depend on it for legitimacy, and to tell it so well that even I began to believe it was true.

The inheritance from my father was in a safety deposit box in Switzerland, and the key was in the hands of his attorney, Tony Griswold—Uncle Tony—whom I had not seen for almost six years. If I was going to buy a farm, I needed to find out exactly what my inheritance was, and what it could buy me. That meant a trip to Switzerland. But first I had to make contact with Uncle Tony, who by now was himself under surveillance. He found it increasingly difficult to get around without being followed, but he wanted to see me, and was determined to hand me the key in person. Via notes in the pockets of clothes purchased and delivered to his office, telephone calls made from restaurant phones and train tickets delivered to a post office box in Pietermaritzburg, we arranged to meet.

At that time, flights to Europe departed from Johannesburg, and the safest way to make the journey to Johannesburg was by overnight train from Durban, which was a six-hour drive from Lungile's homestead in Zululand. Uncle Tony arranged to travel to Durban for a business meeting a few days earlier, and once he had been seen to conclude his business, he would take the train back to Johannesburg. We agreed that I would be on the same train, and that we would meet once in transit.

I made the six-hour journey from Lungile's homestead to Durban in a rickety farm truck. My driver was an American hippie who had dropped out of college and come to South Africa to support the ANC. He had no clue what he was involved in, and I didn't have either the patience or the energy to explain it to him. He was a sweet boy—but that didn't stop him from being arrested, and then disappearing.

I mention him because his arrest and eventual discovery may give you a sense of the time we lived in. It wasn't just black South Africans who were in jeopardy—it was anyone who supported the cause of freedom. The regime was violent, angry and frightened, and we lived with fear from morning until night. That fact influenced all aspects of our lives and defined the choices we made.

I remember seeing the boy's parents on the international news, seeking information about him. They found nothing—but a few years later his broken body was one of many discovered inside a barbed wire compound that turned out to be one of the Special Branch's hidden interrogation centers. It was in a restricted rural area outside Johannesburg, and contained locked cells, instruments of torture, and gory evidence that they had been well used.

While in Zululand my hair had grown out. Now I dyed it light brown, with blond highlights. One of the few things Lenny and Khabazela had in common was that they both loved my mouth—I was self-conscious about my lips for years after Lenny told me that they were like ripe fruit. To deflect attention from them, I used the palest pink shade of lipstick I could. At the nearby Indian market I found a cheap suitcase, and then went into the city and bought a few changes of clothes—just enough to get me to Switzerland. Wearing a pair of narrow, Brigitte Bardot sunglasses, a pastel blouse and capri pants with matching pumps, I boarded the overnight train to Johannesburg. Sitting in my compartment as we pulled out of the station, I thought back to the last time I had seen Uncle Tony.

Khabazela may have told you already that as I drove back from the Rhodesian border after dropping him off to recuperate safely after he had been shot, I was arrested and held without trial. Despite the fact that they had no evidence to charge me with, Lieutenant Viljoen, who had been at my father's house that night, refused me permission to attend my father's funeral. I was pregnant with you, but they kept me in isolation, and I was permitted no contact with Lenny. Viljoen is long dead, but his callousness fueled my anger for years.

You were born several months after I was released, and all I wanted to do was spend time with you. Eventually I was able to leave you for short periods, and one of the first outings I made was to see Uncle Tony, who had been a fixture in my life throughout my childhood. He lived alone in a large, gracious home in Saxonwold, and he gave wonderful parties. My parents may have suspected that he was gay, but back then homosexuality was never discussed in polite company. He was short and funny, sported a small grey mustache, and dressed faultlessly in the most conservative of British suits. His one concession to a hidden flamboyance was that his bow-ties were always a little—just the tiniest bit—too colorful.

We met in his legal offices in downtown Johannesburg. He ushered me into his study—a strange mixture of dark panels and pastel-colored fabrics—closed the door, and took me into his arms. There were tears in his eyes and on his cheeks when he finally released me.

"Who would have thought it would come to this," he said. "Little Michaela Davidson in jail. And they wouldn't let me see you until after your father was buried. I tried everything, Michaela, but they had you in isolation."

"I know," I said, trying to smile. "I was there. And I haven't been Michaela Davidson since I married Lenny."

"Of course," he said.

We sat down and went over my father's estate. I had not counted on much of an inheritance, but he had run a dental practice for thirty years, and I was surprised that there was little beyond a bank account, and a small stock portfolio. The house, which was worth a fair amount, was highly mortgaged.

"Your father was a very cautious man, Michaela. You know how uneasy he was with the political situation. He was so sure the country was about to explode that he planned to take your mother overseas once they retired."

"Where to?" I asked, feeling offended. "He never said a word to me."

"After she died it became a non-issue—without her, he really didn't want to go anywhere. And now all the resources he put aside for his retirement fall to you."

"All the resources he put aside don't amount to much, do they?" I asked. "How was he going to live?"

In answer he went to one wall of his office and unlocked a safe, from which he withdrew a small brown envelope.

"His retirement," he said, unfolding the envelope and taking out a small key, "is in a little box in a Swiss bank. I have no idea how much is there, and he never told me. But I imagine there's enough. Most of it is in cash, and there are a few uncut stones that probably aren't worth much. But he's been adding to it for twenty years. And when he didn't have the cash, he would refinance the house and take out a bigger mortgage." He refolded the envelope, replaced the key, closed the safe and spun the lever. "I'll keep the key here, along with the account number you'll need to get access to the box. It'll be in a sealed envelope in your name, in the event anything happens to me. But whenever you need to get into the box, Michaela, just call, or get a message to me. I'll arrange to get it to you." He looked at me for a long moment, in silence, his eyes trying to tell me something. "Wherever you happen to be," he said softly.

That was the day he offered—almost insisted—on giving me a ride. He said that his chauffeur would drop him at home, and then take me wherever I needed to go. When we went outside, his car was waiting, and leaning against the door, in a khaki uniform, was his chauffeur. It was Khabazela, whom I hadn't seen since I dropped him at the Rhodesian border. I began to realize then that the idea of serendipity is appealing, but in life there are few coincidences. And no mistakes.

Almost six years had passed since that last meeting with Uncle Tony, and the landscape of all our lives was changed beyond recognition. You and Lenny were gone; we were living in Zululand, fugitives from the law. Uncle Tony had morphed from one of the most respected liberal attorneys in the country into a man suspected, at best, of harboring anti-government sentiments, and at worst, of treason and sedition. The fact that we had to meet on a train, and that we had to so carefully arrange the meeting, would have been unthinkable a few years earlier.

Once the train was on its way and the conductor had come by to stamp tickets, there was a knock on the door. Uncle Tony came in. He took one look at me, apologized, and swiveled on his heel as if to leave, convinced that he had the wrong compartment. I giggled at his embarrassment and he stopped, turned and looked at me, speechless.

"Hello," I said, grinning at him. "Aren't you going to give me a hug?"

In answer he pulled the shade down over the door and turned back to me. "Good God," he said, "I would have sworn that nobody I know could possibly look like you. Thank goodness you have such a distinctive laugh."

He looked weary, but he was unchanged—mostly imperturbable, impeccably dressed, wearing a dark blue suit and a bright yellow bow-tie. I stood up and we hugged each other. And to my surprise, I began to cry. I hadn't cried in the almost twelve months we spent in Zululand; didn't remember crying when my father died and I was taken to prison. But now, despite my best efforts, in Uncle Tony's familiar, cologned embrace, I wept like a little girl. He was the last link to my parents, to predictability, and to the stability my life once had. As he held me in his arms I was overcome by a sense of relief and safety. I thought it was the last time in my life I would feel safe —but I also knew that it was an illusion.

By the time we reached Johannesburg, having already said our goodbyes, I had memorized the name and address of the bank in Zurich, and in my cosmetics case was the tube of Colgate toothpaste Tony had given me. He had unrolled the bottom and inserted the deposit box key inside, re-rolling it with meticulous care, and it looked like any half-used tooth-paste tube, bent and squeezed in the middle. I took a taxi to a shabby hotel not far from the station, and at the registration desk, with my heart in my mouth, managed to identify myself for the first time as Grace Michaels. My hand shook as I signed the name.

I thought of my mother and smiled through the fog of urine as I climbed the hotel stairway. She would have understood and perhaps even envied my living in a hut in Zululand, without a proper bed or a bath-room, but she would have been horrified to see me, dressed like a cheap tart, entering this seedy Johannesburg hotel. For my part, I had forgot-ten what it was like to sleep on a proper bed with a soft mattress, and I looked forward to the luxury, even in this place. But when I reached my room all I could do was lie on the bed, shivering, as alone as I had ever felt in my life.

Switzerland, 1964

The next day I made my way to the airport. Using my new passport and the ticket provided by the ANC, I boarded the plane to Switzerland. By the time I arrived in Zurich, I had settled into being Grace Michaels. I was a young woman excited to be in Europe for the first time, anony-mous, liberated from my history, and about to have the means to reinvent myself. Zululand receded into the distance.

I registered at a hotel my mother would have approved of, took a lengthy bath, and treated myself to an elegant dinner in the hotel dining room. I ordered a half-bottle of French burgundy, and as I put my nose to the glass, I gagged—at the richness of the wine, and at its power to evoke the past. It had been a long time since my last meal in such an environment, and I began to realize that traveling back and forth between two worlds was more complex than it seemed. I had roast duck, served with tender pota- toes, salad, and a delicious chocolate mousse for dessert. I watched myself remembering how to use the right knife and fork, to sit up straight, to avoid warming the wine by cupping the base of the wine glass, and to balance it instead by holding the stem. But I also knew how to eat *mielie* porridge with three fingers, and all these rules seemed like simpering trivialities.

The next morning I removed the key from the toothpaste tube and washed it. The metal retained the minty scent of toothpaste, and at the bank I was suffused with the smell of Colgate as I handed the key to the bank clerk. He ushered me through the barred gate and into a small, locked cubicle, and I found myself sitting in an armchair, staring into the lockbox.

I opened it and looked in. It contained several brown currency enve- lopes, and a letter in my father's hand.

I unfolded the letter and smelled my father's pipe tobacco; ran my thumb over the texture of the paper and remembered the solid, warm feel of his forearm, covered in wiry grey hair. As I read his handwriting I heard his voice, saw the expression in his eyes as if we were face to face, engaged in one of our discussions—he, loving, logical, patient, trying to hide the degree of his concern for me; and I, defiant, self-righteous, and furious that as my role model and greatest supporter, he was unable to see that my way was the right way.

His letter was undated, but I knew that Uncle Tony had made a trip to Switzerland the year before my father died, and he must have vis- ited the bank and left my father's letter there for me. At that time, my mother was already gone, and you had not yet been conceived. My father had made no comment about my subversive activity, and I thought he knew nothing. How wrong I was.

My Dear Daughter,

If you are reading this, both your mother and I are at rest. We have done our best by you—but in some ways, it has not been good enough. We would have taught you differently had we been prescient enough to foresee the deterioration of our country into a rabid police state. For better or worse, how you respond to it will define your life's direction. Based on who you have become, I suspect that it will be for the worse.

Never doubt that I admire—even envy—your commitment. But I fear that your unwillingness to compromise will lead to personal choices that are unwise and painful. It is a relief to me, and it will be to you, too, that neither your mother nor I will be there to witness the hardships this will cause you.

You are always against those in power, constitutionally unable to walk away from defending the defenseless. As a result you are always in the line of fire. But even now, you have choices. Your best chance for a peaceful life is for you to take your family and move elsewhere, far from conflict. That is what your mother and I wish for you, if you can find such a place.

The money we have saved is now accessible to you; it will give you the means to make a new start. Some of it is in a form that you may find unusual for a dentist with no financial acumen—but I have had some interesting patients over the years. Be careful not to convert these assets into cash until you understand their full value.

I have no wish to dictate from the grave, and I have full confidence that whatever decisions you make will be for the greater good, although I might wish that your own personal welfare and comfort were higher on your priority list. The future is yours, Michaela; you have proven that you have courage enough for us all.

  With my love

  Papa

There were four currency envelopes. The first three contained banknotes in English pounds, South African rand, and U.S. dollars. It seemed that my father was keeping all his travel options open, and there was enough cash—several thousand pounds sterling—to get me comfortably wherever I wanted to go, and to keep me there for at least awhile before generating some other means of support. In the last currency envelope there was another lockbox key, this one different in appearance from the first, and detailed directions to another bank.

  That afternoon I followed the directions and made my way to the second bank, which turned out to be several blocks away, and sat again in a cubicle before another closed lockbox. This one held only a single item: a small, black leather purse. I untied the purse-strings, drew it open, and looked inside. It was lined with purple velvet, and at the bottom there was a nest of small, rounded stones. I poured them out onto the padded black velvet mat on the desk and counted them. Seventeen. Several were yellowish, a few had red or blue tones, but they were all dull, and they looked like cheap glass pebbles.

  I imagined my father receiving the stones from patients who had little else to give, and smuggling them one or two at a time across the ocean with great care and much anxiety. I couldn't imagine how much money and effort he had wasted on them, and I was saddened for him, and angry, and then disappointed. But he was a dentist, after all, a trusting man who sometimes took sacks of coal, or chickens or bushels of fruit as payment for his services. What could he have known of precious stones?

But my father was wiser than he seemed. I had never seen uncut diamonds before, and I should have had more confidence in who he was. I took the stones to three appraisers recommended by the bank, and despite small differences in their valuations, all three men assured me that my father's rough stones were high grade uncut diamonds. Several were flawless, and although some were small, others weighed in at more than three carats.

I went into a little café to absorb my good fortune over a coffee and a Swiss chocolate pastry. The numbers were so far beyond what I had anticipated that I didn't quite know what to think. The appraisers estimated that I could sell the rough stones for three hundred thousand dollars. That translated to about two hundred and fifteen thousand rand. To give you an idea of how much money that was, after my father's death my parents' home in Cyrildene sold for eight thousand rand. In 1964, you could buy good farmland for a hundred rand a hectare—which meant I could afford to buy a medium sized farm and still have most of my money left.

I sold eight of the stones and transferred funds to the account of Grace Michaels at Barclay's Bank in Durban. When I departed Zurich, there were nine uncut diamonds left in the safe deposit box. I liked the idea of keeping my options open.

nineteen

MICHAELA

Natal, South Africa, 1965

Khabazela would have been just as happy on a sugar cane farm closer to Zululand—but I had no interest in farming sugar cane. The farm I liked best was in the Midlands, about three hours inland from Durban. It was owned by a Scottish family who had used it as a hunting lodge since the 1890s. The current generation was more interested in buying upscale property in Johannesburg and holiday homes in Cape Town, and they wanted to sell.

Luckily for me, one of Khabazela's brothers and members of his mother's family lived in a village close to the farm; several of his relatives already worked on the property. The main black foreman, the farm *induna*, was his uncle. As a result we were able to make the point to the ANC that we had natural local support, and argued strongly for this location.

I have vivid memories of discussions leading up to the purchase of my farm, discussions that today seem laughable, in which I was encouraged by some members to relinquish my bourgeois attitudes and my money, and allow the Governing Council to decide where I should live. In the process I learned much about the inner workings of the ANC. Some members of the Council belonged to the banned Communist Party; others were adamantly capitalist and wanted nothing to do with anything that smacked of socialist or communist doctrine. Still others wanted to divorce themselves from any white organizations and all white people— while the most pragmatic group was willing to include whites who could be useful, until such time as they were no longer needed.

At the end of the day, however, this would be where I made my life. I listened to all the Council's suggestions—but I made it clear that since this property was to be purchased with my money, I was determined to make the final decision about where I felt most comfortable. Khabazela and I might be able to pretend, at least under cover of dark, that we lived together, but we all knew that the reality was not so clear. He and I could not be seen to be living together, nor could we be seen in public as anything other than mistress and servant.

My strongest argument was that the farm would succeed secondarily as a safe house for the ANC only if it fulfilled its primary purpose as my home. I kept referring back to my life in Johannesburg, when I took part in banned and illegal activities—and the only reason I was successful for so long, I thought, was that I lived a relatively conventional, suburban life. At least, that's what it seemed at the time. I turned out to have deceived myself, blind to the obvious reality that it was impossible to live a normal family life, and at the same time to break laws, shield fugitives, and participate in activities that threatened an already beleaguered totalitarian regime.

Even if I had wanted to, I could never have anticipated what my daily routine in the Midlands would be like. As life on the farm took shape, I began to see it in terms of yield, just as I learned to evaluate the calving yield of the herd each spring, and the sorghum yield, and the yield of the corn fields, and the apples and pears we grew. I realized how absurdly grand my expectations of home had been, and I began to see, in the yield of our lives, how little of what I wanted was possible, how much less was probable, and, at season's end, how meager my actual harvest was. In comparison, my life in Johannesburg, masquerading as a clandestine revolutionary, turned out to have been an idyll of stability and peace.

The old hunting lodge became my farmhouse; the large, open central room became the place I lived. It had a huge fireplace open front and back, so that it also served to warm the kitchen in winter, and one wall of the living room opened onto a verandah overlooking the stream that ran through the property. Just across the stream, the foothills of the Drakensberg began, and on clear days, the soaring shape of the reclining giant and the outline of the amphitheatre jutted up through the line of horizon. It was a place of vast beauty and solitude, its fertile valleys rich in wildlife, and in a different world, a different time, Khabazela and I might have chosen no place more perfect. But all we had was our time, and in our world there was no perfect place. So we settled in, and began the life we were allowed.

While the purchase of the farm was taking place and final papers changed hands, he was absent—out of the country, setting up a military training camp somewhere across the border, maybe in Angola. I learned that he would tell me where he had been, or where he was going, only if having the information would not compromise me. I learned never to ask where he had been, and eventually accepted that when he came home, he might be in a state of exhaustion, frequently bruised or otherwise injured. Often, in the days after his return, there would be a news release about a border skirmish between the South African military and Spear of the Nation, or a meeting of operatives outside the country. It wasn't difficult to guess that he had been involved.

It took me years to learn what it meant to run the farm, and I would have been lost without the staff of people I inherited from the previous owners. Gradually I came to know the house staff, and those I liked remained on the farm; those I felt I could not trust, I eventually let go.

The farm foreman, Brian McWilliams, was at first invaluable to me. He lived with his wife and children in the overseer's cottage at the entrance to the property, about a mile from the farmhouse. I spent an hour each afternoon with him, poring over the farm accounting books, learning the business of the farm—what our seasonal produce was and the economics of each; where we made our money and where we should be investing; how we bought or produced feed and seed, and where it made sense to risk capital.

At first Mr. McWilliams seemed pleasant enough. He was a burly, sandy-haired man in his mid-thirties, and he had golden hair growing in tufts from his open shirt collar and on the back of his hands. He had clear blue eyes and a sun-roughened face, and a thick beard through which his lips were barely visible. While at first I thought he had a humorous mouth, I came to recognize that what seemed like a good natured smile was actually a sneer. I think he wore the beard as camouflage because without it, he knew that he would have difficulty hiding what he felt. He spoke excellent Zulu, and I saw that with the farm workers he was authoritative and demanding, but that he treated them with what looked like a distant respect. It turned out that there was less respect than a need to keep his distance. He neither knew nor cared about them, and although he did not fear them as individuals, he was dependent upon their cooperation, and he feared their numbers. For their part, they seemed to understand the equation, venerating his position, while showing neither interest nor respect for his person.

Mr. McWilliams was kind to me, and respectful, and eager to explain what I did not know—but I sensed in him some kind of anger; a predatory quality I was unused to, and it made me uncomfortable to be around him. I knew soon that he would eventually have to go. He was too integral to the management of the farm, too involved in the daily running of the place, and too intrusive. There was no way we could use the farm as a safe house with him as overseer, and it would have been impossible for Khabazela and me to live the way we intended.

On my first day at the farm, McWilliams and I stood beside the chicken run, and he explained to me how the eggs were collected, how many were used on the farm, and the arrangement we had with a local collective to sell the remainder. As we spoke, a black man in his mid-fifties approached. He was unusually short and compact and he moved with the compressed energy of a short man—but his back was straight and his shoulders visibly muscular, and his loping stride said that there was nothing small about him. He wore baggy khaki trousers and a torn khaki work shirt that was too big for him, and he moved easily, bouncing on the balls of his feet and laughing as he greeted the women casting feed to the chickens. When he reached us he stood between McWilliams and me, and he removed the stained, khaki hat from his head. He had a pointed gray beard and an easy smile, and bright blue clay discs, about an inch in diameter, were inserted into his pierced earlobes.

"This is Solomon Mavovo, your *induna*," said McWilliams. And then, in Zulu, he introduced me as the new owner. Solomon looked only at me as McWilliams spoke. His eyes were bloodshot, piercing without being intrusive, and there was warmth in his glance that told me he knew something more about me than he was willing to let on. When McWilliams was through, Solomon gently reached out his right hand to me, and, in the way of Zulu address, placed the fingertips of his left hand tentatively on the inside of his right forearm as he did so. It was a sign of respect and an offering of peace from the distant past, when placing both hands before you was the only way to indicate that you concealed no weapons, and intended no harm. I took his hand.

"*Sawubona, Nkosikazi,*" he said. Hello, madam. I see you. And he did.

It would have been inappropriate for Solomon to mention Khabazela to me—but I knew that he was Khabazela's uncle. I felt comfortable with him immediately, and he turned out to be a wonderful presence in my life, unfailingly protective of me, upbeat and encouraging. He had started on the farm as a young boy herding cows, and his knowledge of the place was invaluable.

When he was giving instructions to the workers on the farm, speaking Zulu, he talked and moved in double time, a coiled spring, illustrating with his body where he wanted them to go, how he expected a shovel to be wielded or a tractor driven. While he was gesturing, the discs in his earlobes shook and bounced as if he were orchestrating their dance.

But to me he spoke slowly, his movements gentle and abbreviated as if I were an easily startled child. At first I found it irritating, thinking that he was talking down to me, making fun in his own way of this ignorant white woman who had enough money to buy a farm but had no idea what to do with it. It soon dawned on me, however, that this was his restrained way of showing respect. I don't know how much he knew about my relationship with his nephew, or about the work we were doing, or about the dual role the farm was intended to play, but these turned out to be irrelevant questions.

Solomon was a simple man. He had never been to the city, never seen a cinema, never ridden a bus. He walked several miles to the farm each morning, or rode there on the back of a tractor pulled wagon. He lived in the village with his three wives. He had no idea what a communist was, or why communism was so feared, and he would have laughed at the idea of putting a man under house arrest. But Solomon knew everything there was to know about the running of the farm, and he had eyes everywhere.

Each morning Solomon walked a different part of the farm with me so that I could discover precisely what I had purchased, learn the nature and the boundaries of my property, and meet one by one the men and women who worked for me. Sometimes we walked part of the farm perimeter; we spent other mornings with the workers harvesting potatoes in the fields, or with the cowherds, who shyly introduced me to the cattle, and told me the name of each of my cows. The farm workers didn't know quite what to do with me—and I had the sense that the previous owners were unlikely to have shown much interest in either the workings of the farm, or in the people who made it possible. I was increasingly grateful for the year we spent in hiding, when I had been forced to learn Zulu. Even so, there were times when Solomon had to intercede because even though I had some language, there were cultural barriers that could not be crossed with words alone.

While I was alone, Solomon insisted upon sleeping in the servant's quarters behind the house instead of going home to his family. Nothing I said would change his mind, and I will admit that I felt safer knowing that he was there. I didn't quite understand how this came about, but years later Khabazela admitted having told his uncle that we were lovers. He asked Solomon to watch out for me when he was away, knowing that the request would not be taken lightly.

One morning before dawn, three weeks after I moved onto the farm, I was woken by Solomon calling me from the kitchen. I dressed quickly and went to him, thinking at first that he had news of Khabazela. He beckoned to me from the kitchen door where he waited, holding my field boots in his hands.

"What is it, Solomon?" I asked, stepping into the boots.

He shook his head in disapproval. "It is not good, *Nkosikazi*. Come, I will show you, and you will see the problem that has come to sit on our doorstep."

Carrying a glass of water in his hand, he took me across the yard, past the rooms where he and the cook and the housemaid slept, through a clearing and into a grove of trees. A black man whom I assumed at first to be one of the farm workers sat slumped against a tree, a bloody bandage on the side of his head and his arm in a makeshift sling. There was blood on his clothes, and his face was drawn in exhaustion and pain. He tried to rise as we approached, but Solomon gently pushed him down and placed the glass of water in his hand. The man drank greedily.

"Here is Grace Michaels," said Solomon. "Tell her your story."

"Khabazela told me if I was in trouble, that I should come to this farm and ask for you," he said, looking at me. "Trouble has come, this you can see. And so I ask your help."

"When did you see him?" I asked.

"Less than ten days from today," he said.

"Where?"

He lowered his eyes in thought, and then looked up at me, attempting to smile. "On a hilltop in Zululand, not far from the homestead of your mother, Lungile."

I smiled back at him—it was the code we had agreed upon.

"This trouble that has come to you," I asked, "will it be bringing others behind you who are also in trouble, or are you alone?"

"I am only one, *Nkosikazi*."

"Can you tell us what has happened to you?"

He shrugged his shoulders and grimaced at the pain. "I have been wounded—shot through the arm—a week ago. I was making my way to my home, and I stopped where my sister works so that she could shelter me for the night. But the farmer she works for found out about me and he came to her room to beat her for taking me in. He was very surprised that I would stand up to him, but I could not allow her to be beaten, and so we fought, and I have cut his throat."

"*Cha*," said Solomon, clicking his teeth. "This is a very bad thing. How do you know that you are not followed? And what of your sister? You have not brought her with you, have you?"

He shook his head. "No, no, she is far from here, gone in the opposite direction. I am not followed—this thing happened three night's walk from here. I have been hiding in daylight, so although they are looking, they have no reason to come here."

"The danger is not here, yet," said Solomon, turning to me. "But it will come if someone sees him or talks about a stranger. Then, word will spread and police will arrive. It will not be good for us. We should hide him until he is strong enough, and then he must go."

"Get him to one of the servant's rooms for the day, then," I said. "He can rest, and tonight we can help him out to the field we were at yesterday—where the cowherds shelter in the rain."

"No, no," said Solomon, "there is a much better place. Go, *Nkosikazi*. If you are seen here it will raise questions. I will hide him today, and tonight I will take you to see him."

I walked the fields alone that morning, wondering how this man came to be three days walk from the farm, and whether he was telling the truth about his injuries. I wondered where they had met, and tried to guess where Khabazela might be. He could be undergoing military training—or torture—in as distant a place as Tanzania or China, or he could be sleeping in the servants' quarters behind the farm. Either way, I would know nothing until he chose to tell me. This may have been his way of protecting me—but while it probably afforded me a measure of physical safety, I felt isolated and lonely, high and dry, and fully exposed emotionally.

As I walked between two shoulder-high corn fields, sweating in the mid-summer sun, I realized that my feet hurt because I was kicking clods of dirt from the path carelessly, and in anger. The arrangement was not working, and, I thought, it would have to change when he returned. I couldn't even say "when" with confidence. Until he came home, it would be safer to say "if."

That night, long after dark, Solomon came to get me. I carried my first aid kit, which contained everything from antibiotics and cough syrup to needles and sutures. Solomon carried his stick in one hand and a bag of food over his shoulder, and he had a long flashlight protruding from his pocket. We walked silently through the deserted yard adjacent to the servants' quarters. Slits of yellow light shone from beneath closed doors, and sounds of muted voices and laughter drifted through the darkness as we passed. Solomon led me along a path I didn't know, around a grove of thorn trees and through a pasture. The moon was half full in a cloudless sky and it was easy to see our way, and I followed him easily for about fifteen minutes until we reached the base of a steep hill and the path seemed to disappear into the undergrowth. It didn't—but the foliage was so thick that no moonlight penetrated, and the path simply wound its way up the incline, around the trunks of huge shade trees. Solomon turned on the flashlight and focused it on the ground ahead of us.

The hill was steep, and I was breathless when we reached the top. For a few moments at the summit we were in moonlight again, but I followed Solomon down the other side and into the darkness again. He took my hand and led me off the path through the undergrowth towards what appeared to be a wall of rock. Within seconds we were in absolute darkness.

"Wait, *Nkosikazi*," he said, releasing my hand, "while I turn on the light. We are here."

In the glow of the flashlight I saw that we were in a narrow crevice that opened in the rock wall, and I followed Solomon deeper into the crevice until it closed over and became a cave that widened and rose around us. It was about twenty feet across, and at the highest point I couldn't touch the roof with my upraised arm. At one side of the cave, lying on a blanket and looking up at us, was the man I had seen that morning.

Solomon untied the sack and showed him the contents, enough food to last for several days. I knelt beside him and gently unwrapped the bandage around his head. He had a deep laceration along the side of his skull, but it was clean and healing well. I washed it, spread antiseptic on the wound, and redressed it. I did the same with the sling around his arm, and Solomon helped me roll him onto his unharmed side so that we could treat the wound on his shoulder.

The bullet had entered his upper arm just above the bicep and off to one side, so that it ripped right through the back of his deltoid muscle. He was unable to move his arm, and I had no way of telling whether there was any damage to the bone or shoulder joint. I could have drawn from memory the structure of the shoulder—but it didn't help me ascertain how badly he had been hurt. And even if I had known, what would I have done? The nearest hospital was hours distant, and anyway, that wasn't an option since I had yet to meet the local doctor and determine whether he was to be trusted. All I could do was clean and bandage the wounds, and make sure that he had a place to rest and enough to eat and drink. I felt helpless, and I knew that if this was to be a part of my life, I would need to either learn more about healing, or find someone to rely on who was more knowledgeable than I.

By the time I was through, my patient had fallen asleep again, and I repacked the first aid kit and rose to my feet. Solomon stood beside me, flashlight in hand.

"What is this place, Solomon?"

"It is just an old hole in the rock," he said, "a cave, where I came to play as a child. Very few know of this place—but I have brought many to hide here. The cave does not know a good man from bad; it cannot tell a black man from white, or a Zulu from some other, and so it shelters all. Once it hid the little hunters, so that they could make their paintings on the rock. Look," he said quietly, pointing his light at the wall.

I followed the light up to the top of the rock, where a series of painted figures leaped out at me—Bushman paintings of hunters, pursuing antelope and impala, and, lower down, and more recent, what were unmistakably the figures of two larger black men with rifles, battling against several Bushmen with bows and arrows.

I looked up at the rock paintings again, to see in them the only remnant of a vanished culture. The first people in the area, the Bushmen, were killed by fiercer, more sophisticated tribes who wanted to farm and hunt; they were unable—or unwilling—to find a way for their cultures to coexist. Then the Europeans came, and once they had helped annihilate the remaining Bushmen, they turned their superior firepower on the Zulu. And now, the players slightly different and the objectives slightly altered, we were still engaged in a continuation of the same struggle.

I went back to the farmhouse and spent the night tossing in my bed— it would never be a marriage bed, even if it played host to a man who was husband in all but name—kicking at the lonely, yet-to-be-consummated sheets, asking myself what I was doing with my life. But the next morning the phone rang, and my question was answered. We had a party line back then, and I knew that there could be any number of people listening—and

a voice I didn't know told me that the tractor starter motor I'd been waiting for had arrived, and would be delivered in a day or two.

Khabazela was the starter motor, and he was coming home.

We had barely seen each other since leaving Lungile's homestead.
Khabazela knew of my trip to Switzerland to access my father's funds, but
he had now been away for six weeks. I missed him with a physical longing that lived in my chest like a deep ache.

Like a lovesick Sheba in wait for her king, I mooned about the farm,
alternately ecstatic and tearful, at one moment thinking about the welcome home sign I would hoist, and the next furious that he had not yet
arrived, and that such a celebratory gesture was out of the realm of possibility. I wanted to have my hair done, wear my most revealing gown,
make up my face and dab perfume lightly on my neck, between my
breasts, on my thighs. I daydreamed of holding him, of being in his arms.

But while in my mind the husband of my heart was returning to my
bed, to most people he would be just another shabby worker in soiled
clothing returning to the farm, and it wasn't conceivable that he and I
could mean anything to each other. So I did nothing and went about my
business, and I hid my longing and excitement beneath a veneer of impa-
tience and the appearance of activity.

I first saw him the next afternoon, as I stood in the yard talking
to Brian McWilliams. The end of summer was approaching; there were
fields that needed to be prepared for planting, and crops ripe for harvest.

As McWilliams explained his harvesting plans to me, Solomon drove through the gate and into the yard in an ancient, mud-caked narrow-wheeled tractor, a man sitting on each of the rear mudguards. He stopped the tractor at the door to the shed, and one of the men jumped down and went inside. The other man moved slowly—he seemed to be waiting for Solomon, as the elder, to dismount first.

When they were both on the ground, Solomon, no higher than the other man's shoulder, took his elbow and led him toward us, speaking softly as they approached. The stranger wore a black cap and brown farm overalls that were worn in the knees and too short for him, and he walked with rounded shoulders, his eyes on the ground.

My body knew that it was Khabazela before I recognized him, and I felt a tremor of excitement and then a flush of warmth in my face even before the stooped stranger raised his head cautiously and glanced at me from under his cap. I stopped breathing as I looked directly into his eyes. McWilliams, noticing that I had glanced away from him, followed my eyes.

"What is it, Solomon?" he asked brusquely. "Who is this?"

Solomon nodded politely to McWilliams, but when he spoke it was to me alone. McWilliams didn't like it.

"*Nkosikazi*, this is the boy of whom I have told you, my sister's son. He has been in Durban, cooking in the big houses, and if you wish, he will work for you in the kitchen, and he will be in my room here on the farm. His name is Mandla Mkhize, and it will be good for me to leave him here, to watch over you when I am away."

I listened to Solomon's little speech, made for McWilliams' benefit, and I was mortified, at first for Khabazela, and then for myself. I looked at him, wondering what he was thinking, but his face was a mask, his mouth expressionless. Only in his eyes did I see any evidence of the man I knew was there, and I might have imagined even that—the impression on a stone surface of a sudden, fleeting ripple that quickly disappeared, leaving no trace. I looked at him again, trying to find some indication of how he wanted to handle this moment, but there was still nothing.

How we handled this first interaction in front of the farm overseer was important, and it would set the stage for what followed. Khabazela didn't want to initiate discussion—it would have been obvious that something was off. So he stood back, allowing me to control the conversation as I would have done in any normal interaction with a farm worker. Like all black people in South Africa, he had learned early to play the game of self-abnegation, to make himself smaller than he was in any conversation with a white person.

But now that I was in the game, too, I had to play the role life had assigned me—and I had to find my own way of playing it. I didn't know whether Khabazela was stepping back because he thought I would do better without his interference, or because he was testing me—trying to find out whether I would be dismissive and belittling, or whether, playing the white farmer to his black farmhand, I would find a way to be courteous and respectful. Either way, I realized that this was the beginning of what our public life would be, and while I wanted to make it as palatable as I could for him, it also needed to be real to anyone watching. It was a tall order, and I had not anticipated that McWilliams would be our first audience.

"*Sawubona*," I said.

He nodded, looking at the ground.

"Mandla, you are the son of Solomon's sister?"

"Yes, *Nkosikazi*."

"Then you are Mandla Mkhize, of the Mavovo, Gcwabe and Mumbo clans," I said.

For the first time he dropped the false slouch, raised his head and stood tall.

"It is who I am," he said, and for a brief second he showed me his warm, humorous mouth. Only I knew that his expression was in acknowledgement of the fact that I had remembered his clan names from a ceremony in Zululand. Solomon smiled widely, but McWilliams looked at me with raised eyebrows. This was the first time I had spoken Zulu in front of him, and he was unable to hide his surprise that I knew Solomon's clan names. He would never have given a moment's thought to the family names of his workers. But I was enjoying myself.

"These are ancient and honorable clans," I said. "This land is honored to have your uncle here as *induna*, caring for the farm. You would honor me if you took his advice and came here to work in my home."

He removed his cap, twisted it between his hands, managed to squeeze a shy smile from his face. I had never seen him do anything shyly, and I found it charming.

"That would make me very happy," he said, still smiling, "to come and cook for the *Nkosikazi*."

For a brief moment he glanced up at me, and I was shaken by the conflict I saw in his eyes. Humor and mockery; humiliation and self-control, and underlying all, a burning fury. And then, in the same smooth, servile voice, "she will be also happy, too, because I am a very good cook."

McWilliams laughed loudly as he turned to Solomon. "Your nephew thinks a lot of himself," he said.

"He is young still," said Solomon softly, "and he will learn." He smiled. "But he is right about his cooking. He has learned well in Durban."

Then, before McWilliams could respond, Solomon turned back to me.

"I will take him to my room, and get him some house clothes," he said, "and then I will have one of the girls show him the kitchen until you come back to the house. Come."

Khabazela nodded slowly to McWilliams, meeting his eye. Then he nodded in my direction and followed Solomon to the servant's quarters behind the farmhouse.

"He's an arrogant one," said McWilliams. "Shows what happens when these country boys leave Zululand and go off to the city."

"Thank you for your concern, Mr. McWilliams," I said, "But I think I can handle it. And if he doesn't work out in the kitchen, perhaps we'll find another place for him."

"Let me know if he gives you any trouble. If Solomon doesn't keep him in line, I can always find a place for him in the fields."

My new cook prepared and served me dinner that night, working side by side with Selina, the housemaid, who had been doing the cooking since I arrived, and who was relieved to have someone else in charge of the kitchen.

He picked a red rose from the garden and placed it in a vase on the table, and wearing the white jacket he had found in the pantry, with one eye on the kitchen door, he served me alone in the dining room. As he placed a half grapefruit before me, with a cherry at its center, he lightly brushed my hand with his. And when he returned to replace the grapefruit plate with salad, he paused briefly, his back to the kitchen door.

"I have missed you, my Michaela," he murmured.

"Nothing like the way I've missed you," I whispered, and then loudly, "thank you, Khabazela."

When he came in to remove my salad plate and serve me a dish of stewed chicken and vegetables, he touched the back of my neck.

"Each night away from you I have fallen asleep with your face before me," he murmured, "and with the feel of your skin beneath my fingers."

"Thank you," I said again, loudly. "Your uncle was right—they taught you well in the big kitchens in Durban. Where," I whispered, "did you learn to cook like this? And how can I eat your food alone, while you whisper love in my ear?"

"Very well, *Nkosikazi*," he said loudly, grinning. "I will leave you to eat in peace. But," he murmured, "I come to you after midnight, and then we will whisper together, when there is no food standing between us, and when you will find it easier to reply."

"I won't need anything else tonight. And please let Selina know that she can go for the evening." And then, in a whisper, "thank you."

When I was through I carried my dishes into the empty kitchen, rinsed them, and left them in the sink to be washed the next day. I made myself a cup of tea and sat out on the verandah in the breeze from the river, reading a three-day-old newspaper. I watched the sun fall slowly behind the hills, dragging shadows behind it, until the hilltops were lined in golden slivers of light that gradually dimmed and then went out, leaving me to sit in darkness, listening to the night sounds on my farm. The cicadas droned loud and rhythmic; stream frogs added their intermittent dark hum. There were distant barking dogs and the lowing of cows, mournful bird cries from the hills, and the human sounds—drumming, and the faint sound of Zulu harmonies from the village; laughter and quiet talk from behind the house, where the servants were eating their late supper, Khabazela among them.

I sat quietly that first night, my heart throbbing with anticipation at what the darkness held for me. I didn't know what to do with myself, and realized how hard I was gripping the arms of my chair only when my wrists became numb. I tried breathing deeply, attempting to take the African night into my body; willing it to absorb me into itself. I loved this place, and I wanted at that moment to be nowhere else—but it refused me, and I sat alone in my separateness until just before midnight. Then I rose and went inside, hoping that, when he came to me, he would be able to take me out of isolation, erase my loneliness, and make me feel as he always did—part of a grand, unknowable design that gave meaning to the little lives that are all we know.

As I write this to you, Steven, I have wondered whether to include the intimate details of my life as a young woman with Khabazela in this narrative; wondered whether you would find it inappropriate, disturbing, or even worthy of mockery or disgust. By now you are aware that young mothers have sexual thoughts and experiences; that they long for their men and for the intimacy of physical congress. I recognize now that because the relationship between us was forbidden, sexual thoughts of each other, making love, and the act of intercourse itself, were imbued with a dark power and with an intensity much greater than any sanctioned love I have ever experienced with another man. And because the hidden relationship we had was conducted in the dark of night, our intimacy was perforce sexual.

The girl I once was is gone; I write this as an old woman to a middle-aged son, and the reality is that neither of us knows the other. At this point, the worst you can do is refuse to read further. If I include intimate details here and perhaps elsewhere, it is in the hope that you will find them not just revealing, but illuminating. I do so knowing that you may find them instead distressing, or worse. They are a part of my own journey; a necessary part of your discovery of who I am, and who I have been.

I left the kitchen door unlocked, undressed in my bedroom and put on my robe. From the laundry closet I took two fresh bath towels and set them on the wooden stool beside the sink, drew myself a bath, and made sure that both the windows and the curtains were closed. When I first moved into the house, there were two shoulder-high wrought-iron stands

on the verandah, and I had them carried inside and placed at each end
of the bathroom. On each one I mounted three candles in brass holders,
intending to use them for just this event. I lit all six candles, removed my
robe and hung it on the back of the door, and turned off the tap and the
electric light. In the suddenly softened glow and the absence of sound, I
stood naked before the bathroom mirror, looking at the shadowed, darkened curves that were my body. I raised the hair off my neck and pinned
it around the top of my head, and then examined myself in the flickering
light.

At thirty-one I was slender; my belly betrayed no sign that I had ever
been pregnant or given birth, and my waist was still narrow above hips
that widened just enough to make me attractive in a womanly, rather
than a girlish, way. My breasts were small, but full and round, and to me
they seemed unchanged from what they had been before being milked by
a baby boy who was now nine years old. Having reassured myself as well
as possible that I was still as desirable as I had been a year earlier, I turned
from the mirror and submerged myself in the warmth of the huge, white,
claw-footed bathtub.

Khabazela came silently through the kitchen into the empty house,
and he was already naked when he slowly closed the bathroom door
behind him and stood shadowed in candlelight. He was all at once dark
and brightly gleaming, curved and straight and arched, delicately made
and thickly muscled. He was elongated and squat, smooth and yielding,
and as firm and shaped as chiseled stone.

I reached for him as he lowered himself into the tub, and he sat facing me in the flickering shadows. Our eyes locked onto each other, he
raised his fingers to my earlobe and traced down the side of my neck to
my shoulder, across to the V of my collarbone. I knew where his fingers
were going, and at the anticipation of his touch I felt a shudder of pleasure run through me. And then his fingers submerged, to trace the shape

of my body beneath the surface. The water was warm, but his touch was warmer, and when I soaped my hands and went to wash him, the heat coming off his body made me gasp.

We washed each other gently, in silence; he let me soap his hair, and he leaned back in my arms so that I could rinse the shampoo from his head. When I was done he remained lying back against me and I ran my hands gently down his sides and his belly to where he emerged from the surface hard and thick, and I held him in one dwarfed, transparent hand, while with the other I twined my fingers in his tight curls and felt underneath where the skin of his scrotum loosened in the warm water.

When we were through washing, we rose up out of the heat and into the cool air and stood in the draining bathtub in a wet embrace, his body hard against the entire length of me, and with one arm hard about my waist he raised me just enough to enter me and we made love while I stood with my arms about his neck and one leg curled about his hips, pulling gently at his lips with my teeth, and kissing his full mouth with mine.

We dried each other and he led me to my bed; we pulled down the covers and made love again slowly on the cool, white sheets. The only sounds we allowed ourselves were those we could not prevent, and it was anyone's guess as to which of us was less disciplined, or more pleasured, than the other.

When we were through we lay in each other's arms. I lay with my head on his chest, the warmth of his skin on my cheek, the sweet acrid smell of our fresh lovemaking in my nostrils, and it was all bound together by the beating of his heart in my ear, by the echoing vibration that followed each beat, and by my astonishment at the delicacy, and the power, and the resonance of the muscle that pushed life blood through this man's veins.

"So, Michaela, here you are on your farm. Now that you have it, are you happy?"

"It's not the farm alone that makes me happy," I answered, "but having you here with me. Can you tell me where you've been? Or how long I have you before you leave again?"

"I can't tell you much," he said as he ran his fingers lightly through my hair. "Only what cannot harm you. The Special Branch can extract information from a stone—and if you are interrogated and they take from you information about where I've been, you'll be charged with treason along with me." He paused. "I have already once been responsible for landing you in jail. If it happens again they will discover that Grace Michaels is really the escaped terrorist, Michaela Green, and this time they will make sure that there is no escape."

"I know you want to protect me," I said. "I don't need to know the details of the operations you're involved in. But you can't expect me to live in complete ignorance, worried about where you are and what you're doing. We didn't get into this so that you could be the wandering freedom fighter and I could stay home and tend the fire. For the last six weeks I didn't even know whether you were alive or dead, Khabazela. And the first news I had of you was three days ago. That's not fair."

"Solomon told me about Jonathan, the injured man up in the cave. You were determined to tend the wounds of your patient." He smiled, stroking my neck. "You are your father's daughter."

His fingers on my neck stopped short, his body stiffened, and the smile disappeared. For a moment I saw on his face the uncompromising harshness that made him a successful commander for the ANC.

"Jonathan has acted foolishly, and we are all endangered by what he has done."

"But he was trying to protect his sister," I said. "Should he have let the farmer beat her?"

"He endangered his sister in the first place by going to her for help. Others would have helped him—but he was not thinking clearly. For us, it doesn't matter that he did away with a farmer who would have beaten his sister and killed him, but his actions have had other consequences. Now his sister is a fugitive without a job; the police are on the hunt for a murderer, and you can be sure that the Special Branch has been called in." He paused, searching in himself for the softly spoken lover who had been eclipsed moments before. Eventually I felt his body relax, but the lover was gone, and in his voice there was still the anger of betrayal.

"The time will come when this kind of attention is inevitable," he said, his voice dropping to a whisper, "but we're not ready. We're training fighters in camps across the border; there are operations planned inside the country that will target military and government installations. Our objective is not to kill people, Michaela, but to show them that we have the power to make the country ungovernable by destroying the infrastructure. This is not about random violence, or revenge; it's not terrorism, where people are rightly afraid of being killed in their beds, and we don't want to give the government the ammunition to label us as terrorists. We can have much greater political effect if we are seen as an organized military operation with discipline, a command structure, and an overall plan."

He stopped and swallowed, took a deep breath. "Jonathan acted without thought. But it will not happen again. He is now a liability for us, and I have had him taken back to his home near Eshowe. He is not happy with my decision, but we are done with him."

"But he's badly injured. I've been taking care of him, and he can barely walk. How are you having him moved?" I sat up angrily, his eyes and then his hand moved to my swaying breasts. "No," I said as I took a handful of sheet and covered myself. "How could you do this without talking to me first?"

There was a smile on his lips as he raised himself up on his elbow, but it was not a smile I had seen before. He took the sheet and slowly, very firmly, pulled it from my hand until I was fully exposed, and as he passed his eyes over my body the trajectory of his vision left a burning sensation on my skin, like sunlight through a magnifying glass. Then he knelt between my thighs and, with the palms of his hands on my shoulders, he pushed me onto my back.

"This bed will serve many purposes," he said softly. He was no longer whispering; his face was inches from mine, and I felt his voice reverberate in my chest. "But it will never be a place for you to question my command decisions. Not ever."

Then, tenderly, with a relentlessness that frightened me but that I could not oppose, he lowered his hips to mine, and that night I knew what it meant to be possessed by a man, and to be fully known. It exposed me fully; laid me bare, deprived me of every shred of personhood and individuality, even of the social convention of consent. I was surprised, outraged, pleasured, all at the same time. I wanted to eject him and throw him off me, pummel him with my fists, wind my arms about his neck and embrace him, and all my ambivalent impulses converged in my constricted throat and came out as a huge gasp.

Had I resisted him, Khabazela would have stopped. But although I wanted to, I could neither oppose him nor struggle against him. To my astonishment, and in the midst of my fury, I was content in that moment to watch the expression on his face, and to be his vessel.

twenty

MICHAELA

Natal, South Africa, 1966

My first summer on the farm came to an end with the last apples on our trees, as the temperature dipped and frost appeared. As the dry winter approached, the grasses began to fade. The sun set earlier; once it began to dip behind the mountains, the warmth of the day quickly dissipated, and nights were bitterly cold. We had no central heating then, and late each afternoon Selina lit a fire in the fireplace so that I could add kindling as the evening wore on. First thing in the morning when she came in, she made sure that it was lit again.

Khabazela was away when I received an invitation to a meeting of the local ladies club, which went by the name of The Cultural Society.

Under normal circumstances I would have declined. It was the last place on earth I wanted to be, and it was a given, I thought, that I would find no like- minded people among them. On the other hand, they might consider it strange for a new woman in the community to want no part of them, and it was important that I not stand out. I was also lonely, and it was beginning to dawn on me that if I didn't begin building a life in the community, I wouldn't have one. So I accepted the invitation.

I went out of curiosity, not realizing that they had invited me for the same reason. The members were almost all of Scottish and English descent; the Afrikaans farm wives were not included. They didn't know who I was or where I came from—but I had bought a farm from one of their long-time Scots neighbors and they wanted to find out what I was up to. What they saw was an attractive, well-turned out young woman who lived alone, and ran a substantial farm without the presence of a husband or father. They had no difficulty letting me know how they felt about me—but at first, I had no idea that for many of them, the threat I posed was too much to bear.

I had spent almost three months on the farm with little socializing, and arriving at the polo club was reminiscent of the culture shock I had felt when I returned to Durban after spending a year in Lungile's homestead. I gave my coat to a blue-and-white uniformed maid, and as I approached the clubhouse, I heard the sound of women talking and laughing. For a moment I felt glad to be there, optimistic about the possibility of friendship. Then I entered the clubhouse, and I knew I had made some bad choices.

There had been no one to consult, no one to ask what the women would be wearing. In the absence of information, I decided that I would wear my bank suit—which is how I thought of the beige linen suit that I bought in Switzerland before I visited my father's safe deposit box. The suit was simple and elegant, with a cropped jacket, a narrow knee-length skirt, and matching beige heels. The sleeves were three-quarter length, and the whole ensemble had the Jackie Kennedy look that was in vogue in America. It had been months since I wore any makeup, and something in me objected to giving this event too much importance. So I wore pale pink glossy lipstick, and nothing else. My hair, dark and short, fell naturally to my neck. I should have recognized that the look was too stylish and too urban—that it made me look overly tall and fashionable; more attractive and younger than any of my neighbors were willing to have me be.

The women wore full-skirted, flowered and print dresses belted at the waist, some with puffed sleeves and sweetheart collars, or light colored blouses and darker, pleated skirts. Several wore small hats with little veils, and white lisle gloves. They were sitting at little tables, sipping tea out of blue and white china cups. On each table was a teapot, and a platter of sandwiches—watercress or egg salad on white bread points. They recognized me as I arrived, the only unfamiliar face, and as each table took note, all heads turned towards me. Sound and movement slowly evaporated, and the room filled with silence.

One of the women rose nervously and walked toward me.

"You must be Grace," she said.

She looked to be in her late forties, with graying hair above a round, youngish, face. She wore a pink and yellow flowered print dress, a shiny red belt, and a small, brimless eggshell colored hat secured by a dainty hat pin to the top of her head.

"I'm Eileen," she said with a tense smile, "Eileen Gregory." She took my hand and shook it. "I'm so glad to meet you. We've all been a little remiss in not welcoming you before now. Let me take you around and introduce you."

I had already met several women at other meetings or at the cooperative, and as we went around the room, a few greeted me warmly.

Most, however, were curious and distant, even cold. We came to a table at which all but one of the women reached over and shook my hand. She waited until I had greeted her table mates, and then looked up at me. She was probably a little older than I was, overweight and red haired. She didn't introduce herself, and she kept hold of her teacup and saucer, making clear that she had no intention of extending a hand to greet me. Her voice was brassy and loud—either she had no idea how loud, or she felt so insignificant that she would do anything to make herself heard.

"You met my husband, Graham, at the Cooperative," she said. "Graham Collins."

I remembered him—a big man with a soft voice, a nice sense of humor, and hungry eyes. "Yes," I said. "We talked about sorghum and cattle feed. He was very kind."

"He remembers you, too," she said grimly. "In fact, he thought you were quite the thing. Very sympathetic, he was, with the difficulty of your new situation."

I was puzzled for a moment, wondering what I had unwittingly revealed. Then I remembered telling him my cover story—after my husband's death in an accident, I sold our farm in Rhodesia and returned home to South Africa, resumed my maiden name, and made a new start.

"Yes," I said, "it's quite an adjustment, but I'm learning to manage." I paused; no one spoke. "Thank you for inquiring," I continued in my politest voice.

"If there's anything I can help you with," she continued, "you can ask me."

"Thank you," I said. "That's most generous."

"But my husband," she continued quickly, unable to hold back the words, glaring at me through thickened lashes, "has his hands full managing our farm."

I was startled by her vehemence, and by the openness of her jealousy, and I'm sure it must have shown on my face.

"Oh, I'm quite sure he has his hands full," I said eventually, managing a smile. I would have said more, but Eileen Gregory took my arm and pulled me away.

"Let's move around, dear," she said. "Everyone else wants to meet you, too. I'm so sorry," she whispered, her round cheeks flushed with embarrassment. "Please, don't take Madeleine too seriously—she means no harm."

Madeleine Collins was unpleasant, and it would be a long time before I spoke to her again. But she posed no danger—her lack of subtlety made her an open book. At the next table, however, I found Phyllis McGowan, a woman much more sympathetic to my manufactured plight. She was older than I was, and half a head taller, with pale, delicate skin and fine features. Rising to introduce herself, she took my hand in both of hers.

"Nice to finally meet," she said, pulling me closer, as if we had already made a connection. "I've heard so much about you." She had large green eyes, and she fixed them on mine. "You've been through quite an ordeal," she said. "You're a very brave young woman, to start over the way you have."

Had I been less concerned with hiding the truth about myself, I might have felt her interest in my story comforting, but her compassion was laced with questions.

"Must have been so difficult for you to pick up and sell your farm," she said. "We have friends in Bulawayo—were you near there?"

"We were closer to the northern border," I said.

"Oh," she said with surprise. "I didn't know there was much cultivation in that area. What did you farm?"

"We had a cattle farm," I said uncomfortably, making up the story from what little I had been told about the area. "We grew *mielies* and sorghum and sweet potatoes, and my husband planted grape vines, too. He always wanted a vineyard, but he was killed before the vines matured. The new owner will probably go back to staple crops, and the vines will go for firewood." I paused for effect. "But that's no longer my affair."

"No," she said, "but it would be nice for you to know what they decide to do. Are you in touch? I could have my friends in Bulawayo contact them for you."

"I know how to contact them if I need to," I said. "But I do appreciate the offer."

"That's good," she said, and to my relief, she dropped that line of enquiry. But she moved quickly on to the next. "So here you are, all on your own. I think it's wonderful that you chose this area to resettle. Do you have family nearby? I mean, are your people from here? It's difficult enough to manage as a woman in this community, but you need people to call on if you have problems. Running a farm without a man's hand can be terribly difficult."

"Some of us manage quite well," said a voice at my side, and I felt a solid hand on my shoulder. "Come on, Phyllis, we all want a chance to meet her."

Phyllis's pale face flushed with indignation, and I smiled as I turned away, relieved.

"Forced rescue," whispered the newcomer in my ear as she took my elbow and led me away. "Phyllis will milk you dry of information, and without even a bloody cup of tea for sustenance. Come on, let's get you set up."

She took me to the table furthest from the fireplace where two women watched us approach, sat down and patted the empty chair beside her.

"Letty," she said, "pour Grace a cup of tea while I make the introductions."

Across the table, Letty, with short grey hair, high cheekbones, and no makeup, took the instruction benignly, smiled at me, and poured. My rescuer continued.

"That's Letty MacGregor, Grace, pouring your tea. I'm Jane Williams. You don't know us yet, but you will. You've seen the sign for Glen Acres Farm on the way to the co-op? That's ours—we're a hop, skip and jump from your door."

I turned to look at Jane. She had a wide, elfish smile and big, clear blue eyes; her face was round, with a ruddy complexion, and her sandy hair was chopped short. She was solidly built, with a big bosom, and I was surprised to see that she wore khaki trousers, a print shirt with yellow flowers on a light red background, and a creamy silk ascot around her neck. She was not dressed for the occasion—but she was so confident, and she had such a pleasing manner, that she was, in her own way, appropriate.

"Thank you so much," I said. "If you hadn't turned up when you did I might have bolted."

"Wouldn't have blamed you," she said. "That woman's a vacuum cleaner for gossip. But you're not out of the woods yet—you still have to satisfy our curiosity."

"No you don't," said Letty, pushing a cup of tea in my direction, and looking at me out of calm grey eyes, "unless you want to. Be still, Jane, she'll bolt yet if you keep it up."

"Doesn't look much like a bolter to me," she said, grinning.

"You're being rude," said Letty. "You still haven't introduced Anna."

"Please, excuse my bad manners," she said. "Grace, that genteel lady across the table, who's been waiting patiently to be introduced to you, is Anna McWilliams, the better half of Brian."

I turned to look at her, surprised to see my foreman's wife at this gathering. I knew that Brian had a family, but Anna had not yet come to the house to introduce herself, and I didn't want to be intrusive, since the cottage they lived in was on my property.

"Hello, Mrs. Michaels," she said in a high, breathy voice. "I have meant to come by and introduce myself—I set aside some homemade peach jam for you. But I've been so busy with the children." Her face was long and narrow, and her hair, lank and pale, fell straight, hugging her scalp and her neck. She stared at me over the table. "We have four children, you know."

"Do come by," I said. "And bring the children, too. I've already met your oldest boy, Michael. Your husband brought him to the farmhouse last week."

She pushed her chair back and rose and her dress hung on her, a skinny woman with fleshless arms. She stood behind her chair, gripped the backrest with white knuckles, and fixed her eyes on me.

"I wanted to meet you, Mrs. Michaels, and I didn't want it to be at my home or yours. That's why I came here today." There was a nervous quaver in her voice. "To meet the woman Brian works for. And now I have, so I can go back to my husband and my children." She paused. "We have four, you know. Four young children."

Then she turned and rushed out, and there was a shocked silence at the table as we watched her go.

"Perhaps I should just leave," I said eventually, "before someone throws a teapot at me. What's the matter with these women?"

"You've created something of a stir in our little backwater, Grace," murmured Letty.

"But I haven't done anything," I objected.

"Not quite true. You've upset the natural order of things. Jane and I sometimes set people's teeth on edge, too—but they don't respond this viscerally to us."

"Apparently," said Jane with a wicked smile, "one woman living alone is more of a threat than two women living together."

"We're not after their husbands," said Letty, "and they know it. That's the difference."

"Oh," I shot back, "and you think I am?"

Jane laughed. "Don't be daft," she said.

"My dear, it's bad enough that you're single," interrupted Letty quietly, "but you're more attractive and younger than most of these women. If that weren't enough, you own your own farm. What Jane and I think doesn't matter—what matters is that you're enough of a threat to raise the hackles on most wives' necks."

"I assure you that I have no interest in their husbands. Graham Collins seems nice enough but I have no designs on him, and I can't imagine being interested in my foreman."

I was angry and defensive, and on the verge of telling them that I was quite happy with the man I had. But I bit my tongue.

"That's good to know," said Jane. "But Letty's trying to tell you in her very roundabout way that it makes no bloody difference to us. We've been looking forward to meeting you. We were saying over breakfast this morning how delighted we are that you're here, if only to divert some of the gossip from us."

"By and large this is a lovely place to live," said Letty, "and people don't have a choice but to put up with us. We don't need them—and I'm the eighth generation of my family to be farming this land. We belong. Besides, we do a lot of good in the community."

"You, on the other hand, are a newcomer," added Jane, "and you don't fit into the family stereotype. That makes you fodder for the gossip mill. Until you lose your looks or get a ring on your finger, they'll watch you like a hawk. Might as well be a witch living in the dark ages. Just get used to it, and choose who you spend your time with carefully." She reached over and patted my hand. "You're always welcome at our place."

"Right," said Letty. "In fact, I think you should come for supper next week. We'll have Andrew there, too—my brother—he says he hasn't met you yet. But he's the local sawbones—and you need to be on good terms with him if you're going to run a farm around here, so far from the nearest clinic."

"That would be wonderful," I said, grateful for the invitation, and for the opportunity to meet her brother, whom everyone called Doctor Mac. It would be useful to meet him socially, before I had a call for his medical skills on the farm. "When next week?"

"Wednesday night," said Jane. "Don't dress for dinner, and don't bring anything with you. Just show up. We have drinks at six."

I went home that night, had an early supper, and threw myself into bed, exhausted. I had made two friends, encountered a few hostile women who didn't know me from Eve and had no desire to, and I now had a new context in which to think of myself. Until then, I had seen myself only through my own eyes—as a woman living by choice in isolation, with no neighbors and no community, doing clandestine work and waiting, always waiting. It was the life I had selected and I was not unhappy with it—but it did have a bleak aspect.

Now, however, I knew that I had a place. Like a witch in the dark ages, to which Jane had compared me, I had a position in the community. But my position was tricky, a mixed blessing. I was a challenge to my neighbors' competence and their femininity; they saw me as young and beautiful, moneyed and able to compete with—and for—their husbands.

It was difficult to reconcile this image of myself with the other images I carried, because I was also escaped fugitive and lawbreaker; terrorist;

adulterer and marriage breaker, deserter of children and husband. I was a clandestine Jewess, white lover of a black man and, perhaps most difficult of all, I was a fraud, pretending to be someone I was not.

I lay in bed, wondering which of all these things I would choose to be if given a choice. To survive without going crazy, I knew that I would have to meld them into a single whole, and to reconcile them into a coherent version of myself. It may not yet have become completely true, but I believed with all my heart that I had traveled too far to ever go back to being only one thing, and that I had made my decisions. The time for choice was over.

The next day, after more than a week away, Khabazela came home. That night we lay together and I told him what happened at the ladies' tea. My bedroom was in darkness but for the firelight reflecting off my dressing table mirror. It cast soft shadows on everything in the room, and in the flickering dimness I could see his expressions. He smiled as I spoke, and his eyes moved over my face.

"You still define yourself through the eyes of other people," he said as he stroked my cheeks with his fingertips, "even though you know that you are invisible to them. This is a new experience for you," he continued softly, "but for us, it is a part of the life we live every day. Can you imagine how it would be for your *induna*, my Uncle Solomon, if he saw himself only through the eyes of the white men for whom he works? Or if I based my worth on your foreman's opinion of me? We would not survive, Michaela. In our world, the people we live among think us valueless; they have no idea who we are or what our lives are like. Imagine what it would be like if we depended upon them for our sense of self."

He was lying on his side with my head on his arm, and he ran his hand across my waist and down the side of my thigh.

"And now you have joined that world. You need to learn to walk among them the way we do—as if you were walking through water."

"Water?"

"Yes," he said. "They must be as transparent to you as you are to them."

The following Wednesday evening I took the old, faded army-green Jeep across the valley to Glen Acres Farm. It was only a ten-minute drive and I had passed by the entrance many times, but never turned down the dirt road that led to the farmhouse. It was lined with eucalyptus saplings, interspersed with the occasional old hardwood that towered over the road, and there were *mielie* fields on both sides.

Unlike my workmanlike operation where the farmhouse was cheek by jowl with the yard, Jane and Letty had a much more elegant setup. At the end of the long track the road forked, and the farmyard with its machinery, barn and chicken run were out of sight down to the right. Off to the left around a curving driveway was the old stone farmhouse, and although it was winter and the light was fading, the flowerbeds were still awash in color, and trees on the front lawn were covered in yellow and white blooms. I was envious—there was no time in my life for flowers.

As I walked up the path to the front door, I thought of Khabazela's reaction when I told him as we lay in bed together that I had been invited to dinner with Jane and Letty, and that Doctor Mac would be there.

"These are good people," he said, yawning. "Especially Doctor Mac. You know, they call him the White Zulu."

He stretched, and as he did his belly flattened and the muscles in his torso swelled and tensed. I ran my eyes down his dark body, taking in the contours of his chest, the sparse hairs around each bluish nipple and the narrow line of hair along his breastbone that pointed to his shadowed navel, and further down to the glistening nest at his groin. With my hands I retraced the path my eyes had taken, and I felt the heat emanate from him, through the smoothness of his skin, and the hardness beneath. His mouth opened into a wide smile, and I thought he was responding with pleasure to the touch of my hands. I willed him to reach out and respond in kind, but it was late, and he was weary.

"Tell the White Zulu," he said as he rolled over, "that Mandla Mkhize sends greetings."

I curled up behind him, full of forgiveness, and lay my arm across his hip. "How did he come by that name?" I asked. "The White Zulu?"

"Ask," he replied drowsily, and I could tell that he was still smiling. "He will tell you, and you will find his story very interesting."

I was still thinking of the smile on his face when Letty opened the door and ushered me inside. I handed her a bottle of red wine.

"I have no idea what it is, or how it tastes," I said, "but the previous owners left dozens of bottles of wine in the root cellar, and I thought we might try some."

"I'm sure it will be delicious," she said, leading the way into the sitting room. "Go on in and meet my brother—Jane's in there, too. I have to tend to the lamb."

She hurried off to the kitchen and I went down the hallway until it opened into the sitting room. A fire was blazing in the wide stone hearth, and Doctor Mac was sitting on a well-used leather couch beside Jane. They both rose as I came in.

"Hello, Grace," he said, stepping toward me. "We meet, finally. I'm Andrew."

He extended a huge hand, and as I went to shake it he enveloped my hand in both of his. I was surprised by the genuine warmth I felt from him. He was a big man in his mid-forties, solid and energetic; he had unruly dark brown hair, and his face was long and handsome, with a full mouth, cheeks shaved smooth, and eyes so wide that he seemed to wear a constant expression of surprise. But it was camouflage; I never saw him actually surprised by anything. When he looked at me through striking blue eyes, there was nothing ambiguous about his expression. He was intrigued by me, and his eyes revealed that his interest extended beyond mere curiosity. There was a masculine vitality to him, but he had a kind of gentleness that made him entirely unthreatening. Letty and Jane had invited me to dinner for more reasons than one; and I found myself wishing, despite Jane's instruction not to dress for dinner, that I had worn something more attractive.

"What can I get you to drink, Grace?" he asked. His shirtsleeves were rolled up and he wore a deerskin waistcoat, and as he rubbed his big hands together, I watched the muscles in his forearms bunch beneath graying hair, and was reminded of my father's thick arms and his big, deft hands. "It's a little nippy out there. How about a glass of sherry?"

"That would be nice," I said. "Thank you."

"The ladies in our community have apparently given you a thunderous welcome," he said, offering me the glass of sherry and sitting down beside me.

"Thunderous would be an understatement," said Jane. "And it was hardly a welcome."

"The good news is that I don't feel ignored," I said, "although I would have been happier with a smaller splash."

He looked at me. "Yes," he said, "I believe you would."

"Well, here goes nothing," said Jane, uncorking the bottle of wine I'd brought. "The previous owners of your place used to have quite a cellar—most of it imported burgundy, although the parents had a stake in some of the Cape wineries, and they used to bring bottles around for us to try. This one is French—let's see if they left you anything worth drinking."

She poured, swirled, sniffed, and tasted. "Not too bad," she said. "I'll take it into the kitchen and decant it—needs to breathe a bit."

"Wonderful," said Andrew. "We can drink it with dinner." We were sitting together on the couch, and he turned to face me. "I've always lived here, Grace, and our family's been on this farm for generations. I can't imagine how difficult it must be for a single woman to find her way into this community. So, educate me. How've your first few month been? It can't all have been as nasty as it was last week at the ladies club."

"Not at all," I said. "I've had a lot to learn, and it's been busy. But it has been a bit lonely at times, and I'm glad to have met Letty and Jane."

"Very different from each other, my sister and Jane," he said, "but they make a great team." He paused, looked down and retied the laces on his worn, soft leather walking shoes. "They're lucky to have found each other. Letty wouldn't have kept the farm going on her own, and I couldn't run it and a medical practice at the same time. We would have been forced to sell, and that would have been difficult—we've eight generations buried in this turf. Jane's made it possible for us to keep the farm, and I'm very grateful for that." He looked at me again. "Tell me, Grace," he said quietly, "how are you managing?"

I thought I heard condescension in his voice, and an assumption of familiarity that I was not prepared for. "I've done this before, you know," I said stiffly. "I have a competent foreman and a wonderful *induna*. We're doing well, thank you."

"Yes," he said, still speaking softly, but insistently. "I know Brian McWilliams; I've treated his family. And hard though it may be for you to believe, your *induna*, Solomon Mavovo and I grew up together."

"So that's how you know my cook. When I told him I'd be here for dinner tonight, he asked me to give you his greetings."

"Yes," he said, smiling. "Your cook. Mandla Mkhize. Please give him my best. Khabazela," he said pointedly, "is a fine, fine man."

I'd never heard a white man refer to a Zulu with such respect, and I was puzzled.

"I understand that they call you the White Zulu," I said.

"So, Khabazela has been talking," he said with a smile. "Yes, they do. And I'd be happy to share my story with you, perhaps after dinner. It's a longish tale."

He took a final sip of sherry and placed his empty glass carefully on the coffee table. I was leaning back, and he placed a hand on the backrest and turned to me. I had the sense that he was looming over me, much closer than he had been before.

"Tell me about your farm up north," he said in a low voice. "I understand from Phyllis McGowan that it was up close to the Rhodesian border. Your husband tried his hand at growing grapes there?"

"Yes," I said, feeling uncomfortable. I was angry that she had asked me so many questions, and that I had felt obliged to answer them. "I'm so glad she reported to you correctly. What else did she tell you?"

He looked straight at me and spoke softly, close enough so that I felt the vibrations of his voice. "She told me that you were charming and beautiful. But she also said that there was something about your story she didn't believe, and she asked me what I thought."

"And what do you think?" I asked, raising my chin, "about me and my story?"

"She was right on all counts. She also said, by the way, that she thought you were too good to be true."

"Really?" I said.

"Yes." He waited, smiling thoughtfully. "She was right about that, too. You're way, way too good to be true."

I hated the fact that he was able to make me flush to the roots of my hair.

"That wasn't what I meant," I said.

"Anyway," he continued, "I told Phyllis that I thought your story held together perfectly, and that I found nothing unbelievable about it."

"How nice of you," I said. "I suppose I should be grateful."

He shrugged. "That's up to you," he said, and leaned in even closer to me. I instinctively backed away. He grinned. "Don't worry," he said. "I just wanted to tell you two things. First, drop the grapes from your story—they don't grow that close to the border. The fact that you might have tried to grow grapes only raises unnecessary questions about your competence as a farmer."

I was about to object angrily that I didn't have a 'story', and that he had no business questioning my competence or telling me what to do, but I simply couldn't fake it convincingly in front of him.

"Second," he said, "you should know that neither you nor Khabazela are the only ones who are other than what they seem." He held up a hand to silence me. "Don't waste your indignation. You don't have to defend yourself, or him, against me. When you get home, just ask him about our work together."

"Your work?" I asked in a whisper. "What work could you possibly have together?"

"Ask Khabazela," he said, rising and turning his face to the kitchen. "From the smell of it, the lamb is ready. Let's go in, and I'll tell you my story. I promise not to bore you."

He stood aside for me as I rose and, feeling dazed, preceded him into the dining room. "Don't worry, Grace," he said in a low voice, patting my shoulder. "You're among friends."

Andrew and Letty grew up on the farm, their father being the only son of Scottish immigrants who settled the land in the 1860s. When Letty was born, their mother fell ill. Her illness was never given a name, but when Andrew was born five years later, she was unable to breast-feed him. In a local village his father found a young Zulu woman who had just given birth, and they hired her, bringing her into the house with her baby. She became Andrew's wet nurse and doubled as his nursemaid; in time, Andrew began to call her *mama.* His birth mother turned out to be depressed and anemic, he said, and showed little interest in him, even after he was weaned.

"I was suckled by a Zulu mother," he said, "nourished by Zulu milk. While I was at one breast, my Zulu brother Sbusiso was at the other, and we were breast-fed, as was the custom, for almost four years. We slept together in the same cradle, and when we started to investigate the world, the first thing we laid eyes on was each other. My first words were Zulu words, and I spoke Zulu fluently before I spoke English. At the age of seven I was sent to school, and when I was told that I had to go without Sbusiso, I wept with grief. I remember the sense of loss, and the frustration at not being able to fathom why he couldn't come with me.

"But I went, barefoot, refusing to wear the shoes my father had bought for the occasion. We'd never worn shoes before, Sbusiso and I, and they were uncomfortable on our calloused feet. I left them under a bush outside the schoolhouse. Inside, I stood respectfully to greet my teacher the way I had learned was courteous and polite. At the end of the first day I went home, and that night my father asked me how it had been. I gave him a noncommittal response—something short that wouldn't bring me to tears in front of him. He patted me on the head. He said, 'It's difficult, my son, but you'll get used to it in a few weeks. We all do.'

"Later that night, as our mother was giving the two of us our bath, she couldn't help but notice the welts on my back. 'What happened?' she asked. 'Did the big boys fight you?' I think she had expected me to be teased—the other boys knew that Sbusiso was my closest friend. I told her that the teacher put the marks on my back. She thought I must have done something terrible, although she couldn't imagine what it was, and she was furious, in her quiet way—in her culture, children were never beaten. She asked me, again and again, 'What did you do, Andrew, for her to do such a thing to you?'

"Sitting in the bathtub and looking up at her, I raised my arm solemnly and said, 'Sawubona.'

"'Why do you say Sawubona to me?' she asked, frowning. 'This is not a game, Andrew. Tell me what terrible thing you did to make your teacher beat you so.'

"I said that I was just showing her what I had done at school—I had greeted my teacher politely, raising my arm in the Zulu way, as I had been taught, and I had said, 'Sawubona,' I see you.

"She lifted me out of the bathtub. 'What was the woman thinking,' she muttered as she spread a salve on my back, 'to beat a child so?'

"'She said she was teaching me, mama.'

"'Teaching?' she asked with quiet smile. 'We do not raise a child by raising welts on his skin. What was she teaching you?'

"'She said that I was a white boy, not a Zulu—and she was going to teach me never to use that language in her classroom. But it does not hurt me, mama,' I told her, trying to comfort her, 'and it will be better tomorrow.'

"'It will be better tomorrow, yes,' she said. 'But we will see about her.'

"'What do you mean, mama?' asked Sbusiso. He stood behind me, gently tracing the welts on my back. She said nothing.

"My teacher was a hard, obese woman with a sour disposition, powerful from carrying around her huge weight. She used her strength in the service of her frequent irritation with the children in her classroom, and as a result we cowered before her. She had given me my first lesson in Afrikaans cultural tolerance, her only teaching tool a bamboo cane, and I quickly found ways to avoid her anger. After a few weeks, Sbusiso and I forgot about the incident, I learned to wear shoes, and as my father had predicted, I became used to going to school. But all was not right with my teacher, who began to behave strangely.

"At first she was hot all the time," said Andrew, "and we laughed behind our hands as she stood before the open window waving a handkerchief before her face, flushed and sweating in the winter wind that blew down from the mountains. Then she began to lose weight, as if there were malevolent fury in her body boiling her from within, rendering her flesh the way fat is rendered in the fire. She simply melted away, and her skin hung loosely from the framework of her bones like pigskin, softened by use. Her cheeks, once glutted and oily, became dried and shriveled as they caved in, and they slopped down beneath her jawbones like desiccated udders that swayed back and forth as she moved her head.

One day she appeared at school leaning on a cane, and she walked painfully, struggling for breath. We watched her dying, fascinated and appalled, and we were relieved when she stopped coming to school. She died within the year.

"At the funeral, *mama* was serene and solemn, but her eyes gleamed with silent knowing. Sbusiso and I looked at each other, remembering what had happened, and we knew with a terrible certainty that *mama* was responsible. We never discussed it, but it remained a shared secret between us that she had visited a diviner or a sorcerer and invoked the help of the Shades. I was her child, and she had harnessed their anger in my defense."

Andrew said that it was both comforting and terrifying to think that *mama* had such power at her disposal. He would have done anything for her, but the fact that she had been willing to go to such lengths to protect him cemented his identity as a Zulu. From that point on, there was never any doubt in his mind that he would do anything to protect either her or Sbusiso, and by extension to stand up for whoever—or whatever—was important to them.

"It was a defining moment for me," he said, "the moment I knew that the Shades of our ancestors live among us and influence our lives; that beneath my white skin is an African heart; that I have Zulu blood and a Zulu spirit. I knew that I belonged as much to the Zulu people— the People of the Sky—as I do to my father's people. It was years before I recognized that this knowing was as deep as bone, but *mama* had fed me from her body, and she knew long before I did that I was a white Zulu."

By the end of the evening, I understood that the work Andrew referred to doing with Khabazela was wrapped up with the ANC, and that he was as committed as we were. He was not on the Governing Committee, although he could have been had he wanted to. I think even the most diehard separatist blacks would have welcomed him. But he preferred to make his contribution surreptitiously, as the eyes and ears of the organization.

In his role as a physician to both English and Afrikaans-speaking whites, and to the Zulu community, Andrew was privy to much that would otherwise never have been revealed. He knew who was affiliated with which political movement; he knew who could be called on for help, and who should be avoided. He knew every child born, every incident of family violence that required medical care, every altercation between young men of different villages; he knew who was raped and when, and he knew who was behind many of the acts of violence that were never reported. If the legal system failed to punish the perpetrators of random violence or gratuitous theft, others often did, and Andrew was frequently the force behind the thief who repaid his victim, or the young tough who came to the door of the man he had beaten, offering to help with the farming until his injuries healed.

These roles Andrew would have filled no matter what the political circumstances, but in addition, because he traveled around the community, he had an excuse to be anywhere at any time. He was above suspicion, and he was a huge asset to the movement. He also turned out to be a very good friend.

My initial response to the revelation that Andrew was one of us had been anger at Khabazela, who had given me no indication of what to expect. I walked into a living room expecting to be welcomed as Grace Michaels, only to find myself exposed. Andrew hadn't simply seen through my disguise—it had been totally invisible to him because he already knew precisely who I was.

He knew that I had never lived on a farm near the Rhodesian border— but did he also know that my farmer husband was a fiction? I couldn't follow the trail any further in my mind without knowing how deeply involved Andrew was in the ANC, but I wondered for how long he had been a hidden factor in my life. He might have had a hand in planning the event that resulted in our arrest; and he may have been instrumental in the decision to break me out of prison along with Khabazela. I wondered whether he knew that we had been in hiding for a year in Zululand, and whether he had perhaps followed our activities while we were there. Did he know that we were lovers?

I knew very little about Andrew, at least at the start, but he was privy to some—perhaps many—of my secrets. Khabazela had given me no preparation at all; allowed me to enter a situation completely unprepared for what I might find. It put me at a distinct disadvantage, and I left Glen Acres Farm at the end of the evening furious with him.

But by the time I drove down my dirt road into the farmyard and climbed out of the Jeep, my fury had evaporated. Khabazela had played me by sending me into unfamiliar territory and seeing how I would handle being unmasked. Both he and Andrew had kept from me the fact that it was a safe situation, and when it happened I felt far more vulnerable than I actually was. I handled the situation as well as anyone could have, and I was willing to let them conduct their test at my expense. But I was also relieved, because for the first time since arriving on the farm, I felt that we were not alone. There was someone else who knew me for what I was; someone else before whom I didn't need to be on constant alert.

Brian McWilliams's wife, Anna, never did come to pay her respects. When I occasionally saw her in town, I was struck by the fact that she was almost pretty, but circumstance and her own temperament had failed her. She had discontent written all over her pale, narrow face, and I never saw her smile. Her mouth would have been beautiful, but her lips had been sculpted with a knife blade, and most often she held her mouth pursed in an expression of determination or distaste. Like most farm women, she cut her hair herself, and it hung in an uneven fringe over her forehead. Beneath large, pale blue eyes she had dark rings that spoke of depression or lack of sleep, and by all accounts, she had reason to suffer from both.

The McWilliams lived at the edge of the property where the farm road met the tarmac, and I passed it every time I left the farm. Sometimes I saw Anna over the waist-high stone wall that surrounded the foreman's cottage, wheeling a pram in the back yard, or sitting on the porch with the maid, shelling peas or husking *mielies* as the children played on the small enclosed lawn. One day I saw her hanging laundry, her arms raised to the washing line, and she was so thin that I was sure she must be ill. Today we would conclude that she was either anorexic or that she had

AIDS. But back then we didn't know about anorexia and there was no AIDS, and Anna McWilliams was just another bony, flat-chested, over-worked farm wife who bore too many children too soon.

Brian McWilliams was apparently not a bad husband or father, but he was not to be trifled with, especially when he was drinking. It seems he loved his scotch, and it didn't take much to turn him into a loud and vin-dictive drunk. In his defense—a thin defense, I thought—it was said that he seldom beat her, but she was afraid of him, and the story was that she hid his liquor. He accepted it, perhaps relieved that she was protecting him from his worst self. But that didn't stop him from trying to locate her hiding places, which she changed often. I shuddered to think what her life must have been like as he searched for his drink, as she waited for him to find it, and then watched as he changed into the person she was trying so hard to keep him from becoming.

The McWilliams had four children under the age of six, and Anna always had one of them on her back, on her hip, on her lap. Sometimes Brian relieved her by bringing the oldest boy, Michael, with him to the farmhouse, where I gave him a cup of tea and a biscuit as his father and I discussed the day's work. He was a serious child with a thick mop of wheat-colored hair, and he would sit with his tea on the verandah in his short pants, his chapped, little-boy knees clasped together, watching us silently out of big brown eyes. I became fond of him, and he enjoyed com-ing to the relative peace of my home, so different from his own.

Several months passed without incident. Khabazela came and went, and while I loved it when he was home, I was determined not to miss him when he was gone. I spent several evenings with Letty and Jane, and sometimes Andrew joined us; on a couple of occasions Andrew and I went for a long tramp through the *veld* along the low berg, where the winter grass rustled in the silence.

There were still families of baboons wandering the *veld* then, and small herds of impala. The sky, always clear in winter after the sun evaporated the morning mist, was filled with heron, and multiple species of water birds landed on the small ponds that dotted the flatland. The air was filled with dragonflies and buzzing with insects and flying beetles. Whenever we came across an herb or a plant used by the Zulus, Andrew would point to it with his walking stick. We would kneel down beside each other and he would show me how to identify it, and describe how it was used. He pointed out plants whose roots or flowers were used to cause vomiting or to relieve constipation, to heal sores and cure blindness or ringworm or pimples.

While some of the botanical knowledge he had was practical, some was simply superstition, and I found it fascinating to see how the two coexisted. The herb *Icishamlilo*, for example—the extinguisher of fire— had dark purple flowers, and traditional healers used its roots in a concoction to relieve pain. But some healers also sprinkled it around the homestead as protection against evil, and on hut roofs as protection against arson. He showed me *Umabophe*, a shrub whose leaves and roots were used in court proceedings to prevent a plaintiff from making a clear argument. It either made the recipient mute, or made him say things that were not relevant to the case. I laughed.

"You may mock," he said, "but I've seen it happen. When someone knows that he's taken the medicine, we can say that it works only because he thinks it will. But I've seen it work when it was given to a witness without his knowledge."

"You can't believe that, Andrew," I said. "How do you reconcile it with your medical training?"

"I'm trained in western medicine," he said, "but many of my patients are Zulus. I've seen these medicinal concoctions work in ways that confound western scientific thinking." He shrugged, squatting on his heels and supporting himself on his stick. "I don't try anymore to reconcile what I don't understand—I just accept that there are some things our science doesn't yet know."

I looked at him skeptically. "Like your first grade teacher being bewitched and melting away?"

I was kneeling beside him, and for a long moment he returned my glance without speaking. Then he pointed with his stick at the plant between us. It was an herb with narrow leaves and a richly scented white flower.

"This is the *Fairy Bell Pachycarpus*," he said. "The Zulus call it by a name that means 'to forsake one's mother'. The root is used as a love potion—it's said to ensure total devotion. Some Zulus swear by it, and I've seen its impact on them." His mouth widened in a gleeful, boyish grin, and he rose to his feet. "I know it works on western-trained white Zulu physicians," he said, looking down at me. The grin disappeared and became a tentative, concerned smile; the lines around his eyes vanished as his eyes opened wide. "I wonder if it might also work on a ravishing young woman," he said, speaking the words in a low, gentle voice, "whose real name is Michaela Green."

I placed my palms down on the ground and scrambled to my full height, my legs shaking, chaos in my belly, anger and fear fighting for mastery in my head.

"So you know my name," I said, trying to contain the trembling in my voice. "Who are you, Andrew? What is it you really want from me?"

He rose to his feet and took a step back. "I've already told you," he said, "I'm a friend. And what I want from you is your trust."

"Why?"

"Because part of my job is to keep you safe—and it's a lot easier to do that if I have your trust."

"Is there anything else you know about me that I should be aware of?" I paused and glared up at him. "Or is it your goal to keep me off balance by dropping intimate little details about my life at strategic moments?"

"Grace, the last thing I want is to keep you off balance and frightened."

"If you think this is fear, you're way off the mark," I snapped.

"Well, if the truth be told, I'd rather have you angry than afraid of me. But I'd prefer it if you were neither." He managed an uneasy smile. "Where politics and medicine are concerned, I'm as silent as the tomb. When it comes to friendship, however, I'm very uncomfortable with secrets. And we have a problem, because we've become friends." He looked at me, waiting for me to agree.

"What of it?" I asked.

"Well, I consider you a friend," he continued, "and I'm uncomfortable with what I know about you. I wanted to bring it out in the open before it has a chance to create tension between us. Which it will, eventually." He paused in the silence between us and looked around at the little pond, glinting in the winter sun, the sound of birds' wings audible against the water as they landed. "I'm sorry," he said. "I could have handled this better, and I should have dealt with it sooner."

"Yes," I said. "You could, and you should. What else do you know about me?"

"You're not going to make this easy, are you?"

"No."

He sighed. "Michaela Davidson, born in Johannesburg. Your father was a dentist; your mother a teacher, both politically liberal, active members of the Jewish community. You graduated from Witwatersrand University in 1954 with a degree in music. Married Lenny Green, civil engineer; one son, Steven, born in 1955. In 1962 you were arrested along with Mandla Mkhize and sent to prison for treason and miscegenation. You received a ten-year sentence; he was put away for life. You didn't spend much time in prison. The ANC wanted him out, but he wasn't about to escape without you, and the ANC agreed to his terms. Following your escape, a phone call was arranged with your husband from a secure telephone near Durban, and he told you that he was taking your son and leaving the country. They left for Boston shortly after, and you haven't seen your son since." He stopped. "I'm so sorry."

"Steven was seven when they left—he's almost ten now." I said it as matter-of-factly as I could. "There's no reason to be sorry—it is what it is. Go on."

"You and Mandla Mkhize were transported separately to Zululand, where you stayed in the homestead of one of his kinsmen. You remained there for just over a year, after which you were provided with a false identity and papers, and you traveled to Europe to retrieve funds your father left for you in a Swiss bank account. Your intent was to purchase a farm from which you could assist in the work of the ANC by providing him a cover, and at the same time provide safety and transportation out of the country for dissidents and those being sought by the government."

I was angry before Andrew expanded upon what he knew of me, and I felt exposed and taken advantage of. But now I knew what it was like to feel so revealed that humiliation and shame made anger impossible. I covered my breasts with my arms in a gesture that revealed a sense of nakedness beyond what clothing could mask.

"You've had me under surveillance. All the time we were in Zululand, and in Europe. And on the farm."

"Yes," said Andrew. "And I'm so sorry it had to be done surreptitiously."

"You have people watching me—us—on the farm, too. How could we have been so bloody stupid?" My voice was hoarse. "We thought we

could come up here and live our lives with at least a semblance of privacy."
Then a thought struck me, and my blood ran cold. "Does Khabazela
know that we're being watched?" I looked up at him, squinting into the
sun, unable to see his expression.

"You have it all wrong, Grace," he said quietly, placing his hands on
my shoulders. "No one was watching you in Zululand. And when you
were in Europe, whatever surveillance the ANC provided was for your
own safety. For God's sake, woman, you were alone in an unfamiliar city,
walking the streets with a sack full of diamonds. Khabazela wanted to
be sure that you were protected. The organization also had to protect
itself—they didn't know whether you were being watched or whether
your identity might have been compromised. The Special Branch might
have been on the alert, waiting for you to lead them directly to the ANC
leadership when you returned."

"That leadership being you?"

"Don't be ridiculous," he said. "There are no whites on the executive
council. I'm small potatoes in the organization; they tolerate me because
of what I can contribute."

"So why are you so involved in my case? Why so privy to the details
of my life?"

"Because I'm here, Grace. Because I'm a doctor and I help when people are in trouble. It's not for nothing they call me the White Zulu. I love
this country, and I'm committed to this struggle." He paused, looked at
me with a pained expression, and continued in a voice that was resigned
and sad. "The council leadership was willing to have you come out here
and help Khabazela, but they were unwilling to put your lives at any
greater risk than necessary. They wanted someone close by to watch over
you, someone you could talk to and perhaps confide in. They needed to
know how you were dealing with the strain. You live a double life, which
is stressful enough—but when he's traveling, you're isolated, too, and

the fact that you're involved in dangerous work increased the strain even more. They just wanted to make sure that you were coping, Grace."

"And if my coping skills were less developed than they'd like?" I asked, tasting in my throat the acid that I couldn't hide in my voice. "What would they have done then? Dispensed with my services? Gotten rid of me?"

"There's a life and death struggle being played out here," he said sharply. "We're trying to rid the country of a terrible regime, and you must have realized by now that working for the ANC carries lethal risks. This government has already tried to chew you up and spit you out. They failed, but they won't fail again. If the Special Branch knew where you were they wouldn't hesitate to put a bullet in your head—after you told them everything you know. And trust me, Grace," he said grimly, "before they were through, you would have given them all the information they wanted. Then they'd make it look as if you'd been raped, mutilated and dismembered by a horde of bloodthirsty Zulus, and leave your body where it would create the greatest fear among already terrified whites."

He took my arm and led me gently to a rock outcropping, brushed the dirt away with the flat of his hand, and sat me down. He lowered himself to sit beside me, and softened his voice. "The leadership of any underground organization has to know how its members are doing. Anyone who can't cope with the stress endangers everyone he has contact with. Of course the council is concerned about you—not only for your own safety, but for Khabazela's. On every mission he undertakes, the man you claim to love steps into nothingness. Every time he leaves you he takes the risk of not coming back." Andrew paused. "The council wants to make sure that at least when he's with you, he's safe."

Late afternoon was upon us by the time we started back. I walked in front of Andrew, my arms clasped about my chest. The thick cardigan I wore should have warmed me, but the freeze extended through my flesh and into my viscera. The cold felt as if it was coming from within, emanating outwards. The evening chill of winter was in the air as the sun quickly dropped towards the distant mountaintops, and the quality of the light was stark and cold. The dry *veld* grass, wheat-green and pale, was tinted with silver as the wind turned its face and wove wide ribbons towards the horizon and back again, and the silvered swaths matched the backlit silhouette of the mountains.

My conversation with Andrew was an eye-opener—it forced me to recognize how much was at stake, and in how much danger Khabazela walked every day. It was almost as if I couldn't tell which role was real, and which was the cover. In some ways, the role of country lady farmer had become my real life, and the challenges it posed had become my real problems. Living undercover had come to feel like a charade, with pretend dangers, unreal cloak-and-dagger hide and seek, and my clandestine nights of love part of an exciting fantasy, without potential consequence.

I kept to myself for the next few weeks as I came to terms with the reality that Andrew had pointed out. It wasn't clear to me at first how— or even whether—I needed to adjust my thinking or my behavior. But everything I did or said was informed by the realization that we were under observation by friends, and that the danger posed by enemies was much greater than I had been willing to acknowledge.

And it made a difference—I became harder, more focused; more suspicious than I had been before, able to trust no one. I didn't know what

I was looking for, but I was on constant alert for anything that might reveal the presence of someone watching me, and I wondered whether I would have the courage to take any action in the event that I discovered a spy. Until Andrew revealed that I was being observed, I had no doubt that I was coping well—but once I knew that I was being watched I became far less trusting, and it crossed my mind that I might be showing signs of paranoia.

To the farmhands I was cold and distant, and instead of talking to them when I was tramping the fields, I preferred to stand and watch them from the field's perimeter. They waved; I waved back. When I walked the farm in the early winter mornings with Solomon Mavovo, I found him looking at me with concern in his reddened eyes.

"The *Nkosikazi* is not well today," he said, shaking his head.

"What do you mean, Solomon?" I asked.

"Her spirit is elsewhere, I think," he replied.

Even Brian McWilliams was aware of a change in my behavior, and he surprised me as we sat together in my office one morning going over the books.

"Are you unwell, Mrs. Michaels?" he said, leaning forward on his chair.

"I'm fine, thank you, Brian," I responded, not looking up from the ledger.

"I don't mean to be personal," he said, "but you do seem distracted. Even the farmhands are talking about you, wondering if you're ill, or worried about something." He paused, looked down at his shoes. "I hope it's not something I've done."

I laughed. "I'm not that easily upset, Brian. From what you know of me," I said, "do you think I'd hesitate to let you know if you'd offended me?"

"I've not offended you," he said quickly. "That's for sure. I've done all I could to stay on your good side." He brushed his hair from his forehead with a self-conscious gesture, rapid and secretive. "And I'd not upset you for anything."

"I appreciate that," I said.

Brian McWilliams' boyish eagerness to please was sudden, and surprising, and I found it hard not to smile. I wondered for a moment whether I had misjudged him. But as he rose from his chair and walked across the rug between us, I knew that this was more than a desire to please me, and I knew that I should have anticipated it. I rose quickly, not wanting to be seated as he stood above me, and found that I was facing him, and that he had stationed himself much closer than was comfortable. I raised my hands before me, fingers outspread, in a clear gesture that said he was too close. He took my hands in his.

"I had hoped that if you were upset, it was because you were thinking the same things I was."

"That's enough, Brian," I said sharply, pulling my hands away. "Step back, please. And I'd appreciate it if you would keep whatever you were thinking to yourself."

"It's you, Grace," he said, ignoring me. He placed a hand on my shoulder and I shrugged it off, but he seemed not to notice. "You're all I think about," he said urgently, "up here in the farmhouse. All alone. I thought, if you were having a hard time because you were lonely, I could keep you company." His voice was breathless. "No one would ever have to know."

"Don't be ridiculous," I said as sternly as I could. "You're a married man with four children." I pushed past him to the open door. "As far as I'm concerned, this conversation never happened. I'm leaving now—and when I get back I expect that you'll have gone home to lunch with your family. I'll see you tomorrow."

I walked out through the great room and down the hallway to the kitchen, where Selina was making my lunch. I didn't look back, and I heard his boots on the floorboards as he made his way slowly down the passageway and out of the house. His overture was unpracticed and immature, and the fact that he had made it should have been reason enough to dismiss him immediately.

In a life filled with sins of commission, there are a few things I should have done, and didn't. Of these, not replacing Brian McWilliams as fast as I could stands out as one of the greatest.

twenty-one

MICHAELA

Natal, South Africa, 1967

Khabazela was away for two weeks; all I knew was that he was out of the country. There were articles in the news about a meeting at which leaders opposing repressive regimes throughout Africa had gathered in Lusaka, and I suspect that he was among them.

As usual, we had no contact while he was away, but there were moments when my yearning to have him with me was much greater than usual. At first I put it down to circumstance. I was ill for several days, nauseous and unable to get out of bed, and my wish that he was there to help me was followed by the stark recognition that even if he had been home, there was little he would be able to do other than bring me toast and tea. Even that would have been a comfort, but it was his absence that finally got me up and dressed.

When I saw Brian the day after our conversation, he behaved as if nothing had happened between us. I was satisfied that he had heard my message, and I congratulated myself on having put an end to any expectations he might still harbor. But a few days later I woke sometime after midnight to the sounds of raucous laughter and shouting outside. I put on my bathrobe, went to the kitchen and looked out the window.

Brian McWilliams stood in the silent yard, drunk, swaying shirtless in the winter night. His knees were bent, his trousers pulled halfway down his backside, and his pale chest and belly bleached white in the moonlight. His arms were outspread, a bottle in one hand, and he stood facing the house, singing and shouting at the kitchen door. I didn't need to understand what he was saying in order to be disgusted by his actions, furious at the spectacle he was making of himself, and of the shame he was bringing to his family.

Before I could decide what action to take, Solomon came running into the yard with another man, and together, talking quietly, stroking his shoulder, they stilled Brian and gently led him back around the house. I watched through the office window as they supported him out of the yard, one of his arms over each of their shoulders. Solomon started the Jeep and the other man sat in the back with Brian as they drove him back to his wife. The next morning I asked Solomon about the incident, curious to know what happened when they arrived at the foreman's cottage.

"This thing you speak of," he said innocently, "that happened last night, I think perhaps you have dreamed it. I was at home with my family, and I did not come here to the farm."

I looked at him, not yet understanding.

"I was not dreaming, Solomon," I said, "I was awake, and I saw Mr. McWilliams drunk in the yard, singing and shouting. You were there with him, and you took away his bottle and I saw you sitting him in the Jeep and taking him home—"

"We do not speak of these things," he interrupted quietly, his voice respectful as always, but firm. "It brings only sadness and pain to his wife, and it will shame him before those of us who work for him. No good can come of it." He waved his hands in the air as if to dispel a bad odor. "It is over, *Nkosikazi*. Let it be done and forgotten."

Under normal circumstances it would have been difficult to forget, but as usual in my life, I was overcome by the looming pressure of current events. The following morning, crouched nauseous over the toilet, as vomit erupted from my mouth and streamed from my chin, I counted the days since my last period.

When I told Solomon as we walked the next morning that I wanted to visit Lungile, he was not surprised, but I was shaken by his reaction.

"Lungile will be very happy to see this daughter," he said, pointing at me and then rubbing his hands together in anticipation of our reunion, "and she will be full of joy to see that she is becoming a grandmother."

"Solomon, what are you saying?" I asked. "I have told nobody of this."

He laughed in response. "I do not need to be told, *Nkosikazi*. I herded the cows when I was a boy. Now I walk with them every day. I look among the cattle to see which cow is ready to calf, which calf to be weaned, and which cow stands patiently by, waiting. I am an old man, rich in wives, and daughters, and grandchildren," he said, smiling gently. "Do we not walk the fields together, side by side, in the morning when the heaviness is upon you? Do I not see you?"

He pointed with two spread fingers of one hand at his eyes, and then turned the fingers to point at mine. "There would be no wisdom in this old man if he could not tell that a child is being molded within you." He stopped and turned to me. Cautiously, but firmly, he placed a hand on my wrist. "You are with Khabazela's child. This is not an easy thing. But when the child is born, I will be grandfather to the child, as Lungile is mother to you. When we are among others, I will address you as we are accustomed, in the formal way of mistress and servant. But when we are alone, my daughter," he continued without a pause, "it will not be right for me to address the mother of my grandchild so."

This time, the journey to Zululand was familiar, but no less difficult. Solomon gave me directions to the road that came closest to Lungile's homestead, and he told me where I would find a thick copse of trees that would keep the Jeep secluded while I was away. He arranged for a boy to meet me after dark, and he sent word to Lungile that I was coming. I arrived at the meeting point just as the sun set, and had time to drive deep into the trees, to obscure my tire tracks, and to camouflage the Jeep with fallen branches. As I finished and turned to the *veld* that rolled upward before me, I saw the silhouette of a donkey against the nearest hilltop, following a boy no taller than his neck.

I had brought a knapsack loaded with supplies, and the boy secured it to the saddle blanket on his donkey. On this journey, I was determined to walk, and even if Sthembiso had come to meet me instead of the boy, he would have been no match for the determination I felt. Remembering my last journey, among the supplies I had brought for Lungile were two thick blankets. I offered one to the boy, wrapping myself in the other.

We arrived at the homestead after midnight, to find Lungile waiting at the fire, as she had waited for a stranger almost two years earlier. But this time we were not strangers, and we embraced, wordlessly. She led me to the hut that Khabazela and I had lived in, with the same chairs and table, and with a fire burning in a circle of rocks at the center. She sat me down and placed in my hands a bowl of steaming *mielie* porridge, and in the mix were small pieces of meat. This time I needed no instruction, and I ate with my fingers, ravenous for the food and for the caring it represented.

Lungile sat with me, silent, watching as I ate. When I was through, she lay me down on the bed and covered me with a blanket. I heard the sound of her feet slapping on the mud floor as she left, and went to sleep in the warmth of the fire, with the musky smell of old smoke in my nostrils. I was four hours from the nearest road, without electricity or running water, in a silent, doorless hut—but I slept the deep, secure sleep of a child in her parents' home.

The next morning we ate together, and I offered Lungile the gifts I had brought—blankets, Red Roses tea, a pound of sugar, enameled mugs, candles, matches, several kinds of soap, hand towels and washcloths, and hooded sweatshirts for the children. She looked at them all approvingly, and she was most taken by the hand soap. It was perfumed with lavender, and she breathed it in with delight. Then she boiled water and we sat down together around her fire to drink hot tea out of her new mugs.

"You have come," she said.

"Yes, mother. It gladdens me to see you."

"It is good that you bring gifts. But what can this old mother offer you?"

"I am confused," I said. "I come to ask for your wisdom."

She looked down at my belly, and then up into my face. "It requires no wisdom to see that a child is being molded within you." She paused. "The child of Mandla Mkhize."

"Yes," I said, "Khabazela's child."

"As the *sangoma* predicted." She paused again, looking into my eyes, and I was unable to bear her scrutiny. I dropped my head. "Raise up your eyes, my daughter, and tell me about this confusion inside you."

She waited for my answer, and I looked up again into her sun-wrinkled face. From the deep calm of her eyes shone the sure knowledge of answers to all things important. And I remember thinking, how is it possible for this woman, who knows so little of the world, to know so much? Whether right or wrong, she knew the world worked in certain ways; she knew the fixed principles that govern human behavior and destiny. The knowledge passed down to her from her fathers and mothers was unassailable. I envied her certainty then, and I remain envious today.

"The child will come," she said into my silence, "when it is his time. You need do nothing but prepare."

"Prepare?" I asked. "Where do I prepare, mother? That is my confusion. Should I prepare for him on my farm, or here, in your *kraal*? And after he is born, where will he grow? Where is the right place—where is it safe—for the child of a Zulu father and a white mother?"

She thought for a moment, swaying back and forth in the firelight as she quietly sipped her tea, both dark hands cupped around the white enamel mug. With her eyes closed, she turned her head to face the far side of the hut, to the area reserved for the Shades, as if she were listening. I waited. When she had her answer she opened her eyes and turned back to me.

"You ask questions about things that do not concern you." She raised a hand to silence my objection. "Before we plant the seeds of the sweet potato," she said, "we prepare the ground. Then, we plant. When the ground is dry, we give water, but the seed grows underneath the earth. We do not decide whether it will shrivel or grow, or how big, or when it will be ready to be dug. It is so with a child. He grows within you.

Each day will lead to the next. It is enough to know that a child is coming. Make ready for him slowly. At each step, the Shades will help you to know what to do next."

Two days I stayed with Lungile. I watched the sun rise and set. We ate *mielie*-meal together and drank tea at her fire, and I talked and laughed with her daughters-in-law as they prepared food and cared for the *kraal*, one eye always on the older children looking after their younger siblings. I left in darkness before dawn on the third day, and Lungile walked part of the way with me. She placed her hands on either side of my face and then stood back, arms folded across her breasts. When I turned for a last look at her, the sun's first rays beamed skywards from beyond the distant mountain tops, and she stood unmoving on the crest of a hill watching me leave, a small, dark shape cut out against the bright, cold light of a winter day.

When I was at university in Johannesburg, the newspapers were full of the horrific events taking place to the north of us, in other parts of colonial Africa—places like Kenya, Tanganyika and Nigeria. For most people, stories of political upheaval and the liberation struggle generated a lot of talk and much anxiety, but it all came down to wondering how we in South Africa would be affected.

The newspapers, eager to be relevant and pandering to racist paranoia, centered their front page stories around trusted domestic servants who suddenly turned feral and murdered the families who employed them, adults and children, in their beds. Some people began to arm their homes, or to carry weapons in their cars, but most of our neighbors stopped short of such extreme measures. Instead, following the fashion, they installed massive wrought iron gates in the passageways leading to their family's bedrooms. Intruders might break into the house and take the silver, but, went the logic, the bedrooms would be inaccessible, and in the event of a break-in, the lives of the family would be saved.

The gates were often elaborately made with detailed floral motifs, and they were sometimes painted in light colors to match the décor of the passageway. But no matter how intricate, nothing could camouflage the gauge of the metal or the security of the lock, or the intent, the fear it was meant to assuage.

Prior to the installation of these security gates, each morning, before the master and mistress of the house were up, at least one of the servants would have risen, put on a pink or blue pinafore and white apron, and with the house key she had, would have unlocked the back door, collected and polished the shoes from outside each bedroom, made tea or coffee and perhaps delivered it to the master bedroom. But now the servants were locked out of their white employers' bedrooms until someone rose and unlocked the gate. So who, really, were they protecting themselves against if not their own employees, the men and women who cooked and fed them, cared for their children, cleaned up before and after them, had access to everything in their homes? These were the people they were afraid would tip-toe up the passageway in the darkness and murder them all in their beds.

When I moved into the farmhouse, the only security was the locks on the front and rear doors. Wrought iron gates were not yet fashionable, but none of my neighbors would have thought it strange for a white woman living alone to install a security gate in the short passageway leading to her bedroom and bath. I could have justified it on other, more private grounds, too—it would have provided additional protection against discovery when I was not alone. But I thought such a gate would be an insult to my Zulu employees, and that it would give the wrong message; that if I wanted to be respected, to be seen as independent and self-reliant, I needed to show that I was not afraid. It turned out that I was overly concerned with the appearance of valor, and not conscious enough of the need for discretion.

Khabazela returned to the farm late on the night before I arrived home from my visit with Lungile. I had no idea when he would be back, and because we had not anticipated that I might be gone when he returned, we had not established a system that would allow me to easily leave him a message. For the first time, I was simply absent, and he was distraught to find me gone.

When he came to me after midnight, I was already in bed. I heard the key turn in the lock, and his footsteps in the kitchen, and then he was in my bedroom, freshly showered and wearing the silk robe I had bought him. I jumped out of bed and we embraced, and there was something desperate in the way he held me hard against him.

"I came back to find you gone," he said. "I've been worried sick, Michaela. Selina knew only that you were away, and there was no word for me anywhere. Where were you for three days?"

"I went to visit Lungile," I said.

"Lungile?" he asked. "Why? Did she call for you? Is she not well?"

"There's nothing wrong with her," I answered. "She's fine. And she didn't call for me."

"So what was your sudden need to visit her?"

"You were away," I said, "and I didn't know when you'd be back. I was alone. I felt lonely. I went to see her. It was that simple." I paused. "But I also had some questions to ask her."

He could have asked me what questions I had for Lungile, and that would have given me an opening to tell him our news. But he was exhausted from his trip, and oblivious to my needs. I noticed that the sleeves of his robe were rolled up, and on his left forearm was a thick bandage.

"What happened to your arm?" I asked.

He ignored my concern. "You didn't tell me that you were going," he said in the subdued voice we had become accustomed to using at night. "Not a word. No message. Nothing," he said accusingly. "You could have left word with Solomon, or given him a note for me. It was very thought-less of you."

His words hit me like a blow—the last thing in the world I was towards him was thoughtless. It was the first time I had heard petulance from him, and I put it down to weariness and whatever he had gone through while he was away. I decided to ignore it.

"Solomon knew where I was," I said. "He helped me get word to Lungile. Why didn't you ask him?"

"Solomon told me nothing about where you had gone. If this hap-pens again, you should remember that he may be my uncle, but you're his employer, and besides, he feels great affection for you. Without clear instruc-tions from you to share information, even with me, he will remain silent."

He lowered himself slowly to sit on the side of the bed, and I could see how weary he was. He looked up at me.

"Of course I asked Solomon where you were. He told me that you were safe— he's very protective of you. But he said it was up to me to ask you myself where you had been."

"I'm sorry," I said, sitting down beside him. "I didn't mean to worry you—I just needed a woman's company." I took his hand.

"What about your friends?" he asked. "Jane and Letty? Couldn't you have gone to visit them for the afternoon instead of leaving the farm for three days and traveling all the way up to Zululand?"

It was a reasonable question, but I was in no mood to have my decisions questioned or my actions judged. I didn't want to be scolded.

I had been alone for two weeks, I was pregnant with his child, and I wanted loving attention from him. I wanted to share the news with him quietly and tenderly, but I saw that he was exhausted, and he was holding onto his arm as if in pain. I thought that if I tended to him first and made him comfortable, he would be more receptive.

"Can I get you something to drink or eat?" I said, rising to my feet. He shook his head. "OK," I said, "Tell me what happened to your arm. I need to know so that I can help you take care of it."

He sat straight and offered me his forearm. I stepped toward him and looked at the bandage. It was grubby and unsanitary, and it was wet, as if he had showered without covering it. Gently I unclipped the two metal clasps and began to unwrap it. Khabazela seemed to be watching me, but when I glanced at him it was to see that he sat with glazed eyes, focused on something not in the room with us. When he eventually spoke, I jumped at the sudden sound of his voice, hoarse and low.

"It wasn't a military mission," he said. "It was a closed conference, out of the country. No one but the participants knew where we were meeting. If we had succeeded, we would have moved the struggle forward a decade, with greater outside funding and support than we could have imagined a few years ago."

I rerolled the bandage as I removed it, wetting and separating the layers slowly to avoid pulling at whatever was underneath.

"So what happened?"

"Have you heard of the Civilian Cooperation Bureau?"

I shook my head.

"It's our government's latest tactic in sponsored terror," he said. "It's not enough for them to stifle free speech—now they're infiltrating all the major opposition organizations and spreading lies about us to each other.

And what's worse," he said bitterly, "is that we're all buying into their lies."

"They're scared," I said, "we're all scared. But we could have anticipated this—they'll do anything to discredit us. What happened?"

"They got to one of our delegates. He went home one night to find his family gone. They rounded up his wife and children, his mother and unmarried sister; took them to an isolated camp somewhere in the bush. He was told that unless he gave them what they wanted, they'd execute his family one by one, starting with the children."

"What did they want?"

"To know who we were meeting with."

"And he told them?"

"Everything. Where we were meeting, and when, and how many guards, and what we were negotiating."

"Did he have a choice?"

"How do you make a choice like that? I don't know. But what he revealed was costly. Several good men have been exposed, and at least six of ours were killed. They, too, had families. I can only hope the Special Branch kept their word and released his family."

"So, are you all discovered now?"

"No, we're still secure. We were meeting on foreign soil, so they had to use a proxy force. They paid off the local police to come in and do their dirty work. Two dozen local policemen, afraid and untrained, many of them too old to be effective. They had no idea what they were up against." He shook his head slowly. "There were only fourteen of us, all well trained. And we couldn't be taken alive. So I escaped, with eight others. But one way or the other, Africa loses. Black policemen from one African country, fighting black freedom fighters from another, on behalf of an apartheid government. They must be laughing in their beer," he said bitterly.

"And the man who betrayed you? Was he there?"

"He was. But he will never have to decide again between his family and his brothers in arms."

"You executed him."

His eyes glazed over again, and in silence I continued to unroll the bandage.

"No, Michaela," he said quietly. "He was one of the men we lost."

I reached the end of the bandage and took it into the bathroom, where I dropped the wet roll into the rubbish bin, reminding myself to dispose of it before morning so that Selina would not see it. Then I returned and forced myself to examine Khabazela's wound. On his forearm, just below the vein in his inner elbow, were several thick gauze pads, all hardened with dried blood. And on the back of his forearm, just below the elbow, was a similar mass of bloody gauze.

"Oh, God," I said, "it went right through your arm. Did you get it properly treated?" Before he could answer I put a hand out to help him up. "Come into the bathroom so I can get this gauze off," I said. "What was it, a bullet or a blade?"

He rose easily without assistance and smiled at me. "That's the kind of attention I was hoping for," he said, "instead of finding myself in the servants' rooms tending my own wound."

"You didn't tend your wound very well, by the looks of it. But we can fix that." I ushered him into the bathroom and sat him on the side of the tub, with his arm extended over the sink. "Khabazela," I said, trying to distract myself as I worked on him, "there's a very good reason why I don't want to feel bad about my visit to Lungile, so be careful not to make me feel guilty."

"I'm sorry," he said. "I'm not trying to make you feel guilty. But when I got here and found you gone, I was shocked." He stopped, watching as I gently wet and loosened the gauze.

"You were shocked that I was gone?" I asked. "Why? You go away all the time. I don't like it when you're away, but that's part of the life we've agreed to live." I was irritated, and allowed myself to tug too hard on the gauze. He grimaced as he felt the torn flesh pulling beneath my hands. "I'm sorry," I muttered. "I didn't mean to do that."

He watched me again for a moment, lowered his head and kissed my hand. His voice was quiet, and slow, as if the words were being manufactured as he spoke them. "I was not shocked to find you gone, Michaela. I was surprised by the intensity of my feelings. What shocked me was how deeply I felt your absence." He paused again. "Don't ever doubt that I love you," he said.

I looked up at him and smiled and he grinned back at me, and I saw it in his eyes.

"I know," I said. "Now tell me what went through your arm."

"The local police were armed with outdated weapons," he said. "British rifles. World War II Enfields, with attachments." He paused. "Bayonets."

When he explained what happened, he did so with the dispassionate precision and curiosity of a small boy describing how a live grasshopper came apart in his hands.

"The policeman holding the rifle was aiming the bayonet at my eyes," he said, "but I was holding my arm in front of my face." He showed me with his hands what he was describing. "When he jabbed the thing at me, the tip of the bayonet caught me on the inner side of my forearm, and the force of the thrust pushed it all the way through my arm. In the plane coming back, the medic said he thought the ulna might be cracked, so it should be splinted. But he didn't have any splints. All he could do was disinfect it, sew me up, and give me a tetanus injection."

I took the last of the gauze off, exposing his arm. The wounds were only an inch or two from the elbow, and they had been roughly stitched, but the flesh was badly bruised and discolored.

"We're very lucky," I said. "See how close it came to your brachial artery? You might have bled to death."

"The bayonet was wedged between the bones," he said quietly. "I had to grip the rifle stock between my boots in order to pull it out."

Then, into the silence between my finishing with his wound and beginning to speak, there was a sound from the kitchen—the clicking of the lock turning, and the distinctive squeal of the ungreased door slowly opening.

I turned to him soundlessly, my eyes wide and alarmed.

"Did you lock the door?" I whispered.

He nodded his head and I responded by asking, "You didn't leave the key in the lock, did you?"

"No," he whispered. He inserted his uninjured hand into his pocket and withdrew the key.

Selina was the only other one with a key, I thought, but she never came into the house at night.

"Something must be wrong," I said. "I have to go and see."

I gestured with my hands that he should remain in seclusion in the bathroom. He agreed, sitting down on the lowered toilet seat and I left, turning out the bathroom light. As I reached the bedroom door I stopped and gasped, as into my narrow vertical view came a man's boot. Shoulder. The side of his head. The face. Brian McWilliams' face.

"How did you get into my house?" I asked, startled. "It's after midnight. Is something wrong?"

"Nothing's wrong." And then he said my other name. "Grace."

It was wrong in his mouth; he was uncomfortable saying it, and it sounded awkward, but he said it because in the circumstance he had created for himself, he believed that calling me by my first name was an expression of the deep affection he felt for me, and for the attraction he was sure I must feel and could not help but acknowledge now that he was standing before me. He tried it again.

"Grace."

Again it sounded clumsy in his mouth, a glove that didn't fit, a pair of pants that hung down below his feet, ungainly and embarrassing, his father's clothes, too big for him. But he pushed on.

"I had to come to you. I couldn't stay away. And I know it's the right thing to do, because you can't be happy all alone here, a lovely woman like you."

I ignored his comments. "How did you get in?" I asked again. "I know I locked all the doors tonight before I went to bed."

He laughed softly at the question, and I realized that although he may not be drunk, neither was he completely sober.

"I stole it from Selina's room while she was asleep," he said proudly, "and I had a copy made. Otherwise I would've had no way of coming to you."

"You have a wife and children," I said. "I've told you before that I'm not interested. I'm perfectly happy living here on my own. Now go home."

He ignored my words, stepped closer to me. I put my hands on his shoulders to stop him and when he kept coming I pushed on one shoulder and pulled on the other trying to turn him around, in the opposite direction, out of the bedroom and away from the bathroom where Khabazela watched.

But the moment I touched him I realized that I had made a huge mistake. He raised his arms, held his hands against mine, and pulled me toward him. His hands felt massive, and he crated mine up inside his big palms, hot and hard and rough against my skin, and at the same time clammy and unwholesome.

Holding my hands and bending them backwards as he lowered his head, he tried to place his mouth on mine. I stepped away in disgust, pulling one hand from him and pushing at his chin but he resisted, his mouth still on mine. Then with all my might I dug my fingernails into McWilliams face, drawing three lines of blood down one side of his nose and across his cheek.

He stumbled back with a cry, one hand to his face, and with the other he lashed out, catching me on the side of the head with his open palm.

Khabazela, already tensed to explode from the bathroom, was on his feet before the sound of the blow reached him. He hit the bathroom door with such force that it crashed open against the wall behind it with a noise like a detonation.

In that moment, McWilliams, cradling his wound, wore a look of such surprise that Khabazela, now in his stride, felt a grin taking shape on his face and the sound of a laugh forming in his throat. But after a delay I finally reacted to the blow and stumbled sideways into his path and he had to stop and catch me.

At that instant McWilliams stepped forward and we were all so close together that there was no room for action. Khabazela steadied me with his good hand while he automatically readjusted his feet so that he could move rapidly when he must, because now the worst had happened. We were discovered, and this man held our lives in his clumsy hands.

"Fuck," muttered McWilliams, removing his hand from his face and forming fists before him. "Fuck, you bitch," and his face screwed up and big tears fell from the corners of his eyes and dribbled down to merge with the blood trickling in three strands from his nose and cheek down to the corners of his mouth where it seeped in between his lips and colored his saliva and his teeth pink. He looked at me as I stood with a hand on my head where he hit me.

"So," he spat, the words bubbling pinkish from his mouth, "you're happy here on your own? Not interested in me?" He pointed a finger at me, still crying. "You're a liar," he says, "you're not alone, you just prefer the company of this *kaffir* farmhand in your bed." He looked with disbelief at the bathrobe Khabazela wore, the richly colored, luxurious robe I brought back from Europe for him. McWilliams laughed, a broken sob. "You think you can hide his stink and his filth with a white man's clothes? You must be mad."

Thinking and moving very fast but experiencing it all as if he was in perfect control, Khabazela knew that he was yet invisible to McWilliams. McWilliams' fury was aimed at me, and if I could speak well, perhaps the worst could still be averted.

"You have it all wrong," I said urgently. "Look at his arm—I was just bandaging it for him. He was hurt last night and came knocking at my window."

"You're a liar," he said. "But you're done now. I'm taking your boy here with me—and where I'm taking him he's not coming back from. Starting tomorrow you'll do whatever I want. If not, believe me I'll make a police report and you'll end up charged under the race laws." He wiped his face with the back of his hand and swayed first to one side and then to the other. "You ready to lose your farm and go to jail because you were ready to drop your panties for Mandla Mkhize? For—" he gestured with contempt "—for this?"

The courage scotch that he drank just before coming into the house was taking effect and as he breathed a jagged sigh the smell of it surrounded us all. He reached out and grabbed Khabazela's bandaged arm, holding it hard, the way you grip a thick tree branch before heaving it over the fence.

"Come on, you," he said, expecting no resistance, and with his other hand he reached out to push me aside but I would not be pushed.

"Can't we sit down and talk?" I said. "This is not what you think, Brian, and it really doesn't have to be so dramatic."

Our eyes met and Khabazela gave me an imperceptible nod—we agreed that I would try and talk my foreman out of his madness.

"So now I'm being dramatic," McWilliams said. "Now you want to talk, now that you're in trouble."

He looked for the first time at Khabazela, standing frozen at his side, breathing slowly, barely aware of the tortuous grip on his wounded arm.

"Look at him," said McWilliams, full of contempt. "Look what you took in your bed—he's so shit-scared he can't move. This is what I've been up against? You chose this over me? A filthy dumb *kaffir*? In his whole life he couldn't have imagined such a thing—that he would have the chance to fuck such a gorgeous woman—even a beautiful one so damn stupid that she would want to sleep with him. Look at him now that the fucking is over—he's too frightened to stand up for you. God damn it," he shouted, enraged. "I could have stood it if I lost you to a decent man. But not this. Did you have to risk your life and your freedom and your farm—everything—on this garbage?"

No, thought Khabazela, don't do it—but he knew by the look in my eyes that it was too late and I would not remain silent.

"He is a decent man," I said quietly. "I love him. And if I risk my life I do it by choice."

I could not help but speak; McWilliams could not contain his rage; and Khabazela would not stand by and watch this enraged man strike me. Before McWilliams could even clench his fist, Khabazela recognized that he was about to lash out at my face with his free hand, and he launched his left knee into McWilliams' groin. As he felt it connect he put his left foot on the ground and catapulted his right knee upward. McWilliams doubled over, slamming his forehead into Khabazela's jackhammer knee with a dull, blunted crack and the big man toppled to the floor like a piece of lumber and lay there, groaning.

And then, from being lost and wavering, I moved into the state Khabazela had spoken of, the slow motion of calm and absolute certainty that kept him safe when he was in the midst of violence and the only thing he could count on was the unexpected. I knew exactly what I must do and why. And I knew where my certainty came from. Lungile, who spoke of sweet potatoes and children, said, "each day will lead to the next; it is enough to know that you have planted a seed or that a child is coming. Make ready slowly. At each step the Shades will help you to know what to do next."

Khabazela sat on the bed cradling his wounded arm, dazed and exhausted, watching me, wondering what to do as Brian McWilliams lay not a yard from his feet, groaning.

I rushed from the bedroom through the short hallway, and in the darkness of the kitchen I went straight to the metal hangers above the stove on which hung pots and pans. I reached up with both hands to unhook the big blackened cast iron frying pan that Selina used for browning meat and making gravy and fried chicken and her delicious crisp potatoes. It weighed about twenty pounds and was an awkward shape, but I returned to the bedroom, hefting it in front of me as it banged against my thighs, one hand on the long, thick handle and the other at the opposite side, holding onto the smaller wooden grip.

As I reentered the bedroom Khabazela looked at me quizzically and I saw his eyes travel from my face to the frying pan at my waist and back again.

"Michaela?" he said, but I didn't answer because I was focused on the body of Brian McWilliams lying on his back on the floor, whose sporadic groaning was now louder than it had been when I left a moment before, a semi-conscious moan, and I knew I didn't have much time to do what I knew I must. I walked toward him and lifted one foot over him so that I stood astride him and again Khabazela repeated my name, in a question, but this time he knew the answer and he said it again, differently.

"Michaela?" And then, hoarsely, "Michaela, no."

But again he made no move to stop me as I took the handle of the cast iron frying pan in both hands and hoisted my arms straight up above my head and held it there, poised as I took a deep breath, looking down at Brian McWilliams.

His eyes slowly opened. He looked up at my face, dazed, and after a few seconds raised his glance to the frying pan held high above his head. When I saw the terror take shape on his face I paused briefly but couldn't stop. I bent smoothly at the waist and brought my arms around in a wide arc and with all my might I hammered the underside of the frying pan down on his head, thinking of a steel ax-head driven deep into hardwood timber.

The frying pan bounced from his skull and the impact vibrated up my wrists, shooting through my arms into my shoulders like steel against steel without any shock-absorber to cushion the blow. Three times I raised the cooking utensil and by the third time my strength was sapped and it fell with the force of gravity alone and its own weight which was enough, and this time there was no bounce and I heard not the hard boom as it landed on the split and bleeding flesh at Brian McWilliam's hairline but the crack of shattering bone.

My knees collapsed. I sat on his chest gasping and reached down to take his heavy wrist in mine. Before he took his last breath I lifted his hand, holding the fingers out straight. Raising my head, I dug the dead-weight fingers into my neck and drew them down so that my skin and then my blood caught beneath his scrubbed fingernails, and my night-gown shredded to reveal my breast, bruised and scratched.

"Oh, Michaela."

I heard in Khabazela's voice a deep despair as I rose from the body and slowly sat on the bed, taking his hand in mine as I had taken the hand of Brian McWilliams and as I pulled his hand towards me I felt him shrink back.

"No, no. Just give me your hand," and I placed his reluctant hand on my belly and looked up at his face.

"My Khabazela," I said softly as I gently rubbed his open palm against my belly, "We are going to bear a child."

He looked down at his hand, puzzled, and I saw that he could not reconcile this information with the actions he had just witnessed.

"You're pregnant?" he said and with relief I saw him begin to pull himself together. I nodded my head, pushing his hand against my belly.

"That's why you went to see Lungile," he said, and again I nodded my head and he turned from me to look down at the floor. "But why this?"

"He saw you," I said patiently. "He knows who you are. He would have gone to the police. Even if they didn't believe him they would begin to watch you. And what if they started an investigation? They'd find out everything. We had no choice."

He nodded his head slowly up and down, and understanding became hopelessness as he took his head in his hands.

"Enough," I said, startled by the sharpness of my voice. "We've been here before. Do you remember the real reason we were convicted of treason? We slept together. They couldn't abide the fact that we loved each other and they put us away. We escaped once—but if they find out who we are they'll kill you and put me back forever. I won't let that happen. Not to us and not to our child."

"You've solved the problem of our being discovered," he said, raising his head from his hands to look at me. When he continued, it was in a calm and rational voice. "This rubbish on the floor will never reveal that we're lovers. Our secret is secure. All we have to do is get rid of the body and wait." He paused. "Until you give birth," he said. He stood and looked around and I could see that he was planning. "They may not know who I am, but they'll know what you've been doing. How are you going to bring up a colored baby, Michaela? Did you forget the law? We have to get him buried. And you have to get an abortion."

I rose to stand in front of him. "No," I said fiercely, grasping the lapels of his bathrobe in my fist. "I will not abort our child." With my other hand I pointed to the scratches on my neck and chest. "Why do you think I did this to myself?"

"I don't know why you've done any of this," he said, "but we don't have much time. It'll be dawn soon."

"We're not getting rid of the body," I told him. "It's staying here until the police arrive."

"What?"

"I will tell the police," I said calmly, staring back straight into his eyes, "that my foreman made advances to me, and I rejected him. I'll explain that he broke into my house after midnight and raped me. I'll describe how he tried to force himself on me a second time but I fought him off and because he had been drinking I was able to unbalance him so that he tripped and fell. He knocked his head on the footboard and while he was lying on the floor I went into the kitchen and grabbed the heaviest thing I could and ran back and hit him before he regained consciousness. I'll tell them how I didn't mean to kill him," I said softly, "but I didn't want to risk being raped again."

"Oh, Michaela…"

"You keep repeating my name," I said through gritted teeth, "as if it's all hopeless. Stop it."

"I don't know what else to say," he said wearily. "And I don't know where this is all going."

"I'll tell you. In a minute you're going to leave, and you're going to stay away for a few weeks. The police will come to investigate and hear my story. Everyone will know all about it. And when I begin to show they'll look at me with sympathy instead of contempt."

"They'll feel even sorrier for you when you give birth to a black baby," he said bitterly. "Did you forget that under this government, law trumps biology? If it's illegal for us to make love, then having children is illegal, too. It's bad enough that you're willing to hide our child behind rape, but that doesn't change reality: bringing up a black child as your own is illegal. He'll be taken from you and brought up by a colored family, or by a black family closer to his skin color. By strangers. What kind of life are you condemning our child to?"

I was suddenly unable to breathe, as if the air has been sucked from my body. This was a nightmare, and I began to see that it might have no end. I allowed myself to consider Khabazela's suggestion that I get rid of the baby, but it passed quickly as I remembered Lungile's face, and Solomon's expression, and my father's constant admonition to never forget who I am. Instead, I began to think about the sequence of possibilities, and how I might handle each one.

"We don't know how dark our child will be," I said aloud, "or what kind of hair he'll have."

If he's very light, I thought, there'll be no issue. If he's a little dark but has straight hair, they'll assume he has my coloring. But if he's a little dark with kinky hair they'll subject him to the pencil test—put the pencil in his curls and if it stays there then he'll be guilty of having black blood somewhere in his past, either in McWilliams's family or in mine. What will happen then? Or worse, if he's very dark...

I felt rage rise in me at the infamy that forced me to give a value to the child I carried based on curls and coloring, on the way his hair fell or the richness of his skin. And then the rage evaporated and turned to fear for how terrible my child's life might be if he had rich, burnished skin or tight, shining curls and we failed in our fight to make things change.

"How the hell am I supposed to know? There's no rule book here—no right way. We have to make this up as we go along. If we decide that it can't work," I said softly, rising from the bed, "that he wouldn't have any kind of life here, I promise I'll take him and go somewhere else. We'll leave the country." I paused. "And you'll come with us."

He didn't respond to my words, but he rose to stand facing me and I asked him a question, dreading his answer.

"Aren't you happy—even a little bit," I asked, "that we've made a child together?"

He tried to laugh off my question, and looked surprised when he heard what emerged from his own throat—something between a groan and a sob, harsh and pained.

"Happy?" he asked, placing his hands on my shoulders. "You kill an unconscious man with a cast iron frying pan, and I sit by as you mutilate yourself with his still-warm fingernails. You pick that bloody moment to share with me the news that you're carrying our child. Then you explain how you plan to accuse the dead man of rape to hide the fact that the child is ours. And you intend to raise our child without me, because it's illegal for us to live under the same roof, have a child, or raise the child together. And you ask me if I'm happy?"

"It was a stupid question," I said. "I'm so sorry. I didn't mean for you to find out like this."

In the ruin of my bedroom, he embraced me. "This is the way it is," he said.

What hurt me most was the resignation—even defeat—in his voice. In response I threw my arms about his waist.

"You're having our child alone, Michaela," he said softly, speaking into my neck. "You have less than a slender hope of making it work, and

I'm excluded from this picture. You're conducting an experiment, and it terrifies me, for the child's sake, and for yours. And I'm frightened for us." He pulled back and looked at me. "A lot more frightened than happy."

That he was fearful for us gave me pause, but we had no time. I kissed him hard and he kissed me back. I tore myself from him and pushed him out and watched him walk across the yard to his room in the servants' quarters through the dull yellow gleam of light reflected from the kitchen window.

After a few minutes he emerged carrying a bag under his arm, looked quickly towards me at the kitchen window and nodded. Then he slipped away across the yard and into the gloom, and as he disappeared, fingers of darkness seemed to crawl into the yard in an attempt to swallow up the light.

I shivered and turned back, gathered my shattered life and my ripped nightgown tight around me, and walked down the hallway to the phone. I put the receiver to my ear and rotated the ringer handle. Cassie, the night operator, picked up.

"Hello, Grace. Is there a problem?"

"Better get the police out to my farm." I paused, clearing my throat. I was yet unpracticed in this kind of deceit. "It's McWilliams, my foreman. He raped me. I think I've killed him."

twenty-two

MICHAELA

Natal, South Africa, 1967

The policemen who arrived at the farm before dawn were both shocked and impressed by the damage I had done to Brian McWilliams. They stared at his broken and bloody head, commented quietly on the blood and brain matter smeared on the underside of the cast iron frying pan I had left lying beside the body. Then they turned to me, asked lots of questions and took detailed notes.

I was sitting on a chair in the dining room, and the older officer, a man in his fifties, knelt at my side, gently examining my scratched face and torn robe.

"You might want to have your doctor examine you," he said, rising to his feet. "I know you live alone here—would you like me to call anyone for you?"

I shook my head. "No. I'll be fine."

"I know you will, Miss," he said, smiling, and I frowned at him. "I know this must be very difficult for you, but you can take some comfort in knowing that, pardon my language, this bastard picked the wrong woman."

They called the police station and waited with me until the wagon arrived to collect the body. I took a bath and dressed, and the only evidence of my ordeal was the scratches on my face, covered by the purple of mercurochrome. By then the word had spread, and by the time I emerged from my bedroom, Jane and Letty had arrived and were in the kitchen, making tea. Once I had convinced them that I was fine and that I would do best if allowed to go about my daily routine, they praised me for my fortitude, and left.

In truth I was far from fine. My back and shoulders hurt from the effort it had taken to raise aloft and crash down the frying pan, and I was filled with guilt, unable to reconcile what I had done with who I was. I had staged my own rape and lied about it, and yet the pain and anguish I felt belonged to a woman who had actually undergone the experience of being forcibly penetrated. The irony was that my violation was self-inflicted.

I got through those early days one moment at a time, reminding myself constantly that there had been reason and purpose behind my actions. And I held my breath whenever the phone rang, or I heard a car approach, waiting for the announcement of an inquiry into the death; waiting to hear that the police had questions because the medical examiner had found no sign of seminal or vaginal fluids on the corpse, and no indication of sexual activity.

But it was all in my imagination. As far as the police were concerned, it was an open and shut case. I was a convincing and sympathetic victim and they accepted my story at face value. As a result of the report they filed, there were no questions raised about what had happened. I don't think the medical examiner even looked at the body, and there was no inquiry of any kind into Brian McWilliams's death.

I insisted upon maintaining my daily routine, and each morning Solomon came by to collect me and we went on our rounds. At first he did his best to distract me, but as the days passed he became increasingly distant and silent. We walked silently side by side, speaking only when the subject was cattle, feed, crops, fences or machinery. He said nothing about what had occurred and he asked me no questions, but I was aware that he was unable to meet my eye.

On the day Brian McWilliams was buried, I returned from my walk with Solomon to find Anna McWilliams sitting ramrod straight on my verandah. She had come straight from the funeral in her darkest jacket and skirt, and she wore a little grey hat to which was attached a veil that she raised as I arrived.

Selina had offered her a cup of tea, and was just placing a tray loaded with a pot of brewing tea, two cups, and a platter of shortbread biscuits on the table. I had not seen Anna for weeks, and although she looked drawn and weary, there was about her a kind of energy that surprised me. She seemed not quite as dowdy as I remembered her, and she was confident and well put together, her hair clean and combed, her eyes bright. I had been dreading this meeting, expecting a tearful and resentful widow, and after my initial reaction at seeing her, which was to turn and run in the opposite direction, I was relieved to see that she was so composed. It was almost as if in some way, Anna McWilliams had been freed by her husband's death.

"Hello Grace," she said calmly, looking up at me. "You don't mind, do you, if I call you Grace?"

I had deprived her of her husband and her children of their father, and taken from them what little comfort they might have had from knowing that he died a good man. I had no idea how to treat this bereaved woman.

"No," I said, "of course not."

"That's good," she said, "because I'm not sure how to address the woman who killed my husband." Her lips parted in a brittle smile. "Whatever he did or didn't do to you, the result of your action is that I have no husband. Worse, my children have no father." She leaned forward in her chair and reached out to the teapot. "May I pour you a cup of tea?" she asked.

I nodded, forced myself to sit down beside her. I had imagined being in complete control during this meeting, having to tone myself down, to be gentle and calming. Instead I found myself at a loss.

"Milk?" she asked, and I nodded. She poured a thin stream of milk into my cup, added tea, and handed it to me as if this were her garden party and I a guest. I don't recall whether she actually was, but she might as well have been wearing white gloves. She picked up her own cup and leaned back in her chair. Slowly she took a sip, and sighed.

"Such a lovely morning," she said. "I sent the children back with the nanny—I just couldn't bear to go right back to the house after burying Brian, and everyone I know was at the funeral. Except you, of course. So I thought, why not pay you a visit?"

"I'm glad you did," I said. "I wanted to speak to you, but I didn't know how. There's no protocol in this situation, is there?"

I sipped my tea, wondering what she was doing in my home. From the way she was acting, she felt she held all the cards. But what were the cards? Did she know something with which she could blackmail me? It hit me that perhaps her husband had known about us—that he had been spying around the house previously, managed to see inside, heard us talking, and that he had told her. But then I remembered his reaction when he saw Khabazela in my bedroom.

"What are you doing here, Anna?" I asked as gently as I could.

She feigned surprise. "Doing?" she said. "What do you mean? We're having tea together on your verandah." She took a bite of Selina's shortbread and a delicate sip of tea, and placed her cup and saucer on the wrought iron table. Then she leaned back, crossed her ankles, and laced her fingers on her lap. "We need to make some plans. I have four children, Grace, and now it's only me. I'm going to need some help."

Money, I thought with relief. What she wants is money, and then she'll go away.

"I'm sure you're going to need help," I said. "If you need staples just come to the farm. And if you run short and need cash to tide you over—you know, until you decide where you're going to go—please, just ask me. I don't want this to be any more difficult for you than it needs to be."

She shook her head. "Sounds very generous, Grace, but I'm not going to make it that easy for you." She smiled. "I think it's about time we learned about each other. All I know about you is that when your husband died, you sold your farm up north and bought this one. You have money. You're educated."

She paused.

"You don't know much about me, either, but I'm going to tell you a few things. I grew up fifty miles from here, in farming country. We were poor white—and that means very poor. My father did odd jobs for the smaller farmers, and most often he was paid in livestock and food. Brian McWilliams was the way out of my father's house. Turned out he wasn't much of an escape—all I did was exchange one hell for another. By the time I realized what I'd done, it was too late. Now he's gone. All I have is four children to raise, the furniture that sits in the foreman's cottage on your farm, and a collection of half empty liquor bottles hidden all over the house. Whatever savings we might have had, he just drank away," she said simply. "He left me nothing, and now I have to go to work."

I calculated in my mind how big a check I could write her, and whether it would be big enough to purge my guilt. I wanted her off the farm—and I didn't want her around when my child was born.

"How much do you need, Anna?" I asked.

"You don't know me," she said again, the quiet smile still on her lips. "You think if you pay me enough I'll take my children and go away. But I don't want money. And I'm not going anywhere."

I felt my heart sinking at her words, and it must have shown in my face.

"I don't want to make trouble for you, either," she said quickly, as if she had been waiting to say the words before I refused her. "But I want something I never had. I know I have to work—but I want a job that gives me a chance to be someone, to do something useful. I need a decent place to live with my children. And I want a good life for them, with schooling, and music, and to be around educated people."

"You're living a fantasy, Anna," I said. "I don't have that kind of life myself. How could I possibly provide it for you?"

"I'm not living a fantasy," she said, rising from her chair and looking down at me. She reached up and lowered the veil. She was smiling, a serene expression on her face, and she was suddenly, surprisingly, beautiful. "You're the kind of people I want my children to be around," she said, "but I'm not sure how to make it happen. We should talk again in a few weeks, after we've both had a chance to think about it."

She leaned across the table, emptied the tray of shortbread into her open serviette, folded it over neatly, and dropped it into her bag. "For the children," she said. "Thanks for the tea, Grace. I'll get the serviette washed and returned. Goodbye."

I watched her walk down the driveway past my standing roses, bag over her shoulder, hips swaying gently inside her dark skirt, grey hat on a head held tall. Where the garden stopped and the fields began, she turned, and then disappeared behind the tall *mielie* plants that towered above her on both sides of the road.

What she wanted I didn't know, but I was full of admiration for her courage and her audacity, and I fully supported her desire to get the best deal she could for her children and for herself. What I didn't know was what it would cost me, and I was completely unable to penetrate her agenda.

She came to mind often in the next few weeks, but fleetingly. I was busy with the farm; watching and feeling my belly grow, remembering what it was like to be pregnant. It was an emotionally rich time, full of expectation and dreaming. But it was also filled with uncertainty and fear of what the future might bring, and loneliness, and with the ache of absence. My parents were gone; Khabazela was somewhere in hiding or playing out roles in his life from which I was excluded. And being pregnant again reminded me of the first time, of my joy and pride when you were born, of how much I missed you.

Several weeks after Anna appeared for her impromptu tea party, I ran into her at the general store. I was about three months pregnant, just beginning to show, and when she greeted me briefly, she glanced at my belly. The sudden surprise on her face disappeared quickly, and she said nothing. Before we parted she asked whether she could drop by the farmhouse that afternoon, and we agreed that she would come around teatime.

She walked briskly down the road between the *mielies*, and up the driveway, at precisely 4:00 o'clock. I was reading the newspaper. When she appeared I had just glanced through the glass table top and noticed that I was tapping my foot nervously. She walked onto the verandah and sat opposite me.

"What a lovely day," she said.

"Hello, Anna," I answered. "I was just about to pour myself some tea. Would you like a cup?"

She nodded and I poured us both tea as she sat with her face raised to the sun, eyes closed, as if our being together was the most natural thing in the world.

"I'm glad to see that you're so relaxed," I said, placing her cup on the table. The sarcasm in my voice was unmistakable, but the only acknowledgement she made was to sit up straight, place her cup and saucer onto the wide armrest of her chair, and slowly take a sip of tea. Then she smiled, the same serene, knowing smile she wore on our previous meeting, and again I was struck by how beautiful it was on her pinched face.

"We all have secrets, Grace," she said, "and since we're on the way to being friends, I'm going to share one of my secrets with you. It's something I would never have told you while Brian was alive, but now that he's gone I have nothing to lose. And I think you'll find this interesting." She sipped her tea. "Brian and I didn't have much in common, but we were young and we had a lot of energy, and we loved sex. When he was sober, we were wonderful in bed."

"I don't need to know this, Anna," I interrupted.

"Oh, yes," she said fiercely, glaring at me. "You absolutely do. Just be quiet and listen."

"All right," I said, taken aback. "I'm listening."

"Even if we'd wanted to," she continued calmly, "we didn't know enough to prevent pregnancy. But for four years I didn't get pregnant. We couldn't understand it, and the sadder I got, the angrier he became. That's when I discovered how nasty he could be when he was drunk.

Swore at me. Called me liar, fraud, sterile bitch. He knocked me around and then the next morning he would be all tears and repentance. I stopped loving him. One weekend when he was off hunting, I ran into a boy I'd been friendly with. We had a beer together and ended up in his car. Then we were out on a blanket in the middle of a field, under a big moon. Within weeks I knew I was pregnant."

She leaned forward, elbows on the table, and looked at me.

"Getting pregnant was the easiest thing I ever did. It happened four times, whenever I slept with someone else. Like clockwork. Brian came to my bed several times a week, also like clockwork. But he never gave me a child. We had four children; none of them are his. He could knock me around, but he never knocked me up."

She smiled brightly over her teacup. "He may have been weak, Grace, and a bully, and he was violent when he was drunk. But he loved to fuck, and he was good at it because despite everything, he actually liked women. Even at his worst I doubt he could have raped anyone. And the closest he ever came to fertilizing anything was when he told your Zulus to spread cowshit on the fields. Yet here you are, fucked and fertilized—and, you say, forced." She held her arms out, as if in surprise, and said, "I just don't know what to make of it all."

Then she slumped back against her chair as if she had no bones, rolled her eyes, and exhaled loudly. At the corners of her mouth she wore the hint of a smile, and around her crinkled eyes there was a mischievous expression.

I said nothing at first, speechless at her lack of restraint, and furious to see that she was actually taking pleasure in this little charade. The fact that most of my story was a lie didn't make her description any less invasive or unfair, and I felt violated. Even in the moment, that irony was not lost on me. And I couldn't even begin to think about the implications of what she was saying.

"So now you know what I've been hiding. I've risked telling you this because I need you," she said with the earnest quality of a young girl, "and I want to start out on an honest footing with you. If you were vindictive, you could do some damage to me in this community even though Brian's dead. But you won't, because I think you have more to hide than I do."

Perhaps for lack of a better alternative, I found myself laughing, and Anna looked on, puzzled. She thought my secret was that I'd had an affair with someone, perhaps Brian, perhaps another married man in the community, and that I was trying to protect either him from the charge of adultery, or myself from being seen as an unmarried mother and a loose woman. She had no clue what I was really concealing, or on how many levels I was living a lie. And she had no idea that if Brian was not actually the father of his four blond children, then it was at least plausible that he might be the father of my not-altogether-white child.

"What's so funny?" she asked.

"Even with your vivid imagination," I said, wiping my eyes with my sleeve, "you couldn't possibly imagine what's so funny." I looked at the compelling mix of manipulation and innocence in her face, this young mother, alone. "You've been through some hard times, Anna, and you're letting your fantasies run away with you. You're talking a lot of nonsense—but I do admire your spirit, and you're right. We could both do with a friend." I paused. "I think we can probably work something out."

After the incident, Jane and Letty began dropping in unannounced to check up on me, and to make sure that I was recovering from my ordeal.

"You've been through an awful thing, Grace," said Letty one day. "But you just seem to take it in stride and keep going."

"I have a farm to run," I answered. "You can't dodge what life throws at you. All you can do is wipe yourself off and soldier on."

It's what my father used to say to me, and I felt a sense of relief that what I was sharing with them was a truth from my real life. I was living so many lies, and I hated myself for the untruths I was forced to tell these two loving and generous friends.

"My father used to say I was so stubborn that I wouldn't go around an obstacle. The only way I knew was to go straight through, regardless of the consequences."

"I've heard that before," muttered Letty, and she smiled back. "My father used to say it to me. And he was right, too."

"Yes," I agreed. "It's the direct route, but it tends to exact a high price."

"The older I get," she said, "the more inclined I am to take the long way round. I find I like to arrive in one piece."

We all laughed together, and that was the day they both watched me walking. I saw them exchange glances as I unconsciously draped my arms about my belly. And the next morning Andrew dropped by.

He was uneasy as he greeted me and although it wasn't hot, there was the sheen of perspiration on his forehead. He refused any refreshment, and I led him into the study, where we sat facing each other.

"Been some time since I've seen you, Grace," he said. "But I hear from Letty that you're fine."

"Really?" I said. "And did she also mention that I was pregnant?"

"She's not a meddler, Grace. She and Jane are concerned about you."

"Well, at least I know why you're here this morning."

He leaned forward in his chair, reached into his pocket for his handkerchief, and wiped his forehead. He was clearly uncomfortable. "Your pregnancy is not the only reason I'm here today," he said.

"Yes, you have many reasons for being here, and multiple responsibilities. You needed to see for yourself that I'm pregnant, and you're probably going to insist on examining me, aren't you?"

"I do think it's a good idea for you to get some prenatal care."

"Which you'd be happy to provide?"

"I would, but you're free to select another doctor if you prefer."

"That's not very practical, considering the nearest doctor is more than an hour's drive. So tell me, Andrew," I said, "when you examine me, will it be as my physician? As a medical operative for the ANC? Or will you perform your obstetric exam as Mandla Mkhize's medical representative?"

"That kind of nastiness is uncalled for," he said softly, "and it's unworthy of you, Grace." He glanced down at my belly. "Now I'm here I see you're about three months pregnant." He paused, his forehead creased in thought. "And the incident took place how long ago?"

"The incident," I said, "was a rape, and it took place two months ago. So you're mistaken. This is what two months pregnant looks like."

He smiled. "Save the fairytales for your neighbors," he said. "Perhaps you can fool them. But in the last twenty years I've delivered a thousand babies, and I know what two months pregnant looks like." He pointed at me. "That's not it."

I leaned back into the cushion and crossed my arms over my belly. My anger was gone, replaced by exhaustion and anxiety. I realized, suddenly, how difficult it was going to be to keep all my stories straight.

"I'm really tired, Andrew," I said, "tired of all this. Why are you here? What is it you want from me?"

He rose quickly and came to sit in the straight-backed chair at my side. As he did so he picked up my wrist and took my pulse with a practiced hand. When he was through he lowered my wrist, but he kept his warm hand on my arm.

"I'm here for several reasons, Grace, none of them particularly pleasant, except for my wish to see you. Unfortunately, the other reasons I'm here will probably negate any pleasantness."

"What do you mean?" I sat up straight again, panic surging. "Is he in trouble?"

"He's fine," said Andrew, waving my concern away and gently pressing my shoulder back against the chair. "Now, are you going to have me guess what's going on, or do you want to tell me yourself?"

"You've probably guessed already," I said, "unless he's told you himself, in which case you know anyway."

"What I know is what I see, and what my experience tells me—that you're pregnant, and that you were already pregnant before you killed Brian McWilliams in the commission of an attempted rape."

"Attempted?" I said.

"Other than your word and a dead body, there is no proof of a rape."

"So," I said, aware of the harshness and anger in my voice. And the fear. "You don't believe me?"

"I didn't say that I don't believe you. I'm just telling you what I know—and believing something is different from knowing it's true."

"Words of wisdom," I murmured. "From the White Zulu. *Sangoma* of Science."

"There are a few other things I know are true," he said, ignoring my insult. "Would you like to know what they are?"

"Do I have a choice?"

"Yes, you do—you can stop me anytime. What I know is that you're going to have a baby in six months, and that the community will believe Brian McWilliams is the father. But I also know the only way he could be the father is if you slept with him at least a month before you killed him. And I don't think that happened."

"So what did happen?"

"I'm not sure," he said. "But I'll make a prediction. When you give birth, we're going to have a hell of a time making sure that the baby stays with you, because it will be some combination of a most beautiful, light-skinned mother, and a tall, black, very handsome father. And I'd put money on the fact that the race police will have questions about the baby's complexion."

I turned away from him. "You're so bloody smart," I said.

"Yes," he said, gently squeezing my arm, "I am. And you have no idea how hard it is to be so smart and yet have no answers. If ever there was a right time for this, and if ever there were a better combination of parents, I can't imagine it. Since I realized that the child is his, I've been trying to find a way to carry it off in a way that won't upset the authorities." He stopped and thought for a moment, his hand still on my arm. "We won't know until the child is a few months old, but it's possible that he—or she—will be light enough to avoid raising suspicion."

"So what do we do?"

"We wait and see."

I turned to look at him, intending to be sarcastic, but instead I found myself smiling at him as the tears streamed down my cheeks.

"Sorry," he said quietly, folding the handkerchief in his hand back on itself and wiping the tears from my face. "I can understand why you're weeping, but why the smile?"

"Wait and see was exactly what I planned to do, although I didn't think of it as a plan. I just couldn't think of anything else. Either you're not so smart, or else I'm smarter than I thought I was."

"You're definitely smarter than you think you are," he said, still smiling, and then his eyes clouded.

"What's the matter, Andrew?" I asked.

"I'm here to take care of Grace Michaels and her baby," he said, "both because of what you call my multiple responsibilities, and because I've become very fond of you. But what I have to say now needs to be heard through the ears of Lungile's daughter. This is a thing of the Zulus, and you need to hear it with Zulu ears. It's not something Grace Michaels— or even Michaela Green at her most radical—would be able to understand or accept."

"Sounds pretty awful," I said. My heart was racing. Whatever it was, it had to do with the part of Khabazela that was beyond my reach; the tribal part of him that connected him to a tradition I could never access.

Andrew smiled again, warily. "Perhaps not that awful, if you're a traditional Zulu woman," he said. "But it's not good."

"What is it?"

He cleared his throat and sat forward in his chair so that we were a head apart.

"One of Khabazela's goals is to enlist the Zulu community here; to show them why they need to take control of their own future, and to give them the tools to do it. He can't do it without first becoming a part of the community. And that's proving more difficult than anticipated."

"Why? He's already part of the community. Solomon is his uncle, and he has an extended clan in the village."

"All true. But to have stature and influence, a man needs to be like other men. The people need to see that his future—as well as his present—lies in the community. He needs to put down roots, Grace." He paused. "He needs children."

I put my hand softly on my belly, fingers outspread. "He will have a child," I said. "Soon."

He shook his head. "That won't be enough."

"Our child?" I said, looking up into his face. "Won't be enough for what?"

"Grace, you're not making sense," he said quietly. "If you're going to give out that the child is the result of a rape, it can't also be his child. And even if you want the Zulu community to know the truth and to be able to claim the child as its own, it may have the wrong skin color."

"So our child will be either too dark to be accepted by the white establishment, or too light to claim a place with his father's people. How is it possible for two people to bring a child into a world where he has no place? And you tell me that *I'm* not making any sense?"

As I stared at him, waiting, I remember thinking how masculine Andrew's face was, with a heavy jaw and a full mouth. The pity filling his blue eyes made me want to weep. He tightened his hold on my forearm, and reached over with his free hand to enfold mine in his.

"Grace, he's taken a girl in the village as his wife. Her name is Miriam." And then, as an afterthought, "she's carrying his child."

The chasm I was staring into opened even wider.

"She's carrying his child," I said. "As well."

"Yes," he replied, still holding my hand with one of his and my forearm with the other. "She is also pregnant with Khabazela's child."

I pulled myself awkwardly to my feet and headed toward the kitchen. "I'm going to make tea," I said over my shoulder, not wanting Andrew to see the stricken expression on my face. My voice was unrecognizable—it came from somewhere high in my throat, just behind my tongue, the thin voice of a woman unable to breathe. "Wait here, please—I need a few minutes."

The kitchen was deserted. It was early afternoon; Selina was on her break. I put the kettle on the gas flame and stood over the kitchen table, trying to absorb this new disaster, trying to measure the contempt Khabazela must feel for me to be able to do such a thing—without even telling me. I couldn't begin to measure what this would mean for my life, and for the life of our child.

I wasn't aware of the kettle, but after listening to its whistle for a few moments, Andrew came to investigate. He found me bent over the table, supporting myself on one hand, the fingers of the other buried in my hair. He didn't know that, having tried to weep and failed, in my anger and fear I dug my fingernails so deeply into my scalp that I drew blood.

Without a word he made the tea, set it on a tray, and carried it into the study. Then he came back to get me, led me gently out of the kitchen, sat me down, and placed a steaming cup on the table at my side. We sat together for a long time, and he waited until I was ready to break the silence.

"If I were alone right now I'd tear the house apart," I said eventually.

"I'd be tempted to do the same in your place."

"You might be," I said. "On the other hand, you've come here as another man's proxy, to deliver the message that I'm not enough for him. He's marrying another woman, and she's already carrying his child. And in a minute you're going to start trying to convince me that I shouldn't chuck him out, sell the farm, pack up and leave. That makes me furious with you, as well as with him."

Andrew smiled.

"There's nothing funny in this," I said sharply.

"Plenty of irony, though," he replied. He relaxed into the armchair, his thick forearms crossed over his chest. "Look at me, for example. I couldn't have begun to imagine being here, another man's proxy, as you put it, yet here I am. And the reason why I might want you to accept what he's done and stay here has very little to do with my responsibility to any person or political movement." He paused, looking at me with eyes wide and unconcealed. "That's why I'm not going to try and convince you of anything. You know your own mind, and you'll make your own decisions."

"Before I make any decisions I need to know precisely what message you're here to deliver," I said.

"I don't have a message from him, Grace; he didn't ask me to come talk to you. Doesn't even know I'm here."

"So you think he's just dropped me out of his life? That he was going to let this happen and have me find out after the fact?"

"No, no. He'll tell you in his own time. But I thought it would be easier—that it would work out better for all concerned—if you already knew about it when he came to speak to you."

"Why?"

"Because I think it's important for you to be reminded of how he views this."

"It's pretty clear that he views his relationship with me as over. Does he even plan to acknowledge that he's the father of my child?"

"Acknowledge?" he said harshly. "To whom? The apartheid government? Don't be ridiculous, Grace. You forget we're in South Africa? This is why I came to you—because you can't count on anyone else to be honest with you. No one else knows enough about you, or about all the circumstances, to tell you what you need to hear. He certainly can't."

"What do you mean?"

"Well, for starters, what makes you think that he views his relationship with you as over? That he would even consider dropping you from his life?"

"Are you insane, Andrew?" I asked, glaring at him. "He's going to marry a woman in the village. How could you possibly think I would share him with another woman?"

"What I think is not the issue here. It's what you and he think that matters. But you're not thinking straight, Grace. You might not be interested in sharing him—but that doesn't mean he wouldn't be quite happy to share himself. You've forgotten that the man you're in love with is a Zulu, and the times we live in make it impossible for him to discard traditional values. You ask whether he'll even acknowledge fathering your child—I think he'd be dumbfounded by the question because it would never enter his mind to deny that your child was his. But he might be asking himself different questions: what good would it do the child to know that a Zulu man named Mandla Mkhize fathered him? What can a black father offer to his colored child in the South Africa we live in? And they're reasonable questions. He can't offer much, and his fatherhood would need to be kept secret until the child is old enough to be trusted—probably as a teenager. And then there's the question, Grace, of whether a boy or girl of fifteen or sixteen, having been raised in a white or colored community, will even want to acknowledge a black father. Have you considered that?"

He stopped to sip at his tea, by now long cold. And again, in the silence between us, I wondered whether I was doing my child a grave disservice by bringing him into a white world.

"There's more," continued Andrew. "You forget that he comes from a polygamous culture. Where he grew up, most of the men have more than one wife. Did he ever lead you to believe he intended to be faithful to you? I don't think so, because that could never have been his intention. You entered into this knowing that you could never marry—that the time you spent together would be short and infrequent. Did he ever tell you that the limited possibilities open to the two of you were sufficient for him to forego the comforts of home and children? He probably believes this is a non-issue—that there's no reason why the life you have together, and the work you do, should change." He stopped and looked at me. "If he were standing here now, he would say that he's not what stands in the way of making the relationship between you work. You are."

In the forty years I've had to wonder why I stayed, I've come up with many answers. None of them are good enough to explain or justify what ultimately happened.

I stayed because I loved my farm, and the people who worked on it, and the land. I stayed because of the corkscrew-horned kudu on my property, and the steenbok and the impala; because of the sun setting over the Drakensberg Mountains, and the long, pale winter grasses dancing with the wind. Because of Solomon and Lungile and the *sangoma's* predictions, and because South Africa was my child's birthright, and because I didn't want to deprive my baby of the opportunity to live in the new South Africa, the one I firmly believed was coming. I stayed because I had developed a small community of friends, and because if I went anywhere else, I would have to start from square one.

And where would I go? In the 1960s there was no place in the world—at least no place I knew of—that would welcome a single white mother with a black child. Even in Boston, New York and other enlightened places in the northeast United States, the civil rights struggle was just getting underway. I thought I was devoting my life to destroying a corrupt and evil system, and the realization, from my spot at the tip of the African continent, that the world seemed to offer no better place to go, was both frightening and humbling.

Despite this, I thought of going to Boston and starting over. Lenny didn't want me, so I would be alone—but at least I would be close to you, Steven. Then I imagined Lenny's anger and outrage were I to arrive with my colored child, and your resentment at having to put up with a half-sibling. Today, I realize that going to Boston might have been the wisest thing I could have done. It would have been difficult, but nothing as difficult as staying has been. Lenny is basically a good man, and he would probably have overcome his anger; you were still a child, and would probably have followed your father's example. But I was still young, then, and going to Boston felt like defeat and humiliation.

As a younger woman, I would have argued that all cultures were equally valid; that the responsibility for our problems rested with our political and economic systems—apartheid, and communism, and unregulated capitalism. Time has cured me of that belief; time, and loss, and the Taliban, and Sharia law, and our awareness of the treatment of women in most of the world. But when I was pregnant, I recognized that Andrew was right. I might be angry and feel betrayed, but I could not fault the tribal value system that made it possible for Khabazela to marry another woman and still expect to have me.

I don't know what I would do today—but back then, I stayed because I loved him, and because I knew that I would continue to love him, though I would never again invite him to my bed. And because, to tell the truth, the greatest horror I could imagine was having to start over again. So I stayed, and I planned. I waited for Anna McWilliams to make her demands, and for my child to be born. And I waited with anticipation and dread for Khabazela's return.

twenty-three

MICHAELA

Journey to Swaziland, 1968

For weeks I waited, watched for messages he might have left. When the wind blew at night and the windows rattled in their frames; when floorboards in the hallway creaked in the early morning hours; when the dogs barked at the scent of a stranger or the sound of birdsong suddenly stopped, all my senses came alive to the possibility that Khabazela was approaching. But his arrival, when it did happen, was not what I had expected, and it was for reasons far different from anything I could have imagined. Once more in our lives, the personal and the political collided, and as usual, politics took precedence.

That day, the radio reports were full of news about a raid outside Johannesburg, on the secret headquarters of Spear of the Nation. Among the documents discovered in an open safe was a detailed military plan to bring down the government. All those present were arrested, and eight leaders of the organization were taken into custody. It was, said the news reports, another major victory for the Special Branch, and a major defeat for the resistance.

I was concerned —but Khabazela had never discussed his rank in the paramilitary wing—in fact, he had never admitted to having any official rank, and I had no way of knowing whether he was senior enough to have been at the meeting. When the footsteps came that night, I was not surprised—but they were not his.

Solomon was never comfortable coming into the farmhouse—he had never been further than the kitchen. I was already wide awake when the floorboards creaked, and when the sound was followed by his whispered voice, I was out of bed and at the door in an instant.

"What's happened, Solomon?"

"*Nkosikazi*, Khabazela waits for you at the cave of the little hunters. He is with other men. Important men, I think. Will you come?"

"Of course," I said. "Are any of them injured?"

"No *Nkosikazi*, but they came tonight from Johannesburg. All day yesterday and tonight they have been running from the police. There are guards, also. They are hungry and thirsty. I have water for them, and food. I will wait while you make yourself ready."

I changed quickly, put on my boots, and followed Solomon through the chilly darkness to the mouth of the cave. In a cloudless, pitch-black sky the brilliance of the stars seemed to cast their own light, and the sliver of moon just above the horizon seemed dull by comparison. There was just enough light so that I could see each of the four men we passed on the path, each one in battle fatigues. Three carried high-powered rifles;

one carried a sub-machine gun. In all my encounters with this secret and unlawful paramilitary, I had never seen such an open show of force, and I wondered who they were protecting, and against what opposition. Solomon greeted each man with a murmured word, and I thought, not for the first time, that there was more to this simple man than first met the eye.

Khabazela was standing at the entrance to the cave, dressed in worn khaki fatigues and holding a flashlight in one hand and a pistol in the other. He was tense and alert, tall and muscular, and I loved him. I wanted to throw my arms around him; grind my fists into his face. I did neither, but he briefly placed his arm about my shoulder, looked at my belly and gave me a quick, unsure grin. Then he turned and I followed him to the back of the cave.

In the beam of the flashlight, three men sat on upturned logs. All wore creased suit pants and dirty white shirts that looked as if they'd been slept in, and each had been given an old khaki jacket to guard against the cold. There was a tall Englishman with a graying mustache, swept back hair and blue eyes, and a stocky, powerful black man with an afro, a wide smile, and an American accent. They both looked weary, and greeted me without rising. The third man, by contrast, sat erect on his log, and he rose and bowed to me when I entered. When I looked at him and realized that he was Chinese, I must have shown my surprise, because amusement registered at the corners of his mouth. I had never seen a Chinese man in Zululand, but I was not responding to his presence alone.

We were only one day beyond a devastating raid; the government had publicly accused Spear of the Nation of receiving financial and military backing from China, from the international communist party, and from other left-wing organizations in the UK and the United States. And here, in a darkened cave decorated by long-gone Bushmen hunters, an Englishman, an American and a Chinese man happened to show up a day later—one day's drive from where the raid occurred. Their appearance was no coincidence, nor was the fact that they were protected by a grim contingent of guerilla fighters from Spear of the Nation.

Solomon knelt on one knee, opened the knapsack, and drew out a bag of apples, a loaf of bread, a block of cheese and several canteens of water. He lay it all out on a blanket on the floor of the cave, and as the men drank greedily and helped themselves to the food, they listened.

"I apologize for the accommodations," said Khabazela. "This is not usually how we entertain our guests. But you are at least safe and dry, until we leave here after dark tomorrow. This is Grace Michaels, your hostess, and she will also be your driver. We will do all we can to get you all out of the country and home in one piece. In the meantime, Solomon will take care of your needs; as you've already seen, the guards outside are well trained, and they will keep you safe. It's been a long day—you should rest while you can."

He ushered me outside, beyond the entrance to the cave, where we sat together on a fallen tree trunk. We were in a darkened clearing surrounded by a dense tangle of overhanging trees, vines and brush. There was nothing silent about the night—it was filled with the murmur of windswept foliage, the sounds of cicadas, wood frogs, and night birds, and by the troop of silver vervet monkeys on the alert, indignant about our invasion of their territory. He took my wrist in his hand and ran his thumb along the underside of my forearm. It was an intimate gesture, gently done, and it was all I wanted from him.

"Are you well?" he asked in a low voice.

"I'm fine," I said, carefully withdrawing my wrist from his hand. "Who are these men?" I asked.

"Better if you don't know," he said. "As far as the world knows, these men are not here now, and as soon as we've returned them to their own countries, they will never have been here."

"We've hidden plenty of people up here, but never with armed guards. Who's after them? Were you at the meeting with them?"

"Yes," he said. "We were all there. I was watching out for them, and I was able to get them out. The Branch knows that several of us escaped—but they have no idea who, or what powers these men represent. Every one of our leaders is in custody as a result of the raid. It's been a terrible loss—but if those three are captured, it will be far worse. Foreign governments will have to deny their support for the resistance, and they'll be pressured to withdraw funding. Even worse, it would make the regime even more paranoid. They'd close the country down. That would mean more isolation, more restrictive laws. It would set us back twenty years. Whatever it takes, I have to get them out of the country."

He looked at me in the darkness; I could see the whites of his eyes not six inches from my face, and the smell of his sweat and exertion was strong, and very familiar.

There were only three ways out of the country—by foot, on a five day hike over the Drakensberg Mountains into Lesotho; by sea, picked up on an isolated beach close to the northern border; or by plane, out of some remote airfield. My belly tightened and I felt the excitement that always kept me awake on my midnight trips to the border with hidden human cargo. But this was different. It wasn't just me I was putting at risk. The tightening in my belly took on another meaning—perhaps it was my baby tensing at the thought of what I was about to put him through. And I was not the only one with misgivings.

"This is very dangerous, Michaela; more than anything we've ever done. And the stakes are higher. I don't want to involve you, especially now—but I have no choice. They may be looking for us; they've already set up police roadblocks and random inspections. We're going to be stopped, and your face is the least likely to cause problems."

"You say the Branch doesn't know who escaped. What makes you so sure they're looking? And why here?"

"I have to assume they're looking everywhere. There was an informer at the meeting, and now they've taken everyone at the farm into custody—lookouts, farm workers, secretaries. If any one of them knows anything, the Branch will eventually extract it—and they'll go to any lengths to catch these men. All we can hope for is enough time to get them out of the country."

"So where are we taking them? To the coast?"

He shook his head in the darkness. "Too well watched," he said, "and the ships we have access to can't outrun naval patrols. We have to stay inland. We're flying them out."

"What airfield?"

"Across the border. Swaziland."

I envisioned the journey across two hundred miles of mostly unpaved roads, over sometimes mountainous terrain, in the dark. Once we crossed into Swaziland, we would still have to locate the airfield—and then I would have to get back across the border and return home before anyone noticed my absence.

"If we're lucky," I said, "it'll take twenty-four hours, and we won't be able to stop for fuel. We'll have to carry enough petrol for the journey there and back. We've got some extra supply here, but the main tank is low and the supply truck doesn't come until next week."

"I don't want you to use petrol from the farm—we don't know if anyone at the distributor is keeping track of what you use. We've already arranged to pick up several full drums on the way out," he said.

"Good."

"The police are on high alert," he continued. "They may be watching the farm. If we're delayed or run into trouble, you'll be away for several days. You may need to explain your absence."

"I've already thought of that. I'll say I took a holiday in Cape Town."

He shook his head. "If they investigate your story, it would be easy to prove that you lied. No. We need another alibi for you. In fact, we need two. One in case the police come here to investigate. And it has to be an alibi that keeps them from following us, because if they follow us they'll figure out who these three men are. But we also need a story that we can tell the police if we're stopped on the way—one that they're likely to believe. I've already spoken to Andrew," he said awkwardly. "If the police come here, they'll be told that you're having a difficult pregnancy, and that you're on bedrest for a few days at the clinic. He'll be able to keep them away."

"So you've been in touch with Andrew," I said, unable to hide the hostility in my voice. "That's nice. I'm so glad that you have a way to keep updated about my pregnancy."

"Don't," he said quietly. "Not now."

"When?"

"When this is over," he said. "We have a lot to talk about."

"You bet we do," I said. "I've waited for over a month—I suppose I can wait a few more days." I breathed deeply. "So, let's talk about tomorrow. We have three passengers to hide—but the concealed compartment in the trunk is only big enough for one."

"That's one of the things we need to discuss," he said. There was a pause, in which he reached out and took my wrist again. "I knew I could still count on you."

Again, I withdrew my wrist, this time, not so gently.

Andrew was probably correct—Khabazela would think it normal to marry a traditional Zulu wife, and still have me on the side. It was consistent with his tradition, which he was unable and unwilling to discard. But he was also a product of Western culture and values, and he was intensely aware that he had betrayed my trust and my love. He said nothing about where he had been, or what he had been doing during his long and silent absence, but he didn't have to. The word "still" gave him away, and told me all I needed to know.

That night, in the farm work shed, Solomon wired together a wooden frame just wide and high enough to comfortably hold two men. When he was satisfied that it would maintain its shape, he secured it over a mattress to the bed of an open-backed farm truck. He piled sacks of potatoes in layers on top of the framework so that the truck appeared to be fully loaded, but he arranged for the sacks on one side to be easily moveable so that the men could get out quickly if necessary. Before we left, the Chinese man and the black American lay beside each other on the mattress, and Solomon showed us how to reload the sacks to hide any evidence of their presence.

Andrew arrived with a passport for the Englishman, and the cassock of an Anglican Minister. The passport said that he was Father Peter Fitzpatrick, visiting Zululand from London, on an educational mission. He was a passionate ornithologist, and he had his binoculars on the dashboard within easy reach. We were going birding up north, and would be stopping at several Anglican mission schools along the way to deliver our potatoes.

It was a reasonable story—and from my experience teaching at the mission school in Sophiatown, I knew what the police attitude would be. They were disdainful of anyone interested in feeding and educating black children, and if we were stopped, they might sneer and joke at the purpose of our journey—but it would be believable enough for them to wave us on.

I drove the truck, and beside me sat Father Peter Fitzpatrick in his cassock. We left just after dusk, travelling in convoy, keeping as much as possible to the farm roads. I was behind, driving the open-backed truck. A few minutes ahead of us was an ancient closed van driven by Solomon, who had somehow converted himself into an inoffensive, elderly, round-shouldered Zulu in shabby grey overalls. He carried with him his pass identifying him as an employee of one of the gold mining syndicates, and a form from his employer giving him permission to be on the road.

The back of his van—the cargo compartment—had been converted into a makeshift bus with wooden benches along both sides, and it contained five men. Four were mineworkers who had allegedly been injured in a tunnel collapse a mile underground. They had been rescued and treated, and were being transported back to their villages, now unemployable until they were again fit for work. One had a broken leg in a splint, another a shoulder in a sling, a third—Khabazela—had a thick bloodied bandage around his head covering one eye, and the fourth lay on a stretcher on the floor, his chest bandaged. The fifth man was another mine employee along for the ride, to tend to the injured on their journey.

Beneath the benches, hidden behind blankets in which they had tied their belongings, were the high-powered rifles they had carried the previous night. And within the splint and the bandages and the sling were concealed other weapons—knives, knobkerries, short spears. Equally lethal, but silent.

Beneath the dashboard of the farm truck, Solomon had attached a two-way short distance transmitter. In the back of the van, the others could hear whatever took place in the farm truck. If we ran into trouble, they were only a few hundred yards ahead.

At several points along the two-lane road we encountered barriers manned by the local police. They stopped random vehicles and checked identification and, in the case of black drivers and passengers, pass books.

We had no trouble with these—the police didn't give our mineworkers a second glance, and they were courteous to my Anglican minister. As we waited in line behind the truck to get through one roadblock, we overheard conversation through the transmitter as officers approached the truck.

"Out of the truck, you. Open up the back."

"Yes, *baas*."

Solomon opened the driver's door and we watched him shuffle slowly around to the back, where he struggled to undo the latch. There were two officers standing between us and the truck, and one of them, a head taller than Solomon, shoved him roughly aside. Solomon seemed to totter, almost fell, and then recovered himself. He said nothing. The officer fiddled roughly with the latch, opened it, peered inside, and stepped up onto the footrest. We heard him gasp.

"Shit," he said. "Smells like something died in here."

"No, *baas*," said Solomon, straight-faced, "these men are not dead. The ones who died when the mine collapsed, we sent them back to their homes in a different truck."

Laughing, shaking his head at Solomon's stupidity, the officer stepped through the open door into the truck. Through the gloom, I saw him standing above a figure lying on a stretcher, the bloody bandage on his chest clearly visible. The officer thrust his foot at the man's leg, forcing his knee off the stretcher, and there was a deep groan of pain.

The officer backed out of the truck and his companion straightened his cap, pulling it down over his forehead. "Come on," he said. "This bunch isn't hiding anyone—they don't have enough brains between them to piss straight. Most of them are just going home to die. Let's move on."

Solomon closed the back door, tested it several times to make sure it was secure, then shuffled around to the front of the truck and took his time getting settled. Then, very slowly, he drove off. I inched forward and stopped at the barrier—but the two policemen were still laughing at Solomon's comment about the dead men, and they glanced at our identification papers and waved us on.

As a result of these relatively easy encounters, we approached each police barrier without much concern. But roadblocks closer to the Swaziland border were manned by members of the Special Branch, and they were less courteous and far more thorough than the local police. They examined us with increasing suspicion and urgency as we approached the border; scrutinized us as if they had been instructed to match our faces to images or descriptions they'd been given earlier.

"It's almost as if they're expecting us," I said at one point, after the men in the truck had been forced to a standing position, two of them having had to lift and then support their comrade on the stretcher.

"They suspect something," he said, his voice from the truck muffled by the speaker. "They're on increased alert along every possible escape path, or else they've been told that we're headed in this direction."

Each roadblock was constructed differently. We were pulled off onto the right side of the road, and then onto the left; we sat in traffic as vehicles were inspected directly on the road, one at a time. We were questioned inside the car, and forced to stand ten feet back as they did their work. We'd been examined by one officer alone, by two working together, and been distracted by three working on us at the same time, each one doing something different.

The Special Branch officers manning the barricades wanted to keep people off guard, and their strategy worked. Not knowing what to expect raised the anxiety level and increased the odds of someone making a wrong move, especially someone with something to hide.

Just before 2:00 am we bypassed the little town of Piet Retief, about ten miles this side of the Swaziland border. The road was completely deserted, and there had been no other vehicles for miles. As we went around a sharp curve we came suddenly upon a barricade, and with no time to slow down and put space between us and the truck, we arrived thirty seconds apart. As we arrived the inspectors were standing around casually, and one of them was at a field table pouring coffee from a large thermos into tin cups. To one side, there was a small enclosure delineated by several wooden barriers and by two black Special Branch vans. They directed Solomon into the enclosure, and waved at me to follow. The light inside one of their vans was on, and we could see a wire fence separating the baggage compartment from the back seat.

"They've got search dogs," came a whisper from the transmitter. "Michaela, this is no time to play hero. Watch for us—if we come out of the van, you and Peter drop to the ground."

Five Special Branch officers in brown uniforms and flat, hard-topped caps stood back from our two vehicles, bright flashlights in hand shining directly into our faces. One of them had a megaphone, which he lifted to his mouth.

"Turn off your engine."

I obeyed, as did Solomon. With both motors stopped, we could hear the muffled sound of the dogs barking in the van. I knew the Special Branch dogs. They were Alsatians, German shepherds with thick, rough coats, dark brown and black; handsome, powerful animals. We had two as I was growing up, and they were gentle, loyal and intelligent. But the armed forces trained them as search dogs, eager to smell out contraband; and the police used their hunting instincts to terrorize the black population. The residents of Soweto and Sophiatown, and the workers on my farm all swore that police dogs could smell a black man at a thousand feet, and I knew the violence these animals could do. In the minds of many in the resistance, these dogs, and the free rein given them by their masters, were an emblem of the brutality and fear by which the government was able to function. An officer approached my window, and out of the corner of my eye, I could see that another was simultaneously approaching Solomon.

"Get out please, Miss, and your passenger, too. Bring your identification with you, and step to the rear of your vehicle."

Carefully I opened the door and stepped down, identification papers in hand. Peter did the same, walking carefully to avoid tripping on his cassock. We met at the back of the truck, where the officer waited for us, sub-machine gun slung casually over his shoulder, one hand resting on the stock. A second officer stood waiting for Solomon, watching impatiently as he hobbled slowly around his van. The two men examined our papers in silence for what seemed like an interminable period, then looked at each other and began interrogating us, their questions choreographed to keep us off guard. I answered those directed at me, but all I was aware of was a succession of loudly barked questions that came fast and furious.

"What work do you do at the mine, old man?"

"Where in England is your ministry, Father?"

"When did this mine accident take place?"

"What is your connection to the Anglican Church, Miss Michaels?"

"How many injured miners are you carrying?"

"Which mission schools are you going to visit?"

"Tell me the name of the place you're taking these injured miners."

"You're a farmer, Miss Michaels. Why don't you show these schools how to grow their own potatoes? Instead you're wasting your time, making our natives more dependent on foreign religions. The Anglican Church doesn't have any business doing charity here in South Africa."

This question was directed at me, but Peter Fitzpatrick—or whatever his name was—straightened the cassock on his left-wing shoulders and answered for me. He did so with the kind of fierce gentleness that took me back to my time in Sophiatown, and for a moment I felt as though I was standing beside Father Huddleston.

"The Anglican Church, and every other Church, my son, including your Dutch Reformed Church, has business wherever there is hunger. And if we don't belong wherever governments repress their own people, then we have no ministry and no purpose."

"Thank you for the homily, Father," said the officer with a sneer, readjusting the weapon on his shoulder. "I'll be sure to tell my Predicant what you said on Sunday morning. I suppose while I'm at it, I should also inform him that you want to give blacks the vote, and make it so one of them can stand in his place and preach in our church."

"That would be a fine idea," said Peter calmly.

"You people," he said in disgust. "Communists, all of you. We ought to make you live with our *kaffirs* for a month. Then you'd change your bloody tune."

The other officer watched this interchange, listening in silence. Now he looked at Solomon.

"Let's see your miners, old man. Time to open up the van." Then he turned halfway around and shouted something to one of the other men.

Suddenly the whining of the dogs increased in volume as the back door of the van they were in swung open. Their handler stood in the opening, wearing black-padded gloves and a black-padded jacket over his white shirt. In one hand he held a short, braided leather whip. Wrapped around the other hand were dog leashes, and from the back of the van three animals jumped to the ground, circling and snuffling the air. The handler knelt down beside them and released them. All three headed towards us, barking and whining. Solomon, still trying to open the van door, was clearly terrified.

"Please, *baas*," he shouted over the barking. "They frighten me, your dogs. Please, take them away from me," and he turned and ran in his slow shuffle back to the front of the truck, hopped up to the driver's seat, and slammed the door.

They strutted about with their sub-machine guns, laughed, made light of Solomon's terror. Nosing something other than potatoes, the dogs circled, sniffing intently underneath my truck. The other officers closed in, watched as the dogs worked themselves into a frenzy of excitement.

"Hah," said the handler. "They've found something here."

"What else are you carrying up to give to your mission students, Father?" said the officer who had questioned us. "You bringing them banned books? *Dagga*? Or is it worse than that? Weapons, maybe? You have something in these sacks, and I'm going to know what it is."

He beckoned angrily to two of his junior men who quickly stowed their weapons beneath the field table and leaped up into the back of the truck. They began throwing sacks down to the ground, where a third man ripped them open as they landed. The handler whistled and one of the dogs jumped up as well, to stand at the top of the pile, pawing at the sacks, tearing the burlap with his claws, whining as he detected the scent of the two men below.

All eyes were on my truck, waiting to see what the two men and their dog would find. It would not be long before we were discovered. I turned to look at Peter—and as I turned I saw Solomon's officer walking toward the driver's side of the van. Out of the corner of my eye I watched the officer pull open Solomon's door, grab a handful of his overall, and drag him out of the truck. Solomon stumbled, held on to the door to support himself, and then, as the officer pulled at him, let go and allowed himself to fall forward. As he fell, he reached down to his chest and held onto the officer's wrist for support and they rolled to the ground together. From where I stood I saw what took place in the narrow space between the two vehicles, and I felt a surge of fierce joy at the look of surprise on the officer's face as his inoffensive victim gathered himself and changed from a shrunken, stumbling old man into a nimble compressed powerhouse.

But the officer's expression of surprise was short-lived. Solomon pulled something almost invisible from his overall—a foot-long bar of slender, quarter inch thick tempered steel, sharpened to a fine point—and in a single powerful motion he covered the man's mouth with one hand and thrust the point directly into his eye. He drove it through the small opening in the bone behind the eye, severed the optic nerve, and as he inserted it deep in the brain cavity, he jiggled it back and forth within its bony fulcrum.

In the darkened strip between the vehicles, like a kneeling night ghoul, Solomon withdrew the bar and wiped it on the dead man's uniform, and as I watched I shivered at how easy and mechanical this work of horror was.

But it had only just begun. Solomon crept towards me on his knees, steel bar poised at shoulder level. One of the dogs not on the truck was nosing at a tire, and as he sensed Solomon's presence he growled and charged. Whether he intended to attack or to simply stand guard over Solomon I don't know because Solomon—so seemingly cowed a few moments earlier that he had run away—dropped and rolled directly towards the approaching attack dog, reached out under the open jaws and thrust his steel bar deep into the animal's chest. With a whimper the dog dropped to the ground and Solomon withdrew the bar, wiping it clean on the dog's coat. And then, in the midst of absolute chaos, with our lives hanging in the balance, he reached out with his free hand to close the dog's dead eyes. Then he banged the bar three times on the side of the van.

The back door flew open and Khabazela and his men exploded silently from the van. There was such an eerie absence of sound that my mind was unable to reconcile what was seen with what was unheard.

Time stopped. I became a frozen spectator to an ancient silent movie as the scene played itself out frame by frame. I watched my Anglican priest drop to the ground as we had been instructed, but I didn't have the presence of mind to move, and so stood like a target in front of the truck. Not a shot was fired; none was necessary, or possible. I don't recall seeing Khabazela or his men carrying rifles; they wielded only the silent, lethal, weapons they had hidden on their bodies.

Solomon was already halfway across the clearing headed towards the officer furthest away as the van door opened. As each man left the van he scanned the scene and picked his target. Khabazela was out first, saw where Solomon was headed, and made for the next closest officer. He covered the ground in an eyeblink. The second man selected the next closest and went directly for him. It was the first time I had seen precision killing, and it achieved its objective: none of the highly trained members of the Special Branch had time to raise or cock a weapon, or to alert any backup. They were taken down almost simultaneously: one grabbed at a throat slit back to the spine as he fell, blood coiling from his neck; another was speared through the chest at close range and the *assegai* quickly withdrawn as he fell, and his heart pumped itself out onto the dirt. A third had the side of his head bashed in with a knobkerrie. When all members of the Branch lay on the ground, Khabazela gathered his men in the center of the clearing to take stock. The two remaining dogs stood by their fallen handler, snarling, and I turned away as they were quickly dispatched.

Then it was over. Within minutes they piled the bodies—human and canine—into one of the black Special Branch vans and doused them all with petrol. One of the men wanted to take the weapons, but Khabazela insisted that they be added to the pyre. He wanted no sign of the night's events traceable to us. Before we drove off, the men knocked in a few windows to allow for quick combustion, and set the van alight.

We watched the fire rise into the darkness behind us as we drove off, and after a moment there was a huge detonation as the petrol tank exploded. It was highly visible, an operation that would not be easily hidden. But we had yet to cross the border, send our passengers on their way, and return home—and it was certain that the forces arrayed against us would now be magnified a thousand fold.

We crossed the border into Swaziland without incident—it was less a border than an unmanned signpost—and five miles into the landlocked protectorate of the Swazi people we came upon a sandy landing strip that ran between two fields. The plane was already there, waiting in darkness for us.

As Khabazela's guerillas silently heaved potato sacks from the sides of the truck to release the two men concealed beneath, I was already planning the route home. The journey back would be far more hazardous. We would have to drive by night, sleeping in safe houses during the day, and it would be too dangerous to travel together. We would have to separate, and I would be travelling without support or company. It was far more than I had bargained for.

But he was way ahead of me. As our passengers clambered down, stiff and sore, and stood beside the truck stretching, Khabazela was already instructing his men to reload the potatoes.

"What are you doing?" I asked. "I can't go back with a full truck—we have to get rid of the potatoes."

"There are plenty of people in this country who need the food," he said. "My men will see that it goes where it is needed, and then go underground until it's safe to return."

"I don't understand," I said. "You want me to wait here while they deliver the potatoes?"

"They're taking both vehicles," he said patiently. "We're not waiting for them. When they can return, they'll bring your truck back if it
doesn't seem too dangerous. Otherwise they'll leave it here."

"So how are we supposed to get home?"

In answer he pointed to the plane, now heading down the runway
towards us.

"You're going back to the farm in that," he said, "via Maputo."

The pilot flew us north in the two-engine prop plane whose owners
were never revealed to me. I slept most of the way through Swaziland and
woke as we entered Mozambique airspace. We landed at a private airstrip
in a sandy field outside Maputo, and our three passengers were immediately whisked off to be flown out of the main airport. There were a half
dozen uniformed guards patrolling the airstrip, and while they ignored
me, they treated Khabazela with distant respect. I don't know whose airfield it was, or who was protecting us, but for the first time I was aware
that Khabazela was relaxed and calm.

Servants came and went with food and drink, and we spent the day
in the shade, sleeping under a huge canvas awning, waiting for nightfall
when it would be safe to enter South African airspace. The pilot stayed
with his plane at the far end of the runway, and I saw him from a distance wandering around the aircraft, making sure that all was ready for
our flight that night, and overseeing the refueling truck that appeared at
dusk.

We didn't say much to each other until after dark, when we took off
again, headed out over the Atlantic. We were the only passengers, and it
was the first time we had been alone.

"Khabazela, where are we going?"

"We're flying south," he said, "down the coast of South Africa. Before we get to Durban we'll turn inland, staying low to avoid radar. I don't know where we will land—but there are many small runways within a few hours of the farm, and the pilot knows which ones are safe. There will be a car there waiting to take you home."

"So I'm going home to my farm," I said, looking at him. "What about you?"

The passenger cabin was small, and we were sitting against opposite bulkheads, facing each other. There was a table between us, and behind each of us was a mirror, angled slightly down. I could see the back of his head, tightly curled hair cut short to the shape of his very familiar skull. And I could see myself, a weary young woman with uncombed hair and dark circles beneath her eyes. I didn't like how I looked—puffy, unhappy, demanding; not very attractive. He, too, was exhausted and drawn, and his lean face showed it. Beneath the arches of his cheekbones his cheeks were hollow; his mouth closed tight, lips sad and turned down at the corners. He looked at the hands in his lap as if they were not his, picked at the fingernails. I watched him, waiting, unwilling to make it any less difficult.

"It was too hard, Michaela," he said finally, speaking slowly, still avoiding my eyes.

"What was?"

"Living apart from you, and meeting only in secret. I could do it, because I knew it was just as difficult for you as it was for me—so long as I was still able to work effectively. But what some of the leaders told me all along came to be true. I thought I was strong enough to do what I came here for—but my strength alone is not enough to bring about sweeping changes. For that, I need to be someone the people can identify with; someone who comes from among them, and also lives their life."

He paused uncomfortably, shifted in his chair. "It means having a *kraal* in the village. And it means a traditional family, wife and children." He lowered his head, sighed deeply, and, finally, looked up to meet my eyes. "You know already that I have taken a wife, Michaela," he said. "That night at the cave, it was clear to me that you knew—I could feel your anger. I supposed that Andrew told you, but it was not the time to talk. Andrew is smitten by you, you know." He grinned, weakly. "Or I thought it might be Solomon who told you. He is torn in half by this—he feels as much loyalty to you as he does to me, which is a great tribute to you."

I looked at him, clenching my fists in my lap, filled with fury. "Don't you dare try and charm me," I said. "Do you think so little of me? You imagine that I can be flattered into accepting this?"

"I'm sorry," he said softly. "I didn't intend to offend you."

"I suppose I should congratulate you. Both on your marriage and on your virility—you have two women pregnant at the same time. How proud you must be. Which child will be your firstborn," I asked. "Hers or mine?"

"Don't, Michaela," he said.

"Don't what? Complicate your life?"

"This is difficult enough. Don't make it worse."

I laughed harshly. "How could it possibly be worse?"

He had no answer, and for a time we sat in silence. I don't know what he was thinking, but I was searching for an escape from a situation that seemed, for that moment, awful beyond words, and inescapable. The drone of the engine filled the space between us, and I finally calmed myself sufficiently to have a conversation.

"Her name is Miriam, I hear."

"Yes."

"You didn't think for a moment that I was just going to go along with this, did you?"

"I hoped," he said. "But I thought not."

"But you went with her anyway, and when she became pregnant you married her, in the traditional Zulu way."

"Yes," he said. "It is the Zulu way."

"But you know that even if I wanted it, the Zulu way has no place for me. When we had each other, I felt no need to have a place in your tradition. I had you, and that felt like enough. We could combine forces, live a secret life, and imagine that we had won a small victory against all the forces that want to keep us apart. But for me, alone against Zulu tradition, there's no winning. Not if I don't have you at my side." We looked at each other. "And you can't have us both at your side, you know."

"I know," he said.

"So what plan do you have for me now? Where do I go?"

"Go?" he said, looking at me with bewilderment. "We still have work to do. You belong on the farm. And I can still come to you." He took one look at me and his smile disappeared, stillborn. "No," he said. "I suppose not."

"No," I repeated. "No more."

The emptiness of no more night visits hit me, and I was filled with sadness. We had conceived a child together, but nothing was permitted us. Aside from the immediacy of love and the urgency of our work together, there was little else important enough to unite us. I felt hopeless and defeated. Even though his people might never be able to wholly accept me, I had thought it within my ability to wholly accept them.

Now, for the first time, I had evidence of my own limitations. Whether they were the result of having been brought up in a western, Judeo-Christian culture, coming from a Jewish home, or having parents who believed that men and women were truly equal, I was unsure. But whatever the reason, it was beyond my capacity to accept being a sec-ond wife—or a mistress—in a culture where men were permitted what women were not, and in a political environment where either way our relationship would have to be hidden.

twenty four

MANDLA

Natal, South Africa, 1968

I have left it up to your mother to decide how much she wishes to share with you about the early part of our relationship. For me, it was a dangerous time, but filled with excitement. It was disorienting as well, because I played many roles, and eventually it became impossible to keep them all straight. Ultimately, I had to admit to myself that I could no longer function effectively. It was only a matter of time before I made a mistake that would place Michaela, or the men in my command, or our entire operation, in jeopardy.

Without being a part of the community, I was unable to have the kind of impact I needed to have. And once I realized that I was the cause of the problem, I had no choice but to change things. So I married Miriam, a young woman in my mother's village. We have been together now for over thirty-five years.

As might have been expected, Michaela did not take the news of my marriage to Miriam well. She felt that I had betrayed her, and she wanted nothing to do with me. I told her that my love and admiration for her were unconditional; that my being married need not change anything between us. But there were limitations to what she could accept.

"You live as if the opportunities available to you are endless," I told her, "as if you can go on making choices without consequences. Well, you're already living with consequences. In order to come live with me, you had to leave Steven. That had consequences. In order to make you and our child safe, and to make our work here possible, I had to marry. That has consequences, too, for all of us. But there are reasons—very practical reasons—why my marriage might be advantageous."

"For you, maybe," she said, filled with anger. "You have someone to cook for you and a warm bed to go to when you're not with me. It makes you one of the boys; when you meet with the traditional leaders you can impress each other with the number of your women and your children. Yes, it makes the work you do easier if these leaders respect you—but don't insult my intelligence by telling me how your Zulu wife will make my life better."

"It may not make your life better," I told her patiently, "but it will make your life—and our child's life—safer."

We had these discussions over several days, and it became increasingly apparent that our time of intimacy and closeness were over. But if that was the case, there was a way in which my having a Zulu wife could make her life better, and might also provide an acceptable reason for me to be around the farmhouse.

"You're going to need someone to take care of the child while you run the farm," I said at one point. "Have you thought who you will hire?"

She looked at me as if I had lost my mind.

"You're not serious," she said.

"Why not? You need to have a woman who's trustworthy and competent, someone who you can be honest with. In this situation who could you be more honest with than my wife? You'll need someone you like, and you and Miriam will get along very well."

"You are serious," she said. "I can't believe it. You want me to employ your wife to come take care of our child in my house?"

"I would like you and Miriam to meet, and yes, I would like you to consider having her work for you. You may be angry with me, Michaela, but you cannot be angry with her. She has done nothing wrong, and she intends you no harm. There is much she can learn from you. She is a lovely young woman whose company you will enjoy, and like you, she will soon have a child."

"So my house will become a little like your private *kraal*, where we two women can raise your children together. Is that what you envision?"

"No," I said firmly. "It is not. Your house will be your home, in which you raise your child as you see fit. You would have a nursemaid for your child who lives in the servants' quarters, and who will sometimes have her child here with her. What happens beyond that is completely up to you," I said quietly. "What I want is for you and for our child to live in safety and security, and for Miriam and her child I would like these same opportunities. In this world, where am I more likely to find them than in your house?"

You will find that your mother is a stubborn woman, Steven, but she is not dogmatic. One of her many admirable qualities is her ability to change her mind when she sees a better way, and she has the moral strength to admit when she is wrong. In this case, she recognized that I was right, and she was able to see that her argument went counter to the goals we were trying to achieve.

I knew that all she had to do was to meet Miriam, and the deal would be done. Miriam had just turned twenty. She was slender and energetic, with smooth brown cheeks and fiery eyes, and a smile that would have melted glass. She did not have much education—it would have been difficult in the village to find a girl who had completed high school. But when I met Miriam, I knew that she was a good match for me. She was highly intelligent; she had a very strong sense of herself. She was one of those people—I have seen this quality mostly among women—who understands how the world works, and who manages to function within the system while somehow rising above it. I knew that she would be able to work in Michaela's house without becoming a servant. In her own way she was as determined as Michaela, but she could be obstinate with a sweetness that brushed most obstacles out of her way. I had been completely honest with her, and by the time I suggested that they meet, I knew she had an instinctive understanding of how difficult it all was for Michaela.

I thought it best that I not be there when Miriam first went to the farmhouse, and Michaela arranged it at a time when they could be alone in the kitchen. Afterwards neither woman spoke much about their meeting, other than to say that it had gone well. But over the years, both of them have dropped little pieces of information, and I've been able to piece together a picture of what happened.

I know that at first it was awkward for both of them. This was not the normal interview of a prospective nursemaid by a farm wife. They sat down together in the kitchen, and Michaela made tea. They were nervous;

both mistress and servant pregnant, and aware that the children they carried had the same father; and aware also that if their secret became public, none of our lives would be exempt from the ensuing disaster.

They talked at first about what the job would entail, and what were Michaela's expectations. At the start, Miriam was in awe of this tall, beautiful white woman who ran the farm alone, who had had the courage to follow her heart and love me despite the risks, and who, she knew by then, had the strength of character to end our relationship when I married. But it didn't take her long to see that Michaela was also heartbroken by the course events had taken, and that beneath it all, she was just another woman in the world, about to have a child, and, like so many other women she knew, about to have a child alone.

At one point, pouring from the teapot, Michaela knocked a cup off the table. The hot tea splattered and the cup shattered on the wood floor. As they stood together at the sink, Michaela trying to remove the stains on Miriam's light blue blouse with a wet cloth, Miriam noticed that there were tears in her eyes, and she instinctively put one comforting arm around your mother's waist.

"It will be good for our children to have each other," she said quietly. "And so that we will not be each of us a mother alone with a child on this big farm, it will be good for us, Madame, to be sisters. When Khabazela comes, he can see both the children." She looked at your mother and her eyes were dark, and shining, and the white part was pure and innocent. "And he can see you, too."

Michaela was taller than Miriam, and she looked down at her, slowly wiping her eyes. "If we're going to be sisters, Miriam," she said, "you can't go around calling me Madame. I think you'd better find me another name."

I remember every word the old *sangoma* spoke, and over the years, as the events she predicted have come to pass, I have found myself repeating her words and remembering the sound of her strange, tortured voice as she channeled the Shades.

The *sangoma* said that Michaela and I would have a child, and she said that together with another mother, Michaela would raise two children. It happened just as she predicted, and I found myself in the enviable position of having the two women I loved bringing up my two sons in the same house. It would have been unconventional anywhere, but in that poisonous world, it was beyond anything I could have imagined or hoped for.

They were born two months apart, Simon first, and then Thulani. Our good friend Andrew, the local doctor, attended both births. On any other farm, one of the boys would have lived in the farmhouse and the other in the servants' quarters. On this farm, Simon and Thulani slept in the same crib, and whether it was in Miriam's room behind the house or in the baby's room Michaela had prepared for Simon, all the two boys cared about was that they were together.

Andrew—whom we all called the White Zulu—was smitten with your mother, and they became very close after Miriam and I married. By the time the boys were two years old she was ready to move on with her life, and Andrew moved into the farmhouse. They were a good match. He was a powerful personality, his integrity was absolute, and they shared a commitment to our cause. More than that, they shared a strange need, which I never understood, to become what they could never be. I believe they found happiness in each other, and they lived together for almost twenty-five years, until his death a few years ago.

I was relieved to know that there was a man in the house, because in those years the degree and frequency of political violence increased beyond anything we could have previously imagined. In addition to my other work, I was frequently called on to mediate, and my deepest regret is that I was absent for much of those years.

My greatest concern about having a child with Michaela was that the authorities would come sniffing around, and that they would make an arbitrary decision regarding the race of our child. They might decide based on some bizarre measure that the child was black, or colored, and he would have been taken from Michaela to live with another family in a different racial district. We are only a few years from that Kafkaesque world, where we lived in fear of arbitrary decisions based on inhuman distinctions among people, but even to me it seems hard to believe that for so long it was the norm we lived with.

Both boys were healthy, and both were beautiful. Thulani had his mother's full cheeks and big dark eyes; he had my mouth and my smile. There was no question about his parentage. That was not the case with Simon, who had warm brown eyes, curly hair, and a complexion that could have been Mediterranean or Indian. His ancestry might have been Corsican or North African. His full mouth, much like your mother's, would have suited an infant in a fresco on the ceiling of the Sistine Chapel. But there was no place for possibilities or uncertainty under the race laws. In that benighted environment, it was better not to stand out. So Michaela kept his hair cut short and made sure that he stayed out of the sun, which would only have darkened his skin further. When he did go outside he soon became used to wearing a cap with a brim that protected his face.

Luckily, it was far easier to make him invisible on the farm than it would have been in town, just as it was easier on the farm to have the two boys essentially living together. When Miriam took Thulani home with her, she sometimes took Simon, too. I don't think Simon knew there was a difference between them.

My mother was still alive then, and living in the village; she made a great fuss of both her grandsons. And they had the run of the farm. They moved easily from the farmhouse to the servants' quarters, and when they were old enough to explore further afield, there was always someone looking out for them. They were inseparable, deeply loved, and the irony was that despite all our fears, they lived charmed lives, in absolute safety.

If ever two little boys might have thought that they owned the world, these were they. As they grew and became more independent, the radius of safety around the farmhouse expanded, and along with it, Michaela's— and my—fear that Simon would be exposed. We agreed that the only way to ensure that they were not separated, and that they were safe, was to keep them close to home for as long as possible.

It was not a long-term plan; we knew that we had to take each day as it came. But what really gnawed at me and kept me up at night was the fact that I could not give my two sons the same education. The only schools in the area were for white children, and there were no black schools anywhere. But this was not, as Sophiatown had been, an area of dense population that was highly visible and under constant police scrutiny. I wondered how we could capitalize on the fact that we were instead a rural community covering a vast area, and we had sparse police coverage. And I came up with an idea that turned out to offer multiple benefits.

In Sophiatown, it was impossible to hide our forbidden schools, so we camouflaged them as social clubs. But Michaela's farm in the Midlands was in many ways a self-contained community, separated from other farms and other people by vast expanses of growing fields and grassland, and by hillsides, scrub and forest. It was the perfect place to start educating the children of the farm—not just my two boys, but the children of farm employees as well, both black and white. And when I returned from a lengthy stay out of the country and suggested it to Michaela, she laughed loudly and asked me to come by the old barn the following day.

The next afternoon I made my way to the farm. The barn was a good ten minute walk from the farmhouse, but anyone approaching it had to go past the farmhouse first. It was secluded behind a grove of close-growing trees and vines, and the only way to access it was via an overgrown tractor path. The barn was used to warehouse outdated farm machinery, and when I had last seen it the barn door was hanging from one hinge. As I approached I saw that the door had been repaired, and when I pushed it open, the barn was empty of machinery. There were old benches stacked in the center, and a wood stove at one end.

At the far end of the barn Miriam was whitewashing the walls while Michaela swept the floor. In one corner there was an old table surrounded by several chairs, and a third woman sat with her back to the door, cutting and pasting sheets of paper, and writing letters of the alphabet with a big marker on each page. Simon and Thulani were laughing and running around at one end of the empty barn, playing a game with a little girl of about six. I walked across the barn towards them and when the boys saw me they shouted and ran to me, and the little girl followed. The boys jumped at me and I lifted them both, one in each arm, and continued walking towards the women.

"Good morning, Mandla," said Michaela. She spoke in her public voice, presumably because of the third woman in the room, but her eyes were smiling. "This is the room I was talking about, where we will have classes for the children. I'm pleased to see you—we can use your help arranging the benches around the walls." She spoke to the third woman, who had turned her head to look at us. "Anna," she said, "I think you know Mandla. Mandla, you remember Mrs. McWilliams. She's going to be helping us. And this is her daughter, Helen."

I had not seen Anna McWilliams since shortly after the boys were born, and I almost didn't recognize her. She had been a thin, unhappy woman with stringy blond hair; she looked always as if she had been beaten, or was afraid that she would be. There had been something unhealthy about her; something almost unclean. In any event, she was almost unrecognizable. Her hair and clothes alone made her look like different person. She had gained weight, her cheeks were round, and she was smiling. She looked at me over her shoulder with a curious expression.

"Hello, Mandla," she said.

"Hello, Madame," I said, feeling awkward with the two boys wriggling in my arms.

"You have a very handsome son," she said.

"Thank you, Madame," I said. "He is a good boy."

"He and Simon are lucky to have one another," she said.

Miriam came up from behind me and put out her arms to Simon, wanting to separate us before this woman who was watching so closely.

"They play well together," said Miriam. "Come to Miriam, Simon."

Simon waved her away and put both arms about my neck. Thulani giggled, and Simon did the same.

"Yes," said Anna McWilliams, "they do play nicely together. The only thing that might separate them would be if you had another child, and gave Thulani a brother. Are you ready for your next child, Miriam?"

It was the kind of invasive comment that a white woman could make to a black servant without thinking twice about personal boundaries. But in this case, after she spoke, something flickered across Mrs. McWilliams' eyes, and her cheeks paled. Both boys still had their faces buried in my neck, and she looked from my face to the back of Simon's head, and then from Simon's head to Thulani's and back again. By then Michaela had put her broom down and come to stand with us. She quickly took Simon from me. Anna recovered herself and the color returned to her cheeks.

"I think Thulani doesn't need a brother," she murmured. "And neither does Simon." She turned to look from Michaela to me. "They have each other, don't they?"

There was much that I did not understand about the relationship between your mother and Anna McWilliams, and I did not know what their friendship was based on. But whatever concerns I might have had about our security turned out to be groundless. Perhaps, when you come to know your mother better, she will tell you the whole story. It might reveal much to you about how committed she is to what she believes in, and the lengths she has been willing to go for those she loves.

twenty-five

MANDLA

Natal, South Africa, 1982

Michaela was a most protective mother, but by the time the boys were fourteen, she had made the decision that keeping Simon at home raised too many questions in the community. She recognized that it was time for him to face his world, and to learn what he needed in order to negotiate it, and she sent him off to the central white high school.

He was tall and slender, a handsome boy; his short curls had somehow loosened as he reached puberty, and if he had a dark complexion, his manner, his open smile and his obvious intelligence were enough to convince even the most diehard proponents of racial separation that he couldn't possibly be anything but white. He had a wonderful sense of humor and a good sense of himself, and besides, he was strong and muscular. He would be able to defend himself if challenged, and he could certainly withstand any comments about his complexion. And if he couldn't, then it was time for him to learn.

For the boys, the separation was difficult, as it was for Michaela, and for me. The change we had hoped would come to the country was nowhere in sight, and I found it even more difficult than I had imagined to accept that there was no way my two sons might live similar lives. I was close to Simon, and I loved him; if he felt a closeness to me that was beyond what he might have expected, he probably attributed it to the fact that I was his best friend's father. But Michaela and I had decided that it was not yet the time to tell him the truth, and there was always between us the tension of what could not be disclosed. He was so curious about everything else, but Michaela said that Simon never asked any questions about his absent father. His lack of curiosity surprised me—but it should have alerted us to the possibility that he already suspected the answer.

The two boys were the same height; Thulani slightly bigger in the shoulders. Michaela was much taller and bigger-boned than Miriam— but Miriam's father had been a huge man, and perhaps Thulani's bigger build came from his grandfather. I loved to watch them together, whatever they were doing—they were the face of the country we knew would someday be born. Sometimes, remembering that when Michaela told me she was pregnant, I wanted her to have an abortion, I felt the heat of shame in my face, and I was filled with gladness that she had the determination to go ahead with her pregnancy.

We could have sent Thulani to school, but it would have meant a boarding school far from home. Neither of the boys was prepared for the complete separation that would mean, and Miriam did not want him to leave home yet—he was a young fourteen, she said, and she wanted him close by for a few more years. So he remained at home, spending mornings in the Barn School, and afternoons learning about the workings of the farm, either with Michaela, or with my uncle Solomon. We planned to send both boys to university—if necessary, out of the country. Michaela made sure that she duplicated as closely as possible the syllabus being taught at Simon's school, so that Thulani didn't fall behind.

On the rare evenings I was on the farm, I was privileged to watch the two boys doing homework together. Sometimes we sat outside, Miriam and I, when the weather was warm, in the yard behind the farmhouse. Sometimes we sat together in the farmhouse kitchen or in the little room with the fireplace next to her bedroom in the servants' quarters. Less frequently, we went home to our house in the village. I read the newspaper; she peeled vegetables for the next night's dinner, or she ironed, or she darned. When she was done, she, too, read the paper, and then we talked about the news, and about what was occurring in the country. But wherever we were, we would both be focused on the two boys, who often sat within earshot. We listened to their conversation as they sat together, their heads bent over homework. Simon was the bookworm; historian, philosopher, poet. Thulani, on the other hand, was the realist. Math came easily to him, and science; he thought like an engineer. We listened to their quiet voices one evening as they went over the day's assignments.

"I don't get it," Simon said. "Why does mass multiplied by acceleration equal force?"

"It's just a formula," Thulani explained. "Everything follows from the basic concept. All you have to do is understand it."

"I understand multiplication," said Simon impatiently. "But I don't get what mass has to do with acceleration."

Thulani's smooth forehead crinkled as he frowned, and then smoothed again as he broke into a smile.

"There's your 'why' question again," he said. "Sometimes you just have to accept that a fact is a fact, Simon. It's not complicated like your chicken or egg question—either it's true or false. And this is true. So just accept it."

"I can't just accept it, Thulani," said Simon, "until I understand it. If it's that easy for you to understand, then explain it to me."

Thulani thought for a moment.

"We know that if an object is accelerating," he said, "it's because something is exerting a force on that object. This is just a way to measure the force. The fact that we're dividing force by mass—instead of multiplying—tells us something about the relationship between the two. Know what it is?"

"That the greater the mass of an object, the more force is needed to move it?"

"Exactly!" He shrugged. "That's why force is equal to the mass of an object multiplied by its acceleration. It's just the way the universe works," he said. "Accept it."

Simon did—and he understood it, too. Whether the concepts had do with Pythagorean theory, or Euclidean geometry, or the basic laws of gravity or physics, Thulani had an instinctive understanding, and an ability to make it comprehensible.

But if Simon needed to understand the "why" in any scientific discussion, the need he had to question did not extend in the same way to literature. As long as the world created by his author was convincing enough, he found it easy to suspend disbelief. The giant squid wrapping itself around a submarine in *Twenty Thousand Leagues under the Sea* was quite believable to Simon—but Thulani found it foolish. They ended up wrestling on the grass, Simon's legs gripping Thulani's waist like the giant squid, and they laughed together until one of them gave in.

I seldom involved myself in their conversations—I was content to sit and listen as they worked out their differences, as they taught each other, and as they grew in brotherhood. It filled me with pride. But sometimes they came to ask me questions, and as they matured, I found myself more and more frequently pulled deep into conversation with them on political issues about which I felt great conviction.

One of these issues was the internecine bloodshed we lived with. It was horrendous—and once it started in earnest in the 1980s, it was difficult not to be drawn into the conflict.

When the underground military wing, Spear of the Nation, was established in 1960, the leadership of the organization, including Nelson Mandela—who himself went to Ethiopia for military training in 1962—made clear that our mandate forbade violence against civilians. We believed that a government incapable of delivering power, water and communications cannot govern, and the theory was that by disrupting the infrastructure, we would force them to the bargaining table.

But the violence we experienced, which intensified in the 1980s, was not directed at the government. The newspapers called it black on black violence. It was politically motivated conflict, in which the two most powerful anti-government parties struggled for dominance in what they all hoped would become the new South Africa. The policies that distinguished the ANC and the Inkatha Freedom Party from each other will be disputed long into the future. But the basic distinction between them was tribal.

The Inkatha Freedom Party was founded by Mangosuthu Buthelezi, a Zulu prince and Chief of the Buthelezi tribe, and it was understandable that tribal Zulus would gravitate to him. But Buthelezi was seen as a man willing to compromise with the regime, while Nelson Mandela was not. In 1985, responding to public pressure, the government offered Mandela freedom from a life sentence in prison if he would renounce violence. He responded by saying that the organization had only adopted violence because other forms of resistance were no longer available, and he refused. This kind of integrity, and the commitment it implied, was one of the reasons that the ANC had a wide appeal nationally.

But Michaela's farm was in the Midlands, not far from Zululand in the area now called KwaZulu Natal, and it was an area where there was an almost virulent tribal loyalty to the Inkatha Freedom Party. It made the work we had to do for the ANC far more difficult, and placed us and those working with us at great risk.

The tragedy is that both parties forgot their common enemy, and allowed themselves to be manipulated. The Special Branch understood this, and took advantage of the mistrust between them to create chaos. It was just another example of the attempt to continue the age-old strategy of divide and rule that the apartheid government had applied so success-fully. Agencies of the government even went so far as to commit political assassination and mass murder, leaving behind false evidence that these were acts of revenge by members of one party against the other.

As Michaela and I watched the political conflict intensify, we reminded each other of the prediction that a time would soon come when brothers would shed each other's blood. And they did. In the years that followed, in ones and twos and groups of five and ten, more than 20,000 of our people would be killed.

At school, Simon was exposed to the regime's view that the Zulus were uncivilized and violent, and that the violence meted out was either the result of old tribal hostilities, or a primitive response to the demands of the modern world. This position was motivated by fear, and there was no place in it for complexity, compassion or understand-ing. And I had to be careful in my conversations with my sons to give sufficient information without revealing the depth of my involvement in the conflict.

When the boys were fifteen, an incident at a railway station between Johannesburg and Durban caused deep divisions amongst urban and rural Zulus. It was discussed for weeks in the news, and it became a topic of discussion at school, in every village, and at the farm.

More than a dozen members of the ANC were murdered in gruesome fashion on a train travelling to Durban—and there were signs left at the site that members of the Inkatha Freedom Party were responsible. When this was reported in the press, angry members of the ANC took revenge, and several members of Inkatha were killed. They were executed using burning necklaces—gasoline filled tires put over their necks, and set alight.

I was seldom home in those days, but Simon and Thulani came to me the next time I was at the farm. It was a summer evening; Miriam and I were sitting outside. I had told the boys little about my involvement in the ANC; and nothing about the fact that I was high up in the hierarchy of the outlawed Spear of the Nation. But they knew something—it would have been impossible in that environment to keep them completely in the dark.

Thulani was angry and troubled, and I realized that it was time to take them into my confidence. It would have been too dangerous to share the full story—but they were old enough to know more than they did about what was going on in the country, and why I held the views I did.

What I was about to share with them was sufficient to put us all in danger, and it crossed my mind that perhaps I should tell only Thulani, who would honor what I told him as only a son could. I didn't know exactly how Simon felt towards me. Respect, yes; love, perhaps. I had been a constant presence in his life, and Michaela had made sure whenever I was around that the three of us spent some time together, even if it was just a few minutes playing or talking; and she made sure that he saw her treating me with respect, and more affection than was customary between mistress and servant. I suspected that he would honor my confidence—but I was certain that whatever I told Thulani, he would share with Simon. It was better that he heard the truth directly from me.

"I want to respect your opinion," said Thulani, "but it's hard to understand how the ANC can be a good organization when its members tie people up and burn them alive. How can you support this?"

"I told Thulani you don't support this, Khabazela," said Simon. "But you can't know what every member of the ANC does, and that you're not responsible for what they do."

"I didn't say my father is responsible," said Thulani, and he turned to me. "But I don't understand how you can justify being part of an organization whose members are so violent."

Miriam and I exchanged glances, and she nodded to me. She agreed; it was time. She went into her room and came back with a flashlight, which she handed to me.

"Come," I said, rising to my feet. "Both of you. It's time for us to take a walk."

I led them back out through the waning summer light to the base of the hill below the Bushman cave. This was the one area of the farm they had been warned against, and although I couldn't be sure, I suspected that they had never explored as far as the thick foliage; that they didn't know that there was a path leading around the massive trees and up into the invisible crevice that opened into a completely secluded cavern. I stopped at the base of the hill, before we entered the undergrowth, and turned to them. They both looked at me expectantly.

"Where are we going?" asked Simon.

"This is a secret place," I said softly. "I take you here in the confidence that you will never share this place, or the things we talk about here, with anyone. Agreed?"

They both nodded agreement, and I led the way through the thorn trees, into the foliage and around several huge tree trunks until the weak moonlight showed the path winding up the incline. When we reached the wall of rock I reached a hand behind me.

"Take my hand," I said, "and then take each other's hand and follow my lead. It gets very dark."

I led the way, unsure which one of the boys was directly behind me, or whose hand I was holding. They were silent as we climbed into the crevice and the darkness closed over us. When we reached the cave I turned on the flashlight, and their surprised and hushed reaction told me that this was a new place for them. I showed them the Bushmen paintings, gave them some of the history, and then sat them down cross-legged in the middle of the cave.

"I wish it were not necessary for me to share this with you," I said, "but you both know already that we live in dangerous times, and I cannot protect you from that fact. We would all be in even greater danger if I let you grow up uninformed. So, are you ready to hear what I have to say?"

"Is this to be kept a secret even from my mother?" asked Thulani.

"No," I answered. "Not from your mother, and not from Simon's mother. We have no secrets from each other. But that's it. No one else. Okay?"

They agreed, and they sat in solemn silence as I told them about some of the pieces of my life. I found myself wanting desperately to tell them everything, but it was not possible. I could not tell them that Michaela and I had spent a year hiding from the police in Zululand; that we had been lovers. I did tell them that I had been a teacher, and that after the destruction of Sophiatown, I realized the government was beyond responding to peaceful protest. I talked about my arms training out of the country, and told them about my role in Spear of the Nation.

"The details of all this," I said, "are not important—what I do, and where, and how. I'm sharing it with you because I want you to believe what I say, and you are old enough now to ask for more than simply my word. Because of my role as a commander, as a negotiator, and as the representative of the ANC to other organizations within and without the country, I have access to information that others do not. If I tell you a commonly held belief is a fiction; if I assure you that something is true, my words are based on information not commonly available."

"What fictions are you talking about?" asked Thulani. "And what truths?"

"Simon, you are right in saying that I cannot control everything our members do—but as a leader, I bear overall responsibility for their actions. And Thulani, you are right in being outraged. It is true," I said, "that members of our organization have committed terrible crimes in retaliation for things done by members of Inkatha." I paused. "At least, they believe these things were done by members of Inkatha."

"Weren't they?" asked Simon.

"Not all of them," I answered. "One of the things that make it so terrible to live in this time is that we don't know whom to trust. Brothers are pitted against each other; divided loyalties break families apart. And the government knows that we are not united—that we are represented by two organizations with different policies, struggling for power."

"You mean the ANC and Inkatha?"

"That's who I mean," I said. "And those in power will do anything to divide us and cause us to fight among ourselves."

I explained that the Special Branch had a division dedicated to making trouble between the ANC and Inkatha, and that I was certain the train murders were actually committed by Special Branch operatives, who then left false evidence leading back to Inkatha.

"How can we be so stupid," asked Thulani, "to be taken in by such a trick?"

"It is a trick, and a very clever one," I said. "We've played right into the government's hands. They point to us and they claim what Simon is hearing at school—that the Zulu people are primitive, and that we can't govern ourselves without violence. We're not ready for modern politics. It terrifies the white minority; and it provides justification for keeping things as they are."

"Isn't there a way," said Simon, "to show both organizations that they're being played against each other by a common enemy? Then they could get together and present a united front. They'd be much stronger that way, wouldn't they?"

"Yes. Part of my job is trying to convince the leaders of both sides that we could do better together," I said. "Eventually we will succeed— but before we do, things may become much worse."

"Worse than they are now?" asked Thulani.

"I'm afraid so," I said. "It's one thing to convince the leaders—it's another thing entirely to get the word out to every member of the organizations. And even then, it's very difficult to change behavior in every village and every place where people come together. We won't get anywhere until we realize that we can accomplish more together than we can at each other's throats. And before that happens, our losses will have to become even more dramatic."

The flashlight began to dim, and I rose from the ground.

"Come," I said. "It's time to go." Before we left I placed an arm around each of their shoulders. "There are really two reasons why I have shared all this. We're doing everything possible to bring an end to all the killing and I have hope that it will soon stop. I want you to have the same hope. But my identity is no longer as hidden as it once was—I'm too much of a presence at negotiations. And if I'm known, then Thulani is known, too, and by association, you as well, Simon."

I told them how important it was to be cautious; to stay away from unfamiliar places; to avoid people they weren't sure of, and to never be alone. I reminded them never to discuss their affiliation with me or to publicly disparage one party or the other. And we discussed bravery, how important it was under some circumstances, and how foolhardy under others. This was a time, I said, to take every challenge seriously; being brave when the stakes were so high was foolhardy. And, I said, if anyone threatened them, they should come immediately to me.

I placed a great burden on their shoulders by sharing what I had, but I knew it was necessary. They were young and hotheaded; whatever they felt, they felt strongly. No matter how rational they might be, I knew that under the right conditions, they could be pushed into conflict from which there would emerge no winners. I had seen it often enough in the townships and outside the villages, where a whole generation of young men sauntered, enraged with their lives, with the government that oppressed them, and with their leaders, who were too conciliatory and whose protests and negotiations had achieved nothing. These young men were an explosion waiting for a detonator, and I had the unenviable job of trying to defuse every detonator in sight. I wanted to make sure that my sons were nowhere to be found if and when I failed.

twenty-six

MANDLA

Natal, South Africa, 1984

Two years passed. Three combatants of our military wing were convicted of attacking police stations, and were hanged; many others were quietly dispatched without a trial. There were several car bombings outside police stations and military installations. Some attempts on the lives of elected politicians were successful; others were foiled—and then there were the badly planned ones, such as the premature explosion at a synagogue at which the state president was scheduled to speak. The toll of the dead and injured grew, and in KwaZulu, the level of violence rose to an unprecedented level.

My role in mediating local and regional disputes grew to such a degree that the apartheid government began to notice me, and to think of me as more than a terrorist agitator. At the same time, the traditional Zulu leaders I had had such difficulty with before I married Miriam, began to develop a healthy respect for my ability, if not for some of my opinions. I found it ironic that I was called upon by all sides to mediate, discuss and reconcile, and I began to think that we were approaching the point at which peaceful change might happen.

1983 was the year in which 4,000 public leaders signed a declaration for the release of Nelson Mandela from prison. The declaration was initiated by Father Trevor Huddleston, now an archbishop in England. He had traveled far since saving my life in Sophiatown so many years earlier, and it was good to know that he had not abandoned the cause. I couldn't know then that seven years would pass before Nelson Mandela would be released from prison, and that in our lives what was both predicted and unthinkable would happen.

In October of that year, Chief Buthelezi, the president of Inkatha, along with the Zulu King, Goodwill Zwelithini, was invited by the Inkatha Youth Brigade to speak at the University of Zululand in Ongoye, in commemoration of King Cetshwayo.

This was in the heart of Zululand, the center of the homeland, and the area from which Inkatha had come to expect the greatest loyalty. Inkatha supporters made clear that this was to be their day—but just prior to the event students boycotted classes in an effort to have the whole presentation cancelled. They were concerned that the royal entourage would enter the building carrying traditional weapons that were required in the presence of the king, and that Inkatha supporters would attend in great numbers. I knew that most of them would be enthusiastic students, but that among them would be some paid thugs—and I knew that student members of the ANC would be present to protest the agenda of Inkatha. It was a foregone conclusion that there would be bloodshed.

On the day of the event I waited at the farm with Miriam, expecting that I would receive a call as soon as possible after the end of the event letting me know what the fallout was, and whether I needed to do anything to contain it. But before it even began, in the early evening, Hlengiwe, the daughter of Miriam's cousin, ran into the yard calling my name.

Hlengiwe was sixteen, the same age as the boys; they had all played together as children, and I knew that Thulani was close to her. She was a willowy, athletic girl with a pretty face and round cheeks. She kept her dark curls above her head with a colorful ribbon just above her forehead. It showed off her perfect skin. Usually she was quiet and composed around me, but on this day she was agitated; she had been weeping, and she was wringing her hands.

"What is it, Hlengiwe?" asked Miriam, ushering her into the kitchen and sitting her down. "What's the matter?"

"Thulani went this afternoon to Ongoye. He said he wanted to hear Chief Buthelezi, and the King."

"I told him not to go," said Miriam, looking at me with guilt in her eyes, as though it were her fault that our son had disobeyed.

"He's old enough to make wiser decisions than this," I said. "You can't blame yourself—just think hard about what you will do with him when he gets back."

"I also told him not to go," said Hlengiwe. "But he said it was time to stop all the violence."

"My God," said Miriam. "The boy thinks he's gone to make peace! Is he mad?"

"How did he get there?" I asked.

"He went with some people in a car."

"What people, Hlengiwe? Tell me what people he went with. Did he know them? People from here?"

"I don't know," she said, shaking her head. "I saw him getting in the car, but he told me not to say anything. He didn't want Simon to know, either."

"Simon?"

"Yes. He knew Simon would come looking for him, and he did, but I wouldn't tell him where Thulani went; I didn't want him to go. He was so cross with me. But he asked everyone, and someone told him where Thulani went, and that he was going to see if he could prevent any violence." She burst into tears. "Khabazela, Thulani will be in real trouble if they find out he's your son. Simon said they don't want the ANC there tonight; and that you told the two of them never to go anywhere alone. Now he's taken Michaela's car and followed, so that he can be there to protect Thulani. I don't think they have any idea how dangerous this is. You have to stop them."

"You did the right thing to tell us," I said, rising and putting on my jacket. "Miriam, there's going to be trouble tonight. I'm going to Ngoya."

"You're not going alone," said Miriam.

"No. I'll get Andrew to drive," I said. "I hope we don't need his doctoring —but he'll get us through any police blockades, and he drives faster than I do."

I didn't say it, but Andrew could also legally carry a weapon, which I could not—and I knew that in the trunk of his car, along with his medical bag, he carried two rifles, a pistol, and several pangas.

I ran to the house to find Michaela and Andrew sitting on the front verandah. They had no idea that Simon had taken a car and gone off, and when I told them, Michaela was furious. She got up from her chair and started pacing.

"Thulani shouldn't have gone, and Simon shouldn't have followed him. What were they thinking?" She stopped suddenly and looked up at me, frightened. "How bad is it? Will they be all right?"

"I don't know. That's why I have to go to Ongoye."

"Give me a minute to get the car keys," said Andrew. "I'm driving."

He didn't have to tell me that his medical bag was in the car.

We had no trouble; Andrew drove fast, and there were no police on the road. I hoped that we would pass Simon in Michaela's car, but he was travelling with as much urgency as we were, and we caught no sight of him. When we left the farm, the sun was shining; by the time we reached the campus an hour and a half later, it was raining hard, and darkness was minutes away. The area differed from the farmlands we had just left—it was at a lower elevation, received much more rainfall, and as a result the vegetation was thicker, and the area around the campus was almost like rainforest. There was a permanent staff employed to keep it at bay, but beyond the parking lot and the sloping grassy mall leading to the main entrance, the forest had encroached on the campus and taken over all but a few yards around the buildings.

The parking lot was full; the police were milling around in their wide black police hats and black raincoats shiny with the rain, watching, waiting for something. There were three ambulances on the grass, emergency technicians visible in the light streaming from their open doors. A half dozen people stood or lay on stretchers outside each ambulance, waiting for attention.

"The blood-letting has begun," said Andrew grimly. "We're already too late."

"We need to find my boys," I said. "Fast. Then we can try and stop it before it gets out of hand."

The royal convoy was not in evidence, and the security entourage that usually accompanied the king and Chief Buthelezi were nowhere to be seen. Before we locked the car Andrew opened the trunk, loaded two pistols and gave me one. I shoved it into the inside pocket of my jacket. He gave me a flashlight which I tested and then put into the outside pocket of my jacket. He did the same.

"You want a panga?" he asked.

"No," I answered. "I'll take this instead."

I picked up the tire iron from the bottom of the trunk and hid it beneath my coat, suspended from my belt. From my years working in garages I knew what a defensive tool it could be. It was also easier to conceal than a panga. Pangas were for cutting and killing, and we were not there to do either. I would have told any other man that he didn't need one, but Andrew understood the issues as well as I did, and if he was more comfortable with a panga, I was not going to tell him he was wrong. But he didn't want one. He put the pistol in his pocket and closed the trunk, and together we walked across the parking lot towards the main door.

Andrew knew the police officer in charge, Andreas Kurtz. He introduced me as a concerned parent, said we had come by in search of two boys, and to offer any medical help in case it was needed.

"It's needed already," said Kurtz wearily. "Nowadays it's always needed, isn't it?" He looked at me. "More parents like you should be here tonight, Mandla. Your young people are killing each other in such numbers that it makes the white people afraid. They say, these Zulus think so little of their own lives; how much less will they think of ours?" He shook his head. "It's not good, all this angry killing. Has to come to an end."

"My son Thulani came here this afternoon thinking to make peace," I said, slowly and calmly, looking him in the eye. "So we're in agreement about that, Officer Kurtz, and so are the boys we're looking for. Do you have any idea where we might find them?"

"Who's the other boy you're looking for?"

"The son of a friend of mine," said Andrew. "From a farm near my sister. Simon Michaels."

The officer had been inspecting the campus buildings around us; now he looked sharply at Andrew.

"A white boy?" he said. "With dark hair?"

"You've seen him?"

"Young fool. I told him to go home—this isn't his fight, and it's dangerous for him to be here. He said he was looking for a friend who might be in trouble, and I told him I hadn't seen any other white boys. He got angry and shook my hand off his shoulder—ran off into the crowd." He stopped. "He wasn't looking for a white boy, was he? He was looking for your son." He hit his forehead with the back of his hand. "His friend, your son. And they were both coming to make peace. Ag, I'm so stupid. I should have seen it. How old are the boys?"

"Both sixteen," I said.

He shouted to his men and they gathered around him quickly.

"You saw that white boy who ran inside about twenty minutes ago?" A few of the men nodded. "He's here looking for his friend—what's your son's name?"

"Thulani."

"He's here looking for his friend, Thulani. This is Thulani's father. Both boys are sixteen, and they think they're here to make sure there's no fighting. Let's find them before they discover that this is not your average rugby match. Go! Go! Search every room in the place again! Carry rifles cocked—and be cautious. Some of these buggers are carrying pangas."

The men headed off into the buildings straight ahead of us.

"We'll take a quick look in the building first—if we don't find the boys we can move outside," I said to Andrew.

"You want to stay together or separate?"

"Let's go in together until we know what we're dealing with."

"You're not going in there," Kurtz objected.

"We would rather do it with your permission," I said, "but we're going in to find the boys."

Kurtz looked at us both, and I could see the confusion on his face— that we were actually going to go looking; that I was giving instructions and Andrew was about to follow them, and that I had the audacity to contradict him.

"We'll be fine," said Andrew.

"My men are trained, and they're carrying cocked rifles," he said. "Don't be foolish, Doctor; you don't want to go in there unarmed."

Andrew smiled and withdrew his pistol. "I know these young men and their families as well as Mandla does," he said. "I'm carrying this but I don't think I'll have any use for it."

Something dawned on Kurtz as he realized that we were not simply a white doctor and a concerned black father. "Suit yourself," he said. "You're on your own."

"Thank you," I said as we headed off towards the building.

The rain had stopped, but the air was moist and warm. As we headed towards the entrance we passed small groups of young people—mostly men, a few women. Some were standing aimlessly; a few sat silently on the wet grass. The more seriously wounded had been carried or dragged to the ambulances—but many of those remaining had ripped clothing and were bleeding from wounds on their faces or arms. They were all in shock.

At the entrance to the building, protected from the rain, five bodies lay side by side, their faces covered by random pieces of clothing. I removed the coverings and glanced rapidly at each face. Children, all; not one over twenty. I had seen it all before, many times; and I had thought of each death as if it was the death of my own son or daughter—but this time I was searching for my sons, and I understood that it was not the same.

I recognized none of the faces—but all had been savagely beaten and hacked, and they were lying in their own blood. This was not the work of angry students or members of the Youth Brigade; this was the practiced slashing of professional killers, mercenaries who for a price would kill their mothers and sell their sisters for meat. I knew them; had watched them in action and seen their absence of anger and fury; witnessed only the cold pleasure taken in the act of dismembering, disemboweling, severing human life from the cord. Killing in cold blood is the most debased human act I have witnessed, and the most horrifying.

Inside, but for the running footsteps of the police, the building was silent. In the small vestibule, they had split into two groups—one group went off to search classrooms along the corridor to the left; the other group did the same on the right. Straight ahead was a short, unlit hallway leading to the assembly hall. Through the open double-door came sounds of muted conflict—struggle, and gasping, and the very particular sound of blows landing on flesh and bone. There were suddenly four policemen standing behind us, alerted by the sounds. We peered into the semi-darkened room. Halfway down and to one side of the hall four men bent over bodies on the floor, their arms rising and falling. I couldn't tell whether they were holding weapons, or simply using their fists.

We ran towards them, and two of the men saw us. They rose and rushed in the other direction and out the far door. We pulled the others off the figures on the ground and the police held them while we looked at the victims, a young man with a split lip and a bleeding head, and a young woman, crying, trying to cover her exposed breasts. Her skirt was torn and her underpants around her ankles.

"Are you all right?" asked one of the policemen. "What happened here?"

"They dragged her in here," said the young man, his voice ragged, "to rape her. I followed and tried to make them stop."

"They said they would teach me," she said, "that it doesn't pay to go against them."

Andrew stayed on the floor to tend them; I rose to face the two men the police were holding. One was a young man, looking scared; the other was older, in his forties—way too old to be a student demonstrator. The only possible reason for his presence on the campus was to make trouble. As I looked at him I thought he was familiar, but I couldn't immediately place him. He was a man of medium height, with a fleshy face and a wide mouth.

"Mandla Mkhize," he said, and his voice was full of hatred. "I hoped to see you here tonight, Khabazela. I hear that you've done well these last eighteen years." He smiled, an unpleasant, mocking smile. "Did you find your son yet?"

"What do you know of my son?"

"You don't recognize me, do you?" he said. "No wonder. It's been a long time, but I haven't forgotten that you sent a wounded man back to his home in Eshowe, in disgrace. Do you remember what my crime was?"

"What do you know of my son?" I repeated, but he ignored me.

"My sister sheltered me in her room, and when the farmer she worked for found me, he was going to beat her. I had a bullet in my shoulder, but

I killed him, and then went where you told me to go—to the farm of the woman who would help me."

"Yes, I remember you. Jonathan. Now, tell me what you know of my son."

A policeman stood behind him, holding on to his upper arms. I stepped closer to him and repeated my question, but still he ignored me.

"This man knows something about my son," I said, turning to the officer. "I need to question him."

"You need to question him?" said the policeman. "Who the hell do you think you are?"

"Mandla Mkhize is his name," said Andrew quietly, rising from the floor to stand at my side. "Be very careful what you say to him, because what you say to him you say to me also." He turned around to the young couple on the floor. "You'll both be all right," he said. "I think you should leave now."

They rose, and, holding onto each other, they made their way out of the hall.

"This man has information about the boys we're looking for," continued Andrew, "and we'll get it from him faster if you're not here. I suggest you see where the other two men have gone. Take the younger one with you—perhaps he knows something useful."

The two policemen looked at each other uncertainly, and one of them turned to Andrew.

"I know you," he said. "Don't I?"

"Perhaps," he said. "I'm a doctor—and I probably helped bring your children into the world. Now go—I promise that Kurtz will authorize this."

"Okay," he said. "Let's go. Come on, you."

He released his grip on Jonathan; together, the two policemen ran towards the back door, shepherding Jonathan's young companion between them. Jonathan stepped quickly to the side and turned around to face the front door, but Andrew was already standing behind him, a hand firmly planted on each arm. Andrew tightened his hold and forced Jonathan's elbows behind his back.

"Remember the password you gave me?" Jonathan spoke through a painful grimace. "To give to the woman on that farm, so she would know I came from you? 'On a hilltop in Zululand, not far from the homestead of your mother, Lungile.' What was that all about?"

"That was long ago—and we don't have time now. Have you seen Thulani or Simon?"

I placed a hand firmly at his throat and squeezed once, quickly. He lowered his head to protect himself, but I kept my hand at his throat and I felt the blood pulsing through the vein in his neck. I wanted him to know that I would exert whatever pressure I needed to.

"I don't know any Simon," he said into his chest.

"Come on, man," said Andrew. "Khabazela doesn't want to hurt you, but we know he will if he has to. Where is Thulani?"

"You had me carried back to Eshowe in shame." He looked at me as he spoke, his voice hoarse, wheezing as he breathed through the pressure of my fingers. "I did nothing but defend my sister, and you sent me back, wounded and disgraced. My son was a good boy, but he lost his way when I came back; he was embarrassed by me, and he ran off. You took my life from me, Khabazela. Now I work for whoever pays. My wife left me after our son was killed in a robbery—he was nineteen, just a little older than Thulani." He grinned through his discomfort. "A nice boy, your son. Interested in learning about the other side of our conflict—the side his father is not on. When I found he was your son I saw to it that he learned everything you failed to tell him, and I arranged for him to be here today." He paused. "He is a stubborn boy."

"Where is he?"

"They took him and a few other boys out to the trees to see if they could educate them. You know, talk some sense into them."

"Who are 'they'? How many of them? And what do you mean, talk? What did you want Thulani to do?"

I squeezed, and he coughed.

"I wanted him to tell them what he knows about your work," he said.

"He knows nothing about my work," I said. "You wanted my son to betray me?"

"Wait," said Andrew. "We need to know where they took him. Jonathan, which direction?"

"They went out the back," he wheezed.

"Let him go," I said.

"Khabazela, my brother," said Andrew quietly. "Don't do this thing. Let's go find the boys."

I thought then that I should have taken care of him eighteen years earlier—either gotten rid of him completely, or forgiven him and let him come back once he recovered from his wound. But I didn't know enough then to realize that one has to either kill one's enemies or make them into friends, and now Thulani was paying the price.

"I showed him compassion once, Andrew. Not again," I said. "Release him."

Andrew did as I asked and Jonathan immediately raised his arms to pull my hands from his throat, but I knew how to use the pressure of his fingers on my wrists against him. It was not the first time I had tightened my grip on another man's larynx; not the first time I twisted my arm, jerked down and pulled to the side. Within his neck I felt something tear, and as the air bubbled and seethed from his lungs as if he were a punctured balloon, he slumped to the floor.

"If they harm a hair on either of my sons' heads," I said to Andrew, "he'll be lucky that he died quickly."

"And if they don't?" he asked as we turned and ran down the aisle to the back door.

"Then perhaps I'll regret it. But either way, he was a mercenary and a rapist," I said. "Look what he was ready to do to the girl."

The campus was not large, and the main buildings sat in a huge oval of light shed by floodlights surrounding the perimeter. As we headed down the path towards the darkness we intercepted the policemen who had just left the hall, and Andrew motioned them to follow us. I was in the lead—I knew that once out of the light, the instincts I had developed over the years would kick in.

We moved slowly, careful to avoid snapping twigs or the sudden movement of vines and branches. Light was visible through the trees, and as the distance closed it became recognizable as the flickering of firelight. Then the sounds started—raucous laughter, shouts, a cry of pain—and we ran towards the light. I don't know how long it took. It could have been seconds, or minutes. If there was a path, I couldn't find it, and even after I turned on my flashlight our progress was maddeningly slow. As I clawed my way through the brush I heard over and over the urgency and alarm in the shouted voices, and awful images of what we might find flashed through my mind.

When we arrived at the clearing we stopped just out of sight, hiding beyond the trees. At each side of the clearing was a flaming torch, and the shadows cast by the flames danced on the faces and bodies in the center. It took a moment to figure out what we had come upon.

There were bodies on the ground; one or two were moving, but it was too dark to see what condition they were in. Several men stood in a circle, two of them holding onto Simon. He struggled to get free, but they restrained him without effort. Beside him stood another boy, also being restrained. The mercenaries were all too old to be students. These were Jonathan's friends, paid killers who called themselves warriors when it suited their purpose.

In the center stood Thulani. Blood ran down his forehead; his nose was bleeding. He was unsteady on his feet, and the fifth man stood before him, taunting him.

I took a second to be thankful that both boys were still alive, but even as I did so the man taunting Thulani drew back his panga as if to hit my son on the side of his head with the flat of the blade. Before I could move Andrew stepped into the clearing with his pistol drawn and shot the man through the head. The policemen followed him, and one of them shot a second man as he reached behind him to withdraw a weapon from his belt.

Andrew, the policemen and I were clumped on one side of the clearing; before us at the center of the clearing were Simon, Thulani and the third boy, and with them, the three remaining men. In the moment it had taken to fire two shots, each of the three men grabbed hold of the closest boy and stood behind him. Using the boys as human shields, they backed away from us in unison, towards the far edge of the clearing. It was obvious that they were planning to take off into the forest.

We exploded across the clearing and reached them just in time to see the last man disappear into the darkness with his captive. We instinctively spread out to cover all three men and dove into the forest after them. They didn't get far; neither did we.

I passed the third boy—the one I didn't know—sitting on a fallen tree; the man holding him must have released him and taken off. I rushed past him and in the flickering light of the torch behind us and my flashlight shining ahead, I saw Simon struggling. His captor was trying to release him and run, but Simon held onto his arm, which the man managed to raise above his head. In his hand he held a hunting knife. I moved toward them through some thick substance that slowed my motion and before I could prevent it the man used the force of Simon's hold on him to create downward momentum, and I saw the knife begin its trajectory.

I burst free of the thickness that held me, intent upon destroying the man who was about to harm my son. With all my strength I thrust the tire iron at him, and I felt the point bury itself in his temple. He dropped like a stone—but not before his blade connected with the side of my brave boy's neck. The man fell. Simon kept moving and I felt a brief surge of relief, but as he turned to his left his blood sprayed in hot bursts from his neck onto my face. As I wiped his lifeblood from my eyes, I knew that in such volume, he would soon bleed out. I followed him to where Thulani struggled with his captor, and again that night I was outside time, held immobile while action took place that I was powerless to stop.

Thulani was weakened by his beating but he managed to twist himself around as the man tried to escape, and to grip him around the neck with both arms, but the man still held onto his panga and he knew—and I knew—that his one best chance to escape Thulani was to use his panga as a flail.

"Thulani, let go of him!"

My mouth opened to scream the words, but no sound emerged. Every molecule in my body was intent on getting to my son before the panga began to rotate. But I was too late. Thulani's captor reached around himself, slashing his panga viciously against the softness of my boy's belly, flailing left and right, and then again left and right, from side to side. Thulani released his hold on the man's neck, and I watched in horror as my son's body opened up and spilled itself on the forest floor, and the rest of him followed. As Thulani released his captor the man stumbled and Simon threw himself forward, blood arcing from the wound in his neck. He fell on his brother's murderer, grabbed the panga from him, and using his own weight he forced the blade down through its owner's throat.

They lay there together, blood mingling, the man holding his throat together as his heart pumped itself out.

I pulled Simon away so that I could see what blood was his. Beside me Andrew reached Thulani, and I heard him drop to his knees.

"Ahhh," he said, "no, Thulani, no." His voice broke, tears running down his throat. "Not like this."

Simon held on to my hand as I cradled him on the ground, holding pressure over the artery in his neck, but it bubbled up hot under my fingers and I watched my life flowing into the earth. I leaned down and kissed his forehead.

"My sons."

I said the words for the first time in my life, unaware that I was talking out loud. The tears fell from my eyes onto Simon's forehead and rinsed a clear channel through the blood on his cheeks.

Simon opened his eyes and looked up at me. There was already blood gurgling in his throat and his eyes were glazed with his dying, but he smiled at me, and when he spoke, it was in a whisper. Through my grief, I leaned down to hear him.

"My father," he said. "Thulani and I talked about this, often. We knew we were brothers. Tell him, now he has to share you with me..."

My tears fell into his open, unseeing eyes, and I nodded, knowing even as I agreed that there was no one left to tell.

"Both my sons?" I said, addressing no one in particular; there was no one left to address. "You take them together? All at once?"

I had never felt so alone. At that moment, whatever gods or shades or spirits I might once have spoken to evaporated from my life like mist under the cruel scrutiny of the sun.

We carried my sons back through the trees to the main building, and there I washed the blood from their bodies and sewed together their torn flesh, thinking to hide the degree of their damage from their mothers. Andrew tried to dissuade me, but he too was heartbroken, and he stood and watched me as I clumsily did my mending. I was not thinking clearly, and perhaps a part of me thought that by sewing up their wounds I might bring them back. But their lives were gone. And mine.

There I sat on the forest floor, my legs spread out before me in the mud, holding my sons one against each shoulder. I wept in a way I never thought possible; heard bellows of animal grief so painful that I looked around me for the source until I realized that the sounds came from my own throat. The only thing worse than the experience of my own grieving was our dark and silent journey back to the farm, where I stood frozen and numb, a weeping rock, and I watched Miriam and Michaela fall on the boys, kiss their dead eyes, keening and wailing. And then they stood together, holding each other upright even though all they wanted was to end the pain of their own grief, fall to the earth and burrow deep beneath it.

This is the first time I have ever told anyone the details of what happened that night, Steven. But it is your right, as Simon's brother. You thought that you were the only son, but now you are the only one living. I hope you will remember that when you meet your mother.

We buried Simon and Thulani on the farm one moonlit night in a grove of ancient trees. They lie side by side, and Michaela has put a picket fence around the graves. I'm sure she will take you there, to show you the little fenced plot where she tends roses and where she grows herbs and grasses. She will not tell you this, but she visits our boys each day, as she has done since the night they were killed.

I don't remember how we managed to get through the days after Ongoye. I was still convinced that the only way to achieve political change was to make the act of governing impossible by the use of sabotage—but the personal cost of doing so had finally become too high.

After that night, I could not find it in myself to even think about taking life. I ceased all my military activity, terminated my connection with Spear of the Nation, and became a full-time negotiator. And it didn't take long to realize that for me, being on the farm or in the village was like a living death. Whether I was in Miriam's room, in the farmhouse itself, or anywhere on the grounds, I heard the sounds of the boys' laughter and their horseplay, and I found myself over and over turning around to look for them—only to be reminded yet again that they were gone.

And for Miriam, it was too difficult to remain in the village where she had raised Thulani. When I suggested that we go elsewhere, Miriam was relieved, and so we began to make plans to move. I was not sure where we would go, and we talked to Michaela as well, because if she had wanted to leave, too, we would have gone somewhere together. It might have been easier for us to move as a unit—she could have sold the farm and bought a property elsewhere, and it would have been quite normal for us to follow as her domestic servants. But she was living with Andrew by then, and he would not have been willing to move far from his medical practice. And they were as happy together as they could have been under the circumstances.

Besides, it would not have worked well for Michaela and Miriam to be too close. Although they would not willingly admit it, they found it difficult to be together. Each woman's grief only intensified the grief of the other, and they were a constant reminder to each other of what they had lost.

Something else happened in the weeks following the burial that made it impossible for Michaela to leave. Hlengiwe appeared at the farm late one afternoon, and when I arrived that evening looking for Miriam, I found her with Michaela and Hlengiwe waiting for me inside. They were not in the kitchen, where I would have expected them to be, but in the main room, in front of the fire. When I came into the room Hlengiwe rose from her chair and turned to me. There was something very serene about her as she came slowly towards me.

"Until tonight, Khabazela, I thought that of all of us, my loss was the greatest. I should have been able to see it, but I did not know until now that Simon and Thulani had the same father," she said. "So your loss is greater than I could have imagined. I am so sorry."

She put her arms about my neck and hugged me gently, and kissed my cheek. It was not what I expected. There was something intimate and unseemly about her embrace, and I didn't understand what had happened or what I was supposed to do. It struck me that this must be a thing among women, and that I couldn't be expected to know how to deal with it. But even as I thought it, I knew the idea was ludicrous.

"What's going on?" I asked. "Why have you taken it upon yourselves to share with this girl something so private? This was not yours alone to give away."

"This is not just any girl," said Miriam quietly. Both she and Michaela shook their heads and gestured to Hlengiwe as if they were deferring to the younger woman.

"I have something to tell you," she said as she returned to her chair. "Please sit down."

We sat down across the coffee table, and Hlengiwe leaned forward towards me. Her eyes were intensely dark and liquid, and there was a fierce intelligence in them that I hadn't expected.

"Thulani was like my brother," she said. "You know that we played together from the time we were little. And Miriam knows that when she brought both boys to the village, we all three played together. But with Simon, it was always different. There was a distance between us, even as children, and I thought for a long time that it was just because he was a white boy. But as we became older I saw that when we all played together, Simon would play with the other children, but with me he was distant. It made me very angry because I thought he disliked me. So I ignored him.

"Thulani knew better than we did what was going on, and he told Simon that I was in love with him. So Simon overcame his shyness, and last year, when I turned sixteen, he took me into the woods and asked if he could kiss me. I told him that all my kisses were his, and that he did not need to ask for them." She smiled shyly, a sad little smile. "He took many, and I do not regret what I gave, because I received more in return."

"I thought that my loss was the greatest of all, because in Thulani I lost a brother; and in Simon I have lost my best friend, and the man who would have been my husband. But I came here today to tell you—all of you—that even in the terrible weight of this grief, we must leave room for living." She looked into the fire, and then turned back to me. "My father, I had to know that Simon was your son, because I am pregnant with Simon's child."

When you visit South Africa, Steven, you will come to Michaela's farmhouse, and you will meet our grandson, Penya. He has his grandmother's eyes, and his father's chin, and I would not be surprised to find that he seems familiar to you. There are good reasons for that. Penya is your nephew; your brother's son.

twenty-seven

STEVEN

Boston, 2001

D ariya sat on the couch looking at me as I dialed the number, standing with my back to the wall as I waited for the call to go through. The ring was unfamiliar, almost archaic. It was late afternoon when we finished reading; it would be about 9:00 pm in South Africa.

"Hello?"

"Hello. Is this Michaela Green?"

"Yes, this is Michaela. What is it?"

The connection was clear, the voice energetic, cultured, with a stronger South African accent than my father had. It was the voice of a competent woman who didn't like being disturbed in the evening, but who was used to being called at inconvenient hours. I felt ridiculous—this was an absurd conversation to have on the telephone, but I knew that the only way to have it was to dive in. I cleared my throat.

"This is Steven." I paused, gripped the phone tightly. "Your son."

There was a pause at the other end of the line, long enough that I wondered whether she had severed the connection. During the pause, I wondered, what does one call the mother one hasn't seen for four decades? Mom? I didn't think so.

"Everything else came true, and now this, too," she whispered. "We had to wait until I was an old woman for you to return from that far distant place."

"What did you say?" I asked, not realizing until after I had spoken that she was referring to the *sangoma*'s prediction.

"It's nothing," she said, pulling herself together. "You're in a far distant place, and your call took me by surprise." She paused. "Stevie? Steven, I mean. Thank God you called. I suppose I shouldn't call you Stevie. How do you like to be called?"

I wanted badly to remember the hushed voice; wanted it to catapult me back into my childhood. It didn't.

"Steven is fine," I said, and stopped. I didn't know where to begin.

"Thank you," she said. "I've been hoping you would call, ever since Khabazela told me you had spoken. I know your father left something for you to read after his death, and I know from Khabazela that he's written to you himself, and that he sent you my—attempt." She hesitated. "I don't know what either of them wrote, but since you're calling me, I assume you've read it all. It feels a little strange, but at this point you know far more about me than I know about you."

"That would be true," I said.

"I was sorry to hear about your father," she said. "I would have liked to see Lenny again."

"Yes."

"Time got away from us. I suppose life got in the way."

I thought for a moment before I responded, not wanting to sound as angry as the child in me felt.

"What got in the way was your youth and your politics, and everything else that stands as an excuse for what you did. Your life might have gotten in the way—mine didn't. It was just upended." Then I asked the question that had kept me up at night throughout my childhood. "Why? How could you have let this happen?"

In the silence that followed I could hear her breathing, swallowing, pulling herself together.

"Every day I ask myself that question," she said hoarsely, "and I'll continue asking it for as long as I live. I can give you many reasons, but even to my ears they sound like attempts at justification. Perhaps we can find an answer together, because so far I haven't found one." She stopped talking and I could hear her taking deep breaths. "Can we meet? I long to see you, and to meet Dariya." She paused. "And Sally and Greg, my grandchildren."

I ignored her request to meet, but took note of the fact that she knew all her grandchildren's names.

"Forty years," I said quietly. "That's two generations. If Lenny hadn't called you, would you ever have made the effort to contact me?"

"When all this started," she said, "our reality was vastly different from anything you can imagine, Steven. We were in the middle of a war; people were dying all around us. I thought of myself as a freedom fighter in the forefront of battle, and I couldn't run away. I felt like an adult, but in retrospect, I was so young—half the age you are now. And what I did wasn't in your best interest; it was selfish. I'm desperately sorry that I decided not to join you in Boston—sorry for the pain it caused you, and the grief; for the burden it placed on your father; for not being there while you grew up and became a man. But the years passed, and by the time you were old enough to be trusted with the truth, I had become a coward. I began to wonder whether you weren't better off without me; whether you'd even be interested in seeing me. After all, I didn't turn out to be much of a mother." She paused. "Did I?"

I was reminded that this woman, who owned the unfamiliar voice at the other end of the telephone, and whose face I would not recognize, was the same one I had loved with every fiber of my being; whatever doubts I might have about her love were newly acquired. They pierced the protective skin that had grown over when I lost her, emerged rough and splintered from my body, a raw, painful presence that had to be acknowledged and dealt with. This was the woman whose bed I had crawled into and into whose arms I had cuddled; the woman whose smell I could still conjure in my mind, and whose lips I could still imagine kissing my cheeks and my forehead. To say she hadn't been much of a mother would be to say that losing her wasn't much of a loss.

"I knew even as a little boy that you loved me," I said, looking across the room into Dariya's eyes. "I couldn't have said it, but even then I understood what unconditional love was. I loved you so much, and then you—you just disappeared. I didn't understand how someone who loved me so much could have gone away. It was like losing a part of my body."

Dariya smiled an encouraging smile at me from across the room.

"Remember that I was deceived, too, Steven," said my mother mildly. "I really thought you knew, and had decided you wanted no contact with me. I thought I was respecting your wishes. Don't I deserve some credit for making contact as soon as I found out the truth?"

I didn't answer.

"I have no answer for you," she continued. "All I can offer—and all I can ask, if I have the right to ask for anything—is the chance for us to rediscover each other." She paused. "I would love it if you would all visit me here."

"We'll have to think about that," I said.

"And Steven?"

"Yes?"

"I don't know what your father told you before he died, but don't be too hard on him. For years he carried the consequences of what I did on his shoulders. I had no right to burden him with that."

"Considering the circumstances," I said, "he didn't do a bad job of raising me."

"I'm sure he didn't," she said.

We agreed to talk again in a few days, and ended the conversation. Dariya rose from the couch and she saw me watching her. She smiled at me again, and I took her in my arms. There was a strange thing trembling at the corners of my mouth, and I didn't know whether it was a smile trying to happen, or an effort not to cry. Perhaps both.

"We're about to have a family reunion," I said.

It took months of planning and negotiation, but in July of 2002, Dariya, Sally, Greg and I boarded a South African Airways airbus at JFK Airport in New York and made the seventeen hour flight to Johannesburg.

As we planned the trip, I shared with Dariya my regret that my father was not coming with us; that he had managed to die before going back. He said he never wanted to see my mother again for as long as he lived, and he made it happen.

"Why would you have wanted him to go back with you?" she asked.

"I would have liked to get them in the same room," I said, "face to face."

"So you want vengeance," she said one weekend in June as we walked on the beach in Dennis. "You're the painter—what would vengeance look like?"

"Don't be so dramatic, Dariya," I said. "This isn't about vengeance—it's about resolution. I would have liked to confront them with what they've done, and see how they react."

"So what would this confrontation look like?" she asked.

"What do you mean?"

"Well, if you can't see it, I'll paint the picture for you," she said. "You get both your parents, in their seventies, in a room. Each of them tells a different story—but both stories are equally true. You decide whose sins are worse, and you extract your pound of flesh.

"The way you're thinking now, maybe it would have been eleven ounces from your mother; five ounces from your father. A few months ago, it would have been reversed. Anyway, you cut it off their bodies accordingly, and you stand there holding this messy pound of parental flesh in both hands, and their blood drips between your fingers onto the carpet, onto your shoes.

"Where are Sally and Greg while this butchery is taking place? Outside playing with the neighbors? Or are they watching? You wanted no more secrets—you want our children free, unharmed by the past. Well, this is the past you're dealing with, and if you take a pound of flesh, either you'll have to show it to them, or conceal it from them. And there is no place on earth deep enough or far away enough to hide it."

I grabbed her on the beach, kissed her mouth in the June breeze, and tasted the sun on her skin. My touchstone. There were oiled teenage girls in bikinis on the beach watching us, close enough so that I could smell their suntan lotion. Their still winter-pale boyfriends grinned in disdain at our middle-aged show. You should be so lucky, I thought.

twenty-eight

STEVEN

Johannesburg, 2002

I was close to fifty, and had been absent from South Africa for forty-one years. The country had changed dramatically, that I knew—and I could only wonder how much of it I would recognize. Once we arrived, however, it became clear that at the age of seven, in crisis and mourning, I had squeezed the essential juice from memory and placed it in airtight storage, to be retrieved at the right time.

We planned to deplane in Johannesburg, transfer the luggage to a rental car, and make the six or seven hour drive southeast to the Drakensberg. My mother, however, had other ideas. She suggested that we spend a few days with Khabazela in Johannesburg first, and this gave us an opportunity to get over jet lag before we saw her. Khabazela said he would come to our hotel—he wanted to show us something of Johannesburg before we went to his home in Soweto.

On our second day in the country, we came down from our room to find several men sitting and waiting in the hotel lobby. Only one could have been Khabazela. He was tall and spare, a straight-backed, vigorous man in his seventies. He was wearing a tailored gray jacket over a yellow tieless shirt, and a dark pair of pants. He sat relaxed and comfortable in a maroon lobby armchair, arms resting on the lustrous upholstery. The contours of his cheeks were a series of concave arcs so that his face was long and thin, and other than the deep wrinkles around his eyes, his skin was smooth.

He had a white goatee and a carefully shaped mustache, and when he saw us emerge from the elevator he bounced to his feet. When he smiled his elegant, somber face lit up like an unexpected sunrise.

"Steven," he said, putting a hand on each of my shoulders. I recognized the deep sonorous voice from our telephone conversations. "I'd know you anywhere—you're the image of your father." He put his arms about me and hugged me hard, and spoke softly into my ear. "It's been a long time, Steven. You have come home. I welcome you."

Then he turned to greet Dariya, Sally and Greg, but I didn't hear what they were saying. It was the first time I had thought of this trip as a homecoming. Not by any stretch of the imagination could I think of this place as home—yet. I was surprised both by his words and by how deeply they touched me.

We had breakfast in the hotel, and I watched how Khabazela won over Sally and Greg, who had initially been shy and a little in awe of this dignified and courtly man. At first he was serious with them, asking questions with real interest. As they grew more comfortable he began to joke with them, and they responded.

neville d. frankel   441

"Greg," he said at one point, as the cereal and sausage and eggs were being cleared away and the coffee being poured, "is looking at me with very serious eyes—and I know those eyes." He smiled. "They have a question in them. Right?"

Greg nodded.

"Well, out with it. What's the question?"

"Dad says that you and Grandpa Lenny were friends," said Greg, "but he seemed much older than you do."

"We were friends a long time ago—when your father was a little child," said Khabazela with a twinkle in his eye. "Your grandfather and I were about the same age, but I think the work I do has kept me very immature."

"I know what immature means, you know," said Greg patiently, "and you're not immature. What work do you do?"

"What do you think?" he asked.

"There are lots of immature kinds of work," he answered. "You could be a clown, or in the circus. But I don't think so."

Sally rolled her eyes. "He does some kind of work with children, Greg. Working with children keeps grownups young. Right, Khabazela?"

"I do work with children, Sally—I'm a teacher. And that has kept me young." He turned to Greg. "And being children, you know that the best teachers are sometimes clowns; the best school sometimes feels like a circus. And that has kept me immature. So you're both right."

"So you knew Dad when he was little," said Greg. "Grandpa's the only one we know who knew Dad back then. In the past."

"You make it sound as if it was the olden days," said Sally. "They did have cars and television and videos, you know."

"Not quite," he answered. "They did have cars—but no television, and certainly no video. And when I knew him it was way before computers."

"Wow, that's weird," Greg said. "So, what was our Dad like?"

Khabazela looked at Greg. "Your father looked just like you," he said with a serious expression. "He was smart, and curious. And he was into everything. When he was a baby your grandmother would put him down, and he would disappear—around a corner, into a closet, under the branches of a tree. And then when he was older, he was sure to find the most dangerous place you could imagine. He was like a kitten—he would climb up farther than was safe, and then he would cry because he couldn't get down. Several times I had to risk my neck to save him."

The children were delighted—but Sally was onto another topic.

"So," she said thoughtfully, "you know our grandmother, too."

"Yes," he answered. "I do know her, and we are very close friends. You will love her from the first moment you meet her. And I'm sure that when she sees the two of you she will fall in love with you, too."

Greg looked at Khabazela with wide green eyes. "Were the two of you ever in love with each other?" he asked.

"That's a very personal question, Gregory," said Dariya quietly, and Greg flushed with embarrassment.

"Friends can ask personal questions," said Khabazela, stretching out a reassuring hand and resting it on Greg's forearm. "And I don't mind answering this one."

I held my breath, not knowing what was coming, but he didn't miss a beat.

"I think she loved me, and loves me still," he said gravely. "Perhaps you'll ask her when you see her. But I can tell you this—I was in love with her. Everyone who knows her falls in love with her."

I attempted to pay the check, but Khabazela waved away my credit card.

"This is mine," he said gently, his hand covering my own. "I look forward to the day when you are part of the landscape, but for today you're my guests."

He pushed back his chair, patted his mouth with a napkin, and placed it carefully on the table as he rose. "But now, I think it's time for a short tour before I take you to my house to meet my family. Shall we go?"

He led the way, a hand on the shoulder of each of my children, looking down at them and smiling as they spoke to him. I watched them go ahead of us, irritated that I felt such a sense of loss. His gentleness, his wry humor and sense of fun, and his wisdom, made me wonder what it would have been like to have him as a part of my life as I was growing up. I began to feel a sense of regret that I lost him when I was a little boy; wondered what it might have been like to have him as a confidante and an example. But there was no going back—there was no back to go to.

The distance from the northern suburbs of Johannesburg to Soweto is only a few miles, but it might as well be half a world away. Many of the homes are little changed from the time of apartheid. Small brick or concrete buildings on tiny lots, the gray, greenish or reddened color of the brick often identifying the period when construction took place. In many lots, shacks of waste wood, board and plywood have been thrown together to house additional family members, and makeshift fences separate each property from the next. Young men played soccer on barren fields; at crowded market stalls, women sold vegetables, and, at one market, the children were horrified to see a woman pushing a supermarket cart filled with skinned sheep's heads.

"Those are called smilies," said Khabazela, amused by their reaction. "Some people think sheep's head is a delicacy."

"Do you?" queried Greg, hoping for a negative response.

"I have eaten it many times," he said, "but it is not my favorite dish."

"Mine neither," said Sally, her nose wrinkled in disgust.

The streets were wide, barren and untended, with few sidewalks, and fewer trees. But the human population was dense. Along every avenue, on every corner, throngs of people sat on the ground or on folding chairs, talking and arguing; they stood around their makeshift shops, buying and selling, or walked along the side of the road carrying boards or boxes or bags of fruit and vegetables. Women gathered outside their homes, tending babies and infants; children played everywhere—along the streets, beside the stalls, on every empty plot of land.

Not all homes were alike. Many had been added to, rebuilt, improved, and were well tended, with carefully grown gardens. There were areas of gentrification, where middle-class subdivisions had been built, and a growing number of larger homes as successful black South Africans decided that they preferred the neighborhood feeling of the communities they'd been raised in, rather than the isolation and electrified fences of the northern suburbs.

Khabazela lived in Orlando West, an area of Soweto on the side of a hill about three quarters of a mile from the house Nelson Mandela once occupied. We passed by the house, a small, brick structure, now a museum, across the street from where merchants had set up tables of Mandela memorabilia, African carvings and paintings.

The house was a modest, two-bedroom brick home with a living room and dining room in front, separated by a well-used porch. There was a low brick wall in front, a vegetable patch on one side of the walk, and a small grassy area on the other. Three children played on the grass, and as we pulled up, several more ran outside and waited on the porch. I parked the car on the roadside and Khabazela ushered us in through the gate.

"Welcome," he said, "I am honored to have you in my home." He beckoned to the children, who came over quietly and stood around us. "Children," he said to his family, "these two are Sally and Greg. They are

Michaela's grandchildren. These four are my grandchildren," he said, pointing, "and the children of my brothers and sisters. And these two," he said, a hand on two of the youngest curly heads, "are my great-grand-children, and also Michaela's."

"Michaela's great-grandchildren?" I asked.

"I know it seems complicated," he said, "but let me explain, and it will become clear. You remember that Michaela and I had a son, Simon, who was killed. Simon left behind him a young woman, Hlengiwe, who was carrying his child. That child is Penya, now grown. You will soon meet him—he works with Michaela at the farm. Penya is married; these are his children, the grandchildren of your brother, Steven, and therefore your grand-niece and nephew."

I knelt down to greet these two lovely children who looked up at me with clear eyes and open smiling faces. Trying to take it all in and to find some connection, I felt both richness at the family I had just discovered, and a profound sense of loss at the brother killed years before I even knew of his existence. Dariya saw my confusion, and she shepherded the other children away. There were smiles all around, and a little girl with huge brown eyes, round cheeks and a bright green headband shyly approached Sally and took her hand.

"Good," said Khabazela. "Now, off you go, all of you, while I take Steven and Dariya inside."

Sally was ready to go in an instant, but Greg looked back at us for confirmation. Dariya gave him a smile of encouragement.

"Don't worry," said Khabazela. "They won't go far. There's a soc-cer game around the corner, and next door is my niece's house. My wife Miriam will give them all lunch while we talk, and then she'll join us. She can't wait to meet you. Come, please. Come inside."

Inside was a comfortably furnished living room with a soft, flowered couch, and two pale green armchairs set around a varnished, dark wood coffee table. On the walls there were several African paintings, framed teaching awards, some family photographs, and a series of more formal photos. As we looked at the pictures, Khabazela pointed us to a group photo of people being addressed by Nelson Mandela. It was dated 1993.

"Nelson was giving an award for the work we did in KwaZulu-Natal. The area we were in was part of what used to be called Zululand," he said. "Do you see me in the photo?"

Dariya and I looked at the photograph. Khabazela was younger, his beard still dark, the lines around his eyes absent.

"Yes," she said, pointing. "There you are."

"And do you recognize the woman on my left hand?" he asked.

I looked at the woman, and an involuntary exclamation, like a stutter, escaped my lips. "My mother," I said.

She was older than the picture I carried in my memory—in 1993 she would have been almost sixty. Her graying hair had been simply cut just below the ears, and her clothing was plain and elegant—a pair of dark slacks and a light blouse. In the picture she was standing tall, her shoulders back, a strong, self-possessed woman, slender and still attractive. I had no memory of how tall she had been when I was seven, but in the photo she was half a head shorter than Khabazela. This was the first picture I had seen of her since discovering that she was still alive, and I recognized her features. If speaking to her hadn't been proof that she was alive, this certainly was. At least, it was proof positive that she had been alive in 1993. But still, I didn't know quite how to react.

"I realize that seeing her must be something of a shock," said Khabazela, "but I thought it better to shock you in little pieces, rather than all at once." He smiled at me.

"That picture," he continued, "was taken near your mother's home. Madiba—Nelson Mandela—was traveling through the country then, and he wanted to thank us for the work we had done to help bring apartheid to an end." He paused. "She made much possible," he said gravely, "that would otherwise never have happened. She saved many good lives; hid both women and men, black and white, from agents of the Special Branch; smuggled many freedom fighters out of the country and into safety. And she did it at great risk to herself, and at her own expense."

I nodded politely, but said nothing. My surprise must have been obvious; my thoughts transparent. He smiled at me, a wise and loving expression on his face, and his reddened eyes, both trapped within and protected by the lines that surrounded them, peered out at me.

"I have seen many things, Steven," he said, "and I can imagine many more—but I have no idea what this is like for you. I would not try to whitewash what has passed between you and your mother, but you must know that I am not her messenger. You will find out on your own what kind of woman she is—far too intelligent to think that her meeting with you can be made easy, or simple. It will be like crossing a raging river—the only way to get to the other side will be to go through it. That photograph lives on the wall—pointing it out to you is my doing, not hers."

I felt the heat of embarrassment rising in my face as he spoke. I was about to apologize when a large woman with a bright, flowered scarf tied about her head came in through the front door. She looked like the little girl with the round cheeks who had shyly taken Sally's hand—but there was nothing shy about this woman.

"This is Miriam, my wife," he said, as we turned from the photograph on the wall to greet her. "How are the children doing?"

"They're fine," she said. "I gave them sandwiches and drinks, and they're playing like long-lost cousins. They're putting on a musical talent show, and I'm going back to keep an eye on them— it gives me an excuse to watch them perform." She grinned widely, and came around the coffee table to embrace us.

"I welcome Michaela's children to this house," she said. "I'm so happy to see you here, after all this time." She placed a warm hand on my cheek and looked into my face. "You have your mother's smile," she said. "It's not a smile that many people see, but those of us who know her well are privileged to see it occasionally." She turned to Dariya. "Steven is the same way?" she asked.

Dariya snaked her arm around my waist. "Oh, yes," she said, grinning. "Steven rarely smiles for anyone but the children. But those of us who know him well are privileged to see it occasionally."

"Very funny," I said.

Miriam laughed delightedly. "I cannot wait for you to see your mother," she said. "I think you will find that you are very much alike."

We spent two days with Khabazela and his family. He wanted to show us the house I had grown up in. I had little interest, but Dariya insisted.

"The children will never have the opportunity to see where I came from," she said, "but it's nice they can have a picture of your history. It will mean a lot to them as they get older. And for me," she said, "seeing where you grew up adds to the impact of what your parents wrote. I think we should go."

So he drove us by the house my parents and I had lived in, and we went into the parking lot of the elementary school where Miss Coetzee and I threw marbles at a brick wall. I remembered none of it, but the children were delighted. On our final day, we stopped outside the home my mother had grown up in, where my grandfather Samuel had his dental office. He showed us the garage where my mother had parked her father's car, covered in his blood, and pointed to the kitchen, where my grandfather had removed a bullet from his thigh on the kitchen table.

On the third day we loaded up our rented four-wheel-drive Toyota wagon and equipped ourselves with a map. Khabazela came by our hotel to give us detailed directions, and to say farewell.

"Thank you so much," said Dariya, giving him a hug. "This has been a fabulous introduction, and meeting your family was a real treat."

"It's been wonderful to meet you all," he said. "Miriam and I are driving up to the farm late next week, so we'll have the chance to spend some more time together. I think Hlengiwe and the children will all be there, too. I think by then you'll feel a part of the family. In the meantime, I wish you a safe journey." He looked at me. "And a smooth reunion."

He kissed Sally and Greg; he and I hugged each other, hard.

"Thank you," I said, and he patted my shoulder.

Then he waved us off, and we began our journey to visit my mother.

From Johannesburg we took the N3 highway, driving southeast towards Durban, on the coast. We went past towns that spoke of the country's colonial past—Harrismith, Ladysmith, and Estcourt. Once we left Johannesburg behind us, the *veld* seemed to extend forever, a rolling flatland of dry, winter grasses ranging in tone from light yellowish-ochre, to a straw color with hints of pale grass-green. It moved in the wind like a huge living thing, like an animal with volition.

Occasionally I saw acres of *veld* grass change direction in an instant; more often, when there was a wind, the grasses seemed to move arbitrarily, a pale sea of disorder waving gently back and forth. The highway crossed multiple rivers and streams, each one breaking the *veld* with a strip of greenery and trees along its banks, and the landscape was increasingly dotted with *kopjies*, small hills, and stark, eroded sandstone formations that increased in size as the elevation began to rise.

Aside from the beauty and grandeur of the landscape, what struck me most was how much space there was, and how few people lived in it. We passed signs for the occasional village, and when we changed from one highway to another we did so by driving through small, rural towns. But for the most part, the only signs of human habitation were collections of small homes or huts in the distance, many of them without an obvious connection to any road.

In Johannesburg, Dariya noticed the particular scent of the air. It was stronger in Soweto, and it was familiar to me at some level that I couldn't identify. It was a not unpleasant scent, mildly acrid, as if something had been burned long ago, and what was left was this residual odor, a thin shadow of the original smell.

As we drove out of the city and through the *veld*, it became stronger, and I noticed that at any given time, there was smoke from a grass fire somewhere—on the horizon, on a hill in the distance, or more often, close to the highway. Khabazela had told us that in the winter season, when there was little rain, the *veld* was like a tinderbox waiting for an excuse to go up in flames. These were precautionary burns to create fire breaks.

It was especially dangerous along the road, where a spark from a discarded cigarette stub could ignite a major grass fire. We drove through many controlled burns along the highway, where smoke obscured visibility, and where we could watch a team of men directing the fire, with a water truck present in case the wind took off in the wrong direction.

After the first few hours of driving Greg and Sally fell asleep, and Dariya and I drove in silence through the majesty of the *veld*, the Drakensberg visible in the distance. Dariya held my hand in hers on the console between us.

"Is this what you remember?" she asked.

"I don't remember much," I said. "And after listening to Khabazela for two days, whatever I might remember has been replaced by other images."

We drove a few miles in silence, and I knew that she was waiting for me to speak.

"You know," I said, "I tried once to exorcize my mother from my life."

"Really?"

"It didn't work, of course. But I've imagined for months how when we finally met, I would tell her the story of how I tried."

"Tell me," she said. "How did you do it?"

I told Dariya what happened to me when, in the eighth grade, one of my classmates lost his father in a car accident.

"He still had his mother," I said, "and the rest of his family. But my mother was dead—or so I thought—and it was my first conscious awareness of how small and intimate my world was. It was terrifying—the first time I recognized that my father and I were our whole universe. We had no one else."

"Didn't your father have any friends?" asked Dariya. "There were plenty of South Africans in Boston. What about people he worked with? And didn't he have any women friends?"

"To my knowledge, he never had any women friends. And he couldn't afford to have any contact with other South Africans. He wouldn't even talk to them—it was the only way he could be sure that no one would ever ask me a question, or discover anything about how Michaela had disappeared. So no, there were no friends."

"I had no idea," she said slowly.

I continued with my story, telling her that when my friend's father died, my first concern was for my father—what would he do if I died? I was a little in awe of the fourteen year old boy I had been—the boy whose first thought was for his father—but perhaps I ought to have been angry or resentful that my father carried his loss, his grief or his longing, in such a way that it placed such a burden on my shoulders.

The crisis in my friend's family gave me a new impetus to attempt a dialogue with my father. I wanted to connect with him; to get access to the parts of him that were walled off. Talking directly about my mother had never worked—but now I had a different avenue of access, or so I thought.

After supper one night as we finished washing the dishes, I readied myself to broach the subject. I wasn't aware of being anxious—but I must have been, because I remember feeling my heart hammering against my chest as I spoke, and wondering whether he could hear it, too.

"I was talking to Billy about his father's funeral," I said as I opened my knapsack and began to take out textbooks. "He's going to visit the cemetery every year, and put flowers on the grave."

"That's a nice gesture," my father responded without looking up from his book.

"His mother says it's a way to keep his father's memory alive," I continued. "And Dad, I've decided that I want to keep Mom's memory alive, too. I'm fourteen, and I don't have any idea where she's even buried. Don't you think it's time you told me?"

Now he looked up, and I saw from his expression that the wall was not coming down anytime soon. I made one more attempt.

"She's not buried here, but couldn't we have a memorial ceremony for her? She wouldn't need a day of her own—she could share Memorial Day."

"The best way for you to memorialize your mother is for you to work hard, be the best person you can, and make a difference in the world, as she wanted to do. And the place to start—" he pointed to my textbooks— "is right there, right now. Besides," he said in a monotone as he looked back at his book, "there is no cemetery. She always wanted her body cremated."

"Wait a minute," Dariya said. Even after all she had been privy to, there was incredulity on her face. "Cremated?"

"My question came at him out of the blue," I said. "How else could he have responded? Anything he said would have been a lie. My mother left him holding the bag—it was his job to keep her alive by not giving her away, and I had convinced myself that she was dead. What was he supposed to say? It was a terrible position for him to be in."

My father could not have imagined what message I would take away from his bald-faced lie. But at fourteen, I was outraged when I realized just how little she had loved me. It was bad enough that she involved herself in dangerous activities that took her away from me so early, but she had seen fit to leave me nothing—not even a headstone in a cemetery where I could go to put flowers in her memory, or to touch the ground where she was buried. The night he told me that she had wanted to be cremated, I woke in a steaming sweat, enraged; when I got out of bed in the morning and remembered, I was furious.

"Anyway," I continued, "if she didn't want to be remembered, fine. I wouldn't have a memorial ceremony—instead, I would have an exorcism, and erase her from my memory."

I told Dariya how I removed my mother's photograph from the frame beside my bed and took it with me when next we went to the Cape. And I took with me a yellow silk scarf—found years earlier among my father's things in an old trunk, assumed to be my mother's, and hidden since in my dresser. At dawn on a Saturday morning in June of my fifteenth year, while my father was still asleep, I made my way down to the beach carrying a little plastic bag. Close to the high tide line I dug a small hole and built up the windward side, and in the cold, moist cavity I lay the scarf. On top of it I placed several pieces of crumpled newspaper, and on top of that I slowly tore the photograph into as many scraps as I could. Then I opened the prayer book to the mourners' prayer, the *Kaddish*. As I read it in my halting and inaccurate Hebrew, not understanding a word but familiar with the litany and the rhythm, I lit a match and, shielded from the wind by the sand barrier I had built, I ignited the little pyre.

I had planned to wrap the remains in the scarf and carry them back to the house for burial in the yard, but all that was left when the flame died was a small pile of ash atop a fragment of wet, yellow silk. I replaced the prayer book in its plastic bag; carefully shoveled sand back into the hole to avoid disturbing the ashes, stamped it down and roughed the surface. Then, confident that I had permanently exorcised my mother, I turned away, went back to the house and climbed into bed.

"What an awful thing to do," said Dariya. "But you can't possibly think of telling your mother."

"I was going to," I admitted. "I've spent a lot of my life thinking about my losses—but now, knowing what we do about her life, I don't think I need to tell her the story. It would be like twisting the knife. All I feel for her is sorrow."

twenty-nine

STEVEN

KwaZulu-Natal, 2002

T
he drive from Johannesburg to the Drakensberg took seven hours, and when we left the highway at Mooi River, we still had thirty miles to go along narrow country roads, only some of which were paved. We were in KwaZulu-Natal.

At one point we took a wrong turn and drove twenty deserted miles through a silent landscape of immense dignity—stark, rocky foothills and fields of grass dotted with cows and the occasional goatherd with his animals. The road was empty, we discovered, because it led to only one destination—Giant's Castle Reserve, an immense natural park. Along the way we passed the rural Zulu village of Mahlutshini, where most of the homes were built of brick or cement, or of the discarded materials from building sites—corrugated iron and wooden beams. But there were still many dwellings that gave a feeling of what the village might have looked like when my mother arrived forty years earlier—rounded, thatched huts; half-spheres of intertwined branches caulked with mud. There were even a few huts where the walls had been painted in traditional Zulu designs.

The village seemed to have been built in an arbitrary way, with houses scattered along the hills in no particular design—but there was an order imposed by the landscape. Some houses were built on the side of the road, but most were situated on hillsides, and on higher ground, and because there was no shortage of space, there was little crowding. This was a poor village, but the magnificence of its surroundings lent it grace and dignity.

On the left the village extended up the hillside, and off into the fields on the right. The road ran right through, and because there were so few cars, the people used it as their main thoroughfare. The day we arrived was a Sunday, and the village road was crowded. Many adults were dressed in white vestments, or in long robes of startling blue or red, on their way to church, and children were everywhere, running through the crowds, riding bicycles, playing with balls, bicycle wheels, tin cans. I drove cautiously, feeling very much as if we were trespassing on a private event. The people were friendly, looking at us with open curiosity as they made their way slowly to the side of the road so that we could pass.

The village had little if any indoor plumbing, but there were hand pumps scattered through the hills, and women and children looked up from their pumping to wave at us as we drove by. We passed several women walking down the road with five-gallon containers of water, or packages, or even huge and ungainly bundles of firewood, balanced on their heads.

Eventually, studying the map, we realized that we had made a wrong turn, and before we reached the end of the road at Giant's Castle Reserve, turned around. We had not seen another vehicle since our first pass through the village, and on the return trip we were greeted by the same smiling crowds, and by some laughter.

"They all think we're idiots," said Sally through a clenched grin as she waved out through the open window.

"Why do you say that, honey?" I asked innocently, thinking the same thing.

"They knew we were lost the first time we went through, and they were just waiting for us to realize it and come back," she said. "And they're right. I feel like an idiot, and it's not even my fault. I just wish," she said into the rear-view mirror, a look of long-suffering on her face, "that I had parents who could read a map."

"They can read maps," said Greg solemnly, and I heard Dariya's words in his mouth. "They're doing their best in a new and difficult situation. Why don't you just stop being so bossy?"

The children glared sullenly at each other for a brief moment, and we smiled sheepishly as we crept along slowly, waiting again for people to make their leisurely way to the side of the road. At the time, our detour felt like a waste—but it gave me some perspective on the nature of my mother's life. She lived a world apart from the reality of our lives in Boston—and compared to what we had just left behind us in Johannesburg, she might as well have lived in another country, in a different time.

At mid-afternoon, having driven back through the general area of Balgowan, we turned left off the paved road and onto a dusty two-lane dirt road that seemed to wind on forever.

"This is where we should be looking for Cleopatra Mountain," said Dariya, checking the directions. "It's the side of a mountain, up at the top of a cliff that looks like the outline of a woman's face."

"There it is!" shouted Sally, eager to be first. "Straight ahead of us!"

She pointed through the front windshield at the mountain looming before us, and we leaned forward to see that at one end, in profile at the summit, there was indeed the outline of a face. Whether it could have belonged to the Egyptian queen is another question.

Leaving the farmland behind us, we followed the gravel road, and Cleopatra Mountain slid off to the side as we began to rise into the foothills of the Drakensberg. At one point the road forked, and we took the right fork up a hill.

"We're very close now," I said. "What color are the walls supposed to be?"

"Grayish-blue," said Greg. "And two big pillars, one on each side of the entrance."

My mother's property was surrounded by a high brick wall, and it was indeed painted a deep grayish-blue. The entrance was between two cement pillars, to one side of which there was a small sign announcing "Cleo's Retreat, Bed and Breakfast. Best Fishing in the Drakensberg. Michaela Green, Proprietor." Tourism had come to the Midlands in a big way, and a few years earlier my mother converted part of the farm into a high-end bed and breakfast, which Penya ran for her. Still, it was something of a surprise to find that the woman who lived the life she had, was also the proprietor of a fair-sized bed and breakfast establishment. I pulled into the parking lot and turned off the engine. There were only three or four cars in a lot big enough for a dozen. We discovered that people left early in the morning, and returned for dinner.

"Well, I guess we got here," I said.

Dariya placed a reassuring hand on my arm, and as usual, our children missed nothing.

"This will be fine, Dad," said Sally. "You don't have to worry."

"Yes," said Greg, putting a small hand on my shoulder. "We're all in this together."

"And if it turns out that Grandma doesn't like you, Dad," said Sally, pinching both Greg's cheeks between her thumbs and forefingers, "all she has to do is look at this boy's handsome face and you'll be a star."

"Hands off the merchandise," he said, garbled and unclear, and we were all laughing as we poured out of the car.

We made our way down a series of stone steps and through a rose arbor, with a well-labeled herb garden on one side and a hedge of white flowering trees on the other. At the bottom of the steps there was an expanse of grass leading to the banks of a narrow, fast-flowing stream, and at the opposite bank forested hillsides ascended steeply, separating into several rounded hills.

The forests petered out halfway up the hillsides and were replaced by long, rough grasses, and at the summit the hillsides coalesced into an imposing façade of eroded sandstone formations. These were foothills, small by mountain standards, but they were majestic and grand.

At the bottom of the steps and to the left was the main farmhouse, constructed of dark, quarried stone, and beyond it, a series of buildings and then plowed fields. To the right there was a large inlet, a pond that had been created by allowing water from the river to pool, and it was surrounded by a series of individual guest houses, and a larger building with a sign over one door indicating that it was the office.

"This is a most beautiful place," muttered Dariya, leaning into me. "I begin to understand why Michaela didn't want to leave here. I wouldn't want to leave, either."

We stood at the bottom of the steps, looking from the farmhouse to the office. I didn't relish the prospect of explaining who I was to a stranger behind a desk. But two huge German shepherds solved the problem for me. They bounded across the grass towards us, barking loudly, and Greg grabbed hold of my hand in alarm. Sally ran towards them, fearless and laughing.

One dog was slow, old and grizzled; he had a torn ear and arthritic rear legs, and his breathing was labored as he did his game best to keep up with the competition. The other dog seemed to have just emerged from puppy-hood—all he wanted to do was play, and for him, everything was a game. He had a thick coat of heavily brushed hair, a curious, intelligent face, and, it turned out, a wonderful temperament. He greeted Sally, jumped up briefly with his paws on her shoulders and licked her face, and then very gently came over and charmed Greg by inserting a cold snout into his hand.

The noise couldn't help but attract some attention. The rear door of the office building flew open, and a young man came towards us. He held himself tall and straight, like Khabazela; his eyes were green, his hair tightly curled, and he had a lean handsome face and a humorous mouth. He was a stranger to me, yet there was intimacy in his smile, and knowledge of me, and in some indefinable way he was as familiar to me as my own children.

"I should have been waiting here to greet you," he said, his voice deep and vaguely familiar. "My grandfather called to say that you would be arriving around now."

"Penya?" I said.

"Yes," he said, giving Dariya a hug. "My grandmother asked me to welcome you all on her behalf. And to Michaela's other grandchildren," he said gravely, turning to them, "to Sally and Greg, I welcome you, too, to your grandmother's home. I am your cousin, Penya. *Sawubona.*"

"We learned what that means in Zulu, Mom," said Greg proudly, looking at Dariya. "It means 'I see you.'"

"That's very good," said Penya, kneeling down so that he was at eye level with Greg. "And do you know how to answer *Sawubona?*"

He shook his head.

"I do," said Sally. "*Yebo.* But I don't remember what it means. Maybe it means Hello?"

"Not quite," he said. "It means 'I am here.' And do you know why we greet each other this way, instead of saying a simple 'hello?'" He rose. "We believe that we all exist only because other people see and know us. So when I greet you, I am saying that I see you; that I recognize your being. And when you reply, you are saying that you are here because I see you. And so, in that way, we acknowledge our need for each other."

Then Penya Michaels turned to me, and for a brief moment he looked at me in silence.

"You did not know until now that I exist, but I have known for many years about Steven Green," he said. "Now we meet, finally."

He placed his hands on my shoulders.

"*Sawubona*," he said softly. "Welcome home, my uncle."

Penya had arranged for our suitcases to be carried down from the car, and showed us to our rooms in the main farmhouse. He sat down with us in the kitchen to a late lunch of grilled chicken sandwiches and salad that was brought in from the main kitchen, and he was charming, knowledgeable, and interested in us all and in our impressions of the country.

But I found myself increasingly agitated. My mother was absent; there was no mention of her or of where she was, and I restrained myself from asking. After so many years of silence, was it too much to ask that she be present when we arrived? I waited until the end of the meal, when the children wandered out to see if they could spot the huge brown trout in the pond.

"When do you expect my mother back?" I asked.

Penya grinned. "She wanted you to get settled and have lunch," he said. "She's waiting for you."

"Where is she waiting?" I asked.

"She's not far from here." He pointed vaguely outside, towards the mountains. "She asked me to take you to her whenever you're ready."

"I've come halfway around the world to see her," I said, rising from the table. "How much more ready could I be?"

Penya rose, too. "Come then," he said softly. "I will take you."

Dariya got up from the table and kissed me lightly on the cheek. "Good luck, Stevie," she said. "I'll see you when you get back."

"You're not coming?"

"I'll stay here with the children," she said. "I think you and Michaela should meet first."

"No way," I replied. "You're coming with me, and so are Sally and Greg. We came as a family, and we're going to meet my mother as a family." I turned to Penya. "There's no reason why we can't all go, is there?"

"Of course not," he said. "It's up to you."

"We're all going," I said. "Let's collect the kids."

We went out to the Jeep, Penya whistled for the dogs, and helped the older dog, Wally, up onto the tailgate. Starburst, the younger, made the leap on his own. I sat in front with Penya; Dariya and the children sat in the back seat. We drove out of Cleo's Retreat and up a steep and winding single-lane road to the top of Mount Lebanon and Cleopatra Mountain. I turned to look at my family and the two dogs in the back, nosing the air.

"How is this for you, uncle?" asked Penya, glancing curiously at me.

"More than strange," I said. "It feels as if I've stepped into someone else's life. A few months ago I didn't know I had a mother. And I've always been an only child. One moment I feel like rejoicing because I once had a brother; the next, I find myself grieving because he died before I knew he existed. And then there are moments when it's simply enough to enjoy being your uncle. These are big changes, Penya, and I will get used to them with time, but it does feel very strange. I think you have the advantage, having known about us."

"I don't feel it as an advantage," he said. "I'm just very happy that you've all come. And I know that my grandmother can't wait to see you."

"I can't say I remember her," I said. "But not being there when we arrived is a strange way of showing how eager she is to see us."

Penya said nothing.

"Where are we going?" I asked eventually.

"It's a ten-minute drive," he said over the roar of the engine, "and it's steep."

He stopped the car, put it into four wheel drive, and we made our way up the hill. We passed only one other inhabited area—the Cleopatra Mountain Farmhouse, a small guest lodge that was famed, and rightly so, we discovered, for its sumptuous gourmet meals. The owners were friends of my mother's, and Penya said it was the last working farm before entering the protected natural areas of the KwaZulu-Natal Reserve.

Eventually we came to a boom across the road, a little guard hut, and a sign for the Highmoor Nature Reserve. Penya greeted the guard and they spoke briefly. The man doffed his hat, gave us a shy, tentative smile, and raised the boom. There was a sign on the guardhouse prohibiting dogs, but he made no comment about our passengers and I had the sense that he knew who we were and why we were there. We drove into the empty parking lot and Penya stopped the car. He opened the tailgate and both dogs jumped down and waited, watching him.

"Let's go," he said. He pointed toward a low hill. I could see nothing beyond it, but the beginning of a path was visible. "Wally and Starburst know the way." He smiled at us, a wide, open smile, and he nodded sagely. "I think you will enjoy the walk," he said, and led the way up the path.

The fact that we had come halfway around the globe to meet my mother was apparently not enough for her. She was going to make us walk through the wilderness to reach her. I was so completely out of my element, and the situation was so strange, so outrageous, that any anger I might have felt was swept aside, and the sense that I was being manipulated seemed to evaporate. Perhaps, I thought, that's the sign of successful manipulation.

The dogs waited expectantly for us at each turn, and then leaped ahead. They ran forward a few hundred yards, where Wally would wait while Starburst came back to ensure that we were following, ready to lead on to the next curve in the path. When we reached the top of the first hill and saw where the path led, I had to stop to take in what lay before me.

In the far distance was the jagged silhouette of the Drakensberg, a six hundred mile escarpment of basalt and granite, rising in places to almost twelve thousand feet. On one side I could identify Giant's Castle and the outline of a huge supine figure, with raised head, chest and legs. But between where we were and the far distance were the grassy sloping hillsides of the Kleinberg, the little berg, the *highveld* that extended to the horizon. The yellow, light-brown grasses, with hints of lilac and green, were like a waving tapestry that had been laid over the undulating landscape, and it was broken only by small ponds and their waterbirds, and by the streams that led into them. Silence seemed to have descended over the landscape like a mist, blocking out all but the sound of the wind through the grass. The sun was warm, and the brightness of the late afternoon light made me glad that I wore my sunglasses.

I breathed in the African *highveld*, and I tasted and felt the vast openness of the country as it entered my lungs. It was sweet and rich from the grasses and the soil, and it contained the acrid odor of distant burns. I sighed deeply, and gave myself over to it. There was little we could do but follow the dogs.

Aside from several hikers camped out in the distance, and a few bird watchers looking for bearded eagles, the area was deserted. The path meandered back and forth across the hills, at times climbing steeply. The dogs led the way over several small bridges. One spanned a brushy ravine, another crossed a narrow stream; a third, longer bridge took us over an area where flowing water encountered a broad expanse of flat granite and emptied itself out across the hillside, the fast, thin flow of liquid over the rocks blindingly bright, flashing and glinting in the sun.

The path divided in several places, but the side paths seemed eventually to reunite with the main track, and Starburst made sure that we were following his lead. The *veld* was dotted with small ponds that had formed in low- lying depressions, and they were surrounded by reeds and tall grasses. The air was so clear and the silence so absolute that as I watched water birds taking off from a pond in the distance, I saw the surface ripple, and heard the delayed slapping of wings on the water as they flapped their way into the air.

The children raced ahead, following the dogs, and Dariya and I walked hand in hand along the path, mesmerized by the beauty and serenity of the landscape.

"We're almost there," said Penya.

Eventually the dogs took a detour off the main path and we followed them up a hill, to a point where the incline was steep enough that the trail had been cut into the hillside. The view on one side was blocked by the rocky hill itself, but on the other side the view expanded as the path climbed, and we seemed to be at the highest point. Just before the summit of the hill the path turned sharply to the right, and as I came around the corner, Starburst was standing directly in front of me, facing a ledge of rock overhanging the hillside. Small boulders dotted the ledge, and on one of them, looking out over the *veld*, was a woman. Wally sat beside her, and she rested her hand on his broad head. She sat with her back to us, a narrow figure with slightly rounded shoulders. She was hatless, and the sunlight shone against gray hair, which was cut short in the back.

"Penya," whispered Greg, pulling at his shirtsleeve, "is that our grandmother?"

"It is," he said, smiling, "and she's waiting just for you."

Greg and Sally looked at each other, and together they ran towards the seated figure, shouting. Sally's hair was wild about her head, cheeks pink with excitement, and her eyes gleaming. And Greg, my dark-haired boy, three steps behind, laughing—aware as always of everything—the tension, the barking dogs, the madness of the situation, the excitement, and his sister's untrammeled joy.

"Grandma! Grandma!" they yelled as they approached her, and she rose in alarm at the noise.

When she saw them running towards her she dropped to one knee, and when they reached her she put her arms around both of them and they all hugged each other, and I saw that she was breathing the smell of their skin and their hair.

"Oh, dear God," she whispered.

After a while the children extricated themselves and Greg took her hand to help her up. We stood and looked at each other. She may have once been beautiful, but I recognized none of what was in my memory. She was thin, with a determined mouth, and a face heavily lined by the sun.

"Steven," she said, "you're the image of your father."

She stretched out a hand to touch my cheek, and then leaned forward and put her other arm about my neck. It was a brief embrace, which I received stiffly, arms at my sides, and then, as she released me, I raised one hand to touch her shoulder. She smiled.

"Thank you," she said softly, and turned to Dariya, who stood silently beside me. "Tell me, how was your time with Khabazela?" she asked.

"He was wonderful with us," answered Dariya. "Thanks for suggesting that we meet with him. It was quite an education."

"Yes," she said. "That was my hope. And now that you're here, I want to learn all about you."

"I think we have plenty of time for that," I said.

Dariya placed a hand on my mother's shoulder and stepped forward, and the two women embraced.

"Thank you, Dariya," I heard my mother whisper, "for helping to make this happen."

I stood to one side, and Dariya, held by my mother, turned her head, searching for me. When she found me she looked at me and smiled, and I had no difficulty understanding the words she silently mouthed.

"I love you," she said.

Tears were streaming down my cheeks, although I couldn't have said why I was crying. It could have been resignation—maybe I was finally coming to understand that there would be no reconciliation as I had imagined it, no real apology or understanding; that any happy ending would be different from the one I had imagined.

For the next few days we stayed close to the farm. We took long walks, sat up late after the children were in bed, talking about the past we had lost. One day we left the farm at dawn and spent a long day on the Durban beach. Khabazela and Miriam were due to visit at the end of the week, along with all the children and grandchildren, and my mother planned to host a huge *braaivleis*, a barbecue, and to invite her friends from surrounding farms and villages.

The day before the barbecue we had lunch, and then the children went off with Penya to fish for brown trout in the pond. Dariya suggested that we drive my mother back up the road to Highmoor, where we first met. My mother thought it a perfect place for an afternoon stroll, and she was delighted that we were so taken with her favorite place.

I drove the Jeep; Starburst sat regally beside me in the front seat, snout raised to the breeze, and Wally, tongue hanging out, lay in the rear. Dariya and my mother sat in the back seat.

Once we arrived, my mother and Dariya walked side by side on the narrow path, and I followed a few paces behind, listening to the conversation about the parallel lives my wife and my mother had lived.

They weren't exactly shutting me out, but they weren't quite letting me in, either. They were comparing notes in that particular way women have. It's always been foreign to me, perhaps because there were no women in my life as I was growing up. It was a way of quickly building a relationship by sharing intimate parts of their lives; finding familiarities and differences; being willing to give up information about themselves, each taking delight in what the other was willing to reveal.

They talked and laughed as they climbed the slight incline to the hilltop, and I quietly slipped away down the last fork, leaving them to ascend to the rocky summit without me. I didn't need company, and it was clear to me that they were content to be alone.

I'm not sure whether I ran down the footpath, or whether I trudged, counting every step. And I have no idea what I was thinking, or for how long I was absent from my body. But when I did come back to myself and look around, I found that I had circled back on the *veld*, and that I was a half mile distant from them.

As I turned to locate myself in space, I realized that the hill was behind me, and from where I stood I could see what looked like a slightly raised rock shelf, and two figures sitting on the boulders that my mother had been sitting on that first day. If they had looked out at the carpet of *veld* that lay unrolled at their feet like a gift, they would have noticed me—but I could see even at a distance that they were deep in conversation.

In Michaela, Dariya found someone on whom she could lavish the care and love that had lacked an object since the death of her own mother. For Sally and Greg, the absence of a grandmother had been significant, and Michaela had already enriched their lives. But for me, the answer was less clear. It was too late for my mother to simply walk onto my stage and replace the woman for whom I had spent my life grieving; and it was too late for me to play the son she had left at the age of seven. What was left was only the possibility of a future not burdened by the full weight of the past.

I had been walking fast, and now I stopped, breathing hard. It was mid-afternoon, and the winter sun was warm on my skin. I loved the fact that I could feel the heat of the sun, and at the same time be chilled by a cool breeze. The *veld* grasses were soft, sunlit, waving gold, and I had arrived at a clear pond on which white-breasted cormorants paddled, ducking for food. Dragonflies hovered and flitted around in profusion, and high above, circling lazily in the currents with dark, outspread wings against the sparkling blue of the sky, were several hawks, and a small eagle with white patches on its underwing.

I glanced back up at the summit to see the two women sitting together, heads bent, talking as they looked down the hill at me. Before going up to join them, I took one last look at the pond. A wattled crane emerged from behind a tall screen of marsh grasses, as if it had been hiding in the wings waiting to make an appearance. The bird saw me, turned its head so that one eye was facing me, slowly raised a stick leg up into its belly, and froze. All that moved was the wattle beneath its beak. I took pleasure in its white neck and shoulders, and in the black cloak fading to grey that seemed draped over its back. We stared at each other for a long moment as it decided whether to take flight. But it was a crane, a wattled crane, relentless hunter of frogs, and its downside was that it could do nothing else. The bird elegantly fluttered its feathers, refocused on the hunt, and turned away, to high-step in delicate and precise slow motion along the edge of the water.

I could have taken the path that wound smoothly around to the summit where Dariya and my mother waited, but instead I jogged up the hill in a straight line, leaped up inclines, vaulted over jagged rocks, and scrambled straight through patches of knee-high thorns. There was nothing easy about being my mother, and I knew, now, that I had always been my mother's son.

acknowledgments

My deepest gratitude to Maurice Mackenzie, a wise and most gracious man whose ability to transcend the limits of race and birth is remarkable, and to Prince Mangosuthu Buthelezi, whose willingness to share erudition and life experience was beyond expectation. Michael Langa, whose life in South Africa makes him a particularly cogent judge of cultural and historical authenticity, validated the story with an enthusiasm and emotion that was deeply satisfying.

Mouse and Richard Poynton, for sharing hospitality and history, for many contacts, and for providing Wally and Starburst; Nick and Anne Nicolson, for an eye-opening view of KwaZulu in the 21st century; Ken Gillings, who guided us around KwaZulu and led us to Cetshwayo's tomb; Major General Chris le Roux, who shared his perspective and his sandwiches with us. Errol Cunnama went beyond the call of duty and introduced us to Moses Mdhluli and Hlengiwe and others who taught us and filled our hearts. And our gratitude to Mr. Mbambelela Zimba, venerable historian and conservationist, with whom we sat in a cow pasture, and who hoped we had come to provide the same protection to his beloved Drakensberg mountains as John Muir brought to the national parks in the United States.

Alfred and Jocelyn Emdon, willing listeners, provided a home away from home; Victoria and Michael Turovsky, and Tibor and Helen Vais provided first-hand research early on; Ann Buxbaum shared with us years of contacts in South Africa.

Heartfelt thanks to those—too many to name—who grappled with the story, made suggestions along the way, and offered unending encouragement. To the many wonderful friends and colleagues whose encouragement and wisdom have proven invaluable: Peter McKenzie, who read an early version; Lucie Prinz, for her editorial wisdom and publishing know-how; David Sloan Rossiter, Leslie Elfant, Jane Leavy and Fred Sperounis; Ginger Chappell; Leon Blum; Simone Kaplan; Linda Kraus; Larry Sagen and Carol Remz, Jill and David Adler, Martha McFadden. And to Carole Osterer Bellman, Gail Chapman Close, Ellen Greenfeld, Kitty Howard, Cindy Lavoie and Caroline Spear—who give new meaning to the term Book Group. Thanks to Janet Silver and Alan Rinzler, for structural advice and editing, and to Marian Brown and Louise Crawford, who calmly and surely shepherded me through the publishing morass and made sure that *Bloodlines* has an audience.

To Jill Greenberg, for years of friendship, partnership and patience, and for allowing me time to write; to my sister Isabel and brother Allan for bedrock support and lifelong validation. To my parents, Betty and Fred, whose example and constant encouragement are gifts to be treasured for a lifetime, and whose prescience in 1960 made possible the life we now live. To my three children: Dani and Mat, whose responses to this story alone made it worth writing, and whose love and devotion, sense of wonder and adventure are a constant source of renewal; and to Jessica, for love and encouragement, for incisive editing, creative brainstorming, for reading more versions of the manuscript than I can count, and for untold good ideas.

Marlene, as inspiration and muse, you brought this tale to life with me. As travelling companion and as first and final editor, your hand is as present on each page as mine, and your love and encouragement are a driving force in my life.

Book Club and Study Guide Questions

1. Was Lenny's decision to leave South Africa a good one? Why?

2. Michaela was given several opportunities to join Lenny and Steven in the United States. Do you think her decision to stay in South Africa was the right choice? Why?

3. In what way is Steven's family life as an adult a reaction to his experiences as a young boy?

4. Of the secrets Lenny keeps from Steven, which one is he most ashamed of? How does Lenny's secrecy shape Steven's responses to the world?

5. How do the relationships with the men in Michaela's life (her father, Lenny, Mandla, Andrew) affect her development as a character?

6. In what ways are Michaela and Steven's wife, Dariya, kindred spirits?

7. How does the loss of Thulani and Simon change the dynamics of the interaction among Miriam, Mandla and Michaela?

8. In order to get through life, we are sometimes lucky enough to benefit from the wisdom of a mentor. Who are the key mentors in the book, and how do they shape the lives of the characters?

9. Can you point to events that trigger changes in Michaela's character as the story progresses? Are there aspects of her personality that never change? How is this manifested in the book?

10. *Bloodlines* is told from the perspectives of four characters—Steven, Lenny, Michaela and Mandla. What is the impact of telling the story from these diverse viewpoints?

11. In your view, what are the major character strengths in Michaela, Lenny, Steven and Mandla? What are their major flaws?

12. In their choice to be together, Mandla and Michaela signal a desire to transcend the limitations of the regimented world they live in—the South Africa of black versus white; African versus Western culture; Zulu versus Jewish traditions. What actions by these characters show that they were unable to completely achieve this goal?

13. Is Steven a main character in the book? What role does he play in the story?

14. What can you say about the nature of redemption in this book? Does Steven eventually find redemption? Would you have ended the story differently?

15. *Bloodlines* centers around loss, the impossibility of reconciliation and the dangers of family secrets. It also contains themes of love, forgiveness and family values. How do these disparate themes coexist?

16. How does the landscape of South Africa take on a character of its own in the novel?

17. In what ways does *Bloodlines* change your perception of South Africa's history?

18. As Michaela and Lenny look back on their lives from the perspective of old age, what do you think each of them would consider their greatest loss or regret?

bibliography

The following books and articles provided background for the story:

After the Party, by Andrew Feinstein, Jonathan Ball Publishers, (PTY) LTD, 2007

Barrier of Spears, by R.O. Pearse, Howard Timmins Publishers, 1982

Buthelezi, A Biography, by Ben Tempkin, JB Publishers, South Africa, 2003

Father Huddleston's Picture Book, Kliptown Books Ltd, 1990

Inkatha versus the Rest: Black Opposition to Inkatha in Durban's African Townships, Michael Sutcliffe and Paul Wellings, African Affairs, Vol 87, No 348, July 1988, pp. 325-360

Long Walk To Freedom, by Nelson Mandela, Little, Brown and Company, 1995

Rivonia's Children, by Glenn Frankel, Farrar Straus and Giroux, 1999

The Destruction of the Zulu Kingdom (The Civil War in Zululand, 1879-1884), by Jeff Guy, University of Natal Press, 1994

The Limits of Manipulation Theory: The Apartheid Third Force and the ANC-Inkatha Conflict in South Africa, Eric Melander, Peace Economics, Peace Science and Public Policy, Volume 8, Issue 4, Fall 2002

The Washing of the Spears by Donald R. Morris, Random House, 1994

Truth and Reconciliation Commission of South Africa Report

Zulu Botanical Knowledge: An Introduction, *by Mkhipheni A. Ngwenya, Adrian Koopman and Rosemary Williams, National Botanical Institute, Durban 2003*

Zulu Shaman: Dreams, Prophecies and Mysteries, *Vusasmazulu Credo Mutwa, Destiny Books, Division of Inner Traditions International, Rochester, VT, 2003*

Zulu Thought-Patterns and Symbolism, *by Axel-Ivar Berglund, Indiana University Press Edition, 1989*

about the author

Neville Frankel immigrated to Boston from Johannesburg with his family when he was 14. After graduating from Dartmouth College, he pursued doctoral work in English literature at the University of Toronto. While in Canada, he wrote *The Third Power*, a well-reviewed political thriller about the transformation of Rhodesia to Zimbabwe. Frankel also received an Emmy for his work on a BBC documentary, *The Hillside Strangler: Mind of a Murderer*. In 2002 he returned to South Africa for the first time in 38 years. Over the next decade he went back several more times, researching what would become *Bloodlines*. Frankel has three grown children and lives outside Boston with his wife Marlene.

Made in the USA
San Bernardino, CA
26 April 2014